Your Bloodline

BY

KC KEAN

Your Bloodline
Featherstone Academy Series #2
Copyright © 2020 KC Kean

This book is licensed for your personal enjoyment only.
This book may not be re-sold or given away to other people. If you would like to share this book with another person, please purchase an additional copy for each recipient. If you're reading this book and did not purchase it, or it wasn't purchased for your use only, then please return to your favourite book retailer and purchase your own copy. Thank you for respecting the hard work of this author.

All rights reserved.

This is a work of fiction. Names, characters, places, brands, media, and incidents are either the product of the authors imagination or are used fictitiously. The author acknowledges the trademark status and trademark owners of various products referred to in this work of fiction, which have been used without permission. The publication/use of these trademarks is not authorised, associated with, or sponsored by the trademark owners.

Your Bloodline/KC Kean – 2nd ed.
ISBN-13 - 979-8682769-23-0

To my girl, my angel, daddy's grass bean.

You are the brightest ray of sunshine, and you don't even see it.

You impact everyone's life, especially mine.

You gave me purpose, drive, passion, and unconditional love.

My beautiful, smart, kind and caring, daughter,

I love you

But even when you're eighteen you sure as shit aren't reading this.

I love you

I love you more

I love you infinity

I love you infinity war

"They all showed loyalty and an intense level of protectiveness toward you, but most of all, they portrayed how much they believe in you. They are not above you, nor are you above them, but together, you have have a very special and rare bond, only bringing out the best in each other.

- Maria Steele, Featherstone Academy

KC KEAN

PROLOGUE
Rafe

These secrets are out of control.

They're ripping me to shreds, blackening my soul.

I want to scream out the truths, tell her everything.

I'm not even sure if I'm protecting her anymore or deluding myself into thinking I am.

But it's time for Luna to open her mind, to unlock what has been suppressed. Hopefully, the memories aren't as bad as she believes them to be.

I just need to find the words to lessen the blows or risk losing her forever.

KC KEAN

ONE

Luna

The white walls that surround me offer the perfect canvas for the bloodshed that fills my vision, taunting me over and over again. I may not be in The Pyramid anymore, but The Pyramid still lingers in my mind.

Rafe got me out of there when the trial was over, and I've been holed up in this room ever since. I don't even know where we are, my mind too focused on everything that's happened in the last forty-eight hours. Between Washington, and what waited for me back at Featherstone, my mind is blown.

"I killed someone," I murmur to myself, the words

tasting dark and heavy on my tongue. That's a sentence I never thought would pass my lips. I killed someone for the first time, and I say that because I know it won't be the last. Not while I remain at Featherstone Academy and as a part of this world.

I killed Tyler, and I don't even feel guilty about it, but I can feel my soul starting to blacken. The worst sight was of my best friend, Red, dangling from the rope as her legs wobbled uncontrollably, trying to stay on her tiptoes. I can still hear the way she whispered my name after I cut the rope, as she gasped for breath, lying helplessly on the floor.

The destruction Tyler left in his path opened my eyes to the new world I find myself in. Death is the most likely outcome for us all. I haven't even considered what happened to the guy in ring two, the dumb fucker who charged me as soon as I stepped into the ring.

I can't really remember leaving Featherstone Academy either, not even the hall. I could only feel the wound on my head and a cut from my collarbone to my navel. I pointed my bloody daggers at Veronica, Rico and old man Dietrichson, promising vengeance, and the rest is all blank.

He smashes me in the face with the brute force of his fist wrapped around his brass knuckles. The pain across my face is excruciating. I can feel blood trickling down my face.

Picking up my fallen dagger with his free hand, he raises it to my chest. I don't squirm away from it, I refuse to show weakness to this psycho. He drags it down, piercing my skin ever so slightly, slicing a line down between my breasts, cutting open my sports bra in the process.

Using the dagger still in my hand, I slam it into the side of his neck. The pain has him lifting his hands, but the shock has his reactions slowed, which gives me time to drag it out and slam it back into his throat from a different angle.

I scream as my fingers wrap around his knuckle duster and I smash him in the face over and over again until he stops breathing.

I try and wipe blood from my eyes to see what direction I even need to turn. I raise both daggers and slice both of the thin ropes at the same time. I hear their bodies drop to the ground.

"My father once told me, never tiptoe through life Luna. Let them hear every motherfucking step you take, Meu Tesouro. With that said, here's your warning, I'm fucking coming for you."

I loved seeing the shock on my mother's face as my words, laced with venom, echoed through the room. I meant every fucking word.

I'm done lying down in this bed, letting the whole event repeat over and over in my head as I stare at the ceiling. I'm emotionally wiped. I feel betrayed. As much as my mother was never maternal, I still thought there would be a sense of family there. Seems I was wrong, blood isn't thicker than water, which makes me snicker because blood is all the Academy stands for.

My heart aches for the lives lost to Featherstone because they deem horrific challenges necessary. For some ridiculous idea of survival of the fittest. Innocent people dying at the hands of one of their trials, because they simply pulled the wrong assignment card. I have to force myself to push away from my morbid thoughts. It's becoming a slippery slope to maintain my sanity.

I know I should leave this room. I've been hiding away since I opened my eyes, allowing myself time to process what I've been through. I haven't eaten a thing, even though Rafe has tried bringing me food. I haven't declined the bottles of water though, not wanting to become dehydrated. At least I haven't lost all of my common sense.

I've paced the floor beside me, screamed into my pillow, and stared into space on repeat and I'm done. I need to woman the fuck up and figure shit out. Everyone has been happy to give me the space I needed, but I have to move past it.

Getting up off the bed, I look down at the state of myself. I'm still wearing Kai's simple rock band tee. I can't bring myself to change, not wanting to lose the scent of him surrounding me, and the silent strength it offers. I think I need him right now, all of them, well, with the exception of Roman, the *true* Acehole. That was all shot to hell and back with the truths that came out in Washington. My soul hasn't caught up that we're anti-Roman yet, and is still crying out for him… for them.

Looking around the room that surrounds me, I see that it's completely bare, no personality. Even the furniture is white, with just a simple full-size bed, dresser and a wardrobe. It's as if it's been sitting here as a blank canvas waiting for someone to claim it. I've officially had enough.

I shower in the en-suite, which comes with every possible self-care product you can think of. Everything is unopened and lined up neatly on the marble countertop. A vanity, toilet and a large shower with all the fancy buttons that make it high end, complete the space.

I feel the grime wash away and mentally push myself to get out of this slump. I have to remember not to scrub my hands down my face since the stitches need to stay dry. The mark down my chest stings under the pressure of the water.

Catching sight of my face in the mirror, I notice the mess Tyler made with his brass knuckles, leaving me to need stitches. The slice he made down my chest, with my dagger, isn't as bad. The pierced skin was glued back together by the doctor instead.

I'd fucking love to go more than a month without getting any black eyes.

It's time to figure out a plan to deal with the mess that is Featherstone.

Throwing Kai's top back on, letting it fall to my knees, I make my way downstairs.

Stepping into the kitchen, I'm completely stunned to find Red sitting at the table with Rafe and Juliana. The laughter that fills the room around them feels like magic, alive and untouchable. I don't know what they're chuckling about, and I don't really care. I'm just glad to see her still breathing.

"Red," I murmur, causing the room to go silent.

She is up and out of her chair, throwing herself at me in an instant. Literally, I'm holding her off the ground. Our arms are wrapped around each other, taking a moment to bask in each other's presence. As much as her hold is adding pressure to my bruised body, I don't say a word. I'm just happy to be able to feel her.

Looking over her shoulder, I see Rafe and Juliana taking us in with relieved smiles on their faces.

"I missed you, captain," she whispers in my ear, making me squeeze her a little tighter. The mark down my chest screaming in protest.

When we finally bring ourselves to pull away, I hold her at arm's length checking her over.

"I'm fine, Luna, just slight markings, that's all."

She brings her hand up to her neck, my gaze following. It's still bruised from the rope burns, all purple and blue. The smile on her face convinces me she's telling the truth, even if she is slightly self-conscious about it all.

"Okay, now that you're finally out of your pit of despair, I'm going to go and get you a large rainbow dust and unicorn sprinkle Frappuccino. Maybe even a cake too," she says with a smile.

"You don't have to do that, Red," I say, but my protest is pointless since she's already heading for the door.

"I know, but I want to. It's only two blocks away, and Juliana has a team of guys downstairs. One of them will come with me, so stop stressing. Sit your cute butt down and eat," she sasses, waggling her finger at me.

Not wanting to make her worry, I offer a nod in response, as I watch her bounce out of the room.

"I never would have pictured you with a best friend so girly, you two are complete opposites. Jess is good for you," Rafe says, as I take a seat at the table.

"She is. The question is, am I good for her?" I mutter in response, looking anywhere but at him as I nervously play with the neckline of Kai's t-shirt, it's mine now.

"Are you crazy? Does she look unhappy to you?" Rafe argues back.

"She wouldn't have been hanging from the fucking rafters if it wasn't for me." I shoot him a glare, slamming my fist against the table, causing his coffee to spill a little. I don't care, I'm sick of him trying to sugarcoat everything.

"If it wasn't Jess, it would have been someone else, no matter what, Luna. She is lucky enough to have you in her corner, willing to destroy anyone and anything to keep her alive. Not many can say that," he says, arms braced on the table as he leans closer to me.

His belief in his own words has me at a loss. I'm too emotionally exhausted to express myself right now, so I say nothing.

"Would you like something to eat, Luna?" Juliana asks, pulling my attention from Rafe, and breaking the tension in the room. Thank god.

She's beautiful, you can tell Rafe is her brother. They look alike in so many ways, except she's not a gentle giant like him. She's closer to my height, and all soft curves. Her brown hair is in a slick ponytail, and her casual leggings and a plain white top don't match the businesswoman I've had glimpses of prior to now.

"Did you know me before?" I ask. If she did, she would know what I am asking.

"I did."

Simple as that, an open and honest response. I can see it in her eyes though, she wants me to ask what she remembers about me, and for me to tell her what I know of her. I'm not there yet. I'm telling my mind I need to remember and learn from my past, but it gives me nothing except blank pages.

Understanding I'm not able to give her what she wants, sadness darkens her face but she manages to carry on.

"So, food?"

"What are you offering?" I question, which makes her smile a little.

"Whatever you want. If I don't already have it, I will have it brought in. Although, I did buy the ingredients needed to make peanut butter and banana pancakes, in case that's still a thing," her voice weakens toward the end, unsure of herself.

Peanut butter and banana pancakes? I blink uncontrollably a few times, unable to move my stare from Juliana's.

They're my favorite. Always have been, always will be. I struggle to find any decent version on a menu, but I know I love them. I just can't remember the last time I had the perfect serving of peanut butter and banana pancakes.

Something tells me my love for them is connected to her.

"If you are going to make them as good as I'm hoping, I can't really say no now, can I?" I offer with a small smile.

The joy on her face is blinding as she jumps out of her chair and starts running around the kitchen.

"You've just made her day with that," Rafe murmurs.

I can tell, but I'm more surprised by the fact that her happiness feels important to me.

"What have I missed?" I ask, changing the subject.

"Honestly? Nothing much."

I snicker at his response. "Vague much? Rafe, I feel like I blacked out after ending my speech. How did we end up here? And where are we?" I ask, looking around the kitchen as if it holds all of the answers to my questions. This feels like a real deja vu moment, again. Recently, whenever I travel with Rafe, I never remember getting in the freaking vehicle. Like when Veronica drugged me to get me to the Academy.

"You did black out, once I got you out of the building and away from everyone." Fantastic. Why does my mind always have to play me like this? "And we are in New York."

"New York?" I ask, glancing around again, like I would be able to tell it's New York by the inside of these walls.

"Yeah, at Juliana's place. We organized everything we could when we were in the box, as everything unfolded," he offers.

"Care to elaborate?" I push, but Juliana humming to

herself over by the stove pulls my attention away from him.

"Do you not want to eat first?" Rafe asks, forcing me to whip my gaze back to him.

"Rafe, if I wanted to eat first I wouldn't have asked. So, get me up to date," I insist. "I need to get my head in gear, and to do that, I need to know what happened after I blacked out."

He stares me over for a moment as he sips his coffee.

"Okay. So, we agreed that Juliana and I would rush you out of there. Reggie had a plane ready for us…"

"A plane? We flew here?" I ask, shocked by this new information.

"Yes, we had a doctor waiting onboard too."

Wow.

I nod for him to continue.

"Betty Morgan tried to get your mother cornered before she could leave the building, but there was quite a bit of commotion. Unfortunately, she managed to get out of there with Rico," he says, with an apologetic look in his eyes. "Maria distracted the Dietrichsons so we could get out, because they were kicking up a fuss about you winning. Kai came to help you down from the rings, and

Parker forced Maverick to bring Jess with us." He raises his eyebrow, likely surprised by the force Parker can have. "Oscar and Roman ran interference with the masses of people present. None of the guys were happy they couldn't come with us," he breathes out at the end.

Trying to process everything he just said, I'm surprised they had time to arrange all of that. I don't actually know how long I was in The Pyramid, so maybe they had all the time in the world.

"Thank you," I murmur, clasping my hands together on the table.

"You don't need to thank me, Luna," Rafe says, placing his hand on top of mine.

"You're still here when I need you, even when everything is going to shit."

"Luna, no matter what, I will always be here. This world is a mind fuck and I'm living in it too. I would never purposefully leave you to handle any of this darkness alone. You are my child to protect, do you understand?" Taken back by his words, all I can do is squeeze his hand in response.

I needed to hear that. I need him in my corner, which means he can't keep holding details back.

After everything that's happened in the past few days, I feel raw looking into his eyes, vulnerable.

"I love you," I whisper.

Tears instantly prick his eyes. I don't recall ever being so open about my feelings with him, but the emotion on his face makes me glad I'm allowing him a deeper glimpse inside.

"I love you infinity, Luna. I know there is still a lot for me to tell you, and I will, I promise. I just don't want to make anything worse."

"Well, I need to know, so I can handle this world. I don't appreciate people like Rico asking me if I remember them, and not actually knowing the answer. I've been laying in bed, willing my mind to open to me, but I'm coming up blank." I sigh, pushing my fingertips into the table.

"We'll get through this together, Luna. We always do," he offers with a smile, as Red comes barreling into the room, hands full of Frappuccino heaven.

"This is why you're my favorite," I mutter, before wrapping my lips around the straw and gulping down the ice cold coffee.

"Well duh, that was my plan all along." She giggles, taking the seat beside me.

Juliana brings over a plate stacked high with pancake goodness. I don't speak to anyone as I devour the plate, finally fueling my body with the most delicious treat ever.

"No one makes them like this," I say, as I come up for air.

"You remember?" Juliana asks, hopeful.

"Err, not really. I just know that this is how they're supposed to taste." I meet her eyes and show my honesty.

"I'll take that," she beams, sitting down beside Rafe.

"I'm already itching at these stitches, can we fast forward to Sunday already?" I ask, needing to steer the conversation in a different direction.

"Suck it up, buttercup. You've got three days left to relax and plan. Deal with it," Rafe says, with a smirk.

"Rafe, be nice to my beautiful girl, or I'll go all Queen Gibbs mode on you and pull rank." Juliana jumps in, giving him a fake glare before offering me a wink. Red chuckles beside me and I join her.

"Well, I could do with a little R&R, and I can't follow through on my threat without a plan now, can I?"

The darkness that takes over Juliana's face tells me she's behind me, whatever needs to be done.

"Whatever you need from me, you just say, agreed?"

she emphasizes, and I nod in response.

"I just need to know what's actually happening right now and going forward. Not my history, that's something I think I need to do for myself," I say, looking mainly at Rafe.

"I promise."

"I'll hold you to that," I say with a stern look, then take a deep breath trying to relax. "Any chance of some pants?" I ask, glancing around the table to find Red smirking and wiggling her eyebrows at me.

"I took the liberty of getting you some outfits, courtesy of Rafe's card, of course."

"If you bought anything pink or floral, I'm getting rid of you," I say, and she just laughs, running to the living room to grab whatever she bought.

Before I follow her, Rafe stops me.

"Hey, have you spoken to the guys yet?"

"No, and I don't plan to." I sigh, looking down at my feet.

"I told Roman not to tell you, Luna. It's my fault." He places his hand on his chest.

I consider his words for a moment, rubbing the back of my neck, embarrassed that we're having this conversation right now. He even said the guys, it's that obvious.

"Rafe, if someone is willing to omit information from me because someone else said so, then they weren't meant for me anyway," I answer, my heart hurting as the words burn my tongue.

I follow after Red without a backward glance.

I don't need excuses, and I don't need the distraction.

I'm out for blood.

TWO

Oscar

I'm going out of my head.

We all are. Five days ago, my baby girl endured that fucking Pyramid. I still can't unsee the blood dripping down her face and the slice down her chest. My girl's breasts on show for everyone to see, yet it's the least of anyone's worries.

She did what she needed to do to survive, saving Jess along the way.

I was too busy running interference so I didn't see her address everyone, but I heard her voice over the speakers. Void of any emotion, yet you could feel the promise of vengeance. When she mentioned her father, my heart was aching for her.

Roman finally explained everything he knew, expanding on the bombs Luna had dropped back in Washington.

Parker, Kai and I dropped everything to get there, the instant Roman had sent the stress text *PINEAPPLE,* but we were too late. Everything had already gone to shit by then. Parker's father, Rico, had shown up to Luna's room with some of his men, while she was still out getting the blueprints needed to complete her assignment.

Apparently Luna had some cool tech stuff set up, and Rafe sent her Grandmother to assist. No one has really explained to me why Rico was there. I do know that his words caught Luna off guard, because he'd been the one to tell her she'd known Roman as a child.

I was a little confused why neither of them had mentioned it. Then, Luna explained in a fit of rage that she didn't remember her life before the age of six. So, Roman had been omitting shit from her, from *all* of us.

Alone in the gym at Ace, I smash my gloved hands into the punching bag before me, trying to get my anger out somewhere.

He had known Luna since they were babies. The Gibbs,

Steele, Rivera and Morgan families were a tight knit group before it was all blasted to hell.

The group was so close that an alliance was agreed upon for their children to be betrothed to each other. I don't know, I don't really understand. I knew it was quite common for multiple families to form stronger connections through marriage, strengthening their bloodlines, but I didn't actually know anyone who had.

It appealed to me on so many levels. To be part of a bigger immediate family unit as opposed to just two. I don't have the capacity to take on someone else's burdens alone, not with everything I already have running around in my head. I've experienced loss, and felt both physical and mental pain for as long as I can remember. When I lose myself to the darkness, I prefer to do so in private. That's why the five of us, together, works for me.

Luna settles me and excites me at the same time. I'm an adrenaline junkie, and she's my latest addiction. We were already a close group of friends, but she just glues us together that much better.

Roman explained that all his childhood memories, until he turned six, involved Luna and West in some way. West has no chance now though. The thought makes me snicker. He'll have to rethink his options because there is no room on the Luna train for him.

The humor leaves my mind as I remember Roman saying that one day, Luna was just… gone, along with her father, Bryce Steele. None of us are any wiser as to why everyone was made to believe she had died with her father, and no one dared ask what happened on that fateful day.

I miss her voice. Fuck, she always brings out my pussy side.

I calm my assault on the punching bag, leaning my head against it as I try to catch my breath. I miss the feel of her skin, and the electricity that courses through my veins when she's near. All this new information is running around in my head, and I haven't laid eyes on my girl, *our* girl, in five days.

Five. Fucking. Days.

It's too long.

Pushing off the bag, I lift my arms and go again, feeling my muscles burn, but it doesn't relieve any of my pent up stress. I know she's with Rafe, and he'll keep her safe. I just need to see her for myself.

My phone chimes from the bench beside me, but I'm not done channeling my anger. It goes off a few more times, and when I finally glance down, it's Roman. The only reason I would stop right now is if Luna was calling me.

The door to the gym bursts open and Roman storms in, relief showing on his face when he sees me. I can tell he's mad that he had to come looking for me, although he's trying to downplay it because he knows we're all struggling.

"Oscar, I've been calling you, man." He stretches his arms out to the side, in question.

"I know," I grunt, not relenting on the punching bag, continuing through the motion.

Jab. Jab. Cross. Jab. Jab. Hook.

He lets me continue for a little longer before he steps up to the other side of the bag and pulls it away from me.

"What do you want, Roman?"

"Rafe called, she's on her way."

Fuck. If he'd led with that when he walked in, I would have stopped what I was doing.

Fucking idiot.

"Did he say how they both are?" I ask, trying to catch my breath as I finally start to feel the toll of my workout. The thought of her being so near has my heart rate picking up.

"He said Jess is bouncing around leaving a rainbow

in her tracks," he chuckles, happy to hold a lighter conversation, even if only for a second. We both know Jess is all sunshine and roses, so that tells us she's okay.

"And Luna?"

"I don't know. He said she was much stronger than when they first left, both physically and emotionally. He tried to broach the subject about us but she just shut him down."

"How long till she gets here?"

I take a seat on the bench, resting my forearms on my knees as sweat pours off me. I've clearly been here longer than I had originally planned. My muscles are already starting to ache, but I enjoy the pain.

"Rafe called when she got off the plane. He thought it would be best if we weren't there when she arrives," he murmurs. The guilt in his eyes shows me how much he is beating himself up over this. As much as I want to beat the shit out of him, I don't need to add to the torture he's already putting himself through.

"What does that mean?" I frown, grabbing my water and taking a sip.

"It means she's about ten minutes away and doesn't want to see us."

"Fuck that, Roman!" I shout, raking my fingers through my hair, gripping at the ends.

"What do you expect me to do?"

Expect him to do? Is he for real? Fuck that hopeless look in his eyes.

"I expect you to fucking stand your ground. She's never going to get past any of this if you don't put up a fight and convince her to listen to you," I yell, and he hangs his head, his fingers fisting in the back of his hair. He's like a caged animal. It's a struggle for him to have someone else hold all the power here.

"I know that, Oscar, but I think I need to give her a minute. I know it's been five days, before you fucking remind me, again. From everything back in Washington with Rico… and me, to fighting in The Pyramid. Rafe said she needs some space."

He's right, I know he is. It doesn't mean I have to like it, and fuck Rafe for giving out more shitty orders.

God, it fucking hurts not being with her right now. I wish I could go back to the beach house with her. Everything was so simple there.

"Have you told the others?" I ask.

"Yeah, they're up in my room, waiting for me to get

back with you. You good?"

I don't answer. I just grab my things and head for the door. We need to figure this shit out because I need my girl.

Rounding the corner for the elevator, I see that it's not on the ground floor, and I don't have the patience to wait for it. So I take the stairs two at a time up to the top level, Roman right behind me.

Parker is standing at Roman's door when we get there, his eyes bleak.

He knew it was the right thing to do to get Luna out of Featherstone, we all did, but he's taking it worse than the rest of us. Parker is slowly sinking. Knowing that his father was behind a lot of this, along with Luna's bitch of a mother, has him at a loss. The only way he'll feel better is with Luna around.

Kai has been quieter than usual. You can see he's troubled by all of this. I'm not even sure if he's slept. He's been trying to hack into the Gibbs' security system, but without any luck. I think he needs to rest his eyes on her, like me.

Roman has just been a grumpy ass, mainly because he knows he really fucked up by not being honest with her. He needs to get a grip on it all because I will not allow this ship to sink.

Standing in Roman's room, the layout is a carbon copy of Luna's. Pity the furnishings scream bachelor pad, instead of Luna's cozy surroundings. The grey wooden floors, white walls and black gloss furniture yells, 'I am man, hear me roar!' My room is a smaller version of Roman's, but that's irrelevant right now.

It's silent in here.

"So how do we play this, guys?" Parker asks, desperation in his voice.

"We have to go at her speed, give her a few days, then charge in. We don't want to give her too much time to get comfortable without us around," Kai says, like it really is that simple.

Nobody wants to wait, it's obvious, but none of us have ever cared enough about anyone to try and put their feelings first. I'm all for charging in when necessary though.

"Any news on Rico or Hindman?" Roman asks, and Kai shakes his head.

"They're good at covering their tracks, the system is constantly running. The second they pop up, I'll know."

A bang outside the door gains our attention. Like lightning, Parker is whipping the door open, and stopping dead in his tracks.

We're all quick to follow his footsteps. Glancing around him, I see her.

Trying to take in every inch of her at once, I don't know where to place my eyes first. I'm drawn to her face, my baby girl has black and blue bruising around her pretty green eyes again. Why do they always go for her beautiful face like that? From the look in Luna's eyes, I can see she had hoped to get in without having to see any of us, and it guts me.

She's not alone, Jess is with her and it's clear she made the bang with a big-ass suitcase. What the fuck's that for? The guilt on her face plays havoc on her features.

Returning my stare to Luna, we all just stand and gape at her, none of us knowing what to say or do.

She looks at each of us, and I can tell she can see the stress written all over our faces. I can also see the hurt in her eyes because of Roman's stupid fucking actions, and that she doesn't want to deal with us.

She turns to walk into her room, when Parker calls out.

"Luna," barely a whisper past his lips, but she hears it.

She can hear the pain in his voice and looks back at him. I see her ache at the devastation in his eyes, and she's unable to stop herself from making her way to him.

Nobody moves, terrified we'll scare her off.

She cups his cheek lightly, and he melts into her touch, leaning his face into her palm as he closes his eyes at the contact.

"I can't make this better right now, Parker. I hate seeing you like this, but a lot has happened this past week. I'm not ready to deal with this yet," she murmurs, leaning into him further. She doesn't even realize she's doing it.

"You just did," he murmurs back, dropping his head to her shoulder, breathing her in.

I'm fucking jealous of him right now.

She holds her hand on the back of his neck, lightly stroking her fingers through the tips of his hair for a moment before stepping back.

Luna offers a poor excuse of a smile before she's gone. Red offers us a grin and a wink before following her inside. Did she make that bang on purpose?

Sullenly, we all step back into Roman's room, the ache in my chest only worse.

Kai throws himself back down into his seat as Roman guides Parker inside with his arm wrapped around his shoulders.

Fuck this shit.

We are more than this, and we need to be a hell of a lot more if we plan to stay by her side.

Firing off a quick text, I leave without even a backward glance, heading back to my own space. I don't need to be around them right now.

I need a cold shower.

Fuck it.

I know that won't work.

I finally laid eyes on my baby girl, and my dick is hard as steel. The warmth that takes over my body feels different this time, but I don't understand why. I just know being in her presence impacts me more than anyone else ever has.

I'm gonna scream her name so loud she'll hear me.

YOUR BLOODLINE

THREE

Luna

"Girl, I'm gonna give you a minute to get yourself comfortable, then me and you are going to put a movie on, eat junk food and finally talk about those boys," Red says, hands on hips, ready for my argument.

"Red, I just—"

"No, Luna. It wasn't an offer. We're going to get into our comfys, I'm going to order you a meat feast pizza and some Phish Food ice cream, and we are going to hash this all out. Understood?"

I nod, knowing she's not going to let this drop, and I haven't got the strength to say no to her right now.

Although, I do know I need to rein my sass in around her. She's picking it up too easily now. I don't like her using it against me.

Looking around the lounge, everything is exactly as I left it before I had to make my way to The Pyramid. The scrap of paper telling me they took Red still sits crumpled on the coffee table.

"Go get yourself sorted, I'll organize in here." There's a pause before I hear, "Luna... Luna?" With a hand suddenly being waved in my face.

"Sorry, I'm good," I say, shaking my head.

She waves her arms for me to get a move on, and I step into my bedroom, shutting the door behind me. I rest my head on the wood for a moment. Taking a few deep breaths, I try to calm myself, when I'm distracted by my phone vibrating in my pocket.

When Red had given it to me back in New York, the group chat with the guys had been filled with messages. I just hadn't brought myself to read them yet.

Pulling my phone out, I have two messages. One from Rafe and the other a private message from Oscar... not in the group chat, huh? The preview that pops up has me opening the message instinctively.

Oscar: I'm going to try very hard to give my baby girl a minute's space but don't ignore me like I didn't dick the hell out of you! The pounding you're in for the next time I get my hands on you will be brutal, alone or not. Really though, baby girl. I'm not afraid to mark my territory, and you're mine.

What the? This guy. I can't help the little bubble of laughter that passes my lips at his words. His big mouth can make things completely worse or brighten my day, and right now it's given me a little spark back.

Damn I needed that, but I won't respond. As much as I want to, I'm still mad. Clicking through to Rafe's text, I welcome the distraction from flirting back with Oscar.

Rafe: Hey, Juliana's trying to straighten a few things out, may take a week. We still haven't had Veronica or Rico pop up, but I'll let you know as soon as that changes. Maria had Dietrichson pulled for business for the next two weeks, make the most of it. Please be careful, and patient.

Luna: Will do, thanks for the update. I'm getting impatient with all this waiting around, tell Juliana to work her magic ASAP.

I leave my phone on my bedside table and quickly slip into a pair of black cotton shorts and a purple tank top. I take a moment to brush my hair through and throw it up in a bun. Now I'm ready to face Red and her fifty questions.

I must have taken longer than I thought because there is a knock on the door as I step into the lounge. Red spots me, but shakes her head.

"I'll get it, you sit," she says, heading for the door. I sprint after her, and push her to the side before she can open it, my heart racing with fear.

The last time she opened my door she was taken. All because Featherstone needed a reason to force me to compete in the games. It was my fault the last time. I refuse to let it happen again.

I swing the door open to Kai standing on the other side. Pizza boxes and a bag hanging from one hand, and a tray of Frappuccinos in the other. My shoulders relax as the tension slowly leaves my body.

His eyes instantly fall to me, and I'm lost in his gaze. I mean he's gorgeous already, but with all my favorite treats in his hand, can he get any hotter than that?

"Sakura, don't worry, I'm not intruding. Jessica is using me as an errand boy," he says, a smile playing on his lips.

"Thank you," I murmur, unable to offer more than a small lift of my own.

I can see he wants to help in any way he can. He's always been able to observe me and understand me, sometimes before I even know myself. Kai is not usually one to force his way in, but I can tell he wants to.

I'm still rooted to the spot as he steps in and places everything on the coffee table for us. He glances between Red and I for a moment when she speaks up.

"Kai, you can leave now. You're imposing on girl time and we're about to gossip about you. That can't happen when you're here, okay?"

I can see the surprise in his eyes by her outburst, but there's a hint of amusement there too. He likes the idea of us talking about them, she's offering him something… hope.

"Sakura," he murmurs with a single nod, then lets

himself out. God, that was hard. The rumble in his voice has me wanting to step into his arms, and let him shield me from this crazy world. It's a pity I've decided his safety is more important than my own needs right now, otherwise I'd be wrapped up in him already.

"Okay girly, let's get our butts comfy. I chose a Marvel movie for you. I didn't want to push you over the edge with girl talk *and* a chick flick," she says with a wink, making me roll my eyes at her lame attempt to get all the gossip.

"Yes, there she is, with that bitchy eye roll I love so much! Woo, come on, captain, let's go."

This girl is crazy, but I find myself getting comfortable on the sofa as she throws a blanket over us and pulls the coffee table closer.

I've barely lifted my first slice of greasy meat feast amazingness to my lips when she's twisting to face me.

"So, you like all the boys, huh?"

She catches me off guard mid-bite, making me choke. She's not messing around with her questions.

I contemplate the best way to answer. I can tell if I say something that can be misinterpreted she'll be Team Aceholes in a heartbeat, if she isn't already.

"I did."

"No, you still do. You're just in denial," she says, waving her pointed finger in my direction.

"I am?" I ask, avoiding her stare, not wanting her to see the truth in my eyes.

"Don't play silly with me, Luna. We both know you have them wrapped around your pinky, and you all love it."

"I can't deny that I did, Red. It's just… a lot has happened in the past week. Enough for me to reconsider all of my emotions and actions. Then for the cherry on top, Roman fucking monumentally lied this whole time too. It's too much drama, and they are too much of a distraction." I breathe out, stuffing more pizza in my face so I don't have to spill my feelings for a moment.

I'm not used to talking about personal stuff so openly. I need to pace myself.

"Okay, I will get back to Roman and his broody ass omitting some truths in a minute, but first, we need to forget the past week."

Is she crazy? I swipe a hand down my face, trying to wipe the pain of it all away.

"That's pointless because before the past week, everything was perfect."

"Exactly, Luna. That's my point. How did you feel this time last week?"

That's a loaded question. This time last week? It was the day after the Fall Ball. God, was that really only a week ago? We'd had the most relaxing day after one of the best nights of my life. Well, after we left the Fall Ball at least.

Grabbing my Frappuccino off the coffee table, I distract myself, gathering the strength to answer her question. That's when I see the black ink scrawled across my Frappuccino, 'Sakura'. Fuck, everytime with the feels, Kai. Not cool.

"Last week? I felt amazing, Red," I murmur, unable to lift my eyes from the side of my cup.

I feel her hand rest on my shoulder, squeezing in comfort. Turning my gaze, I meet her eyes. I didn't think I could let myself relax around anyone like this, but she makes it feel natural to me.

"It's all gone to shit, Red," I mumble, as I avoid eye contact with her, trying to hide my feelings.

"Luna, it only goes to shit if you let it."

"Red, taking Roman's omission of the truth out of the equation, people with a lot of power at this school and within The Ring want me dead. I'm risking everyone around me. It's better if I go back to being a lone ranger anyway, you just won't listen," I say, raising my eyebrow at her.

"Luna, I know this is going to be a shock to you, but this is my pre-warning, okay?" I nod in response, as she lifts her hand from me, and squares her shoulders. "Stop being so self-centered, it doesn't suit you. We are here because we want to be. Trying to push everyone away to make yourself feel better? Well, it makes you bitchy and gives you the appearance of being a narcissist, and I don't like it." She huffs at the end, like that took all her energy.

Well then. I feel like I should be offended. Am I offended?

I stare at her pointy finger still floating in the air and the attempt of a stern look on her face. I know it took guts for her to speak the truth. I respect that, and I love her strength to be honest with me, no matter what.

"It's irrelevant what they want, and safer this way."

"But have you given Roman a chance to explain? Or given the guys a choice in all of this?"

"Nope." I pop the hell out of that p, looking up to the ceiling.

"Do you need a timeout? Your bitch is still showing,"

she murmurs, patting my leg as she stands. "Or do you need another drink to loosen up?"

I don't have the energy to comment on her sass, so I just roll my eyes at her.

"Is there anything stronger?"

"It can be arranged," she says, giving a little shimmy as she heads into the kitchen.

I sit, lost in my own mind, trying to understand how I feel.

Do I want this thing with the guys to be over? No, not really. I'm stuck between Roman omitting the truth and wanting to keep everyone safe.

"So, you're going to push the guys away, to protect them?" she asks, as she waltzes back in with some glasses and the bourbon Oscar had stolen from the limo last week.

"It'll be one less thing for us all to worry about. They need each other, that's what matters."

"They also need you, Luna. We could use their help here."

"We don't need anybody's help, Red. I've got this." I frown. Does she not trust me to handle it?

"Don't frown at me like that. I just mean more hands on deck, and all that."

I don't respond. I just watch her fill the glasses, and hand one over to me.

"Luna, I'm never going to tell you what to say or do, especially because I know it's not your style to listen. I just think you need to remember how they made you feel because I believe you can get back to that in an instant." She snaps her fingers. "You really should give Roman a chance to explain though. Think of the crazy hot make-up sex you could have."

I can't help but giggle a little at her and she joins in, relieved her words didn't upset me.

"The make-up sex would be amazing. I just don't know if I actually want to make up," I say, gulping down the bourbon.

"Well I'm just saying, don't cut off the peen that feeds you, okay?"

I cough on the sip I'd just taken.

"Red!" I splutter, as I check my top for spillages.

"What? Don't even. You have still been holding out on all the details, girl, and I need them."

Is she fucking pouting?

"I am not having this discussion with you, Red."

"Fine, whatever. I'll just ask Oscar, he'll tell me," she

says, sticking her tongue out.

I'm too surprised by her comment to even respond, but she's right. He'd definitely love that conversation.

"Anything else you want to discuss, or can we relax now?" I ask.

"Well, if you're not going to give me any juicy details, I'm not really interested to be honest." She gives me a fake glare but it's not going to change my decision.

She holds my stare a moment longer, before finally giving in.

"Fine, let's watch your action movie, and get some rest. Tomorrow is going to be a crazy day back into the world of Featherstone Academy, and I think you're going to need the energy. I'm staying here tonight though, don't even question it. Alright?"

I wasn't planning on letting her leave anyway. So, I offer a classic Luna nod in response, and snuggle under the soft blanket.

I miss the presence of the guys. I wish they were here right now, but everything is fucked up, and I'm not sure we can ever get back to how things were.

YOUR BLOODLINE

FOUR

Luna

Standing in front of my floor-length mirror, I take in my appearance. The classic black, gold and red colors of my uniform fill my vision. Sadly, my feet weren't injured in The Pyramid so I've had to put my heels on. I refuse to wear makeup. I'm gonna show these fuckers my black eyes and the gash on my forehead. I'm a damn survivor, again, and I'll make sure they know it.

I was worried this morning when Red had to leave for L.F.G. It's the only first period lesson on a Monday, and while I had a free period, Red had a lesson with Wren… alone. She promised she was okay, and not at risk, so I have to believe her. Otherwise, I'd keep her safely away from the drama. Like in a different country, away from it all.

Grabbing my handbag, I straighten my back and head out, ready for whatever this place wants to throw at me today. I take the stairs, slowly, in these stupid heels, and find the guys sitting in the lounge when I get there.

They all instantly rise, eyes on me, and as much as my soul loves their attention, I'm not prepared for any form of conversation. Plus, all the eye candy in front of me has me a little breathless, my brain is close to malfunctioning. Standing in their uniforms with their slightly damp hair, these Aceholes are just too fucking gorgeous. It's infuriating.

Kai is the first to speak, with his hands lifted in surrender because I'm apparently that unpredictable.

"Good morning, Sakura. I promise we are only here to support you. It looks like everyone's been tipped off that you're back at Featherstone because every student that isn't in L.F.G. is outside waiting to see you step out."

I glance toward the door, and he's right. It's crammed with bodies, just like after I was jumped, except Wren isn't there this time.

"They want to see the badass who brought Featherstone to their knees in The Pyramid," Oscar adds, gaining my attention.

I look him over, and his text comes to mind from yesterday. He must be able to tell where my mind just went because this motherfucker winks at me. I can't help but roll my eyes at him. At least he didn't ruin it with his big mouth.

"I don't need you guys to protect me, you know," I murmur, unable to hold any of their gazes, instead glancing back outside to the waiting crowd.

"We know, Luna. Things have changed from when you first arrived. The Pyramid changed everything. You're feared now and they'll want a glimpse of you. Fear equals power at Featherstone, and it'll help if we stand with you," Roman states.

"And why am I supposed to just listen to you, Roman?" I spit out, annoyed that I'm expected to simply take his word for it like nothing has happened.

He sighs as he tries to find the right words to respond. "Rafe said to—" I cut him off with a burst of laughter I can't keep in.

"Because Rafe said so," I mock, glaring at him. "How's

Rafe's last bit of advice working for you?" I snap, angry that I'm allowing my emotions to get the better of me.

Completely done with all of this, I whirl around from Roman, heading for the door and find Parker behind me, despair written all over his face. Any comeback I was expecting from Roman is gone, as I'm instantly sucked into Parker's hazel eyes and the pain that darkens them. Pain. I know deep down I'm the one causing it.

He doesn't move toward me, he just stands before me making me peer into his soul. I offer the smallest nod in agreement, that I'll let them stand with me, and the relief on his face is instant.

"Whatever you need, angel, okay?" Parker adds, and I almost whimper at the rasp to his voice. As if I dunked his head in the dark hole that consumes him and just as quickly pulled him out.

With a final nod, I squeeze his hand as I pass and make my way to the door. It opens automatically, and any chatter is instantly halted. The sun glares down on me as I glance toward the waiting Rolls Royces and spot Ian. I can barely see past the crowd, my skin burning with every pair of eyes on me. I feel the guys gather behind me, showing everyone we stand together.

There are questions on everyone's faces but no one with big enough balls to ask them. So, I'm gonna have to remind them who I am.

"Any particular reason why you're all fucking staring?" I growl. Nobody answers, they're all shuffling awkwardly or looking anywhere but at me. That's when I spot her.

Trudy.

Her blonde hair is curled and falling down her back like she spent hours perfecting it, and she has minimal makeup on. She's not as tall as me, a little curvier, and she fucking owns it.

Remembering my words to her, I relax my posture and address everyone.

"I couldn't give a shit how things are usually run around here. As of now I do things on my terms. If any of you are little minions of Wren's, then please, run it back to her. You all saw what I'm capable of in The Pyramid. You also saw that violence isn't the only way. Unfortunately, I know there will be more blood on my hands. Anyone who makes an attempt on my life will face the same outcome. This is the only fucking warning you're going to get." My voice is booming around us, full of confidence I wasn't fully aware I had right now.

Trudy starts making her way to me, and I'm relieved she is okay. Everyone around us tracks her movement. Where is her brother? As she comes to stand in front of me she must sense my unspoken question.

"He has class, but he's fine."

I offer a nod but don't say a word, not yet.

"Did you mean what you said? Back at The Pyramid?" she asks, and the words are fresh in my mind.

"I promise you after all this. There will be changes around here and you'll be standing beside me, do you understand?"

Glancing around her, everybody is still standing around us as if they're waiting for something *more*.

Looking back at Trudy, I see her fear, worried that I only said what I needed to say in The Pyramid to win.

"Yes, I meant every word."

She gives me a nod, turning to stand beside me, facing out to the crowd.

"The Byrne's stand beside the Steele bloodline, we're done with Dietrichson," she calls out loudly for everyone around us to hear. The students are surprised by her confession, including me.

I feel like she's staking her place in a battle from an old

war movie or something.

Although, it does feel like a war is coming.

"Luna Steele, you know I'm Trudy Byrnes, a Club. What you don't know is, I may not specialize in combat or weaponry, but my family name is the highest of a... different trade. It's nice to finally meet you under better circumstances." She offers a smile, as the crowd's discussions get louder.

"This isn't our fucking war, Trudy!" some guy yells from the crowd. I can't see who it came from though. She rolls her eyes dramatically.

"There's always one with a big mouth, am I right?" she says with a smirk, as I find my eyes drifting to Oscar. They all must have heard her because they're grinning. I'm surprised they've stayed quiet this long.

As if reading my mind, Parker steps forward.

"There's already a war, always has been. Maybe you should clue yourself in on where you actually are. Now fuck off." He grinds out. There's the Ace version of Parker I haven't seen before, the one Red was adamant existed. Fuck me that was hot, although I instantly miss the softer side he lets me see.

Trudy stands in my line of sight to gain my attention,

clearly smart enough not to reach out and touch me.

"Thank you, Luna. For The Pyramid, and for hopefully pulling us all through this shit storm. Here's my number, if you need me, just call. You'd be surprised the following my name comes with. We're having a party out behind the Library Friday night, you should make an appearance," she says with a smile and a sparkle in her green eyes, handing me her card and sauntering off.

Everyone follows Parker's order and Trudy's lead, and scatters.

I keep my eyes focused on her for a moment, her confidence has surprised me now that we're not in the ring. She's not a priority on my list of allies, but she does represent a deeper connection into this world. Trudy is a true example that I made the right decision offering her an out in The Pyramid.

A few guys follow her direction, keeping a tight shield around her.

"You ready, baby girl?" Oscar asks from behind me.

"Yeah," I murmur, glancing over my shoulder at him.

I head for the Rolls I see Ian standing at, not glancing to look who's following. Even though Wren isn't here right now, and one of us could travel alone, I know it won't be me.

"Anybody but Roman," I say, making sure they hear me without giving the other students something to gossip about.

"Miss Steele, I'm glad to see you back," he greets as he opens the door.

"Thank you, Ian. Did I miss anything while I was gone?"

"Apart from them boys moping around like lovestruck teenage girls you mean?" he asks, with a slight lift to his lips.

"Yeah, apart from that," I mutter, even though my heart beats a little faster at his admission.

"Nothing much, if I'm honest. There hasn't been any gossip coming from higher up, but if I get wind of anything I'll let you know."

"I appreciate it," I say, as I slip into the car.

I relax into my seat as Kai steps in beside me. He offers me a gentle smile, not pressuring me into a conversation as the car begins to move.

His presence relaxes me, I love basking in his comfortable silence. His leather and cinnamon scent surrounds me, and I inhale it like a drug. I miss our hands connecting on the arm rest between us but I force myself to keep my hands clasped on my lap.

As we pull up outside Combat, he finally speaks.

"If you need any help burying bodies today, just let me know. I'm down for whatever."

I try so hard not to laugh at his nonchalant attitude as he says it so matter of factly. I don't respond as I step out of the car in front of the Combat building. I prefer it out here, by Combat and Weaponry, where there is so much open space and nature. Enjoying my surroundings is short lived as I hear a girl scream.

"It's about time you showed your face, you fucking bitch. Get over here!"

Wren. Great.

Turning in the direction her voice came from, I see she's not alone. Becky is there with a few others, but obviously there's no Tyler. Wren doesn't look as put together as she usually does. Her makeup is thicker, if that was even possible. Her hair is ruffled too far past the bedhead look.

I glance at Becky, whose blonde hair is scraped back into a ponytail, making it easy to spot the rope burn marks she was unable to cover on her neck. The glare she's giving tells me there's no appreciation for saving her life. You're welcome.

There's a crowd around us, again. Some from just minutes ago with Trudy. Glancing around in search of Red, I see her step toward us, and Oscar places her strategically behind him. Now that I know she's safe, I can address this bitch.

"What do you want now, Wren? I don't care for your childish antics when there's big girl issues to be dealing with," I say, already fed up with this conversation.

"Bitch, you better watch your tone, before someone jumps you in the dark again," she sneers, but her voice isn't as confident as it usually is.

I can't help but laugh, it literally sprouts out of me before I can filter it. This girl, when is she going to catch on? I drop my handbag and step toward her, slowly. My laughter draws everyone's attention further. Becky steps back a little from Wren, who's barely holding her ground right now.

"Girl, are you forgetting what happens every time you come at me? Where's your boyfriend?" I glare, and her face pales. I step right up in her space, ready to show this bitch and everyone else that I mean what I say. I've told her enough times I'll keep coming back harder, stronger.

"I'm done with you and your bullshit, Wren. I'm the fucking predator here, and you're the motherfucking prey. You've seen what I'm capable of. I won't hesitate to put you in the ground, reunite you with Tyler again. You used up all my compassion when I saved your friend's life in The Pyramid. Do you understand?"

I'm mere inches away from her, leaning in, breathing on her face. You could hear a pin drop right now, no one daring to make a sound.

There's a slight tremor in Wren's hand, as she lifts it to slap me. She's never going to learn. I grip her wrist with one hand, while wrapping the other around her throat. Seems this is a common position for us.

Before I can breathe another word at her, Maverick Miller steps into our space, meeting my eyes.

"Let go, Luna," he murmurs.

I take in his words for a moment. He knows what I can do, but he also saw my compassion because he carried Trudy, her brother and Red out of the rings to safety, at my request.

I drop my hands and shove her back, unable to just let go. She stumbles and falls to her ass, grazing her hands on the ground as she loses a heel. I desperately want to laugh, but I look down my nose at her instead.

"Fuck off, Wren, before I don't listen to reason and snap your neck," I say in a bored tone.

"We're not fucking done here, you stupid whore," she screeches as she scurries to her feet, taking off her other heel and running barefoot inside. I ignore her as I turn to double check on Red. She's standing between Oscar and Parker while Roman and Kai stand on either side of them. They've all stepped closer, likely following my steps as I closed in on Wren.

Red offers me a soft smile, as Kai steps forward with my handbag held out for me.

"Thanks."

"It's good to see you, Luna," Maverick says, pulling my attention back to him. His green eyes are filled with respect, as he scratches the stubble on his chin, and his messy brown hair blows with the gentle breeze.

"I believe I owe you a thank you," I say in response.

"You don't owe me a thing. I'm impressed by your approach. I spoke to Rafe over the weekend, if you need me for anything at all just say the word. Although, I would just like to state that I can do big boy jobs too," he says with a smirk, hand outstretched for me to shake.

I'm not sure why he feels the need to shake hands but I reach mine out in return and that's when I feel it, a small object. Keeping my features neutral, I drop his hand after a moment and continue our conversation.

"You sure? You seem like the obedient errand boy type," I say with a grin, and his eyes shift beyond me. I don't follow his line of sight, instead heading inside.

"Don't think you're sparring today, not even with Roman in the corner. You can help me watch everyone's form."

"Are you joking?" I say spinning back around to glare at him.

"Nope, but that won't be a problem now will it, seeing as you're so obedient and all that," he jokes, throwing my words back at me.

Red steps toward me, wrapping her arm through mine and leading me inside.

"It blows my mind how you can go from nearly ripping Wren's throat out, to cracking inappropriate jokes at the tutors, Luna," she says, baffled by the whole thing. I just offer a grin.

Happy first day back to me.

YOUR BLOODLINE

FIVE

I spend the rest of the week surprisingly relaxed. Wren is constantly glaring the shit out of me, and I can see her brain working overtime, plotting out her revenge.

Even the guys have respected my space, though I can see the effort they're using.

Trudy has surprised me, she has some damn reach on this campus from what Red has said. The Byrne's parties seem to be pretty epic and the reason they are so popular. I'm surprised, because for one, she isn't an Ace, or even a Diamond. It has me itching to know what her skillset is. Nobody has attempted to approach me, they're not stupid.

The control Wren usually holds over everyone is slipping.

When I'd told Red that Trudy had mentioned a party on Friday night, she was all in. Practically squealing in delight and adamant we needed to let our hair down and be teens for a minute. Somehow I agreed with her. Glancing at my phone, I have another text from her.

Red: Only 8 hours to go. Eeekk!! I'll be there in 4 hours so we have plenty of time to eat and get ready. No arguments, captain! I'll bring Frappuccinos!

With it being a Friday, I had an early finish while she had L.F.G. again. So, I have four hours to get shit done and relax before she crashes in here like a hurricane. I just have to survive a car ride with Roman first.

My last lesson on Fridays is B.I.C.E. (Bribery, Infiltration, Corruption and Embezzlement) which only Roman and I have. This will be the first time since Washington that I'll be alone with him, and I'm strong enough to admit it has me a little anxious.

Julie, our tutor for B.I.C.E., is still talking us through her examples of bribery. It's all she's done, mumble on about her own examples. I actually wish we had textbooks to read or something because her stories aren't as cool as she thinks they are. I find my gaze constantly drawn out of the window, mesmerized by the trees blowing with the breeze.

My plans for this afternoon are running through my mind on repeat. There's no room for error.

There are about thirty of us in here, all sitting in pairs, and of course Roman is beside me. I can feel his gaze on me, and my body keeps trying to lean into his, wanting to feel his heat. His woodsy aftershave intoxicates my senses, putting me at war with myself.

My brain keeps repeating 'he lied' over and over again to try and keep me in check, but I don't know how much longer that'll work.

Julie is still droning on when the bell rings. I hadn't unpacked a thing, so I grab my bag and make a dash for the door. I need a moment to get my walls back up before we're alone. He didn't speak a word to me in class, but I know that's about to change. He's never going to stay silent when we're alone.

Stepping into the Rolls first, I don't look back. I can feel his eyes on me though, and I know he's close. The second the door shuts behind him the atmosphere that surrounds us intensifies, and I feel like I can't breathe. His scent is even more powerful in here. I almost feel light-headed.

I try to keep my gaze focused out the window, but his sighs tell me he's trying to start a conversation. Finally, he grows some balls.

"Luna, can we talk?" he murmurs, unsure of himself as he turns to face me.

"Nope." My inner bitch loving to pop the 'p' as always.

"Please, Luna, I just need a chance to explain to you…" he says, trying to reach for my hand. I can't let him do that, I'll give in too easily to his touch.

"You don't need anything, Roman. You *want* to give me some bullshit excuse but that's only to justify yourself. I don't care to hear it. So, I'd rather you not open your mouth to talk again," I say, finally turning to meet his gaze. The guilt written all over his face does nothing to help his case.

He slouches back into his seat, swiping a hand down his face in despair.

"Rafe said you're trying to kick start your memories…"

"Wow. Just wow." I laugh, but there's no joy. "Roman, I don't want to have any kind of conversation with you, let alone one about you gossiping about me with Rafe. It's a subject that has nothing to do with you at all," I growl back, my hands gripping the edge of the arm rests.

My palms are getting sweaty, I'm a complete mixture of anger and desire. All I can think about is Red's mention of make-up sex, and that only angers me more. The thought of Roman naked right now, hot and sweaty, my fingers digging into the skull tattoo on his back. Fuck.

I can see the tension in his face, and he's breathing heavily, clearly frustrated that I am not giving into him.

"Can I give you something?" he whispers, not rising to my argument. Fuck him. I want him to yell and scream, maybe go a little crazy, but instead he whispers.

What would make him go so quiet like that? He's usually just as hotheaded as me.

His head is down, chin to chest, but he tilts his ocean blue eyes to look up at me when he notices my silence, waiting for an answer. I process his whispered words again.

"I don't want you to give me anything, Roman." The defeated look on his face intensifies.

"You'll want this, I just don't want to give it to you if you're not ready."

It must be something linking to my past, the past he

knew about and said nothing. When he's not in front of me I miss him, and I can almost forget this bullshit. Then, the second I see the guilt in his eyes, I want to make him suffer.

A part of me wants to tell him to shove it up his own ass, yet the smallest part of me is intrigued to know something from that time. I promised myself back in New York that I would push myself to remember and learn what my mind has forced me to forget.

I continue to scan his face, and the slight drop of hope in his eyes has me nodding subconsciously, my heart beating faster against my chest. It's too late for me to take it back now, and I don't think I want to, especially when his eyes light up in relief.

"I just want to explain to you why I have it first, because it's not mine. I won't explain what it is or anything, just why."

I don't want to hear any of the shit that's likely to come out of his mouth, but my soul wants whatever it is more than I want to tell him to fuck off.

"Go on, then."

"Not here, when we get back to Ace," he says, swiping his hands down his pants nervously.

"Do you have it on you right now?" I ask, frowning at him for trying to drag this out, and he gives me the smallest nod in response. "Then you can give it to me here. I have plans tonight, and I don't have time to waste on this."

I'm not being cruel, I'm just not caring for his feelings either. He must be able to tell that he won't change my mind because he sighs, before turning to face me fully.

"So, when your father died, everyone was made to believe that you had died too. Our families were crazy connected, practically one big happy family, sharing summer homes and keeping things at each other's homes." He clears his throat, nerves getting the best of him, and carries on. "I remember having to go to our summer home to help clear it all out. I think after everything, nobody wanted to sit in those memories anymore, and while I was there I found it. God, it always caught my attention, no matter what, and you would always give it to me."

The sadness that rests on his face for a moment forces me to believe his words.

Reaching into his blazer pocket he holds it out between us.

Cautiously, I hold my hand out beneath his, my pulse ringing in my ears, as he slowly unclasps his fist to place it in my hand. His fingers trace across my open palm, sending a shiver down my spine. I feel the weight of the item he's placed in my hand, and slowly bring it closer to me.

Oh my god.

A peacock brooch.

The vision I had on my way to Featherstone, it was about stealing this peacock brooch. My fingers squeeze it tightly into my palm and I love the feeling of it digging into my skin, my hand molding around it.

The memory floods my mind again, only this time I see the direction I was running in.

I'm dashing through the grass bank, sitting above the beach below, no shoes on, loving the feel of the grass in between my toes.

A little boy sticks his head out from behind a large sycamore tree. I notice his ruffled brown hair and bright blue eyes, his face lighting up with the biggest smile I'd ever seen. I'm overcome with the need to give this little brooch to him. To make him happy, like he makes me.

I slowly open my eyes to see him staring at me nervously, waiting for my reaction.

I don't know how to react. I want to scream at him for lying, cry for the memory I just remembered, and drink myself stupid to forget it all. Instead, I clear my throat and meet his gaze fully.

"Thank you," I murmur.

I can see he wants to ask if I remember, and it's the first time I can actually say yes. I offer myself the satisfaction of a small nod in response.

His eyes light up like it's Christmas, while his hands fidget as though he wants to reach out for me.

The Rolls comes to a stop outside Ace. I'm relieved, ready to leave this intense bubble around us. I step out of the car before the door can be opened for me.

"God, Luna. Are you serious?" His eyes frantically search mine as he stops me entering the building. I can't help but sigh.

"Can we not right now, Roman? That's the first time I've remembered something, but I'm so fucking frustrated with you. I need to relax and get ready for tonight. You giving me this brooch..." I pause, gripping the peacock tighter in my hands, "And triggering a memory for me, doesn't change any of that," I say as I walk around him.

As I'm walking to the stairs, he pulls me toward the elevator. Before I can kick up a fuss, the doors are opening and he's shoving me inside. He's taken me by surprise and I'm a little slow on the defense. Before I know it, he's pressing the button for our floor and caging me in against the side of the elevator. Hands resting on the gold handrail on either side of me.

"Listen here, princess. I know I fucked up. I know, but I'm not going to just let you dismiss me. I've tried the soft approach, given you space and now I've passed my limit."

Fuck me. The tension is coming off him in waves, but I can't help but laugh. Which makes him lean in further, a frown on his face.

"There he is. I was wondering when alpha Roman would finally make an appearance. You've been quiet and obedient this week. I was almost starting to worry," I say with a lot of sass, as I slowly and deliberately reach out to straighten his blazer. Attempting to act unfazed by his close proximity, I'm actually on fire. His eyes track my every movement, making my skin burn to feel his.

I quickly drop my hands from him, my deliberate teasing affecting me as much as it is him.

"Well, I'm done stepping back and letting you lead the pace because you're doing a shit job."

"No, I'm just not taking it in the direction you want me to. You want everything to go back to how it was, and

I don't." He just fucking laughs at me as he moves his face right into mine. His lips so close I can feel their heat.

"Princess, you think I can't see the lust in your pretty green eyes? Sense what your body wants and needs right now? My body is so attuned to yours, Luna. I fucking know."

My pulse is throbbing as I lose myself in his gaze. If he touches me now, I won't be able to stand my ground, I'll give into my body's wants and desires.

He must be able to sense it because he steps in closer, his body flush against mine. My arms start to lift, to wrap around his neck when the elevator pings and the doors slide open.

The noise surprises me and I push him back. He only moves because it's caught him off guard too.

Stumbling a little, I rush past him straight for my room. I struggle to get a grip on the right key, and fumble around at the door. Glancing back at Roman, he finally catches on and steps out of the elevator just as I hear the door click open.

"Luna, I swear to god. Don't fucking run—"

I don't hear the rest as I slam my door shut behind me.

BANG! BANG!

"Luna, open the fucking door!" he yells. My hand still rests against the door, and I can't bring myself to move. "Open the door, princess. I know you're still there."

My feet step in closer to the door on their own accord, my bag dropping to the floor beside me as I rest my forehead against the wood. The cool touch does nothing to calm my racing heart. Taking a deep breath, I turn to lean back against the door, my gaze lifting to the ceiling as my palms lay flat against the door behind me. I make sure my voice is just loud enough for him to hear me.

"None of this matters, Roman. My past, the present, my future, it's all irrelevant because I'm not your problem." I don't know how I manage to keep the tremble out of my voice, especially since my legs are like jelly.

"I want you to be my fucking problem, Luna."

I feel his palm slap the other side of the wood in desperation, and my chest aches. When silence is all that greets him, I hear him sigh. I can feel his presence as though there was nothing separating us. My body imagining the feel of his breath on my neck, willing me to open the door.

"We're not done, Luna. Not by a long shot." I hear the determination in his voice, and I need to move away from here before I give in.

Rushing for the bathroom, I turn the shower on, drowning out any other noise.

This is harder than I thought it would be, and it's all his fault.

Acehole.

After my freezing cold shower, I'm dressed and quietly opening my door. I double check to make sure no one is there. By no one, I mainly mean Roman, but the way they fucking gossip about me, the others likely know he came close to breaking my walls.

I can't focus on that right now. I need to get out of here without any interruption. Happy no one is around, I take the stairs. In my running shoes, I can handle them much better than in my uniform heels. I've also thrown on a pair of black leggings and a loose fitted black top. A cap sits perfectly on my head to hide my face from any cameras. It's likely they would be able to assume it's me if needed, but they wouldn't have solid evidence.

Stepping into the lobby, there's no one around except Thomas who literally sits and greets us all day. I'm not sure what else he actually does.

I spot Ian by a Rolls outside of Ace and head toward him. He's not the closest or first parked Rolls, which is the usual protocol, yet he opens the car door ready for me.

"Miss Luna, is everything okay?" he asks as I approach.

"Yeah, I would appreciate you taking me to the garden please." I offer a smile, not lifting my face too high.

"Of course."

He opens the car door and I slide in. I see him look in the rear-view mirror at me but I don't offer a conversation, he's happy enough to drive in silence.

It's only a few minutes until we're pulling up along the path again, next to my little haven. I hadn't known it even existed until I nearly strangled Wren to death, and Ian brought me here with Kai. Now, I'm here most days.

"Don't grab the door, Ian. I'm fine, and I'll jog back as always."

I don't wait around for his response, I just climb out and stalk between the bushes.

Every day this week after classes, I've had Ian bring me here. I'd even had him arrange a few things to make it more comfortable here, like adding a rattan daybed, fairy lights and a stocked cooler.

This is day five of the same routine, except Red isn't

with me this time. Today I'm not hanging around, this is my cover, my alibi in case anything goes wrong.

Taking a seat on the daybed, I open a bottle of water as I pull out my sketch pad and draw for a while. I'll have more belongings here than in my room soon, everytime I come down here I leave something else. I wait a little longer, making sure enough time has passed before I slip out of my zen garden, heading in the opposite direction from Ace.

Featherstone Academy is so fearless that they post copies of their blueprints freely on their internal school website. Fucking idiots. Not that I really need them, I know where I'm going, but it gave me a better visual for where the guards are. Knowing the best blind spots along this route, it takes me around twenty-five minutes to arrive at the Main Hall.

I walk straight in with purpose, I'm not hovering around or looking nervous. I haven't got time for that, and I don't want to make myself look suspicious. Rafe had someone hack into the surveillance feed for the Main Hall, which I've been monitoring for the past few days.

Coming in from the back means it takes me a little longer to get to my destination, but I can avoid more cameras this way. I have my clicker with me to dodge the security feeds if I need it, as back up.

Turning into the quiet corridor, I pause for just a moment making sure I'm alone. I have my trusty amplifying headphones in, looking like I'm listening to my music. Instead, all I can hear is some asshole munching some chips back in the main open space.

I press my clicker as I slip my hand in my bra, pulling out the key, making quick work of the lock and stepping inside. Shutting the door behind me, it looks no different to the first time I was here.

Dietrichson's office.

When Maverick slipped me the key on Monday morning, amongst the chaos with Wren, I was beyond grateful. Rafe promised I could trust him, and as hard as it is for me to say, I do. When he helped me without question in The Pyramid, I knew I could rely on him. I felt like Rafe was finally helping me, giving me allies and connections to make this a little easier.

Focusing on the tasks at hand, I smooth my fingers across the hem of my leggings. I'd cut tiny slits into the waistband of my leggings and hidden my micro cameras in them. I didn't have much time before the blocker on the security feed would become too obvious, so I needed to move.

I've brought three cameras, a listening device and a chip for her computer with me. I place one in the corner of the bookcase, which will give me a perfect view of everyone that enters the office. The two books that sit below my micro camera make me chuckle, 'How to be an International Spy Training Manual' and 'How to be a Better Leader'.

The second goes in the vent in the corner of the room, almost touching the ceiling, allowing me to oversee the whole room. The final camera fits perfectly in the center of the fake flowers that sit on the windowsill behind her desk, giving me full access to what she does on her computer.

Placing the tiny listening device in her computer mouse, I work efficiently to gain access to her computer with my microchip.

"Yeah, give me a second, I'll be with you. I'm just having issues with Dietrichson's camera feed," I hear through my headphones.

Shit. I need to move. It sounded like it was said from the room above, so I've got a chance of getting out unseen. I quickly retrace my steps to make sure I haven't left anything out of place. The plant sits exactly as it did, the microchip in the computer is completely unrecognizable unless you know to look for it. I straighten the office chair as I glance at the vent. All clear, even the bookcase still has a light layer of dust undisturbed on the shelf. I'm out of here.

I press the clicker off as soon as I get out of the office with the door shut behind me. The steps down from upstairs are luckily in the main space, so I can exit the same way I entered.

As soon as I step outside, I start a slow-paced jog. I don't look behind me, not once. I don't need to draw any attention to myself. I maintain my pace all the way back to Ace, smiling at Ian as I enter.

As I'm heading for the stairs, I hear Parker's voice coming from the gym. Not wanting to be seen, I take the steps two at a time. I manage to slip back into my room unnoticed. Thank god. Now to check the camera feeds and send the access links to Rafe. Then I can focus on getting ready for the party.

Great.

I could do with something much more fun to ease the bit of adrenaline coursing through my veins but I guess dancing will have to do.

SIX

F^uck.

I had her in my hands, and she slipped through my fucking fingers. She wants me, that hasn't changed. I just need us to move past my fucking stupid mistake of not telling her.

I gave up banging her door down after twenty minutes of her ignoring me. I've been pacing the floor in my lounge ever since. How can she possibly feel as though she isn't my problem? She's mine no matter what. I've never wanted to take on someone else's battles before, until Luna, and I refuse to let her continue to push me away.

She remembered. She fucking remembered… and then ran.

I want to know what she remembered, however small it may have been. I *need* to know.

I hear a key turn in the lock and my front door is swung open. Parker, Oscar and Kai step in with Jess trailing in behind them, wheeling a small suitcase. What's that for?

The guys don't look happy, and Jess just looks uncomfortable.

"Hey, what's going on?" I ask, looking between them.

"Tell him," Oscar says, glaring at her.

"I didn't have to tell you, you know? So stop glaring at me, or I'll show you some of the new moves Luna has been teaching me." She glares back.

"Does someone want to get to the point?" I ask, getting frustrated with them. I swear these two bicker like brother and sister. Neither of them move, instead they continue to face each other, battling it out in a fucking staring competition like children.

I can't help but sigh at their antics. Parker must sense my frustration when he finally explains.

"Luna and Jess are going to a Byrne's party tonight out behind the Library."

What?

"But Luna doesn't party," I say, frowning at the thought, which finally gets Jess to turn away from Oscar.

"Well, that was only because she was trying to keep her guard up here. Rafe told me some crazy stories about her. She usually parties if she feels safe enough, or if everything is too much and her mind needs a break. Which do you think it is right now?" She stands with her hands fixed on her hips and glares around at us all.

For a moment my mind goes back to the Fall Ball. When we got back to her room she let her guard down. We all drank together and had a good time because she felt safe.

"Does Luna even fucking know what goes down at a Byrne's party?"

Jess just silently shakes her head.

"Okay. Obviously she's going to clear her mind, but after the Fall Ball, she drank with us because she felt safe. So, no matter what shit is going on right now, we'll be there. That way she can relax her mind and we'll be there to catch her if anything gets out of hand," I say out loud, as I scrub the back of my neck, figuring out a plan.

"So we're gonna let her go?" Oscar frowns, mirroring

Jess' stance, fucking pussy. I don't get a chance to tell him to shut the fuck up because Kai beats me to it.

"Shut up, Oscar. Luna is her own person. We don't tell her what she can and can't do. If she's going, we go too. Simple as that." He nods and Parker agrees.

"Okay, well my work here is done. See you tonight. I plan to get us there after 10, you know, fashionably late and all that." She waves her hand around dramatically. "With the treats I've got planned, you won't be able to miss her." Jess gives us a wink and leaves, dragging the case behind her and quietly shutting the door.

"I think she's trying to help us out," Parker murmurs, staring at the closed door.

"I agree. I think we'll need her," Kai adds.

I nod in agreement. I was all set to come up with a new plan with the guys tonight, I'm done with fucking around. Now it seems we've got a chance to be around her instead.

"Well, I'm gonna make sure I look so good she won't be able to resist me. She won't even acknowledge you dickheads," Oscar says, wagging his eyebrows and heading for the door.

"Fuck off, Oscar," I grumble, throwing myself down on the sofa as the door slams behind him.

"I'm going to go and set up a few surveillance spots before everyone starts showing up so we can always have eyes on her," Kai says, and I grunt in agreement.

"I'll come with you," Parker adds. "I can't handle him when he's all hot and broody." He winks and offers me a grin. As much as these parties can get a little crazy, the thought of being in Luna's proximity has lifted his mood a little.

"You love my brooding. Now fuck off before I find other uses for that mouth of yours." I smirk.

"Screw you, Roman. I took the D last time, it's your turn next, big man," he responds, thrusting his hips a little, and slams the door behind him.

Fuck, now my cock's hard at the thought of us together.

Shit, I need a plan.

Alpha the hell out of her, get her to admit she wants me, fuck for the rest of the night.

Done.

Luna

"Red, I'm not sure about this," I say, looking down at

myself.

"Will you stop? You look hot as hell. Now let me finish your makeup, Luna, or we won't be leaving," Red huffs, pointing the mascara wand in my face.

I'm starting to think that might be a good idea. Stay in and fuck all of this. I'm about to say it out loud when she stops me.

"Don't even think about it. We are going, end of discussion. Now look up."

I sigh but do as I'm told. A few more swipes of the wand and she steps back.

"Holy shit, girl, your milkshake's gonna bring all the boys to the yard tonight," she says with a giggle, making me roll my eyes at her.

"That's not what this is about, Red."

"I know, but damn, Luna. You're absolute fire. Now, give me a few minutes and I'll be dressed. We definitely need selfies before we leave," she says, turning her back to me.

"I didn't sign up for selfies, Red," I stammer, heading for the door in a hurry.

"Don't even, we're making memories, Luna. We don't have a single picture together, why do you gotta play me like that? Your best friend." She turns her head to pout at me, making me tilt my head back and release a heavy sigh.

"Fine."

I step into my bedroom to check my reflection out. Red's latest playlist is still running in the background. Control by Halsey fills the room, something about this song resonates inside of me.

I can't get Roman out of my head from earlier. The peacock is on my bedside table, but I don't know what to do with it or the memory it came with. Mere seconds longer, and I would have been in his room and under him. I still can't decide if it was a mistake or not for me to run.

Shaking my head, I focus on the now, and touch a finger to the mark on my forehead. How is Red always so magic with her make-up skills? You can barely see that I had my head stitched back together last week.

She tried to convince me to let her pull out her contouring skills, but that's just pushing me too far. Instead, she's used my perfect foundation with a little bronzer and blush. My green eyes are framed with pale golds and creams and black winged eyeliner.

I had to stop her when she tried to come at me with her red lipstick, and instead my lips are coated in a pale pink gloss. My brown hair is simple in a bun at the top of my head with a few loose tendrils floating around my face.

What concerns me the most is this damn outfit. I love my body, but I don't usually wear anything so revealing, unless it's lingerie.

A red two piece set. The top is basically a sexy bikini top with thin shoulder straps and a large bow tied in between my breasts. The skirt barely covers my ass and is asymmetrical. High waisted, it's ruched over my hips and wraps around the top of my thighs with a loose frill trim.

It is gorgeous, and I feel sexy as hell, but you can still lightly see the cut down my chest. From my collarbone it leads a straight line down, below the hem of my skirt.

"Red, do you not think my cut is a little too obvious?" I shout to her in the other room.

"Luna Steele, you will own that mark like the survivor you are. Do you understand?" She demands as she saunters in. I turn my gaze to her. She distracts me, offering a twirl in her dress.

"What do you think?" she asks, ruffling her lightly curled hair.

A cobalt-blue bodycon dress hugs her curves like a second skin. Low cut to show her girls off, and finely detailed lines structure the whole front. The back is where the extra sexy is. Criss-crossed straps cover her back in different directions leaving a lot of her back exposed.

Guys are going to be visualizing pulling that zipper down all night.

"You look gorgeous. I think I need to bodyguard you."

"Don't you even, Luna. Now come take a picture with me."

She marches into the lounge, leaving me to follow her. I grab my heels and my clutch, which is only big enough for my phone and room keys.

"Are you sure we have to wear heels?" I whine, taking a seat on the sofa to put them on.

"Yes, Luna." She sighs, as though I'm an annoying child. "I told you, there are dress codes. This isn't some normal college party where you can wear denim and flip-flops. It's about making a statement, so put them on."

I sulk in silence, as I fasten the clasp on my strappy sandal heels. Standing, I take a few tester steps to get comfortable. I don't know why they have to be so damn high, but my moaning is just annoying her so I control myself.

"Take a selfie with me, Luna. Now."

She's standing in front of the floor-length window, with her arm out-stretched ready.

Wrapping our arms around each other, I smile while she clicks away. Giving me an extra squeeze she steps back, pleased with herself.

My phone pings, and when I open it, it's a picture of us. We look happy, like we are actually eighteen and enjoying life. I love it, instantly setting it as my lock screen.

"Let's go, the SUV's are waiting," she says, opening the front door wide to all the guys coming out of Roman's room at the exact same time.

Fuck me.

I think I just self-combusted.

Is it possible to climax without any stimulation, except from what your eyes are consuming?

YOUR BLOODLINE

SEVEN
Parker

Holy. Shit.

I have to take a second to make sure I'm actually breathing with the way my heart is pounding erratically.

Fuck, how can she get any more beautiful than she already is? Standing before me looking every inch the goddess she is has left me speechless.

All I can picture is her hot as sin body riding me, with her pretty pierced nipples in my face. Man, I need to fuck her from behind, hold the globes of her ass as I thrust into her. The thought of my cum running down her leg again, marking her, only adds heat to my vision.

Looking at the guys around me, they all stand frozen in place too. Oscar makes a whimpering sound gaining my attention, and he's already looking right at me.

"Have you seen this, man? I'm about to explode." He looks down, and my eyes follow.

He's literally holding his junk through the skin-tight black jeans, knuckles white with the tightness of his grip. I'm not ashamed to say that turns me on even more because he's not exaggerating, and I'm not far behind him.

Red's giggle has me whipping my head back in their direction.

"You guys are too funny, but can we get a move on?" she asks with an over the top eye roll, and starts dragging Luna toward the elevator.

It takes us a second but we're all rushing behind them at once. Six of us in here doesn't give much room, and we're all trying to nudge past each other to stand as close to Luna as possible. Red is standing near the panel of buttons and presses for us to start moving. Luna is standing beside her, and the four of us are basically hovering as close as possible.

She hasn't said a word, but I'm not stupid, the lust in her eyes is obvious. We just need to remind her of what we had, what we can still have.

"You look stunning, Sakura," Kai murmurs beside me, forcing her eyes to him. It takes her a moment to meet his eyes as she slowly drags her gaze up his body. Her eyes are blown. Fuck. That's hot.

She doesn't answer him, just offering a smile instead. Seems someone else is struggling to form sentences here too, and no one else utters a word.

Roman is wearing a tight black polo top with skin-tight black jeans, and with his thighs, they look ready to burst, so hot I can't help but wet my lips. Oscar is wearing a baby blue shirt with the top few buttons open, and his black jeans. He wasn't kidding earlier when he said he was going all out.

Kai's loose-necked black top and jeans show off an edgier side than we're used to seeing. I've thrown on grey jeans, and my feather tattoo peeks out beneath the fabric of my white short-sleeved shirt.

The elevator comes to a stop, and Red is the one that has to get us all moving again. We follow her lead silently, all of our eyes watching Luna's ass sway in front of us. It's mesmerizing. Oscar is literally tripping over his own feet to get close to her, with Kai and Roman not far behind him.

The SUVs that are used to chauffeur everyone to the party are sitting idling outside. There aren't many people around. These parties start surprisingly early and people actually like to arrive on time to get the most out of it. A Byrne's party is a good time.

A driver holds the door open for the closest SUV, and Luna climbs in first, while Red turns to glare at us.

"You can ride over there with us, but you're not lingering around. Do you understand? We're having girl time that involves shots and grinding. You can drool over her in the corner or something."

She points her finger at all of us and climbs in beside Luna, who typically sits in the corner so none of us could actually sit next to her, except Red, of course.

Roman pushes all of us out of the way so he can sit facing her. Kai goes to follow in after him but Oscar shoulder barges him. I'm standing in complete shock at their actions, yet I still manage to slip in before Kai, who has to take the last seat next to Red.

We're all frowning at each other as the SUV pulls away, clearly blaming each other that we aren't closer to Luna. I'm disappointed by the short journey we've got, I'd like a little more time in her presence.

I can see she doesn't know where to put her eyes, not wanting to look at us but unable to stop herself.

"Baby girl, you look so good right now I could eat you up. Literally, how about we dump these losers and I can make that happen," Oscar says, attempting to use his *purr* on her. I can't stop a little snicker from escaping, and he sends me a glare.

That only makes it worse, forcing out a full laugh as the others join me. Even Luna covers her mouth and looks out of the window, trying to hide her amusement at it all.

"Stop laughing, assholes. Luna, what do you say, baby?" he pushes on, wagging his eyebrows. Luna just gives him a classic roll of her eyes.

"You already sent me a dick pic, Oscar. I'm good for now, but thanks." She barely holds his stare, before she's fidgeting and crossing her legs the other way round.

She isn't fooling anyone. It's clear her pussy's in need of a little friction, but she's too stubborn. She'll refuse herself the pleasure, and us along the way.

"It was a good picture though, wasn't it, Luna?" he says, as he leans forward to place his hand on her bare thigh.

Lightning fast, Red stops his hand from touching Luna,

and suddenly twists it to the left at the wrist, causing him to scream out.

"What the fuck, Jess?" he shouts, clearly shocked like the rest of us, except Luna of course, who's openly grinning at the whole thing.

"Did I or did I not warn you that I would show you some of the new moves Luna has been teaching me if you touched her?" she answers him, a pleased gleam in her eyes.

"Okay, jeez. You wanna let go now?" He glares back at her. She takes her sweet ass time, looking to Luna, who nods, before letting go.

The girls go straight in for a high-five and giggle together, which only deepens Oscar's frown.

"Nice move, Jess," Roman comments, offering her a gentle smile. Even the moody asshole is impressed, and she offers him a smile in return.

I look to Kai, who is leaning against the window, taking everything in around him. He seems extra quiet and brooding right now, and as much as I want to check he's okay, I won't ask with everyone around. He catches my gaze and offers me a silent nod, communicating that he can see my concern but he's fine.

I hope so.

Being in her presence without touching her or basking in her light is harder than I thought it would be, and we're all struggling with it.

The SUV comes to a stop, and all the strobe lighting filters in through the windows. It's like a rainbow exploded in here or something with all the different colors flickering around.

I can see Luna trying to take it all in, and no one moves. No one wants to be separated from her. That is, until Jess claps her hands.

"Laters," she squeals, before reaching over Luna to push the door open. The music instantly fills the space around us.

Luna takes a final look around at us before stepping out, Red following straight behind her. The rest of us don't move an inch, watching her saunter through the crowd.

"We're so fucked, guys," Kai says, and all we can do is nod in agreement.

That's my queen. I just have to make her understand I'll be whoever she needs me to be, as long as it gets me by her side.

Luna

The sun has set, casting shadows all around us as a gentle breeze leaves a trail of goosebumps against my skin.

They sure transformed the hell out of these usually empty grounds. The Library stands alone with plenty of open space surrounding it in the daytime. If I look to my right, I can see the hedges of my secret garden. I need to find five minutes to sit in the tranquility of that place as soon as possible.

Everything else that surrounds me could lead me to believe we are nowhere near the Library. There are five giant gazebos set up, all color coded. A few are opened up while others are fully closed off.

The SUV has dropped us off outside of the white open-plan dance floor, which is a completely elevated stage, with lights fixed into the floor. It almost reminds me of some old school John Travolta shit, but it hasn't bothered everyone already on there grinding against each other.

Looking to my right, there is a blue open gazebo filled

with different seating arrangements. With high bar stools and fancy velvet booths to bean bags scattered everywhere. I want one of those booths. Red better not try and get me on a damn bean bag in this outfit.

Further along is a purple open setup lined with bars and snack stands. God, they're not missing anything out here.

What piques my interest the most are the two closed off gazebos to the left of the dance floor. One is fully caped in red materials while the other is blacked out. There are security guards monitoring the flow of everyone stepping in and out too.

Red links her arm through mine and starts pulling me toward the drinks, but I have to ask about the other restricted tents.

"What's going on over there, Red?"

Before she can answer me, Trudy herself is stopping in front of me with a smile on her face. She looks completely different. It takes me a moment to fully recognize her. Her blonde hair is up in a bun like mine, and her smokey eye makeup makes her green eyes pop.

Her black dress seems almost modest at first, long-sleeved and stopping mid-thigh with an open panel in between her breasts. When I pay more attention, nearly all of the dress is sheer material, offering a glimpse of her body underneath. The fabric thickens over her chest and ass, so at least her modesty is protected. I love this girl's boldness.

"Luna, I'm glad you could make it," she says to me, before turning to Red. "Jess, right? We have Science and L.F.G. together."

"Yes, and we do. Luna was just asking what the deal was with the restricted areas. You want to explain to her?"

Red runs her hand down her dress, not with nerves but more like relief, as she smiles back at Trudy. They clearly know of each other, and are happy enough in the other's presence, but it's obvious they haven't really mingled before.

"Oh, you mean the good stuff? I'll give you a mini tour," Trudy offers with a wink. She looks between Red and I for a moment before stepping around us. "I can tell there's no room in the linking for me. So, would you like to follow my lead?"

With that, she walks just slightly in front of us toward the black zone first, and we follow behind her.

"I really am glad you came. It'll reinforce what went

down the other day, showing everyone we stand by each other. I would like to talk more, but for now I'll show you a glimpse into my world. I also want to mention that Wren is here with her followers. I have eyes everywhere, so we'll know if she tries to make a move," she says, maintaining eye contact as we cover the distance to the entry.

I offer a nod in response which is enough for her. It'll have to be. I may be on her turf right now, and I'll respect that, but I'm the one running the bigger picture.

As the tall guy monitoring the door stops us to chat with Trudy, I glance around, my eyes uncontrollably searching out the guys. It doesn't take a moment for them to come into view. They're in the purple gazebo getting drinks, but they're all watching me.

Glancing away quickly, I turn back to the entryway in front of us. Trudy finishes her discussion and the guy holds the curtain back for us to enter.

Following her lead, Red squeezes my arm as we walk in. I check she's okay and she just offers me a smile. I'm surprised with what I see.

Half of the room is covered in cushions with people laying across them, relaxed. There must be close to fifty people scattered across the space, while the other side is lined up table after table. Someone manning each station, with cash tins on one side and different bags on the other.

"This is our drug supply. We offer guests exactly what they want and a safe place to enjoy it," Trudy says, waving her hand in front of her.

Huh, this is not what I expected.

I'm obviously not surprised that Featherstone has people run drugs, but Trudy has this running smoother than I've ever seen. Back home, there were back street drug dealers and people dying from dirty needles. Well, that's the side I caught a glimpse of anyway.

"Do you dabble? I can offer you a sample of whatever you like. I don't personally, I prefer to keep my nose clean and make sure we run a tight operation, but no judgement here." She stretches her arm in offering, making sure to look at Red too, but I shake my head.

"Thanks, but I prefer fighting and sex, they are my version of hardcore drugs," I say with a smile, hoping she doesn't try to force me. This will all end real quick if she does.

Thankfully, she offers us a smile and turns back the way we just came.

"Let me show you the red area, then you can enjoy

yourselves."

I follow behind her, as I look to Red.

"You okay? You don't have to bore yourself with this if you don't want to," I offer, but she just rolls her eyes at me.

"I've been to these parties before, Luna. I'll have your ass on that dance floor soon enough." She giggles at herself as we step up to the red entryway.

"Are you ready for the highlight?" Trudy grins as the guy guarding the space pulls back the curtain.

It's much busier in here. It's like a casino, large tables set up with different games playing out and bodies crammed in around them. Cheers can be heard from the far end. A red carpet leads a pathway right down the center.

Following Trudy's lead down the middle, the lights start to dim as we move away from the bright lights above the tables. She stops in front of me and I come to stand by her side.

Wow.

They cover all the bases at these parties, huh?

Before me are at least twenty people, in pairs or bigger groups, having the biggest orgy I've ever seen. It's quite impressive really. I don't recognize anybody, but it humors me that I'm paying enough attention to know that. They're all scattered across pillows and what seems to be a floor completely made out of mattresses.

I hope they have a good time, it definitely seems like they are.

The closest group to us is two guys and two girls. One of the girls is being fucked from behind, while going down on the other girl, who's simultaneously having her mouth plowed. The guys are really giving it some effort too. I'm impressed, and now slightly turned on.

I'm ready to get out of here, have a dance, maybe even a small drink. Then I can head back and please myself.

"You seem to have everything taken care of, Trudy. I like your style."

She glows under the compliment.

"I'm glad, I think we can make this work between us, Luna. I'll see you out. Please enjoy whatever you please. Sadly, I have some business to attend to, but if you need anything just say the word. Either my brother or I will come as quickly as possible."

And do what exactly? What could she offer that I wouldn't be able to do myself?

I don't say any of that, instead I offer her a smile as she leaves us at the exit with a wink. She's instantly being dragged away to deal with a group who are apparently not following the rules.

Is it home time yet?

"Shots time!" Red screams, squeezing my arm.

Great, fucking fantastic.

KC KEAN

EIGHT

Luna

Red drags me to the bar area where the guys are standing. Seeing us approach, they turn to watch us, Roman's eyes are undressing me and assessing me all at the same time. Like he needs to check nothing happened in those tents, but he can't get past the idea of me naked. I can't look him in the eyes right now, he made me vulnerable earlier and now I feel awkward.

They all do, I couldn't function on the way over here, not even to tell them to fuck off. Which is what I should have done.

"Who's getting the shots in?" Red says, loud enough to

be heard over the music. They all perk up at her words, but Oscar is the quickest. Slamming his hand down on the bar top, he gains the bartender's attention, even though he's serving someone already.

"I want six shots of Tequila. Actually, just give me all the supplies, it'll be quicker if I do it myself." He looks back to wink at me as the guy drops the glass he was already holding to meet Oscar's demands.

I'm cut off from looking at Oscar, when I feel two hands grip my waist and spin me around. I'm facing a guy I've never seen before. Clearly he's got himself some liquid courage, by the smell of alcohol on his breath and the slight stumble in his step.

Instantly, my instincts takeover and I notice three guys standing behind this prick as support. They're obviously adding to his confidence, because this douche has some balls if he thinks he can just fucking touch me like this.

I don't react straight away, I want to see what this fucker has to say first.

"Little Miss Luna fucking Steele, hmmm? Tyler promised us a good showing in The Pyramid. Said he'd fuck you to death, but here you still are." He licks his lips as he looks down at my body, clearly turned on by the thought, and it makes my skin crawl. "If I can't have what I was promised, I'll just take it for myself," he sneers down at me, as his free hand lifts to touch the scar down my chest.

Before I can even get a hit on him, Parker has his arm wrapped around his neck from behind, like a guillotine, as he growls into his ear. I can't hear what he's saying but the rage on his face takes me back. All I can do is stand and watch, as my breathing becomes heavy with the adrenaline now pumping through my body.

The crowd around us are all watching the scene unfold, none of them seem surprised by any of this or care enough to get involved.

The sweet and caring guy I know Parker to be is not who everyone else sees. I think I forget their reputation and abilities because I see their softer sides. They really are assholes to everyone else, the power they hold keeping everyone at arm's length.

As the guy goes lax in Parker's arms, I look around him to where his group of friends are. Not more than ten feet away from us, the rest of my Aceholes are wreaking havoc without even breaking a sweat. Allowing me a glimpse into what they are known for.

This is not helping. Why am I even trying to protect them when they can handle themselves like this?

Kai hits one of them straight in the face, blood instantly splattering around him. While Oscar is pummeling the shit out of another beside him. Blood coats his knuckles as he doesn't relent. Roman drops the guy he's holding and pulls Oscar back.

I'm not impressed. I missed the fight because I was so fixated on the first prick, now I've missed all of the action.

The bloodied state of them should not turn me on. My need for them increases with their protective aggression. I'm pushing them away and they still want to defend me.

Nope.

Not going there. This is for the best.

Parker drags the guy over to the others on the floor and tosses him on top of them like he's nothing but a used condom. Then he's marching back over to me, not once hesitating to get up in my personal space.

His hazel eyes aren't on mine, they're on my chest, looking at where the guy stroked me, as he brings his lips to kiss the spot. Replacing the memory with his own searing touch.

His finger lifts to the start of the mark near my

collarbone, and slowly trails down the path it leads, stopping at the waistband of my skirt. I can't move, his touch has frozen me in place. Watching the rage take over his face, he finally brings his eyes up to meet mine. The anger that lingers burns deep.

"If that fucker wasn't dead already, I'd have killed him with my bare hands." Parker's words are quiet, but deadly, clearly talking about Tyler. His fingertip is still resting at the top of my waistband, on the last part of the scar he can see. The combination of his words and his touch has me struggling to respond or push him away.

Roman steps up next to Parker, running his eyes over me to make sure I'm okay, while Kai observes me from a distance. All their eyes on me are adding heat to the fire, making me feel like I can't breathe.

I find myself searching for Oscar, but he's strolling toward us with the bottle of Tequila as Red carries the tray of shot glasses, salt and wedges of lemon.

Like none of that just happened.

As they place everything on the nearby table, I look at Red, trying to get her to understand that I'm struggling here. My need for them is rising uncontrollably, I have to get out of their space to calm down. Searching my face, she offers a little nod and stands next to Oscar.

"One shot, then it's girl time on the dance floor, understood?" she sasses, and Oscar reluctantly sighs.

"Fine, better make it a good one then." The smirk on his face takes over.

Kai and Roman both come to stand around the table, not saying a word as their eyes burn trails over my skin.

Parker gently turns me around and stands himself at my back.

Fuck.

I'm trying to stand my ground, but that's difficult when I can feel his shaft pressing against my ass. His legs slightly parted to stand on the outside of both of mine. His hands aren't touching me, but my core really wants them to.

Roman grabs my left hand and licks the inside of my wrist as Kai suddenly grabs my right hand doing the same. With them both touching me and Parker pressing me in, I can't fight it. I'm Luna fucking Steele and I'm standing here all submissive and shit, but my body refuses to move.

Oscar slowly stalks around the table. I catch a glimpse of Red who's smirking at me, she's loving this, likely encouraging it. I'm going to remember this moment, and pay her back one day.

Oscar comes to stand in front of me and hands Parker a shot, while Roman and Kai each pick one up off the table. Leaning in, Oscar licks my collarbone to my right, as Parker licks my left shoulder. I shiver uncontrollably.

Salt is quickly sprinkled on all the spots they've marked me with. I know what's coming and I'm lost to the sensations taking over my body.

"3... 2... 1..." Red calls, then all at once they're all licking the salt off. Holy fuck. I can barely catch my breath as they all take their shots and grab a slice of lemon from the table. I think I might explode.

Oscar steps back with a shit-eating grin on his face, aware of the effect they're all having on me, and it forces me to shake out of it.

Bypassing the usual Tequila process, I grab the final shot off the table and throw it back in one swift move. I don't even cringe. Tequila reminds me of the last time we were all together, and it must remind them too with the heat in their eyes. Keeping my eyes on them, I call out to Red.

"You ready to dance?"

"Hell yeah I am," she cheers, grabbing my hand and dragging me to the dance floor.

Thank god, I need a second to cool down.

They really are Aceholes.

Red pulls me to the center of the dance floor, as 'Change My Heart' by Ummet Ozcan and Laurell comes on. She's instantly singing the song out loud as she moves her body to the beat. I do love this song. Everyone says fighting is like dancing, but for me, it's the other way around, seeing as I learned to fight first.

The space is crowded with bodies, grinding and swaying together. I have no idea who these people are that surround me, and as hard as it may be, I try to make myself relax and move to the music.

The flashing lights above us are enchanting; lifting my hands above my head, I join Red. Clearing my mind, I get lost in the rhythm, and sing the chorus aloud with everyone around us.

I don't pay attention to those around us, but I can tell they've noticed me. We've suddenly got plenty of room to move. I won't complain, you've got to have balls to approach us.

The song finishes, and Billie Eilish 'You should see me in a crown' booms through the speakers, causing Red to squeal with joy.

"It's your song, Luna."

No it's not? The confusion on my face sets her into action.

Stepping back further, and causing the other dancers to also move, she starts to sing the song at me, ass swaying and her finger pointed straight at me. Every fucker is looking, but she doesn't care. Even those that can see from the nearby gazebos are looking. Fuck that, if they're going to look I'll give them something to watch.

My hips roll deeper, my hands leading a show against my skin too as the song plays and Red continues to sing. When the chorus hits the second time, I fucking sing it too. So fitting, I mean every damn word.

I see my Aceholes standing at the edge of the dance floor, eyes locked on me, filled with desire I want to get lost in.

Nope. They're not my Aceholes.

They are a distraction.

Twirling, I grab Red's hand and we dance together, not caring about everyone else.

After a few more songs, I'm ready to relax. As I'm about to attempt to convince Red to stop, Trudy is approaching.

"Please girls, one dance. I think the only way I'll get

five minutes to do so is if I'm with you, because no one will interrupt me." The pleading in her eyes has Red answering for us, grabbing her hand to join in.

I let go, staying with them, but not as close. I like Trudy enough, and I'm glad we're on good terms, I'm just not holding hands and dancing like I'd die for her.

Doja Cat 'Candy' blares through the speakers, and I agree to one more song, everybody in here is going to be up dancing now. Dancing along with everyone, I catch sight of the guys again, and some fucking girl has her hands on Oscar. Who the fuck does she think she is?

I stop dancing, glaring in their direction. Who is this bitch?

I can feel my feet begin to move on their own accord, but stop again instantly when Oscar drags her hands off him and points in my direction.

The girl's eyes widen in fear when she sees me looking, and as Oscar takes in my stance, understanding dawns on his features. The smug ass grin on his face infuriates me more than the fucking girl.

Spinning back around to Red and Trudy, I turn straight into another body. An arm wraps around my waist to catch my fall as they pull me in against their chest. Hands raised ready to push this fucker off, I pause when I realize it's Trudy's brother. He must be able to tell that I'm instinctively ready to attack because he slowly steps back to give me some space, dropping his hands from my body.

"Hey, you reckon I can walk away from this meeting today, or am I going to need to be carried out again?" His grin let's me in on the joke, making me relax, and I play along.

"Mmm, I'm not sure yet, but I'll let you know."

"Aiden, nice to meet you under better circumstances." He holds his hand out to me, all formal, and I shake his hand.

"Luna."

"Duh, I know that. *Everyone* knows who you are," he says, with a roll of his eyes.

Something over my shoulder catches his attention for a moment. I'm about to see what it is when he places both of his hands on my shoulders.

"Honey, you've got yourself some delicious men staring you down. I wish it was me, but alas it is not. I think the closest I've been to Kai Fuse paying me any attention at all was back in Freshman year of high school when I stood too close to him at a urinal. I was fourteen and horny as shit, and all I wanted was a peek at his meat to dream about. Sadly, he looked at me like I was crazy." His hands are still on my shoulders as he pouts down at me.

I can't help but laugh. A full belly, head thrown back, laugh.

"Aiden, I do believe you are missing out," I say with a wink, as I grab his wrists to get him off me. He's not harassing me, it's just uncomfortable with a stranger this close.

"I can tell. He's looking at me worse now than he did then, that's for sure. I think all four of those boys want to maim me. If only they knew I would prefer to see them naked, huh? I mean, you're hot and all but not worth me going straight for." He grins wider. "Want to have a little fun? They look like they need to relax."

Glancing to Red, I can see the concern in her eyes as she assesses the situation, while Trudy can likely sense what her brother is up to and just shakes her head.

"It's your death wish."

I can't help it. If my pride won't allow me to fuck them, then it can at least let me fuck *with* them.

"I doubt it'll take much. Make sure no one wears black to my funeral, okay?" He smirks as he leans in to whisper in my ear, placing his hands on my waist.

"5... 4... 3... 2..." He barely says two, before he's being ripped off me and thrown across the dance floor. Everyone is frozen in place waiting to see what happens next. Seriously, they can't go around hitting everyone who fucking touches me.

Looking at the Acehole who did it, I'm not surprised to see Roman seething in front of me. Hands fisted at his side as he breathes heavily, trying to control himself. Fucking idiot.

Red and Trudy are with Aiden who is laying on the floor wearing a shit-eating grin.

"Are you okay?" I ask as I approach, shaking my head. I don't apologize, he knew what was going to happen and he chose to do it anyway.

"All good, buttercup." He offers me a thumbs up, and the whole thing just makes Roman growl louder.

"Roman, back off."

"Back off? Are you joking? No one touches you unless I say so. He's lucky I don't break his fucking hands," he growls, crowding my space.

I look to my left to see the others are standing beside us, not far off Roman's level of rage. They're not going to be of any use to me then. I sigh and steel my back, I won't take his overbearing shit, especially when we aren't together.

"Screw you, Roman. You don't get to say shit. It's my body, I'll do what I please and there's nothing you can do about it. Remember? I'm not your problem," I hiss at him, and he just starts to chuckle as he gets right in my face.

"You think I don't know he's not into pussy? I know, princess, and he still doesn't get to touch you. Do you understand?" His usually bright blue eyes are dark, swirling with emotion as his eyebrows pinch together with frustration.

"You controlling, egotistical Acehole!"

I'm done. I'm not listening to any more of this shit. I step toward Red, when he grabs my arm and stops my movement.

What will it take for him to listen to me?

I lift my left arm and turn to swing at his chest, not wanting to ruin his handsome face. This is what we both know, violence, but he catches my fist with a smug look on his face.

"Princess, I couldn't give a shit what you think I am, you're mine. The fact that you still call me an Acehole tells me more than you know. You think I don't know you, baby? You want me, you want all of us, but you're too much of a pussy to admit it," he growls in my ear, and I can't control the goosebumps that trail down my neck at the graze of his lips.

Screw him for thinking he knows everything. I raise my knee and hit him square between his legs. He instantly releases me and keels over a little. He doesn't deserve my kick ass fighting skills when he's just being a dick. If he wants to grab me, he deserves to get the cheap shot.

"Fuck, princess," he splutters.

The other guys finally approach, but I've had enough.

"Red, are you okay if Oscar gets you home?" She looks between us all for a moment and nods silently in agreement. Thank god.

Parker tries to stop me, but I shrug him off. Without another word I turn and stalk the fuck out of there, glaring at every asshole who looks my way.

NINE
Kai

A path clears in front of her as she stalks off. I give her a moment, watching to see where she might be going. As soon as she turns left instead of heading for the nearby SUVs, I know where to go.

"I've got this, guys," I say, glancing around at everyone. They all offer a nod in response, while Jess attempts a stern glare at me with her hands on her hips.

"Don't pull a Roman, okay? I can't help you idiots out when you act like that." She glares, and I agree. Roman is too hot headed most of the time, and even more so when it comes to Luna.

"Do us proud, bro!" Oscar shouts as I follow after her, not wanting to let her out of my sight.

I allow her the space and peace she needs, and she doesn't look back once. She either knows I'm following or doesn't care that she's alone in the dark out here. Likely both. My Sakura is fearless and full of strength.

The moment she turns off the path and into the grass, she's slipping her heels off. She steps into our little secret garden and I'm surprised to find it lit with what looks like solar paneled lights. There are little fairy lights on the inside of the hedges, which I hadn't noticed the last time we were here. Larger lamps are scattered throughout the space, giving it the perfect glow.

I watch her as she stands for a moment, loving the feel of the perfectly trimmed grass beneath her feet. Slowly making her way to the gazebo, she flicks a switch and it lights up. That's when I realize, I never noticed the lights the last time we were here because they weren't there.

When did she do any of this? I'm not sure, but I don't like the fact that she's clearly been coming out here at night, alone.

"Are you coming in, Kai, or are you going to stand there all night?" she calls. Who am I to refuse?

Following her path, I'm shocked when I get to the gazebo and see how much it has actually changed.

When we were last here, it was a simple gazebo with a picnic bench in the center. Now, the table has been moved over to the right-hand side with a rattan style daybed set up to the left. I'm surprised it's not cramped, instead it's the perfect setup.

Out of nowhere, she's pulling a cooler out and lifting a bottle of water in the air. Yep, perfect setup.

"Do you want a drink?" she asks, tilting her face at me. Her ass stays in the air as she stays leaning over the box, and it's hot as hell.

"Whatever you're having, please."

"Well, I have water and soda or we can do some vodka shots. What do you fancy?" She's shaking the vodka bottle around enough for me to know that's what she wants me to choose.

If she's willing to let me stay here and spend time with her, then I'll take whatever she's offering me. Especially if she's going to let her guard down.

"Vodka shots it is then," I say with a relaxed smile, as I move closer.

I can tell she's stressed out, but asking her if she's okay

will only make it worse. So I play it safe.

"I can't believe this is the same secret garden from two weeks ago." She looks around at it all with a small smile on her lips.

"Yeah, I've been coming out here when I need some fresh air. I like the outdoors, but I don't want to sit around the blocks with everyone else. So, I had some packages delivered and Ian set it all up for me."

"Ian, as in, Ian the driver?" I ask, as she takes a seat on the daybed. She keeps the vodka bottle in her hand as she nods in response. I'm glad she's got allies amongst the staff too. I'll have to run a little background check on him.

Taking a seat beside her, she naturally moves closer to me, but I don't think she realizes it. She's so hell bent on this not working, yet her body is always leaning toward one of us.

As she holds the bottle of vodka, I'm glad to see it hasn't already been opened. She's her own person, but I don't want her to sit out here drinking alone. She must be able to see something in my eyes when she meets my gaze.

"Don't worry, Mr. Observant. It was here as a just in

case and look at that, here we are." She grins at me, and lifts the bottle to her lips, taking a swig and passing it to me.

I follow suit, enjoying the burn down my throat. She stares me down the whole time.

"I wish you guys would go back to whatever it was you were doing before I got here," she murmurs, catching me off guard. Looking down at her hands in her lap, that's her tell. She doesn't mean her words, but she wants to.

I place my hand under her chin, and lift her face to meet my gaze.

"Sakura, why do you want us all to do that? Why are you trying to make everyone believe you don't want this? Including yourself?" I ask, shuffling a little to face her better. She closes her eyes and releases a heavy sigh.

"It's for the best, Kai," she whispers, swiping the vodka bottle from my other hand, and taking another swig.

I refuse to move my hand, even if it is uncomfortable for her, and she doesn't pull away. I snatch the bottle back and take a large drink myself before placing it on the floor.

"Why do you get to be the one to decide what's best for everyone?" I grumble, trailing my hand down her neck. My fingers wrap around the front of her throat, as I let my dominant side take control.

Her pupils dilate. Even right now, when she's telling me to turn my back on her, she still can't hide her reaction to me.

She's seen the quiet and observant Kai, but I clearly need to show her the other side of me.

"I've spent enough of my life having others make decisions for me, Sakura. I refuse to let you do it too, even if you think you're doing it for the best," I whisper, bringing my lips closer to hers. "You won't protect me, or any of the others from the inevitable. This is the life we have grown up in, we know what to expect, Sakura. So how about you rein in your pride, listen to Roman and we can all move on. Together."

She rolls her eyes, and I apply a little more pressure around her neck. Her eyes widen, but not in fear. The lust in her gaze is unmistakable, she can't look away from my lips.

"Kai," she gasps, want filling that single word.

I'll give her what she needs, when she gives me what I want.

"What do you need, Sakura? Tell me."

Keeping my hand around her neck, I move her further

up the cushions instead of sitting on the end. Looking up at me, she searches for the right words.

"I need a release," she pleads, and I grin at her. I'm one step closer.

"And what will I get in return, Sakura?"

"You'll get a release too."

Shaking my head, I lift myself up and place my legs on either side of hers. Straddling her, I make sure to hold my weight. The combination of my weight above her and my grip around her neck has her panting. Her chest is rapidly rising and falling as she squirms, trying to gain any kind of friction.

She's beautiful when I get a glimpse of her submissive side. She'll swear blind she doesn't have one, but at this moment she's letting me manhandle her like she would never usually allow.

"That's not all I want, Sakura," I murmur, leaning in to run my nose up the side of her face. Her scent is intoxicating, and the little moan she releases goes straight to my throbbing cock.

"Fuck, Kai. Whatever you want, just touch me." Her hands run under my t-shirt, her fingers teasing my skin, but I can't give in yet.

"I want there to be an us again. All of us." I tease a finger down her chest, tracing her scar as I keep my other hand gripped around her throat.

"What? Kai, that's not what this is about right now," she says, frowning at me.

"Ah, well that might not be what this is about to you, but I don't hate fuck. I definitely won't fuck you without meaning, Sakura. So, agree to try with us again, and I'll give you exactly what you want." I kiss just below her ear, a gentle touch above the hardness of my grip, and she moans.

"It's not safe around me, Kai. I won't put you all in danger like that."

"Bullshit. When will you understand that we choose where we stand? Stop trying to take away our choice, Luna," I growl out, which catches her by surprise.

"Luna? You've never called me that. Are we fighting or flirting?"

"I've got my hands wrapped around your throat, what do you think?"

"That doesn't answer my question," she says with a grin.

"Give me what I want, and you'll get your answer,

Sakura." I push her on to her back, leaning over with her. Caging her in, making her pupils widen with the use of her nickname. Hot as hell.

"Kai, please." She wraps her hand around my wrist, pushing me down harder on her throat as her eyes roll back in pleasure. I haven't even touched her core yet and she's already this worked up.

"Hmm, I do like it when you beg me, but that's not what I asked for now is it?" Using my free hand, I pull my phone out of my pocket and press it to dial out.

Placing the phone beside her head as it starts to ring, I slowly inch my fingers across the swell of her breasts, teasing the outline of her hot as fuck little bikini top. She lets out a moan as the phone answers, Roman's gruff voice coming through the speaker phone.

"Yeah?" he answers, but then silence takes over as he hears her moan.

"Tell him you'll listen, and we're a team again, Sakura, and I'll give you exactly what you want." My mouth replaces my fingers and my tongue comes out to trace the fabric.

She lets out another whimper as heavy breathing can be heard from the phone. Still, she says nothing.

"The sooner you agree, Sakura, the sooner you get to climax."

I move down a little, and trail my fingers up the inside of her thigh, but stop right before I touch her core. I can feel the heat already, and I'm struggling to keep it together.

She frowns at my paused movement, and tries to shift her body to force my fingers to touch her sweet pussy. I place a little more of my weight on her legs, restricting her, and she finally meets my gaze.

"Fine, I will hear him out. Now fucking touch me, Kai," she yells, tiny beads of sweat dotting her forehead. I inch my fingers a little further, resting at the edge of her entrance. I can feel how wet she is, and my cock swells even more against the confines of my jeans.

"Almost, Sakura, and the rest. You're so close to pleasing everybody, including your hot little pussy. You can do this."

"I won't... I won't make decisions for you, and I'll listen to Roman. I want to be with you, all of you, but I'm just scared, okay?" She yells in frustration at the end. I can see she hates admitting her weaknesses and fears, but she just did. For me. For us.

I smile down at her as I thrust two fingers into her core,

my thumb instantly finding her clit and pushing down. The moan that escapes her lips is ecstasy, and I want more of it.

Giving her throat one last squeeze, I lift off her, pulling her skirt off and throwing it aside without a care. This is the moment. I'm not holding her down, I'm not hanging pleasure in the air, she can leave if she wants to.

Meeting her gaze, she must be able to see the fear in my eyes that she's about to pull away again, and her features soften.

"Kai Fuse, do not give me this Mr. Alpha vibe, then question it. Did I want to admit my fears out loud to you? No, but you know that already," she murmurs, rising to her knees. "Do I feel a million times better for being honest with you, and allowing myself to be with you? Damn right I do. Now fucking kiss me."

She doesn't need to ask me twice. With my hands on her hips, I pull her toward me. Our lips come together as she wraps her arms around my neck.

I get lost in her touch, in her scent, until she pulls back a little and rests her forehead against mine.

"Now, if you don't make me climax, I'm not responsible for my aggression. Understood?" I can't help but smile, there's my Sakura taking what she wants.

Pulling a condom out of my back pocket, she gets the message, leaning back and pulling her top off. My eyes go straight to her pretty little nipples, all shiny with her jewelry. My mouth goes straight to her peaks as she lays back for me. My fingers caressing over her hips as my mouth slowly trails down her body.

As my mouth hovers over her clit, she pulls my hair, gaining my attention.

"Kai, this is a snack, okay? No making a fucking meal out of it, I need you inside me," she says with an exaggerated stern look. I just grin, I might be quiet and observant but I'm the boss here. She'll learn soon enough.

Twirling my tongue slowly around her sensitive nub, I tease her entrance, forcing her back to arch up. She's so responsive from such a small touch, I want more. I thrust two fingers all the way in, her heat causing me to groan and my cock throb in my pants.

I cup her pussy so she can grind against me as I rub her g-spot, her moans getting louder as she fists her hands at her sides. The tremble in her body becomes erratic, along with her breathing, and I know she's close. So I bite down on her clit while keeping my fingers at the same pace, and my Sakura explodes, like fireworks on the fourth of July, only prettier.

While she takes a moment to catch her breath, I finally release my aching cock from my tight ass jeans. I'm not wasting any time trying to get undressed right now, I just need to be inside her, like we both want.

Just before I roll on the condom, she knocks it from my hand. The dazed look in her eyes and the soft smile on her face takes my breath away.

"If you're claiming me, I'd prefer it without anything between us," she whispers, and I wish I had time to capture her face right now. My heart pounds rapidly in my chest, just from thinking about entering my Sakura for the first time.

She's still not quite come down from riding her high, but I'm done waiting. Grabbing her by the ankles I pull her to the bottom of the day bed and place my knee up beside her.

Glancing one more time to make sure, she gives me a nod, and I sink all the way fucking home.

Oh god.

I need a minute.

Her pussy is so tight, and so hot, I have to force myself to last longer than five god damn seconds. Her head is thrown back in pleasure, and I can't help but tighten my grip on her waist. Panting, I get myself under control and start to move. Slowly, dragging out every last touch. Between us, we are a heap of grunts and moans, and I'm lost to it all.

"Please, Kai, more. I need more," she begs beneath me.

Lifting her legs up, her calves resting against my shoulders, I go harder and faster, giving my Sakura exactly what she wants. Her moans intensify as I reach out my hand and squeeze her left breast, trapping her nipple with my thumb.

Her hands search above her head for anything to grab on to. I'm thrusting so hard we're moving up the bed. With nothing to stop our movement, her head hits the rattan at the back of the daybed.

Without removing my cock, I drop her legs and lift her to ride me, while I'm on my knees. The moment she comes down on me I'm reaching a whole new level of heat. How is it possible for her to strangle my dick this hard?

She grinds against me as I crush my mouth to hers, devouring her lips. My hands clawing at her back, needing to feel her everywhere. I see the moment she reaches ecstasy and orgasms around my shaft. The tightness, her moans, the pleasure etched into every fiber of her being, sends me over the edge. Crashing into wave after wave of my own release.

As we both come down from our highs, she cups my face, bringing my gaze to hers. Leaning in, she places a gentle kiss to my lips. My Sakura is a badass bitch, and she just gave me a peek at her tender side. My heart feels like it may thump out of my chest.

Knowing her affect on me, she offers a cheeky wink before slowly standing. I can't help but chuckle when she tries to stand and her legs buckle beneath her. The fake glare she sends my way only makes me laugh louder.

Caught in each other's stare, we jump at the sound of something shuffling around.

"What was that?" Luna asks, as she tries to step into her skirt.

"Well, I'll be the first to say that I'm all for porn on audio. I didn't even need the visual," Oscar's voice floats through my phone which is nestled amongst the cushions.

I look at Luna, and the surprise is clear on her face, but she laughs at the situation.

"Fuck off, Oscar," she murmurs, as she picks the phone up.

"Hey, baby girl. It's not just me. We just had a dickfest back in Roman's room, and I'm not ashamed about it. Tell her, Parker."

Luna's eyes widen with the knowledge that others were still on the other end of the phone, getting off to us fucking.

"I am very sad I missed that," she says into the phone. Standing in between my legs, her fingers run through my hair at the back of my neck. So good.

"Not as sad as me, baby girl," he purrs back. "Fuck off, Roman, stop trying to hit me."

The commotion on the other end of the phone escalates before the call suddenly ends.

"We're not calling them back," I grumble, knocking the phone from her hands, making it bounce off the daybed.

"Whatever you say, Mr. Secret Alpha," she says with a smirk, and I bite her nipple in response, making her squeal and grab her top to cover up.

"In all seriousness, Luna, I need you. We need you. We have to be a team, okay?" Stroking my cheek, she looks me straight in the eyes.

"I'll try, Kai, it's just hard."

"I know, Sakura, but this is how we are meant to be.

So, get used to it," I say, patting her perky ass before standing too. "Full disclosure, this was always our game plan. Roman was to rile you up, and I was always going to be the one to convince you to come back to us. It just wasn't meant to specifically happen tonight or involve violence. Roman just went a little crazy, and I'm all for seizing the moment."

She gapes at me as I watch her brain try to add up what I'm saying, but she just keeps coming up with the wrong number. She clears her throat and tries to glare at me, it's a shame the slight twitch of her lips gives her away.

"When was this plan devised, exactly?"

"Earlier, and yes, Red was aware. We sent her a text before we left Ace," I say, flashing her my full-watt smile.

"You sneaky fucking Aceholes," she says, shaking her head, as I pull her toward me.

What did she just call me? I can't help but chuckle a little at her.

"Let's get you home, Sakura," I murmur against her lips, and she nods in response.

Making sure her top is back in place, I wrap my arms around her shoulder and pick her discarded heels up with the other hand. She looks up to me with a smile gracing her lips.

I kiss the top of her head, as we stroll back toward the party to grab an SUV. Tonight could not have gone any better.

I got my girl back, my Sakura.

Now I just need to figure out how to keep her.

YOUR BLOODLINE

KC KEAN

TEN

Luna

Sunlight glares through my bedroom window, forcing me to wake up. Stretching, I enjoy the comfort of my bed before I look to my right. Huh? He's not there.

Kai brought me home last night, and I couldn't bring myself to let him leave. He was more than happy to comply so I'm surprised he isn't still here.

God, last night. I don't even know where to begin, or how it even began, but I definitely like how it ended. I shouldn't be surprised that I ended up in the arms of one of my Aceholes, I just thought I had more willpower than this when it came to them. Clearly not.

I need to stop trying to push them away, and finally have this conversation with Roman. As much as I was in the heat of the moment last night, I wouldn't have agreed to any of this if I didn't mean it. Kai just gave me the push I needed, and the orgasms, which definitely helped.

Feeling the sheets beside me, they're still slightly warm. So, he didn't dash as soon as I fell asleep at least. Glancing at my bedside clock, I'm surprised to find it's past eleven o'clock. I know we were up late last night, but my body clock still usually has me awake before eight o'clock at the latest.

I slept so well last night, though. Obviously, pushing them away had been wreaking havoc on my mind, and with Kai beside me last night I was happy to succumb to the rest my body really needed.

Swinging my legs over the side of the bed I get up, grabbing an oversized top from my drawer to cover up with. As I throw my hair up in a messy bun, I head for the coffee machine, and then the bathroom.

Wiping sleep from my eyes, I stalk into the lounge and stop short when I see my sofas are filled. Roman, Oscar and Parker are sprawled across my space in what I can only describe as the grey sweats club. Oscar and Parker are sitting together on the sofa facing my direction, while Roman is facing the tv.

My god. They are all wearing fitted grey sweats, I think I'm drooling. I try to discreetly swipe a hand across my mouth to make sure I'm not, but Oscar catches me.

"Good morning, baby girl," he purrs, leaning back on the sofa with his arms outstretched beside him. His words catch the attention of the other two, who quickly look in my direction too.

Parker offers me a soft smile. I love it when he does that, and I can't help but smile back.

Roman is leaning forward, arms resting against his knees with his head risen. I can see his hands clench, he wants to come over and grab me but doesn't know how I will react. How would I react? We need to talk for sure, and I said I would try. No one will be trying if we're all constantly second guessing ourselves.

My mind made up, I offer a smile in response to Oscar's good morning, but head straight for Roman. The closer I get, he finally realizes I'm heading for him, and I give him a taste of his own medicine. Though, this time I'm the predator and he's the prey.

He leans up off his knees, sitting straight up, the

material of his tight black top pulling against his hard chest. His eyes are scanning my face, unsure of my approach but I still don't say a word.

As soon as I step into his personal space with him having to look up to meet my gaze, I climb into his lap and his hands instantly go to my hips. I don't overthink it, I just wrap my hands around his neck and give my everything in attempting to hug him. Leaning my head against his shoulder, his hands instantly wrap around my waist, squeezing me tight. It takes me a moment, but I relax into him, actually enjoying his hold on me.

Nobody says a word, as if they're surprised by the fact I'm willingly letting them beneath the surface of my hard exterior, with a hug of all things, but it feels amazing. Lifting my head off of his shoulder, I whisper in his ear.

"We have a lot to talk about, we both know that, but I wouldn't have agreed to this if I didn't mean it. I just need your honesty going forward, Roman." His hand rubs up and down my spine gently, and it doesn't feel as bizarre as I expected. Me and Roman, the two biggest hot heads here, having a tender moment.

"I promise, princess, no more secrets. We can talk whenever you want to," he murmurs back. "And you can tell us what the plan is because I know you have one." I offer a slight nod.

"I'm trusting you, Roman, don't fuck me over," I say, leaning back with a stern look. "Now, I'm going to go and brush my teeth and—"

"You're not going anywhere until you've kissed me."

"I haven't brushed my teeth yet." Is he crazy?

"Don't care," he grunts, as he pulls me closer by the back of my neck. His lips instantly touching mine, not a single care about my prior protest. My hands cup his face as I match his dominance for control.

"Eww, can we not be doing this right now? I haven't eaten yet, and part of the agreement for me helping was that you would respect my presence when we were a team again."

I pull back from Roman to see Oscar holding the door open for Red. The grossed out look on her face makes it hard for me not to roll my eyes, when she had a hand in all of this anyway.

When had she even knocked on the door? Huh, these guys made me lose my senses.

I can't help but chuckle at her, and as I try to stand up Roman refuses to let go of me.

"Jess, we need to work on your timing then, so neither of us end up inconvenienced," Roman says back, while grinning at me.

"I'm here exactly when you said to be, in case Luna went crazy that y'all were here. It's not my fault things went better than planned," she says with a cheesy grin on her face, offering me an over exaggerated wink. Roman just smiles at me as she rambles on.

"Do you want to grab some food all together from the diner?" Roman asks, refusing to acknowledge Jess' words.

"Yeah, but I'm gonna need to get ready for that, baby." He gives me his attempt at a pouty face which only makes me giggle. He pulls me in for an extra kiss, squeezing my ass cheeks hard before finally releasing me.

"Go quickly, before I change my mind and follow you." I can't help but stop and consider his words for a moment. "Go Luna." I offer him my own pouty face as I step back into a hard wall.

Parker's arms wrap around me from behind as he kisses the top of my head.

"Good morning, angel." Lifting my head backward, I look up to see him smiling back at me. He clearly wanted to get in on the hugging action. I turn around and wrap my arms around his waist, letting him breathe me in.

"Good morning, Parker Parker," I whisper back, enjoying being wrapped in his sweet woodsy scent.

I feel his body relax at his name as he plants another kiss on my head. Then he's stepping back for Oscar to take his place. He instantly wraps his arms around me and lifts me off the ground, twirling us. I'm not awake enough for this, but I tighten my arms around his neck, holding on while he does his thing.

Finally coming to a stop, he places me on my feet with his back to everyone, blocking us off from them. Gently curling a loose bit of hair behind my ear, he looks straight in my eyes.

"Don't ever push me away like that again, do you understand?" I'm taken back by the tension in his voice. Compared to the Oscar who just twirled me around all carefree and fun. I go to respond but he places his finger over my mouth and shakes his head. "Just a nod will do, I don't want to hear any bullshit."

I offer the simple nod he requested. I am sorry for making him feel that way, so if I can't tell him that, I'll show him. Raising up onto my tiptoes, I crush my lips against his. How does it always turn me on something crazy when I kiss one of them, after kissing another?

His hands squeeze my hips as his lips control mine, and this time I let him. I don't push back for dominance, I give into him. Offering him this as my way of apology, which he gladly accepts. Suddenly stepping back, he points to the bathroom.

"Go quickly, before this becomes an orgy and we really do burn Jess' eyes out," he says with a wink.

"Fuck off, Oscar," she shouts from behind him, and it makes me smile at their constant banter.

Turning for the bathroom, I'm stopped again when Kai is standing waiting by the door. It would be rude not to offer hugs to them all now, wouldn't it?

As I get closer, he holds his arms out for me to step into his embrace, and I go willingly. I may need to wrap my head around all this open affection later, not right now though. Right now, I'm enjoying it.

"Did I overstep?" he asks, looking behind me at the others.

"No, you always know what the right thing to do is, Kai. Thank you," I murmur, as I run my hands under his t-shirt. Loving the feel of his muscles tightening under my touch.

"Good, then I'll let you get ready." Offering a kiss to my forehead, he steps back. "Do you sleep in my top often?" he asks with a smirk.

"Only every night since I've had it." I give him a wink as he looks down at the top he handed me after The Pyramid. He smiles wide, pleased with the fact that even though I'd been pushing them away, I still held on to them in some way.

I finally close the door behind me, and even alone I can't wipe the smile off my face. I go to flick the shower on so it can warm up while I brush my teeth, and that's when I see it.

I scream and run back into the lounge like my ass is on fire.

Everyone is standing and ready to run at the door I just came out of.

"What's wrong?" Parker asks, panic in his voice as he grips my shoulders and checks me over.

"The... There's... There's a sp... spider... in... in the show... shower," I manage to stammer out, shaking from head to toe. Confusion takes over Parker's features as he processes what I just said.

Then the fucking Acehole smirks at me.

"You stay here, angel, and I'll get the big bad spider, okay?" he says, like I'm a little child, and it riles me up.

"Don't you patronize me, that thing is big enough to be paying bills, Parker!" I glare the shit out of him.

As he wanders into the bathroom without a care in the world, I turn to glance at the others. Every single one of them is trying to contain their amusement at the situation. So I glare the fuck out of them too, making them all turn away from looking at me, even Red.

"Red, you know what I'm saying, right? It's massive, like this," I say, using my hands to form a circle to show her the size of it, but she just clears her throat.

"Err no, not really. Spider's aren't an issue for me." She looks around awkwardly, rubbing her hands on her pants like it pains her to disagree with me.

"It's okay, princess. We'll save you, don't worry." Roman chuckles, as he walks toward me with his arms out wide.

I want to tell him to fuck off, but truthfully, I'm too scared and I let him wrap me up. Parker steps out of the bathroom, with his hands clasped in front of him.

"Oh my fucking god. Is it in your hands?" I yell, stepping around Roman. I hear a few snickers, but I'm too freaked out to glare them down.

"No sweat, angel. I'm going to go and run it outside."

"Well, you better run it further than the front door if you're not going to kill it," I shout with my face smushed into Roman's back.

I hear the door shut, and arms wrap around me from behind. Glancing back, I see Oscar finally getting his giggles under control.

"I love me a Luna sandwich." His Cheshire cat smile relaxes me slightly.

"Will you go double check for me, Oscar, please?" I refuse to let go of Roman right now, and he just smiles wider.

"Anything for my baby girl."

Staying where I am, I tilt my head to see Kai and Red still looking and chuckling at me. Bitches. I give them the middle finger which just makes them worse.

Oscar steps out of the bathroom as a knock comes to the door, and Kai lets Parker in.

"All clear, baby girl," Oscar says with a grin, as he flexes his muscles. I roll my eyes at him as Parker steps toward me.

"Kiss her often, fuck her well, feed her snacks and kill

the spiders. I think I'm rocking this boyfriend shit." His grin widens as he wags his eyebrows at me.

"Do not come near me with those spider hands, Parker," I warn, backing away from him.

Trusting Oscar's word that it is all clear in the bathroom, I run back in and shut the door behind me. I can hear them all laugh at my expense.

Motherfucking Aceholes.

YOUR BLOODLINE

KC KEAN

ELEVEN

Luna

Monday morning rolls around, sadly pulling us from our relaxed weekend and throwing us back into the grind of the Academy. It was fun spending the weekend all together, including Red. Although, I'm definitely ready for some alone time to satisfy my needs, preferably with the guys, but it may have to be toys at this rate. Either way, I need to scratch my itch.

Red stayed the weekend, happy to pacify me with her safety. I don't want her alone in another block where I can't get to her quick enough, though she's adamant she's going back to Diamond tonight. With that in mind, I dial

Rafe on my mobile as I slip my heels on ready to head out for Combat class.

"Hello," Rafe's gruff voice answers through the speaker.

"Hey, I was just wondering where you were up to with what we discussed about Red? She's adamant she won't stay here all the time. I know I can't force her, but after they just took her for The Pyramid, it has me on edge, Rafe." I lean against the kitchen counter, tapping the surface nervously with the stress of all this on my mind.

"Hi Rafe, how are you? I miss you so much. What have you been up to? Oh, nothing much? Well *I'm* just too busy to even offer you a normal greeting. Catch you later. Bye," he smarts at me over the phone, making me shake my head. Then the line goes dead.

Did he just fucking hang up on me? Fuck's sake, Rafe. Taking a deep breath, I try again.

"Hi Rafe, how are you?" I try not to sigh at the time we're wasting here.

"Oh, Hi Luna. I'm alright, just getting ready to head down to Inked. How about you?" His teasing is getting on my nerves, fucktard.

"Are we done with the pleasantries now?" I ask, putting my breakfast pots in the dishwasher and slamming the door shut.

"I mean, I got you to play along for a whole five seconds. I'll take that as a win, but to answer your question, West should have the keys to you by the end of the day."

Thank god. I sigh in relief, my brain going into overdrive as I plan how to go about this.

"And there won't be any repercussions or additional expectations?" I need to make sure.

"Juliana made sure of it, no stress. Her dad is fully on board with it too, okay?"

"Yeah. Thank you, Rafe," I murmur, almost saying something else but I don't.

"Whatever you need, Luna. You know that," he soothes down the phone. "I'm monitoring the feed from Dietrichson's office ready for her return. The chip downloaded all the files too. So, we've got someone working on decoding everything on her computer as we speak."

"Great, any news on Veronica or Rico?" I ask, frustrated that they're out playing us. They seem far too good at going off grid then showing up completely unannounced.

"No, nothing, but they'll show up, Luna. They always do."

"I know that, I'd just rather have the upper hand this time, Rafe. Every time they've shown up it's been out of the blue and on their terms. Maybe I should come home, extra eyes and all that." I lean against the counter with a sigh, as I rest my head against the cupboard behind me.

"I know, but we are doing all we can. You need to keep up appearances at Featherstone so we don't look suspicious, you know that." I can't help the sigh that passes my lips as I squeeze the bridge of my nose. This shit is stressing me out.

"Okay, but if we don't start making progress soon, that'll have to change."

"Agreed. Now, can we get to the part where we discuss all the messages Roman's been sending me?"

What? I'm stunned silent for a moment, confused.

"What messages?" I ask, grabbing my bag ready to leave.

"I mean I'm not saying he loves you or anything, but definitely besotted. They were messages to make sure I didn't stop him telling you whatever you wanted to know. Threats really. Do we need to have a talk?" He chuckles.

He thinks he's so fucking funny.

"No, we do not. Stop being embarrassing, Rafe." If I could glare down the phone right now I would. I'm ready to end the call when he stops me.

"Does this mean we can have a talk about Parker now? I know you didn't want to, back in New York, but maybe now?" His voice is much quieter now he's not joking around.

"I think so… I don't know. We'll see. I'm gonna go. Catch you later, bye." I quickly end the call, dropping the phone like it's on fire. I do not need him trying to discuss the guys with me, and I definitely don't need him bringing up Parker. Fuck.

Seeing the time, I grab my phone and head for the door, stepping out into the hall at the same time Roman does.

"Stop texting Rafe. If I get one more of his weird awkward birds-and-the-bees talks again, I'm gonna throat punch you." My finger points at him to make sure he gets it. I've definitely caught him off guard with the silence that follows and the slightest nod of his head.

I really need to work on my greetings.

Sighing, I relax my shoulders and try again.

"Hey, Rome."

The smile that takes over his face touches his sapphire blue eyes, that swirl full of heat and sin. He stalks over to me, and I find myself backed against my door.

"Hey, princess." He leans in, kissing me lightly on my lips, not his usual aggressive self. "I could get used to this submissive side to you as long as I get your fire as well." His thumb trails over my bottom lip while I just stare up at him.

Shaking my head, I gather myself.

"Stop trying to turn me into girly mush, it doesn't suit me, and do not call me submissive."

"Whatever you say, princess." Wrapping his arm around my shoulders, he leads me toward the elevator, and my hand rests on his back feeling his body heat.

Stepping into the elevator, I find the strength I've been looking for.

"Roman, can we talk this week? Not tonight, I'm gonna have my hands full but in the next few days? I think I'm ready to listen, and I want to move past this barrier." I look up to him, and the rare soft smile that plays on his lips melts me.

"Whenever is best for you, princess. I'll do whatever you need me to do. Schedule wise the only thing this week is Kai's birthday on Sunday. I'm going to assume he didn't mention it because he never does, but I thought you might want to know."

Of course he wouldn't mention it.

"Do you guys have any plans already?" I ask, turning into him and stroking my hands down his blazer.

"Apart from our weekend breakfast at the café? No, he usually hides away. He doesn't really like to celebrate his birthday." Sadness creeps into the corners of his eyes. "But that's not my story to tell."

What? If it's not his story to tell, I have to respect that. It just doesn't stop my mind from going a little crazy with wonder. I offer a slight nod and think over my schedule for the rest of the week.

"Would tomorrow be okay for you? I don't want to drag this out any longer." My palms are already starting to sweat thinking about it.

"Yeah, of course, princess," he murmurs, kissing the top of my head. A normal gesture from Parker or Kai, but it feels extra delicate from him... *more*. "What's got your hands full tonight?"

"Ah, well I may need your help. Well, all of your help may be needed, actually." I try and offer a cute smile, but it definitely falls flat when he raises his eyebrow at me in question.

"I'm going to need some manpower, manipulation and your whole Acehole persona. You in?"

"Fuck, princess, when you call me an Acehole it's like you're telling me you care," he says with a grin, making me roll my eyes. "What have you got me signing up for then?" He groans down at me.

"Moving Red into the Gibbs room here in Ace." A genuine smile taking over my face, but he groans at my words.

"You do the talking, we'll be the back-up. I am not dealing with her drama queen tendencies, and you can tell the guys too."

Ah, shit. This is going to be worse than I thought.

"What? No way, Luna. Are you crazy?" Red yells at me from across the table. Other students surrounding us stop what they are doing to see what all the commotion is for.

I decided to wait until lunch to drop the bombshell

on her, hoping the public setting would cool her reaction, clearly I was dead wrong.

"It's for your own safety, Red. Rafe promised nothing changes for you. You'll continue with your bloodline as normal but stay in Ace with us, on the same floor as Kai and Oscar. It's a win-win." I'm trying to remain calm and talk rationally, but she's doing this whether she likes it or not.

"I'm going to ask again, are you crazy? I can't just start living in the Gibbs' room. It's not mine, and I refuse to owe anyone for this." Damn, she's holding her ground more than I thought.

"Look, I know I can't keep you holed up in my room with me okay? But it's not safe with you being in a different block. Not after The Pyramid, Jess. I need you to compromise with me a little here. I've given up any attempt of pushing you away. So let me offer an alternative, where we both get what we want," I bargain with her, yet she still folds her arms on the table and glares at me. A frown line pops between her eyes as she tries to stand her ground.

I don't back down and I don't say a word. I just stare back at her. Finally, with a sigh she relents.

"Okay, but I need more details than this," she says, her

finger pointing at me, trying her best to look intimidating. I offer a simple nod in response, watching as the guys approach, scanning their tickets at the end and moving further down the table to join us.

Parker and Kai kiss me on the head in passing as they sit across the table with Red. Oscar leans in and bites my earlobe, completely catching me off guard. I barely manage to contain a squeal, as he takes the seat beside me, blowing me a cheeky kiss with a waggle of his eyebrows.

Before he can get too comfortable, Roman is pushing him further down the bench, and sliding in between us. Not to be out done by the others, he grabs my chin and smashes his lips to mine.

Possessive as fuck, yet I love it. Their antics have me rolling my eyes, but it does ease the tension at the table between Red and I.

"So, you told her then? We're gonna be neighbors, Jessikins. Which means I can monitor any boys you're not telling me about who try to sneak in and out of your room." He wags his eyebrows at her, which only riles her up.

She squeezes her eyes shut in frustration as her hands clench tightly on the table. The deep breaths she takes are beyond dramatic.

"I really want to punch him in that special way, like you showed me." She looks to me, as if almost seeking approval, but Roman steps in.

"I'll help you out." He offers her a wink, then quickly turns and slaps the back of Oscar's head.

"What the fuck, Rome? There was no need for that." His frown focuses on Roman as he rubs the back of his head. Red giggles, and thankfully relaxes a little.

Roman holds a fist out in Red's direction and she meets him in the middle, bumping fists and wiggling their fingers. What the fuck was that? They both smile, and I think we're in another universe.

"Did you guys just fist bump? I'm confused." Red laughs, unable to contain herself while Roman rests his chin on his hand and flutters his eyelashes at me.

"Don't hate me cos you ain't me," he sasses back, making the guys join in with the laughter too, including Oscar even though he's still pouty.

A server approaches the table with a plate filled with mac and cheese, and another with rather plain chicken and rice, which happens to be mine. I can't eat pizza and pasta all day, every day. I haven't got enough spare time to be in the gym that long to burn it off.

The server returns a moment later with the guys' food, and we fall into a comfortable silence. I can see Red's brain working overtime with questions.

"Fire them at me, Red," I say as I put my plate to the side. I don't need to explain what I mean because she knows.

"Do I have to change any of my classes?" she asks, her head slightly down and her eyes looking up at me.

"No, your schedule stays the same." I relax back in my chair a little, the easy questions I can deal with.

"Do I have to compete in the Games?" She plays with the straw of her drink nervously, scared of what my answer may be.

"Definitely not, Red. If that had been a condition you wouldn't be moving in. I promise."

She nods her head slightly, mulling over whatever is running through her mind.

"How is Featherstone allowing this?"

Well, I was hoping she wouldn't think of that. Clearing my throat, I brace myself for any backlash.

"Juliana has been listed as your guardian, and before you ask, your father is aware." Now I'm nervously messing with the napkin in front of me.

"Oh, cool. I guess." She takes a drink, and leaves it at that. I really expected this part to be a bigger issue.

"Sooo, you're okay with that?" I ask, just to be sure.

"Well yeah. She was really nice when we went shopping to get you some clothes. I get she's freaking ruthless. I heard her on the phone at one point, but she was really nice to me. Plus, she loves you a lot, so I'm not going to complain." The smile on her face tells me she's telling the truth. Although, we're not going to discuss the 'she loves you' part.

My phone vibrates on the table, catching my attention.

West: Hey, I have the keys for you. Any chance we could meet up for a chat, so I can give them to you and discuss everything?

I can't help but release a sigh as I glance at Roman from the corner of my eye. I'm not surprised he's peeking at the text beside me, and if the tension in his jaw is anything to go by, he's not happy.

I haven't spoken to West since The Pyramid. Even last week when I had Weaponry class I refused to even make eye contact with him. He got the hint and left me alone, but now he's ready to push. I don't know what I'm supposed to do here. I needed the keys, obviously, I just know it wouldn't be fair to Roman if I let West explain things before he did. He wouldn't understand, and I can respect that.

Glancing around the table, the others are all having light conversations amongst each other, yet they can sense the tension coming from our side.

Trying to not overthink it, I send West a text back.

Luna: Are you free next period? I'd rather skip a class than waste time moving tonight.

I don't hide my phone. I won't shy away while I'm sitting beside Roman, there is nothing to hide. The tension pouring off him at my response is suffocating. He knows that I can feel him watching and he's pissed. Roman goes to stand as my phone vibrates again. Ignoring my phone, I place my hand over his on the table.

I look up to him, pleading with my eyes to give me a minute. His gaze burns holes in me, but I don't relent. Finally, he takes his seat again as the others at the table quickly glance away again. Keeping my hand on his, I check my phone.

West: I'm free. Coffee shop on the edge of the Square?

Glancing to Roman, I squeeze his hand and send back my reply.

Luna: Yes, I won't be alone.

The storm in Roman's eyes calms as he stares down at me. Clearly we need to work on our communication skills. Placing his hand under my chin, his lips instantly find mine. I let him claim me in front of everyone. I give him the control he's desperately fighting for right now. We haven't discussed the past yet, or how West fits into it all.

Not that I remember, but obviously Roman does, and I assume they both know we were supposed to unite our bloodlines. No one has brought that up, just fucking Rico. That also reminds me that we need to discuss Parker's lousy excuse of a father, it'll just have to wait until later.

Finally coming up for air, I shake myself to get out of the dazed state he leaves me in.

"We're going to head out, I need to get the keys off West so we can get you moved in tonight," I say, mainly keeping my eyes focused on Red.

"Tonight?" she asks, surprised with the quick turnaround.

"I'm not wasting anymore time, Red. I've been trying to set this in motion since we were in New York. You have a free period now, right?"

"Yes."

"Perfect, get your shit together. I've got you four hot guys to help with the moving," I say with a waggle of my brows, and by the look on her face I can tell she's not impressed. Oscar gleams at the description, ruffling his hair and puckering his lips at us all.

"They're all taken." She gripes. "And they're not all that hot." The smirk on her face tells me she's joking, likely trying to rile Oscar up. Kai, Parker and Roman chuckle at her dig, not fazed by her words. Whereas Oscar gives her the response she wanted.

"Hey, you better take that back. I'm Oscar fucking O'Shay. I'm hot as shit," he says, over exaggerating the insult with a hand to his chest and puppy dog eyes.

"Oh Ozzie, I'd love to be able to see things from your

point of view, but I can't get my head that far up my own ass," she says with a wicked smile.

Fuck, that was a quick response. We all burst out laughing, except Oscar who's poutier than ever. Give me strength with these two. Shaking my head, I stand from the table.

"You ready?" I ask, looking down at Roman who offers a nod in response. He stands to join me, as both Parker and Kai pause their tech talk to say goodbye. I can't stop myself from walking around the table and claiming both of their lips. These boys are mine, and it seems like I finally want to publicly claim them all.

"Bitch."

"Fucking whore."

I can hear the murmured insults coming from Wren's table, but I don't pay them any attention. I know things are going to get worse with her, but I'll deal with that after. I have other, more pressing matters to deal with first.

Roman grabs my hand, and brings it to his lips, kissing my knuckles.

"So, do I get to play with your little kitty on the way over?" he asks with a straight face, and my toes curl at the thought. My girl is eager for some attention, and I want to play it out a little more.

"We can walk. It's only on the other side of the shopping strip."

"Or, we can take a scenic drive while I have my dessert." A devilish smile takes over his face.

"I don't know. Is it because you want to please me, or because you want to show up to meet West with me on your lips?" The grin he gives me is even more wicked, and tells me I'm not wrong. Acehole.

"If I said both?"

We slow our pace as I lean up to whisper in his ear.

"Then I might say that I have no underwear on."

The heat in his eyes intensifies, and his speed picks up toward the closest Rolls parked outside.

"You're fucking mine, princess," he murmurs as we fall inside.

Yeah, I think I fucking am.

YOUR BLOODLINE

TWELVE

Roman

Stepping out of the Rolls first, I hold my hand out for Luna to take. The heat and humidity has finally dropped, but it's still dry and still slightly too warm for these damn blazers. I undo the top button of my shirt and tug at the collar. Luna's soft hand slips perfectly into mine, and I squeeze gently as we head toward the coffee shop. I can already see West through the window, sitting in the booth at the back.

Thank god she invited me along. I was going out of my mind back at the cafeteria, worrying he'd get to say his piece before I did. This isn't ideal, having to talk about it with West here, but it's out of my hands. I'll take what I can get when it comes to Luna.

Her hair is slightly mussed, her shirt creased from our little sex-capades in the car, and I fucking love it. If she asks if you can tell what we just did, I'm gonna say no. I want everyone to see her like this. Mine. *Ours*. My dick is still straining against my trousers, but I'm attempting the delayed gratification thing right now. When I'm back inside her it'll be with no barriers between us, and with plenty of time for us to go all night.

This fucker though. He knew she was alive, had clearly been in her life before she got here, and didn't say a fucking word. Once upon a time we were the three musketeers. I still stayed in contact with West after I was made to believe she was dead. Our families are close, but over the past few years we drifted apart. Likely because he's older than me and life changes, but to not fucking tell me? He's at the bottom of my shit list, right along with Rico.

I feel Luna squeeze my hand, gaining my attention.

"Please, try not to go all caveman on me, okay? I know we planned to talk tomorrow, just the two of us, but I need these keys." I nod because I do understand.

Jess is important to Luna, some would say her

weakness, and she knows it. So, we need to do whatever it takes to keep her safe. She encourages Luna to see past the darkness, and really is all unicorns and rainbows for all of us. How that is even the same mellow girl we used to pay no notice to at all, blows my mind.

I hold the door open for her to step inside, and she raises her eyebrow at me.

"Chivalry doesn't work on me, Rome," she says, patting my chest as she walks by.

"I know, but I can be polite, Luna. Besides, I know what works on you. Do you want me to show everyone here how much so?" I ask, grinning back at her, which just has her rolling her eyes at me.

Following behind, we head straight for West.

This place has classic coffee shop vibes. A few red booths and a handful of small wooden tables and chairs, none of which match. Some might say quirky, but it's not my scene. The smell of coffee and the sound of the machines overload my senses. This is why I don't come in here, it's too hectic for my already crazy mind.

West doesn't bother to stand, and I can feel his tension toward me for being here. He clearly didn't think it'd be me she was bringing when Luna said she wouldn't be alone. Tough shit. I can't help but smirk at his frown as we approach. Neither of us greet him, but we approach the table like we own the place, happy to just stare him down. I wait for Luna to take a seat before I rest my hand on the table and lean into her.

"Do you want a Frappuccino, princess?" I don't want to leave her with him, but I can tell they need a moment to break the tension. So, I'll get my girl whatever she wants and give her a minute, that's it.

"She drinks black coffee," West interrupts. My hands clench as I try to rein in my temper, this asshole is just asking for a beating. I don't look at him. I just keep my gaze set on Luna, who also ignores him as she keeps her eyes on me.

"Please, baby," she murmurs, tilting her head back a little further bringing her lips closer to mine. I claim her mouth for everyone to see, making sure I leave her trying to catch her breath. Let this asshole know she's mine.

Fuck. That's the first time she's called me by a nickname that wasn't Acehole, and I like it. My dick fucking loves it. I definitely should have ignored my grand idea of waiting for privacy to rock her world. Now I'm going to be sporting a boner the whole time. Fucking hell. I focus on an image in my mind, of little old people playing naked football. All those loose dangly bits flapping around soon has my cock back under control.

Stepping away from the table, I join the small line to grab the drinks. When the few people in front of me glance my way, they instantly move aside for me to take their place. I don't recognize any of them, but they obviously know who I am. Internally it makes my eyes roll at the lack of backbone these idiots have, yet I'm also pleased I don't have to leave Luna and West alone for as long. Win win.

Stepping straight up to the register, I can't help but glance in Luna's direction. They're talking at least, but I seriously hate not knowing what it's about. West has his arms braced on the table, leaning in toward my girl, who is sitting exactly as she was when I left them. Although, she does seem a little tense. I need to know if he's had his hands on my girl sexually, except I don't want to know if it's not the answer I want.

"Can I take your order?" the girl behind the registers asks, gaining my attention. I barely look in her direction as I say what I want.

"Yes, can I have a large caramel Frappuccino, and something fruity without coffee in it?"

"Err, yeah sure. Anything in particular for the fruity drink?" she asks nervously. I look to the menu, but I don't know what any of this shit means.

"Just whatever the most popular fruity refreshing drink is, yeah?" I'm annoyed with the fifty questions. She nods her head frantically and swipes my card quickly.

"What names?"

"What?"

The fuck she on about now?

"Sorry, what names do you want on the drinks?" she asks, clearly confused at my hesitation.

"Oh, princess on the coffee and... Acehole on the fruity," I say, nodding proudly at myself with that quick thinking. The barista gives me an odd look, but jots it down anyway.

I move further along the line to where a few people are standing around waiting for their orders. All of them stepping back when I approach, again. I can feel Luna's eyes on me. It's bizarre how I know it's her, but the way my skin heats up under her gaze is unmistakable. Tracking my eyes back in her direction, she's staring at me while douche canoe talks.

She's not looking at me as though she needs my

assistance, more that she likes me in her line of sight, like I want her in mine too. Who would have thought I'd be this fucking crazy over someone? Standing in line ordering frilly drinks and shit?

"Princess... and Ace... hole?" someone calls, clearly unsure with what they're reading. I turn to my right to find another server holding two drinks. One is definitely Luna's cold coffee, but what the fuck is in that other cup?

Stepping toward her, she nervously gulps at my approach. She likely knows who I am, and the look on my face will only make her more nervous. She stretches her arms out further for me to take the drinks, but I just stare down at them.

"What the hell is that?"

"Sorry, what?" She frowns, confused with my question.

"I didn't order that," I say, pointing at the other drink in her hand.

"Oh, it's... it's a Dragon drink. You asked for a fruity drink, right? That's what the slip says." She holds the cups out further for me to take them, but I'm still standing staring at it.

"It's fucking pink, and what the hell are all of those floaty bits?" I ask, more to myself than to her.

She doesn't know what to do or say to me, except continue to offer out the drinks. I look for some form of confirmation from the people around me. If I thought they were giving me a wide berth before, they definitely are now. I can hear the gossip mill now, 'Roman Rivera goes cray cray over a pink juice'.

For fuck's sake, I'm starting to sound like Red. I snatch them out of her hands and storm over to Luna. How stupid of me to ask for the most popular drink on the menu. Of course, it's fucking girly as shit. It better not taste like glitter, I swear to god.

Luna is staring at me with her eyebrow raised as I approach, but I just shake my head. I know there are worse things to be dealing with here than the fact I have a fucking pink Dragon drink with floaty shit on top.

Luna moves further round the booth to make room for me and I take a seat at the end. West is staring down at his hands while Luna casually grabs her coffee and sips away, without a care in the world.

"Everything okay? What did I miss?" I stretch my feet out under the table and feel Luna's leg rest against mine. The way it grounds me is unbelievable, at least whatever he's said hasn't turned her against me somehow.

Luna clears her throat, offering me a small smile. "West was just saying how sorry he was for what I went through in The Pyramid." The slight twitch to her fingers clasped around her cup tells me enough. She's getting annoyed, and I'm all too happy to tell him why.

"She doesn't need your apologies, she needed you to fucking warn her this kind of shit might happen. You know, with all that time you had getting to know her again," I bite out, still pissed with this whole situation.

"I trained with her and showed her round all the weapons I could when Rafe was busy. I know she's capable, I just wish she hadn't had to go through it is all." Cry me a fucking river. I just shake my head at him though, he clearly thinks training her was enough. It might have helped, but it's not the same. I've already had enough of him, so I turn back to Luna.

Lifting my straw to my lips, I take a sip of this crazy mixture in my cup. Holy shit. What the fuck is in this? Forgetting the straw, I take off the lid and drink straight from the plastic cup, downing half of it in one go. This shit is good. Crazy good. I need another.

I can see Luna smirking at me, and I stop what I'm doing. Getting back to what's going on around me, I give her my full attention.

"What do you want to know, princess?" I ask, softening my voice, and she relaxes her shoulders. This is hard for her, opening herself up to stories and memories her brain refuses to remember.

"Who do I direct questions at first?" She lightly chuckles under her breath, but it isn't with joy, it's more nerves.

She turns her stare to West and rests her chin on her hand. "You can start by explaining how I've known you for four fucking years and you never mentioned shit."

YOUR BLOODLINE

KC KEAN

THIRTEEN

Luna

He doesn't answer me straight away, instead focusing on his joined hands in front of him.

"Come on, West. After I was attacked, we sat in my kitchen and discussed shit with Rafe. Then you came over to tell me the Dietrichsons were trying to put a hit on my head. That's when you dropped a bomb that you knew me when we were kids. You called me some shit like I'm 'your moon.' You're still a coward, West." I glare, trying as hard as I can not to slam my hand onto the table in frustration.

He knew I would ask questions and he must have known they'd lead in this direction. Yet he's sitting there still not giving me any answers, like he wasn't the one who wanted to talk. I can't help but scoff, making them both look at me weird. I'm not explaining my internal amusement and frustration to them.

"Well? Are you going to answer me, or make a run for it again?"

I meant it when I said I am not fucking around. I have too much going on to waste my time on his silence. His sigh is heavy as he finally brings his eyes to mine.

"Everyone had been trying to track Rafe for years. We were told you and your father were dead and he'd just taken off. Rafe still held up his responsibilities to Featherstone, but never showed up to any gatherings or meetings. It obviously helped that Juliana held the seat at the table for The Ring and the Gibbs bloodline."

He takes a moment, clearly trying to make sure he doesn't fuck this up anymore than he already has. I glance to Roman, he's quieter than I expected. His little outburst earlier is what I was expecting throughout this whole group chat, but I can tell he's trying to rein it in, for me.

Laughter rings out around the coffee shop, drawing my attention toward the table near the entrance. A group of girls are laughing and chatting amongst themselves, like normal eighteen year old girls. Oh, to have it that easy, huh?

I turn my gaze back to West, as I tap my fingers impatiently on the coffee table. He takes the hint and clears his throat to continue.

"Then when I was sixteen, I overheard a conversation between my parents. My mother was crying, repeatedly saying 'she's not dead'. It took me a while, but I realized they could only have been talking about you. They wouldn't have been this emotional about anyone else." He rubs the back of his neck as he finally starts giving me some insight.

Roman clears his throat for him to continue, which just earns him a glare from West but he does proceed.

"When I did finally approach them about what I'd overheard, they made me swear to speak no word of it to anyone else. They feared what would happen if Veronica got her hands on you." He raises a brow, they were right to worry. "So I played along. I said and did nothing until I enrolled in Featherstone Academy. Then I used my classes to strengthen my skills. I trained day and night in Combat and Weaponry to be the best soldier I could be. So Rafe would have one less reason to turn me away.

Then, I came looking."

"Why?" I don't understand the why behind it. I take a sip of my Frappuccino as I run everything he's saying through my mind. I let the sound of the coffee machine distract me from this mess for a moment. It's surprisingly quite relaxing listening to the grind of a coffee machine, you know, if you want a permanent headache. Forcing myself to face West, I wait patiently for an answer.

He eventually responds, "Because you're my Luna Moon."

"What is that supposed to fucking mean, West?" I can't keep my volume down and a few people nearby glance over, but I just glare back.

"It means he wanted you all to himself," Roman grunts. I think that's just his alpha jealousy taking over.

"Shut the fuck up, Roman. It had nothing to do with that at all." He sighs, trying to calm down before he turns to me. "Luna, I last saw you when you were six years old and I was ten. Did I have an understanding that I was expected to have a committed relationship with you? Yes. Did I understand I'd have to share you with Roman? Yes. Did I want to? Honestly, no."

I'm taken back by his honesty, I can see the truth in

his eyes.

"So, what do you mean by your moon?"

"I mean you're my moon, the sister I never had. Tell me a time when I have acted anything other than your friend. I have never seen you in a sexual way, Luna. No offense." He holds his hands up in surrender, and I think for a moment.

The closest time there has ever been anything *almost* sexual between us was when I considered him an easy lay after my fight. Now that seems awkward as fuck, I cringe to myself, but other than that, I do actually come up blank. I nod in agreement and he continues.

"I remember the first time I ever saw you, both of you. I was four, and not impressed by this brat always crying and wanting everyone's attention," he says, pointing at Roman. "Then came another baby, that didn't cry and slept like an angel. I remember looking in your baby basket and your father crouching beside me."

He takes a moment at the mention of my father, but I'm okay right now. No breakdown, yet.

"I'll never forget his words, Luna. He said, 'no matter what, West, we do whatever it takes in this life to protect our girl. She's going to need us even when she believes she doesn't. We fight for our family, and no matter what, that's what we are.'"

He goes to carry on when Roman interrupts.

"I was not a crying brat, West the Pest, take it back."

I don't register his tone or West's response as I'm thrown headfirst into a memory.

Glancing around the lake, I look back to see the large log cabin behind me. All dark wood with a slate roof, sitting two stories high and ridiculously wide. It's like a castle to my child's mind. I see my father, Rafe, and two other couples. One of the men looks like Roman's father, Reggie Rivera. They're all smiling down from the second floor balcony and waving in my direction.

My small hand waves back as I sit on the small wooden dock, my feet dangling over the edge but not touching the water. I'm wearing a bright red swimsuit with little white flowers all over it.

"Come on, Luna. It's not deep, don't be a baby."

I look out to the water where the voice came from, to see the little boy with messy brown hair and bright blue eyes looking back at me with his hands in the air. Roman.

We must be four, maybe five years old? I'm not sure.

The nerves I feel in the pit of my stomach don't allow

me to join him, forcing me to stay exactly where I am. I want to get in and play, I just can't.

"What's the matter, Moon?"

Looking over my shoulder, West comes into view and crouches down beside me. I look down at the dock, too embarrassed to meet his stare.

"Hey, my Luna Moon is always talking my ear off. Don't go quiet on me now." He lifts my chin and tucks my hair behind my ear.

"It's stewpid, West," I murmur, a small pout forming on my lips.

"Nothing is ever stupid when it comes to you, Luna. Now tell me what's wrong so I can help fix it." I feel so relaxed with him, safe. Like I could tell him anything in the world and he would make it better.

"I want to play with Roman, but I'm scared," I whisper, glancing back at the water.

"Tell her, West, she won't listen," Roman groans, splashing the water around him.

"Don't push her, Roman. She has to do things when she's ready."

I don't look up, completely embarrassed that I can't just step in. I hear Roman mutter in the water, but West leans in with his hand held out.

"Princess Luna Moon, would you like me to help carry you in? If you don't like it, I'll place you straight back on the dock."

I think on his words as I stare at the water. I can't see the bottom and it makes my tummy go all queasy. Yet I nod my head slightly at his offer. I trust him when he says he'll put me back up here if I don't like it.

He instantly drops off the dock into the water, which barely goes past his knees. He reaches his arms out for me and I throw myself at him, wrapping myself around him like a monkey, as high up as possible. Scared to touch the water.

"You okay?"

I just nod against his shoulder.

"Okay, I'll walk us out a little to Roman, then I'll kneel down in the water. If you want me to stop, just say the word, alright?"

"Yes," I answer quietly.

As we approach Roman, my heart rate picks up a little. West comes to a stop, and I feel him slowly sink to his knees, forcing me to squeeze him tighter. He doesn't complain, he just continues to slowly lower us into the water.

I feel the water touch my toes, and a small whimper

leaves my lips as I fear the bottomless pit of water, causing West to freeze.

"I can stop," he offers. I shake my head feeling braver with him here to help.

He continues and I feel the water rise to my waist. We don't move or say anything for a moment, as I begin to relax.

"Moon, I promise you. If you release your legs, your toes will touch the bottom from here."

Feeling brave enough to lift my head off his shoulder, I look at him. He keeps his arms wrapped around me, but the softness in his eyes gives me the strength I need to try.

I slowly drop my leg and my toes feel the floor. It's full of stones, and not at all what I expected. I drop my other leg to stand on my own. I let go of West, but he hovers to make sure he's there if I change my mind.

Roman decides he's waited enough and starts to splash the water again, and it gets me straight in the face. The shock has me stuck in place, as West glares at Roman.

"Roman, stop being a brat and let her feel comfortable."

I run my fingers through the water, now the shock of it hitting me in the face wears off a little and a small chuckle escapes me.

"She's fine, stop being bossy, West... the pest..." *Roman says, trying to argue back.*

"West the Pest," *I giggle, as I splash water at Roman.*

"Hey, don't be a brat like this one, Moon. I can't deal with two of you," *he smiles, as I splash water at him too.*

"West the Pest," *we both say in unison, making us laugh harder.*

We spend the rest of the day, playing and splashing and having fun like I never had any insecurities to begin with.

Blinking a few times, I'm back in the café with Roman and West, who are both staring at me with concern. I clear my throat and gulp down my Frappuccino to avoid their gaze for a minute. God that was vivid, but I felt it. The care and gentleness from him, even at a young age trying to be the protector he promised my father he would be.

Roman squeezes my hand resting on the table, forcing me to look at him.

"Hey princess, a memory?" he asks softly, and I nod, placing my empty plastic cup on the table. They want me to tell them what it was about, I can see it in their eyes.

"We were at some cabin, and I was scared to get in the water," I murmur, trying to find the right words to explain the rest.

"West the Pest," West says out loud with a small grin on his face, understanding what triggered the memory, remembering where the nickname came from.

"Yeah. I do believe you called him a brat then too." I smirk at Roman as he catches up to the memory we all share.

"I was not a brat. You were just a scaredy cat." He grins at me, even when I glare at him.

We all sit in silence a moment, remembering the bond we shared until West interrupts the peace.

"So, no, Luna. I don't want to be anything more than your friend, your protector. I will protect you no matter what. Which is why when I showed up, Rafe didn't send me away. He allowed me to help, train you in areas I specialized in better than he did. As much as he thought he'd protected you from Featherstone, we needed to be sure you could protect yourself when we couldn't."

I believe his words, but it does leave me with a question.

"When you showed up in Philly a few years ago when I was on a job, how did you really find out I was there?" I tilt my head to him as I lean back, Roman refusing to let go of my hand.

"I started working at the Academy as soon as I

graduated. It meant using my more extreme skills less, and allowed me to keep a little more in the loop. All galas happen here, and I overheard a phone call with Patrick O'Shay. Someone was telling him about the skills of a thief, what I did hear all linked back to you. So, I followed you to be sure." I nod along with his words, it makes sense.

"Can we get to the part where you explain why you couldn't fucking tell me?" Roman interrupts, reaching his limit for keeping quiet.

West sighs before looking at him. "Look, Rome, it was never about purposely keeping you in the dark. I made a promise to Rafe that I wouldn't tell a soul, and he made me specifically promise not to tell you because you wouldn't have been able to stay away."

"Damn fucking straight I wouldn't have! All our lives changed that day, West. I may have only been six years old, but I still felt the same pain. I still wished she was here with us every single day." He slams his fist against the table with his free hand as he squeezes my hand tight with the other.

The chatter around us dims, as everyone glimpses in our direction at Roman's outburst. The three of us just glare around the room, making it awkward as fuck for them, and they all quickly turn away.

"That's exactly the point, Roman. Rafe was trying to keep the heat off her, to protect her from all of this," West says, arms out wide to force his point.

They're never going to agree on this, and I do get both of their sides. They kept me a secret to protect me from all of this, but ultimately I ended up here anyway.

I'd rather understand the full reasoning behind that from speaking to Rafe or my Grandmother, so I try to change the direction we're heading in.

"Is this why you kept calling me a liar when I arrived?" I look to Roman, he knows what I mean. The first time I bumped into him in the gym, and even when we were fucking he called me a liar. At the time it didn't make sense, but now I kind of get it.

"Yeah. When you showed up with three bloodlines, claiming to be a Steele, I thought you were Totem's heir trying to hide under someone else's identity." The pain visible in his eyes.

"When did you realize I wasn't Totem's heir, and truly a Steele?" I ask, wanting to know how long he kept it a secret for.

"When you were attacked. West mentioned you were

on the phone with Rafe when it happened, then I waited at my door for hours, watching for Rafe to leave. He confirmed it."

So, he'd known for a month before I found out. That night in Washington, he'd asked to talk when I got back. My brain on the way back from DCM Tech had been running through all the scenarios why. He'd said it was important. When I look at him now, I know he was trying to tell me this. I can see the truth in his eyes, but it still infuriates me that he kept it to himself for that long.

My mind has had enough. I've reached my limit of memories and truths for the day. I look to West and hold my hand out for the keys, which he hands over without question.

"I believe your words, West. Now, I need to believe your actions. Has Rafe told you anything?"

"Nothing. He won't tell me anything," he says, clasping his hands on the table.

"Good. You'll know if I want you to, when I trust you completely. Do you understand?" I need to be able to trust him before we can move forward.

"Whatever you need."

I nod. "Good. I want you to gather every piece of

information on The Games as possible. I want your own experience, the whole lot. I want to be prepared going in there. I'm going to take these bastards down, and the best way for me to do that, is from the top."

I don't move a muscle, not even a blink, showing him how serious I am. If West wants to protect me like he claims, he can do so by getting me all the details I need to end them.

"Done."

As simple as that. He stands, knowing there's nothing more to say but hovers a moment and I can instantly sense why.

Rising to my feet, I nod, which makes him gather me in his arms and hug me tight.

He was a large part of my childhood and had come back into my life when I was fourteen. Not once in the past four years had I shown any real care toward him. Yet, he'd protected me as a child and grieved my death. It must have been hard for him, for both of them.

I can't hug him back, my arms are crushed to my body.

"You're stuck with me no matter what, Moon. If this brat or any of the others get out of hand, you just let me know," he whispers in my ear, before stepping back from the booth and leaving the coffee shop.

"Are you okay?" Roman asks, surprisingly calm with his arms stretched out along the back of the booth. If he'd asked me that a week ago, I would have gutted him with a knife and licked the blade afterwards, enjoying the taste of his pain.

Now?

He's my Acehole, as much as I hate it and it scares me. I want to just let myself have this with him, with all of them. The Games are looming over our heads. Rico, Veronica and Dietrichson are all up to some crazy shit. I'm dealing with more than I care to already. I want to trust my gut about him, but he's going to need to do more than eat me out in the back of a Rolls.

"Honestly? I don't know. I want to trust you, and I want to try, but you fucked me over. Just like the rest of them."

"I can understand that, princess. Whatever it takes, I'm in." He smiles softly at me, and my shoulders relax.

"Roman, if you ever keep something from me again, there'll be no coming back from that. I also want to be able to trust you with a few things I need to set in place, but you need to show me that you won't let anyone else dictate what happens between us. I also need your help with the special agent, I'm running out of time with that."

I look him in the eyes trying to let him see the pain that lingers, making sure he knows I won't tolerate anything less from him.

"I promise, princess," he says as he stands from the table, stopping in front of me. "I will be by your side no matter what, Luna. We all will."

He raises his hand to stroke my cheek. Tender moments with him give me tingles, we're usually too hot headed together to appreciate times like this.

"Let's head back, so we can get Jess moved over to Ace, and relax a little."

I nod in agreement. "Shall we get drinks for everyone?"

"Definitely, I need another one of those fruity pink drinks with floaty bits. They're addicting." His eyes light up comically as he licks his lips. Making me chuckle as he tugs me along.

I get lost feeling like a normal eighteen year old with him, even if it is only for a minute.

FOURTEEN

Luna

"I swear to god, Oscar. Stop going through my stuff!" Red screams from the other room, and I can't help but shake my head. All they've done this whole time is bicker, god help them now that they're living next door to each other.

"Well, I need to make sure you're not trying to entice guys over because it isn't happening on my watch," he argues back.

We're in Red's new room, and I'm pleasantly surprised with how nice it is. Rafe has no taste so I know this wasn't his doing, most likely Juliana's. The layout is exactly the same as mine, just smaller in overall size without a dresser.

The lounge is almost rustic. Pale grey walls with brown leather sofas and cream furniture, it's really cozy. There is even an electric log fireplace which just adds to the atmosphere. Her bedroom is all lilacs and floral, way too girly for me but it suits Red perfectly. The bathroom is white, I mean everything. I cringe at the thought of having to clean it, I mean good luck with that Red.

"Get out, Oscar!" A bang follows her yell and Oscar comes running out of her bedroom.

"Oscar, leave her alone. Why don't you order some food and we'll come to your room when we're done here?" Kai says, before Oscar can continue arguing.

"She just threw a book at me. Shouldn't you be asking if I'm okay?" he whines at Kai, before turning to me. "She has thongs, Luna. Thongs. I can't deal with this. You need to talk birds and bees with her, and the dangers of leering men, or I will." His hands are manically swinging in all directions as he tries to explain his frustrations, ignoring what Kai just said.

I think someone is taking the big brother vibes a little too seriously. I look to Kai for help but he just shrugs his shoulders and turns away from us. Thanks, Acehole.

"Ozzie, she's a big girl. You don't complain at my choice of underwear and she's technically older than me. Now, can you please relax?" I stand with my hands on my hips, trying to keep my face straight while we are discussing thongs here.

He strides toward me, bewilderment still written all over his face.

"Yeah, but baby girl, that's you. Jess is different, I'm trying to protect her innocence here, and don't call me Ozzie. I don't like it." His hands come to rest on my shoulders, as though I'm the one that needs some sense knocking into them.

"I'm sorry, what about my innocence?" I question, this fucking Acehole has some nerve.

"Baby girl, we left your innocence at the beach, remember? When I did that thing with my tongue and you—"

"No sex for you now, Ozzie!" I yell, trying to shut him up.

I look to Parker for some help here but he's too busy trying not to laugh out loud at Oscar's ridiculousness. The front door opening has me spinning my head to Roman, who's holding the last box in his hands as he takes in the scene before him.

"Do I want to know?" he asks, with an amused look on his face.

"Roman, Oscar said he took my innocence, can you get rid of him?" I pout, trying my luck, because I know Roman will smack him around the head for me. "These useless hyenas over here just think it's hilarious. I'm getting hangry and none of this is helping." I sigh.

"Oscar, go and order food," Roman says with a shake of his head. What? Is that it? Where's the violence? Maybe he didn't hear me properly.

"Roman, he said he took my innocence. Tell him I'm still innocent." Damn, I don't even know why it matters, but I need someone in my corner. Even if I'm starting to whine like Oscar.

"Princess, I took your innocence in the gym, spread out on the mat, remember? When I ripped your blouse open and released your pretty pink nipples from that lacy white bra. Your hot as fuck piercings in my mouth, as you came from the first thrust of my fingers into your tight pussy. Then pinning your hands above your head as I pounded you into the mat. That was all way before his filthy hands touched you," he says with a grin, and turns to Oscar.

"Food, Oscar."

"Fuck you. Fuck all of you. Sex is completely wiped off the table, my pussy is officially closed," I growl at them, but they just start laughing even harder.

Screw this, we've been at this for hours and I just want to relax and eat. I'm going to go and see what Red's up to, but Oscar is suddenly leaning in to kiss my lips quickly.

"Baby girl, don't do that to me. I miss your sweet pussy as it is. Let me make it up to you. What food does my goddess want me to order for her?" His hands come to wrap around my waist, holding me close like I hadn't just been mad with him.

I hear Roman set the box down and join a quiet conversation with the other guys while I get lost in Oscar's gaze. My hands instinctively glide up his chest and rest on his shoulders. I love the feel of him against me.

"I want something Italian, maybe spaghetti carbonara or pasta Bolognese, whatever they have please." He nods at my words and leans in to touch my lips again. This time he takes his sweet ass time devouring my lips, and I'm a sucker for the intoxicating electricity that shoots between us. I think I just threatened a sex ban, but I can't even last five minutes.

Suddenly Oscar's lips are gone, and it takes me a moment to fight through the sexual fog around me to see what's happening.

Roman is pushing him away from me, and toward the door.

"Luna said she's hungry, not that she wants to be your meal, asshole. Come on." He takes a peek at me over his shoulder as he marches out with Oscar. As the door shuts behind them, I feel Kai and Parker's heated stares, which only ignites my arousal more.

Fuck, I'm overheating. I make sure I have my back to them so I can fucking fan my face, this is all too much. The chuckles from behind me tell me they can see me anyway.

I need to get some space before I dry hump them, so I head toward the bedroom where Red is. Not two steps and my phone begins to vibrate in my blazer pocket. It's Rafe.

"Hey, Rafe. Everything okay?" I ask, pausing where I am.

"Hey, I've got some updates on Dietrichson, if you have a few minutes?"

"Yeah, of course. We're almost done setting Red up and anything relating to that bitch is priority," I say as I grab my bag and take a seat on the sofa.

"Okay, well to start with, she's back. I'm not sure why she was able to cut the trip short but we weren't too worried since you already got in and planted the surveillance. At least now we can start monitoring her better."

"Agreed." I don't want to be anywhere near her, but I'd rather have her closer and be able to monitor her than not know what she's up to at all.

Kai sits beside me, questions in his eyes. This is the deciding moment. Whether or not I truly let them in. Let them know what has already been set in motion.

"One sec, Rafe. We may as well have this conversation on speakerphone so I'm not repeating it." I hold the phone away from my face and look to Parker who's standing beside the sofa.

"You want me to get the others, angel?" he asks, not taking a step toward the door until I answer. As soon as I nod, he dashes off. Kai rests his hand on my knee, I look at him and the emotion I see in his eyes catches me off guard.

"Thank you, Sakura," he murmurs. Appreciation sparkling in his eyes, as he knows this is me truly letting them in, like I said I would. I offer a smile in response, unable to express myself in any other way.

"Red, Rafe is on the phone. Are you coming in or

carrying on with the five thousand things you own?" I ask loud enough for her to hear me from the other room.

"I'm on my way, captain." I press the loudspeaker on my phone and set it on the coffee table.

"Kai is here already, and Parker just ran to grab the others. They'll be a minute," I offer as we wait for them.

"So I get to grill them all too? Damn Luna, you could have given me a heads up. I've not got my embarrassing father questions with me," he jokes over the phone, making Kai chuckle.

"Don't even, Rafe. I'll gut you, or tell Juliana and she'll gut you instead," I threaten, as my cheeks flush with embarrassment. Kai strokes my cheek, watching as they start to go pink, as he smiles softly at me. I send him a death glare, but it does nothing at all.

Parker comes strolling back in with Roman and Oscar trailing behind him as Rafe responds through the phone.

"I'll be the one doing the gutting if any of these dickwads fuck with my little girl, understood?" All the humor has left his voice as his voice booms around the room.

"Yes, Rafe. You tell these suckers!" Red cheers as she steps out of her bedroom. "Especially Oscar, he's the worst. Let me tell you—"

"Alright, you're making us go off track. Can we get to the information please?" I snap. I hope they ordered food, that will definitely perk up my attitude.

Nobody says a word as we all sit and stare at the phone, waiting for Rafe to give us the details.

"Okay, so I was just letting Luna know that Dietrichson is back. We had planned to keep her out of the Academy for two weeks, but with the surveillance Luna set up we're happy for her to return so we can begin monitoring."

I hold my breath. I can feel eyes on me as I keep my gaze locked on the phone. The only person who knows the plan is Red, but I hadn't told her I'd already done it. I didn't want her to worry about it.

"What surveillance?" Roman grunts.

"Well, Luna—"

"Not you, Rafe. I want to hear it from Luna," Roman interrupts, his eyes fixed on mine as I grit my teeth.

Shit. I'm really not in the mood for this. I steel my back and stare him straight in the eyes.

"Before the party on Friday, I slipped into Dietrichson's office and set up three cameras, a recording device and planted a chip in her computer. Problem?" Sometimes his caveman overtakes his common sense, I'm going to assume this is one of them times.

"Shut your mouth, Roman, before you make it any worse," Parker jumps in, before Roman can respond. "Luna knows what she's doing, and we hadn't straightened everything out then. So reel yourself in," Parker says from beside me, arms braced on his knees as he glares at Roman.

"Who said that?" Rafe asks through the phone, making me frown. It's not relevant.

"It was Parker," Red answers, winking at me like this is fun.

"Parker, you are now my favorite," Rafe chuckles through the phone, as Parker sits up straight with a giant smile on his face. "Anyway, we had someone get into the computer and there seems to be some encrypted emails back and forth with one I.P. address. So we are looking into that some more, while we track the offshore bank account we found details for on her computer." He pauses for a moment, and I can hear him shuffling papers around on the other end.

My stomach grumbles through the silence, making everyone look.

"The food will be here soon, baby girl," Oscar says

from the arm of the sofa, blowing me a kiss.

"Sorry, I can't find where the papers went that I scribbled on," Rafe comes through the phone again. "But it's not a business or name we're familiar with so we'll look more into that too. West mentioned he was gathering everything possible on The Games, which is a good idea. It's usually kept hush-hush what games everyone participates in, but fuck them. Gather everything you can. Every time someone is in Dietrichson's office, I will be alerted. Do you want me to send the link to Fuse?" he asks, and we all look to Kai, who's nodding his head.

"Yeah, I'll have Luna send my details across," Kai says with a smile at me.

"Great. Sorry, one sec." He moves away from the phone a moment, but we can all still hear him. "What's up, Jake?"

"Is that Luna on the phone?" I hear Jake's voice come through in the distance, and it makes me cringe.

"Now's not a good time."

"When will be a good time, Rafe? She doesn't answer my calls or texts. Is she even alive?" His voice becomes more frantic, and I can't stop my eye roll.

Everyone is staring at me, raised eyebrows from Red,

Parker and Kai. While Oscar and Roman glare. Fantastic.

"Rafe, I don't have time for this. I need to go," I raise my voice, making sure he can hear me.

"Alright, kid. Don't worry about this end. You guys be safe, protect each other, and practice safe sex." I grab the phone and end the call. This shit's not even funny but the guys are laughing, so at least it boosted the mood.

A knock comes from the door and Oscar jumps up.

"Food, I'll get it! I want to be the one to brighten Luna's mood," he shouts over his shoulder, before opening the door. I relax back into the sofa, closing my eyes as I process the little information we've been able to gain from Rafe.

I feel a hand cup my chin, and I open my eyes to find Kai peering down at me.

"Hey," I murmur, bringing a hand up to his arm, which makes him smile a little.

"Do I start with who that guy was on the phone? Or the fact that you set up surveillance without telling me?" He's not angry, these are obviously just topics he wants to discuss.

"Or, we could discuss your birthday on Sunday?" I counter, and he goes to move back, but I grip his arm, keeping him in place. "Don't do that. Don't pull away. I'm trying with you guys here, I need you to do the same."

He stares down at me, his eyes darkening.

"After breakfast at the café, do you want to head out to the garden? Just me and you for the rest of the day?" I ask quietly.

His thumb moves to my bottom lip, stroking a slow lazy pattern back and forth.

"I'd like that, Sakura."

"Good." I lean up to kiss his lips, moving his hand out of the way. "Now, feed this cranky bitch." He chuckles at me, lifting me from the sofa and wrapping me in his arms.

Parker is staring at us from behind Kai, he must have been able to hear our discussion if the concerned look on his face is anything to go by. He nods, making sure everything is okay, and I nod back.

These guys, they care for each other, for Red… for me.

My soul can't deal with the sense of comfort that actually brings me.

FIFTEEN

Luna

It's been six days since Rafe called with a heads up that Dietrichson was returning, and she hadn't made an appearance once. Not only that, but Wren has been gone. Like not even here, and there aren't even any rumors as to where or why. Something's going on, I can feel it. There is a pit in my stomach warning me this is all far from over, and my gut is never wrong.

Everyone will be here in a minute to leave for Sunday breakfast at the café, and Kai's birthday, so I need to send Rafe a message quickly.

Luna: Hey, any news on Wren? Or any details from Dietrichson's office? Something's definitely off.

A knock comes at the door before I get a response, the surveillance feed on my phone shows me the guys and Red on the other side. I pocket my phone, and head over to the door to let them in. Hopefully, Rafe will respond soon.

My eyes instantly seek out Kai first. After Monday, when I mentioned his birthday to him, I've been worried about how today might go. I don't want to make things worse which is why I want to have some alone time with him. Just the two of us.

"I'm fine, Sakura," he murmurs, stepping into my space and wrapping me in his arms. God, I never thought hugs and affection could feel this good. I know he's trying to put on a brave face for me, but the extra squeeze in his arms tells me the truth.

I lean back a little so I can bring my lips to his, which he accepts with gentleness. A complete contrast to the alpha Kai from last weekend. God, I love it.

"I know he's the birthday boy, baby girl, but I need some lovin' too, you know," Oscar whines, drawing me back from Kai's lips.

Kai gives me a soft kiss on the head as he nudges me in the direction of Oscar. Who picks me up and twirls me around, my legs wrap around him and my lips find his in an instant.

His lips crush mine, as he demands more from me. Taking exactly what he wants, I'm lost to his touch as his teeth sink into my bottom lip. The moan that escapes me is uncontrollable.

Every. Time.

I'm suddenly being pulled off Oscar and thrown over someone's shoulder. I can't help the squeal that passes my lips. The ass that is suddenly in my face tells me it's Roman as the others all laugh around us.

Except Oscar who's whining, "Roman, stop being such a dick. You have to share with me." Making everyone just laugh louder.

"Put me down, Roman."

"No way, princess. I'm starving, and if I set you down we'll all continue to pass you around for a taste," I can sense the smirk on his lips, like he's proud of himself. "Of your lips that is." He smacks my ass for added effect.

Dirty fucking Acehole, getting me all worked up.

He walks us over to the elevator, and I try to crane my neck back to see the others.

"Help me out here, guys."

"But you look so hot, all helpless for a minute, angel. It gives me some ideas," Parker says, stepping closer with a grin on his face. He places a kiss on my open mouth, before stepping around us and into the elevator.

"Morning, captain," Red says, as she leans right in and plants a quick kiss on my lips copying Parker, and following after him with a chuckle. She's a witch, an encourager.

"Remind me why we're friends again?" I grumble at her.

"Cos you love me, so hush."

Roman steps into the elevator behind everyone, happy to keep me here. I mean, it's not all bad, I get a good view of his ass while he walks at least. That's when the thought strikes me, and I slowly slip my hand into the back of his grey joggers. Idiot should have worn jeans, instead I've got easier access.

Slipping my hand inside his boxer shorts too, I palm the globe of his ass.

"Fuck, princess," he murmurs, which just encourages

me. I don't care to imagine what we look like right now, this just turned into some fun teasing.

I move my hand further down until I can feel the back of his balls, stroking them gently. His grip on my legs tightens to the near point of pain, but I don't stop. Instead, I gently squeeze his sack in my hands and he groans so loud, it's obvious I'm playing dirty.

He suddenly whips me over his shoulder and traps me in the corner of the elevator.

"You little fucking tease," he whispers against my lips, before crushing his mouth to mine. His lips dominate mine as he delves deeper, always wanting more from me. I try to nip at his mouth, but he pins me in place, forcing me still while he consumes me. We don't hear the ding of the elevator doors opening, or register the fact that we've come to a stop until Red clears her throat.

"Sorry to break up the sex party, but I'm not holding the doors open any longer."

"Fuck," is all Roman can muster.

I look around and everyone is waiting in the lobby. Red, with her arms crossed and a glare in our direction while the guys stare with complete lust in their eyes. It only makes me want to stay and play a little longer.

Roman steps back and adjusts himself as I watch every movement he makes.

"Come on, princess. As hot as you are, I'm hungrier for more than just your pussy right now." I'm still lost in my sex induced brain to respond, so he takes my hand and pulls me along.

Oscar and Parker are leading the way, and Red has her arm linked through Kai's. He looks back over his shoulder, his eyes bugging out, wanting someone to save him but I just smile to reassure him.

Walking into the garage, Roman squeezes my hand and leaves me standing next to Dot. He heads for the pick-up truck parked a little further along that they always use. It blows my mind how they have Porsches and Ferraris parked up in here yet they always opt for the tricked out black Ford pick-up truck.

Red climbs into the backseat, while Roman and Kai get in the front. Oscar is going to ride his bike with me, we can't leave our babies here on a gorgeous day like this. The sun is out, not a cloud in the sky with the leaves beginning to fall from the trees. It's a perfect day and it would be rude not to take her out for a spin. I can't help but stroke a hand over the seat on Dot, appreciating my machine for a moment.

Going to grab my helmet, I turn to see Parker holding it with a nervous look on his face.

"Parker, is everything okay?" I ask, confused with why he's suddenly anxious. I reach my arm out and squeeze his arm, trying to offer whatever support he needs.

"Angel, I want to try to... err... ride with you. If that's okay with you?"

I'm stunned into silence, but only for a moment because he has me so excited I might explode.

"Are you serious?" He offers an unsure nod, but he obviously wants to try, for me. "Oh my god, Parker, of course."

I'm practically bouncing around the garage, in true Red style. I can't help but throw my arms around him with delight. I'm so freaking giddy right now.

"For real? Parker man, how many times have I asked you to come ride with me? Just because she has the sweetest pussy doesn't mean she gets to take you out first. I've asked so many times, man," Oscar grumbles, with his arms crossed as he glares at us.

"Oscar, stop whining and pass me the other helmet," Parker responds, holding his hand out for it.

"Oh, you mean the helmet I bought for you to come ride with me?"

I can't help but roll my eyes at him.

"Oscar, if you stop ruining my moment I'll let you fuck me over your bike real soon, okay?" I say, trying to give him something to look forward to, and it does the trick.

He stares at me with stars in his eyes for a moment before rushing to grab the other helmet. Fuck, I've got myself worked up thinking about it too.

"I like bargaining with you, baby girl. Anything that gets me in your pants is a win for me," he says, handing me the helmet as he brushes a quick kiss against my lips.

"Yo, what's going on?" Roman calls from the car. I look to Parker for him to answer. I'm not getting involved in this.

"I'm gonna catch a ride with Luna." The three of them in the truck stare at him with wide eyes, and I can see Roman is having an internal meltdown at us both being on what he calls 'the death machine.'

"Let's go, before he decides to get all alpha on our asses," I say, looking up to him with a grin. His hand comes to rest on my hip as he looks down at me with a nervous smile.

"I think that's a good idea, angel. Be gentle with me, I've never done this before." Squeezing his arm, I move him closer to Dot, trying to reassure him in the process.

"Just hold on tight and lean with me. Simple. You're going to love it."

"I swear to god, you better be safe. I'm not afraid to punish you guys if something happens. Understood?" Roman shouts, clearly losing more control the longer he stares at us.

Parker takes the helmet and puts it on, with Oscar and I following suit. I climb on Dot first, making sure there's plenty of space for Parker to swing his leg over too. He gets comfortable, his thighs squeezing mine as his arms hold me around my waist. Just not tight enough. Grabbing his arms, I pull them tighter around me, which has his hips pulling in closer too.

Fuck. This feels strange. I've never let anyone on Dot before. This is a big moment for me, as well as Parker. Letting someone on my girl isn't something I let just anyone do, but if I open my mouth, Roman is likely to stop us. Maybe I'll mention it afterwards.

Flicking up the kickstand, I get the engine going. Oscar takes the lead out of the garage, with the truck not moving yet. Following Oscar, I rev the engine and start out of the garage. There are a few students outside, and when they see us on Dot they all stop what they're doing to watch us pass.

We crawl through the grounds of Featherstone, passing the other blocks and following the trail through the wide open spaces, before passing the Main Hall and picking up a little speed on the entry road. I slow as we come up to the wrought iron gates that protect the grounds, to check in with my passenger.

"Hey, Parker Parker, all good?" I shout, with a squeeze of my hand on his arm around my waist.

"All good, angel," he calls back, and I'm good to go. The second we're out on to the country roads surrounding the grounds, I floor it. His grip around my waist tightens for a moment, but not to the point it's impossible to ride.

I love his trust in me. Glancing in my mirror, I can see Roman is right behind us policing our every movement. Fuck that.

"Let's lose this sucker," I yell above the wind, as I speed off. Take that, Acehole.

Pulling up to the café, I spot Roman leaning against the hood of the pick-up truck waiting for us. Oscar's bike is here, he must be inside with Red and Kai.

That was some drive. Parker wasn't complaining about the ride, so I took a detour and it was perfect. The long windy roads that surround Featherstone Academy are made for bikes. I took the ride around the forest that Oscar had taken me on a few weeks ago, wanting to treat Parker to the spectacular view.

Coming to a stop, I park next to Oscar's bike in the motorcycle bay, hoping Roman gives us a second before he starts with the grumpy shit.

Taking my helmet off, I hang it off the handlebar for a second as I pull my messy hair up into a bun at the top of my head. As I lift to get off, Parker holds me tighter to his body with his arm around me, while he takes his helmet off with the other.

"Go away, Roman," he shouts, causing me to look to my side where Roman is coming from. He stops instantly, and observes us for a moment. I can see he's about to say something, and Parker must be able to sense it too.

"I said—"

"Yeah, yeah. I heard you," he grumbles, turning and

entering the café.

"Did you like it?" I try to turn to get a better view of his face but he's dropped his head to my shoulder. Placing a soft kiss to my neck, my body heats.

"That was brilliant, angel. I think I may be obsessed, but I don't know if I can stand right now." I can't help the chuckle that passes my lips at his admission. The first time on a bike always gives you the worst jelly legs.

"Does my Parker Parker need help?" I try not to giggle, but I can't keep the smile off my face. Lifting his gaze to mine, he's grinning too.

"He does, and he needs food. Lots and lots of food."

Leaning back, he gives me space to get off and I hold my hand out for him. He raises his eyebrow in question but takes it anyway. Standing beside me, he rubs his thighs. Bless his soul.

"That's not going to help, let's start walking. I'll even let you wrap your arm around my shoulders to use me as a crutch if you'd like." I smirk as I step to his side, slowly heading for the door.

"That's just because you secretly like our PDA but are too stubborn to admit it." He winks at me like he's got me all figured out.

Acehole.

I pretend to zip my lips shut and lock the key, which just makes him laugh. Now he's got me being playful.

Double Acehole.

Heading inside, everyone is sitting in the same booth as last time.

My eyes instantly trail to Kai. I can feel his pain. I don't know what it's for or even who, but I know that I want to be here for him. To comfort him. Yet I don't know a thing about doing that, I just want to try. For him.

He's sitting on the end of the booth, his gaze looking off into the distance. I look up to Parker, who must know what I'm about to say because he simply nods with a gentle smile on his lips.

Stepping ahead, I go straight for my target. Planting myself sideways on Kai's lap, he barely brings his gaze up to meet my eyes as I get comfortable. I feel a little of his tension ease as his arms tighten around me, but he doesn't say a word.

I'll take what I can get right now.

SIXTEEN

Luna

The rest of the time at the café went by quietly. The guys bantered between them with Red jumping in, her sass on point. I stayed by Kai's side the whole time, happy to observe the others and just bask in everyone's presence. We followed Oscar home, with no detours this time. Instead, taking the long country road leading to Featherstone, which meant I got to show Parker a little extra speed.

Kai and I hold back in the lobby, letting the others head on up as we head outside to go to the garden. I didn't need to grab anything because I'd arranged it yesterday.

Hopefully Ian dropped off a bunch of snacks while we were out. I plan for us to be there for the rest of the day.

Kai reaches his hand out, his fingers wrapping around mine. I don't recall holding his hand like this in public before, but I like it. His thumb strokes lazily across the back of my hand, just like he would do in the car.

We bypass the Rolls lined up outside of Ace, opting to stroll to the garden in comfortable silence together. A few people stop and stare at us, probably wondering which Ace I'm actually in a relationship with. I want to scream, all of them! They're all mine! But I refrain, for now.

The walk to the garden is prettier than usual. I've never really cared for fall before, but it almost has me feeling romantic, with all the leaves scattering the ground in a mixture of orange and red. With just the sound of the birds chirping in the distance, I get lost in his presence.

Stepping into the garden, it's instinctive for me to take off my shoes and socks, feeling the grass beneath my toes. Kai stands beside me with a small smile on his face, as if he expects nothing less.

I pull him over to the gazebo, where the picnic basket sits on the bench and a few little presents are on the daybed. My anxiety kicks up a notch, worried he will turn and leave.

Nobody has wished him a happy birthday or mentioned it in the slightest, but I want to. He stands beside me looking around, and I start to lose my nerve.

"I can make it all go away, just say the word," I mutter as he takes it all in.

"It's all fine, Sakura. Thank you." He places a light kiss to my knuckles and leads us toward the daybed.

He takes a seat next to the four individually wrapped gifts, and places me on his lap.

"They're nothing crazy or exciting... I just..."

"You didn't have to get me anything at all, this is already too much," he says as he squeezes my thigh. Fuck. I should not be getting turned on right now. Not yet at least.

Leaning forward, I take the small envelope first and hold it out for him. I feel him tense beneath me.

"It's not a card. I made sure to try and avoid the whole celebratory aspect." He relaxes a little again, but he's still unsure about taking it from me.

When he finally does, he whips it from my hands and tears it open quickly, like he's ripping a bandaid off. When the little slip of paper falls out, he calms a little more. Flipping it over, he reads my little print out.

To Mr. Kai Fuse

I'm not sappy and shit, I'd like to prick you with my needle.

So, this entitles you to one super rare Luna Steele tattoo of your choosing.

I promise not to laugh at your choice or make a mockery of your hot as fuck body.

Your Sakura

He smiles a little wider at me as he hugs me closer to him.

"I love it, Sakura. I already know what I want you to do, and now you've said you won't laugh at my choice, you can't take it back."

"Whatever you want. I have the stuff here with us, in case you wanted me to do it today," I say, leaning in to kiss his lips.

"Deal. Let's do it now."

"Open the rest, then I'm all yours." Sitting like this, I could get lost in his dark brown eyes. He could feed me any line and he'd have me agreeing.

Kai offers a nod and I reach over for the next item which is in a gift box. He's a lot more relaxed about it this time and lifts the lid to see inside.

"Wow, Sakura. I love it," he says, pulling the item out of the box. It's a men's black rope bracelet that wraps around twice, with a silver pendant showing the Japanese symbol for strength.

"It's a tracker," I blurt out, not wanting to keep any secrets. "Sorry, I... err... It's a tracker. I'm having different ones made for everyone, including me. Something's coming, I can feel it, and with The Games approaching I want to cover all the bases. If you don't want to wear it, I understand—" His soft finger presses against my lips, stopping my blabbering speech.

"Sakura, this is perfect. I think it's a great idea. It's not like we'll be looking at the locations all the time, but it'll be there if we need it," he says with a smile, kissing my lips before putting it straight on his wrist. Damn, it looks good on him.

Before I forget everything else and just feast on him, I lean over and get the next wrapped gift, which is in a very similar box to the previous. He raises a slight eyebrow at me as I shake the box at him. Wrapped in brown paper with a rope bow, it looks simple yet elegant.

Opening it up, there is the smallest piece inside that

looks like a small cut off piece of cello-tape. He gently picks it out of the box and holds it up to the light.

"Holy shit, is this a tracker? It's practically invisible."

"Better than the one you had Roman stick to the bottom of my boot?" I ask, trying to keep a firm tone to my voice, but my smile gives me away.

"You knew?" he asks, his eyes bugging out a little at me, which only makes me roll my eyes.

"Please, you asked a guy with no tech knowledge to place it on me. What did you expect?" He just shakes his head and looks back to the device.

"The level of metal in it is so small it doesn't come up detected when searched," I murmur, staring at it with him.

"This is amazing, Sakura. We need more of these," he says, grinning at me. "I knew you purposely screwed with your assessment on the first day of Tech."

"I did, and I do have more. It just didn't look as cool when I started trying to put them all in the box."

Placing it back inside, he adds it to the pile of opened gifts he's got.

I reach over for the last item, which ruffles beneath my hands.

"So, this was a joke gift, to try and lighten the mood in

case I'd made it all go to shit."

Taking the gift from my hands, I can see the confusion on his face at the feel of it. He opens it up and it's an extra large bag of cheesy Doritos. It takes him a minute, then he's all out belly laughing uncontrollably.

I sit in awe at the sound, basking in this small moment of joy and laughter with him.

When he finally catches his breath, he says it out loud, "A Dirty Luna, huh?" I just smile in response. It brightened the mood, and that's what I wanted. He can have a hand job for free.

"Thank you, Sakura. For all of this," he says as he drops the chips, and wraps me in his arms.

I don't know how long we stay sitting like that, but I could do it forever. It's kind of crazy how much I like their touches, even the non-sexual one's.

"Sakura, how about you get your stuff set up to tattoo me, and I'll tell you all my issues while you work?" he whispers against my neck.

"I'd like that. No matter what it is, Kai, I want to be there for you." I feel him nod against my neck before he releases me so I can begin setting up.

"I already know what I want. After I saw Parker's, I

drew it and put it in my wallet ready for when the moment was right." His words catch me off guard but make me smile.

I wheel my case out from the storage box behind the gazebo and bring it over to the daybed so I can get comfortable. I methodically set everything up, organizing my copper tattoo guns and foot switch, making sure everything has been sterilized. Happy with my layout, I look at Kai, who has sat quietly watching my every move.

"You want to show me your drawing?" I ask, slightly intrigued as to what it may be.

He places the small slip of paper between us, slightly crumpled from being in his wallet, and waits for my reaction. Before me are three moons, all at different stages. The fullest moon in the middle, with two crescent moons on either side. I desperately want to ask what it represents, but I can feel the heaviness behind it.

"Where do you want it?"

"On my chest," he says, lifting his t-shirt and pointing to his pec over his heart.

I simply nod for him to move closer, as I make quick work of sketching it out while he takes his top off fully.

I prefer freehand usually, but I want to get the sizing

right because I can feel that it's important. Using a bottle of water and a sponge, I transfer the carbon paper onto his skin.

"Are you going to ask what it represents?" he asks, making me peer up at him for a moment.

"I didn't want to overstep," I answer honestly.

"Nothing would ever be overstepping, Sakura. I want to know everything about you, and I want to reciprocate that level of trust." The truth in his words doesn't scare me like I expect it to, so I shake the worry away and ask him.

"What does it mean?"

"They are the moons of people's birth dates," he says, leaning closer to point at the original drawing he did. "The largest in the middle is mine, the smaller one to the left is yours and the most crescent moon to the right… is my sister's."

I process his words. My brain should probably focus on the fact one of the moons represents me, but I'm stuck on the fact he said his sister. He's not mentioned her before. Is that why today is hard? I'm trying to bring myself to ask, I just can't find the words. Seeing the question in my eyes, he gives a slight nod in answer.

This is him opening the door to this conversation, his

way of sharing a part of himself with me. I move nearer to him, and bring my equipment a little closer. As soon as the buzzing starts, I bring the needle to his skin and he begins to talk.

"She was taken, on my birthday." My heart jolts at his words, and I take a moment to wipe his skin, so I don't ruin the ink. I don't say anything in response, wanting him to tell me at his own pace.

"It was my seventh birthday, and we were having a party. My mother had set the back garden up like any child's dream. There were candy stands, bouncy castles, like a mini fairground really." He takes a breather for a minute, watching me work. "Looking back now, I remember my mother and father arguing a lot, but for the life of me I can't remember why. All I do remember was that it involved my sister and wanting to protect her." He sighs deeply.

I lean back a minute and squeeze his leg with my other hand, trying to offer any support I can give. He offers a soft smile, encouraging me to continue with the needle.

"So, halfway through the birthday party, my father comes storming outside with at least eight of his men, yelling at my mother and snatches my sister up. She was nine at the time and she just wanted to be let down so she could come back to playing with me." He shakes his head at the memory floating to the surface of it all. "She was crying non-stop, kicking and screaming as they carried her out of the house all together. I've never seen her since."

"Kai, I don't even know what to say. Has nothing been mentioned since? I'm guessing she's untraceable otherwise you'd have her by now." I worry my words are harsh, but I don't want to sugarcoat the grief he's dealing with. If he could have found her by now I know he would have.

"No. My father refuses to discuss it, except to say it was for the best. He literally took my sister away and returned as though nothing had ever happened. My parents were never the same from then, my mother is a shell of the woman she once was. So I was left to wander our giant home alone."

Kai offers me a soft smile, encouraging me to finish the ink on his chest as he watches me for a moment.

"I've searched everywhere, Sakura. My bloodline is actually more business orientated, running business fronts, organizing mergers that kind of thing, with a small side of tech. I trained myself to learn every inch of the tech world, in hopes it would help find me my sister."

I can feel his pain, and it hurts so bad. I lean back and

swipe his skin for the last time, looking at the now marked skin. His eyes follow mine and look down to his new tattoo, a soft smile playing on his lips.

My phone vibrates from the picnic bench, but I don't want to interrupt this moment between us. I automatically start the process of aftercare for him, as I consider my next words.

"Kai," I murmur, waiting for his eyes to meet mine before I continue. "We'll find her together, handsome. No matter what it takes, okay? I'm all in." His eyes close as he nods his head.

"She would love you, Sakura. Full of fire and always pushing back, she hated wimps," he chuckles lightly under his breath. My phone vibrates again. "I think you better get that," he says, nodding toward the bench.

"It can wait, this is important."

"I know, but someone's called a few times now, what if it's urgent?" Sighing at the reality of his words, I stand to grab my phone from the picnic table when it vibrates again. Rafe's name flashing across the screen.

"Hey Rafe, what's up? I'm a little busy right—" He cuts me off in an instant.

"Luna, where are you? The security system in your

room is going off, I've got an unauthorized person in your room. Plus the detectors are going crazy with other devices active in there." The panic in his voice is clear through the phone. My head whips round to Kai who nods, able to hear Rafe without the phone even being on speaker phone.

"I'm on campus with Kai, just not at Ace," I respond, running a hand through my hair. At some point, I'd like just one drama-free day. I knew something was brewing though.

"How do you want to play this?" Rafe asks through the phone. Kai raises an eyebrow at me, waiting for me to call the shots. Always wanting to support me, knowing not to overtake the situation and go all caveman on me.

"We play it out, I'll head back to my room. I can enter alone, acting as though I don't know they're there, and Kai can stop at Roman's across the hall." I shut my eyes, focusing on what needs to be done. "Kai, get Roman on the phone and make sure his laptop is set up and ready. Can you send access to Kai, Rafe?" Throwing my shoes on, I crack my neck, trying to relieve the tension building.

"Yes, I've got his details. I'll send the links over now. Whoever it is, they are stopping the feed from reaching me. I think it's because I'm too out of range, so if Kai is close enough he should be able to see what's going on while you're in there. Have Kai call me when you get in, I want to be in the know, and be safe, Luna."

"I will," I murmur back, before ending the call.

"Let's go see who's got big enough balls to break into my room," I say to Kai, who nods in agreement before we start to rush back. He speaks with Roman on the phone, but I'm not listening. I'm too focused on the rage pumping through my veins.

Whoever it is. They're going to fucking regret it.

YOUR BLOODLINE

SEVENTEEN

Kai

Who the fuck is so deluded they would step into my Sakura's space without her permission? It's clearly an attack and my gut tells me it links back to Dietrichson.

Walking into Ace, nothing seems out of the ordinary. We're both in a hurry as we head for the stairs. I called Roman on the way over, telling him as little as possible to at least prepare them for us showing up. I just couldn't tell him too much, otherwise he'd spiral into a fit of rage and charge over there without care.

I made sure he got the others, including Jess, up to his room to wait for us. Since that call, no words have been spoken between Luna and I, both anticipating what's to come. Reaching the top floor, we stop and stare at her door, as though it will magically open and reveal what's happening inside.

Giving her shoulder a squeeze, she lifts her gaze to mine and I nod toward Roman's door. I need her to plan a little more with us before she goes in there guns blazing. I know Luna's right, that she needs to act as though they have the upper hand, but it still has me on edge.

As quietly as possible, we step up to Roman's door, and I use my key to let us in. As we step into the lounge, Parker and Oscar are playing a video game completely oblivious to what's going on. Jess sits on the other sofa, questions in her eyes as to why she's here, but I can hear movement in the kitchen, so that's where I head.

Releasing Luna's hand, I step into the kitchen to find Roman pacing the floor.

"Roman, we only have a minute. Get out here." I can't hide the urgency from my voice, which only makes his eyes a little more frantic.

"What the fuck's going on, man?" he asks, but we need to address it as a group, we haven't got time for one-on-one talks. I nod for him to follow me into the other room, which he does reluctantly. Luna is still standing in the same spot I left her in, except Jess is leaning in and whispering with her. Neither of them acknowledging our presence in the room.

"Roman, did you set up your laptop like I asked?"

"Yeah, I'll go and grab it from the desk in my room," he mutters in response. He slows when he sees Luna, and the determined look in her eyes, but pushes on to get what we needed.

Not wasting time with the other two guys, I just head for the socket and pull the plug out, disconnecting the whole thing. It's silent for a beat before the protests come.

"What the fuck, Kai? We were midway through a game that we were winning," Oscar moans, throwing his controller to the side. He looks me over from head to toe, as though his mind is just catching up. "Wait, why are you here? Why aren't you at your secret little sex spot with Luna?"

"Because someone has broken into my room and planted surveillance devices while trying to jam mine. Plus there's a high chance someone is in there waiting for me, and we're going to play it out. I want these motherfuckers to think they're winning, before I tear them down," Luna says, so matter of fact. Her hands are clenched at her side, and her jaw is working overtime as she tries to stay calm. "Any objections or questions?" She looks around the group, and they're all staring at her like she gained a second head.

Roman is standing in the doorway from his bedroom, laptop in hand, and I can see the rage starting to unfold.

"You are not going in there alone, princess," he growls, striding over to me and shoving his laptop into my hands. The others stand from the sofa and move over to us, which just has Luna rolling her eyes.

"You know I'm right, Rome. This isn't me being irrational and hot headed, even Rafe agrees it's the best plan. Let's set everything up so Kai can have as much visibility as possible from here, okay?" The tone of her voice is relaxed, but makes it clear this is the plan. It does nothing to pacify Roman though. Stepping into her space, he grabs her under her chin and forces her to look up at him.

My body tenses at the roughness to his touch, he better be damn careful with my Sakura. She continues to challenge him, her eyes not wavering at all. Glancing around the room, I see both Oscar and Parker are tense too, while Jess is shaking her head in amusement.

"Princess, don't fuck with me. I only just got you back and you keep ending up in harm's way," Roman pleads, but Luna doesn't bat an eyelid. He takes a deep breath and curses up at the ceiling. "Kai, I want everything in that room, do you understand? And you, princess, if anything happens to you in there, I'll kill you myself. Agreed?"

Did he just threaten her? I don't know who I'm more worried for.

"Fuck, Rome. Can you save all this pent-up tension for when I get back? You have me hot and it's kind of a distraction right now. Now, I know what I'm fucking doing, can we remember that?" He drops his hands from her and turns wide-eyed to look at us all. His arms out wide and a 'what the fuck' look on his face.

"You see what I'm dealing with?"

"Our girl. You're dealing with our girl. Who we like exactly as she is, right, Roman?" Oscar says, breaking the tension and stepping up to Luna. "I trust you to get shit done and get back here, okay?" he murmurs to her, dotting little kisses all over her face, while Parker steps up behind her and trails kisses down her neck.

"Stop distracting her, guys. We need her on high alert,

not distracted by sexual tension," I snap, which makes them step back. Although, Luna needs a moment to focus again. Her cheeks are a little flush and it's got my dick perking up. Fuck. Now is not the time. I need to get this moving along.

I place the laptop on the coffee table and start typing away. Everyone comes to stand around me, but no one says anything so I can focus.

"Roman, the suitcase I keep in your wardrobe? I'm going to need it." Without a word he runs to grab it for me.

"Sakura, get Rafe on the phone," I say, still not looking up from what I'm doing. Out of the corner of my eye, I see Parker place a bottle of water beside the laptop. Always thoughtful.

Roman rolls in my suitcase, as Luna nods with Rafe on the phone. I take both of them and continue to work away. I'm really glad I made the decision to set one of these suitcases up in each of our rooms, full of all the essential tech pieces I may need. Rafe stays on the phone and is surprisingly helpful and impressed with the systems I'm using. I need to remind myself to set up these cases for Luna and Jess too.

One last click and I'm all set. I turn to the others, and

they're all sitting staring at me, except Luna and Roman who are both pacing the floor.

"Okay, I can't get an actual visual, but someone is definitely in there. Accessing Luna's surveillance system, I can see a heat signature coming from the kitchen. Scanning for tech is a little harder seeing as I'm not in there, so I'm going to give you a few gadgets to help us out." I look to Luna for her agreement, and the nod she gives will suffice.

"I'm nervous now," Jess murmurs. She's been quiet throughout, but it's not the time to speak up when shit's about to get real. I don't say it out loud because I know it would piss Luna off. Surprisingly, Oscar comforts her, wrapping his arm around her shoulder, all she gives him is a tense smile in return.

Standing, I wave Luna over too. "I have a detection sensor, so while you're in there I'll be able to pick up what they've attempted to install. A listening device, so we know what exactly is going on, and this little thing will stop them from blocking your surveillance feed so we can see where you are and who is with you." She nods along at the three small devices I pull out, and waves her hands for me to place them on her.

"I would have preferred my own stuff but appreciate

this," she murmurs, and I get it. I always feel more in control with my own systems.

"Angel, can you give us a safe word? Something that means you need us over there with you immediately, just in case?" Parker asks, rubbing the back of his neck, avoiding direct eye contact with her. It causes him a lot of stress when he can't protect her, the thought of a safe word definitely helps. Luna must see the stress he is in and nods in agreement.

"Yeah, what did Roman put in the group chat back in Washington? Pineapple?" We all nod in agreement. Pineapple has always been the word that means shit has gone south. "Okay, then we stick with that."

Heading toward the door, she gives us a quick backward glance before stepping out. The tension in the room kicks up a notch as she does.

Oscar instantly regrets letting her go and starts charging for the door, but Jess keeps a hold of him.

"Fuck, Jessikins," he growls as he glares down at her.

"I'm so fucking done with her having to go through everything alone. So fucking done. I'll kill them all, every last one of them," Roman rages, now he doesn't have to put a relaxed appearance on for our girl. He pulls at his hair in distress, struggling with the situation. "Get her surveillance running through the television, Kai, now. I *need* to see what's going on."

His fist slams into the wall in front of him in fury, as I fill the screen with the image of Luna's room, and the person sitting in wait.

Fuck.

She's not likely to be the one needing a safe word.

Luna

Stepping inside my room, I relax my body, forcing myself to act natural. Remembering the training Rafe gave me, I take a deep breath and find my center. Although my mind has forgotten what I would usually do when I step in, because all I want to do is head for the kitchen and see who is here.

Deciding I want Kai to get a feel for what devices have been installed, I head to the left into my bedroom to hang my jacket up in the walk-in wardrobe. I refuse to give my back to the kitchen though, so it takes an extra minute to get into my room.

Pulling my handgun and switchblade out from my bedside table, I stuff the blade in my bra and the gun in the back of my pants. I can't walk in casually carrying them if I'm trying to let the intruder think they've caught me by surprise.

Damn, I just want to tear in there. Trying to act casual is harder than I thought. Fuck it. Let's go.

I wish I'd asked for a two-way device so I could hear them too, find out what they're seeing.

I make myself walk at a leisurely pace toward the kitchen, and when I step into the space, the shock on my face isn't forced.

"Hello, my darling, Luna."

"Veronica," I say, schooling my features from shock to distaste at the sight of my fabulous mother.

She sits at my dining table in another one of her business suits. Her hair is pulled back, with one leg crossed over the other and her hands clasped in front of her, she thinks this is her territory. The smug as fuck look on her face has me wanting to knock her out, be done with it. My fingers itch to pull my gun on her. After everything at The Pyramid, I know wholeheartedly that this woman may have birthed me, but she is not my mother.

I hold off for now, curious as to why she's suddenly out of hiding and sitting in my kitchen.

"Have you missed me?" she asks, in that disgustingly sweet voice she thinks makes her sound fucking loveable.

"Not even a little bit. Care to explain why you're here?" I'm not wasting pleasantries on her. I want to get straight to the point of all this.

"I wanted to see how you were after such a marvelous show you put on in the trial." I didn't think it was possible, but her grin gets wider. She loved watching all that death, damage and destruction unfold.

"If you wanted to see me so bad you'd have stuck around, instead of sneaking off into the shadows like the coward you are. You're here because you want something, and the answer is no." Her face tightens in disgust at my instant dismissal of her.

"Listen here, you little bitch, you need to start showing me some respect. I carried you for nine months and all it's done is cause issues for me ever since," she snaps back. Wow.

I can't help it, I slow clap her for her misfortunes. Stupid bitch. The glare I get for my efforts only makes me sneer back at her.

"Veronica, I'm so fucking done with you it's not even funny. I would love to put a pretty little bullet right between your eyes right now. You better leave before I can't hold back any longer," I taunt, but she doesn't move.

"You've always been an ungrateful little whore. I never wanted you. You were a family agreement, one that made me look a fool. It didn't even come with marriage," she scoffs. "Instead, I had to standby and constantly watch as those two gave you everything, leaving me with nothing."

What the fuck is she talking about?

"Now I've had enough. I've found some men to love me, and in return they want you on their team."

Again, what the fuck?

"Veronica, I have no idea what you're talking about. I understood none of the shit that just came out of your mouth." I sigh, resting my hands on my hips. I want to slip my finger to the trigger of my gun, but like a moth to a flame, her words have me intrigued.

She starts to laugh, and I feel it in my bones. There is something big I don't know about it, she's about to take great pleasure in letting me in on the little secret.

"He's babied the fuck out of you, hasn't he? I knew all the boring shit about you blocking your childhood memories, but the fact that he played along to be whatever you needed him to be is fucking embarrassing." Her cackle gets louder and it sets me on edge. "You want me to tell you, little Luna?" she murmurs, standing from the table and walking around to me.

I pull my gun from behind my back, but she's unfazed as she gets right up into my face.

"You can't remember that dear old dead daddy and Rafe were fucking, can you?" she sneers, her face scrunching as her upper lip curls in disgust at the thought. "Used me as a pawn, everyone fully aware except me. When I found out, I did everything I could to have you aborted, but here you still fucking stand." She leans back and stares into my eyes, waiting for me to explode. I refuse to give in to her.

Forcing my emotions deep down, I act bored as though her words haven't just changed everything.

"Have you finished? Or was there something else you wanted to discuss?" She frowns, furious with the fact she's not getting the reaction she wanted out of me.

Veronica's eyes burn a path from my head to my toes as she gets more frustrated with me.

"I was sent by my lover, otherwise I wouldn't be here. He thought you have the right attributes to stand with the new movement that's coming. I can see that's wasted on you," she says, grabbing her handbag off the table and swinging it over her shoulder as she prepares to leave. Thank god.

"Rico also asked me to pass a message on to you. He *loved* your performance in The Pyramid and his demand is for you to stop opening your legs for that bastard son of his. Rico wants you for himself. He'll know if you violate his wish." She goes to step around me and I'm beyond done with her shit.

Swinging my gun I hit her across the face with it, the crack bouncing off the walls around us. As the impact knocks her to the ground, blood splatters around her. This motherfucker is just making a mess now.

"You fucking bitch, what have you done? You'll pay for this," she screams, and it makes me smile. Crouching down beside her, I rest my arms on my knees with the gun aimed at her.

"Veronica, the next time I see you... I'll kill you, you won't even get to open your mouth and I'll have pulled the trigger. Even if it's a complete coincidence that our paths cross, it'll be too late," I say casually. "Now. Get. The. Fuck. Out." Grabbing her by the arm, she barely manages to get to her feet as I drag her to the door. I can hear her verbal attack, but I'm not actually listening.

Opening the front door, I throw her out, causing her to hit the floor again.

"You're going to regret ever being born, you fucking cunt," she growls, spitting at my feet. How pleasant.

Pointing my gun down at her, I grunt.

"You've got till the count of five before I pull this fucking trigger."

She stumbles as she tries to get to her feet. I can see she's about to say some other shit, but I can't with her right now. So I slam the door, shutting her out.

I quickly pull my phone out, my hands shaking as my emotions finally start to get the better of me. Dialing Kai, he answers on the first ring.

"Hey Sakura—" he starts but I interrupt.

"Where in this room are there cameras?"

"Bedroom, bathroom and dresser, nothing in the main areas. Sakura, after what she just said, it makes me think the cameras may be for Rico," he murmurs gently. Placing my phone on the coffee table, I rest my head in my hands as I take a seat on the sofa.

"Is Rafe still on the phone with you?"

"Yes."

"You tell that fucker I want him here in record time. Understood?" I growl.

"He's already on his way, Sakura. Do you want some privacy or can we come over?"

"Come over." I end the call. Red has a key so they can get in.

Picking up the pillow beside me, I scream into it. It beats stabbing a bitch.

YOUR BLOODLINE

KC KEAN

EIGHTEEN

Oscar

We've been sitting on Luna's sofa, staring at the blank tv screen together for what feels like forever. She's not okay, I can see it in her eyes. We heard every word in Roman's room with the listening device Kai gave her, and we saw everything from Luna's own surveillance system.

The second her bitch of a mother was thrown out of the room, Luna's body language completely changed. Her emotions got the best of her as she processed the bomb that had just been dropped.

How do I even comfort her with this? She's trying to

act cool and relaxed, but I can feel the internal battle she's dealing with by the way her hands keep clenching at her side.

Rafe's on his way, I think that's what she's most concerned with. Although, Rico getting her mother to mention that he wants Luna all to himself is bat shit crazy to me and sickening. That's my priority here. That sick fucker is not touching my girl, he's not even allowed to look at her.

Luna, Red and Parker are all sitting side by side on a sofa while I'm sitting beside Kai on the other. He's running data on the devices that were set up while Veronica was here. He tried to explain in more detail, but that shit just goes over my head. Roman is in the kitchen, still on the phone. I'm not sure who to, I know he was chatting with Rafe and he wanted to speak with his father too.

My phone vibrates in my pocket, but I ignore it. Everyone I want to hear from is in this room. Besides, it's likely my father, and I'm not wasting my time on that right now. He fucked our family up when the scientist in him took over.

He'll forever be lost to Featherstone. I was a sibling of four, now only two of us remain. I'm the eldest, and there is no way my family is losing another child to their fucked-up ways. I have to do whatever it takes to get into The Ring and start making some fucking changes around here. If only so my little sister doesn't have to be subjected to this Featherstone crap.

I subconsciously run my fingers up and down my forearms, remembering the prick of the needles over and over again. Fuck. I do not need to be getting lost down memory lane right now. I need a distraction and so does my baby girl.

I'd usually go down to the gym and box my way out of this mindset, but I'm not leaving my girl right now. I'll be here in silent support for her or I could help distract her too.

"Where are we at with the techy shit, Kai?" I ask, turning slightly to try and see what he's doing, which is pointless because all the lines and dots mean nothing to me.

"Yeah, almost. Give me another sec and I should have them all disabled." He doesn't lift his gaze from the laptop in front of him, until Luna suddenly speaks.

"Do not disable the cameras, I want to send a message." The determination in her gaze is hot as shit.

Not the time, Oscar.

Not the time at all but try telling my dick that. I shuffle around trying to readjust myself without drawing any attention. Luna spots the movement straight away. She doesn't pull her gaze away from the front of my grey joggers, even when Kai responds to her.

"There aren't any listening devices so they can't hear us, but there are three cameras, Sakura. They have all been positioned to catch you in a state of undress. The one in the bathroom is in the corner above the bathtub, catching the whole room. The camera in the dresser is fixed into the lights around your mirror. While the one in your room is in the light fitting in the ceiling, directed down at your bed. I don't think it was Veronica who set them up, but I'm trying to run diagnostics to get the back up feed working from that time."

I get angrier the more he describes the location, it all points to Rico after what that cow said. We all know it, we just haven't said it outright yet because we're worried about Parker. I glance in his direction, and the pink flush flaring up on his neck tells me he knows what everyone is thinking but no one is saying.

"Kai, if you could disable the one in the bathroom and

the dresser, would that be enough for you to play around with? I have plans for the last one." She sounds so sexy when she is all vengeful and shit.

Kai nods in response which seems to be enough for Luna, who turns to Parker and climbs in his lap. Jessikins scrunches her face up at them beside her, and jumps off the sofa, striding into the kitchen. A large part of me wants to tease the shit out of her, but my eyes won't stray from the way Luna is straddling Parker.

"Parker Parker, please don't think that what your father says or does ever has a reflection on you. Understood?" she murmurs, arms wrapped around his neck as she forces him to look at her.

He continues to look in her eyes without saying a word, but I watch as his hands lift to her ass. His knuckles turning white as his grip tightens. Fuck that's hot, especially when my baby girl instinctively grinds against him ever so slightly.

She brings her lips down on his softly, trying to pull him through the fog that takes over sometimes. He doesn't respond to her touch at first, his grip remains the same, his lips not moving against hers.

Leaning her forehead against his, her voice drops to

barely a whisper as her hands cup his face. I can't hear what she's saying this time, but I can see the pain in both of their eyes. Parker's because of what his father is doing to his angel, and Luna's because she's trying to get him out of the hole his mind is creating.

My heart aches for him every time he loses himself to the pain. Roman is usually the one to help pull him out of his funk, but they're all adamant Luna is like magic to him in comparison.

She leans back slightly, dropping her hands back to his shoulders and stares into his eyes. I can't help but hold my breath as I sit watching them peer into each other's souls. I don't know how much time passes when Parker finally leans forward, bringing his lips to Luna's.

I don't know what she said to him, but she made him climb out of his head and come to her. Fuck, I'm shocked at how that level of intimacy affects me.

He grazes his lips against hers, slowly giving her more and more with each pass. It doesn't take long for him to start taking from her. Parker keeps one hand tightly gripping her hip, as the other wraps around her ponytail, pulling her head back for better access.

Fuck, this is turning from a little lip on lip action to hot and heavy in seconds, and my dick is rising to the occasion.

Damn, maybe this is the distraction we need?

Kai and Rome are busy, but I could get down with some share time with Parker. Help take our girl's mind off of all this shit, while we all get some satisfaction.

Parker's hand rises, going under the back of her top and my dick pulses at the thought of touching her skin right there. Luna leans back, stroking her thumb over his lips, making me squeeze myself tight to ease the pressure before I embarrass myself and explode.

She turns her lust filled gaze to me, watching my hand, before lifting her eyes to meet mine.

"Okay, so I need a willing body or preferably two," she murmurs. I'm never going to say no to that. As I nod my head she grins, but her smile doesn't meet her eyes.

"Message number one? Nobody tells me who can and cannot touch me. Ever. So... someone's fucking me with the bedroom camera on."

I stare at her, along with Kai and Parker, who are both frozen in place. Fuck that's a statement to make, and you bet your ass I'm down to support my girl, however she needs it.

"Baby girl, we've had an audience once before, I can

go for another round or four," I say with a wink. Kai and Parker both glare at me like I said the wrong thing. "Guys, we put on the best show at the beach. Right, baby girl?"

I stalk over to her, as she stays seated on Parker's lap. Bending a little, I pepper small kisses down her neck. Causing her to grind down on Parker who throws his head back with a muttered curse.

"Let's get this party started, baby girl. I don't want to be mid-stroke when Rafe shows up."

"You and your fucking mouth. Shut up before I change my mind about you." She glares, and I know when to do as I'm told. Holding my hand out she wraps her delicate fingers around mine.

Pulling my girl to her feet, I glance at Parker as we slowly make our way to the bedroom.

"You coming?"

His hands rub down his thighs a few times as he looks between Luna and I.

Kai speaks up, interrupting us from behind his laptop. "Are you actually asking him to join in while the cameras are linked to his father?" He raises his eyebrow at me as Luna tries to pull me along, but I stand my ground.

"Yes, I am. That dumb bitch didn't say don't let anyone

fuck you. She specifically said *his bastard son*. That means this isn't really a statement unless Parker's involved." Everyone stares at me, processing my words. For once in my life I actually worry about how that sounded. "Sorry man, I'm not trying to push here. I'm just stating the facts. I have your back no matter what, but I'm game either way."

Not wanting to stand and stare at him until he gives an answer, I squeeze Luna's hand and head for her room.

"Are you serious?" Jess screeches. I don't stop as Luna slows her pace, but I do roll my eyes at Jess' rude timing.

"You might want to grab some headphones. I haven't got it in me to be quiet. Even if there are children around, Jessikins." I wink over my shoulder and step into Luna's room.

"Oscar, don't be a—" I don't let my girl finish her sentence as I push her against the wall beside the door and devour her lips. Soft and plump against mine, extra puffy from them being against Parker's just minutes ago.

She lets me in, but fights for power at the same time. As she bites down on my bottom lip, I can't control my moan. Her hands reach up to grip my hair as I grab her hips hard enough to bruise. Fuck yeah.

"Shut the door," Jess squeals, and I want to strangle

her. Not wanting to part from my girl I fumble for the door, when I hear it shut without me touching it. Forcing my mouth from Luna's, I glance to my left to see Parker standing beside us.

"You've sure grown some balls since getting laid, my friend. I'm impressed," I say with a grin. It takes Luna a moment to push past the lust induced daze she's in. When her eyes fall against Parker, they darken at what's in store for her.

Using my current grip on her waist, I spin our girl in my arms to place her between us, facing Parker. I can run this shit, the cocky alpha inside of me ready to rise to the challenge.

Grabbing a fistful of Luna's hair tightly, I tilt her head back to look up at Parker.

"You ready, baby girl?" I ask, my lips pressed against her ear as I speak.

"Yes," she sighs, not even fighting my hold.

"Then let's play."

YOUR BLOODLINE

NINETEEN
Parker

Holy crap. The want in her eyes sparkles back at me like she's screaming to be touched. My angel needs a break from all the shit that just went down. What better way to do it than by saying a big screw you to my father, by fucking what he thinks belongs to him.

Damn, my father. Am I really going to let him watch me with Luna?

Hell yeah, I am. I need to start fighting back, learn to stand my ground. Besides, the things they made me do when he first took me makes this look like a family Christmas photo.

My mother had been his cleaner, classic story. He'd raped her repeatedly and she'd ended up pregnant with me. She ran after I was born, never looking back. My life was sheltered as a home-schooled boy with no friends, until my fourteenth birthday when everything changed.

Turns out I was protected to keep me away from Rico and this lifestyle. His men tattooed me, then threw me in front of my father. I'll never forget the sinister look on his face when he brought in a woman much older than me, and forced me to touch her with my mouth. I had no clue what was going on, but the gun to my head was all the encouragement I needed.

Then they made her blow me as they all watched me cum for the first time at someone else's touch. When I later refused to fuck her, they shot her in front of me before beating me to a pulp. So when I'd told Luna I had never had sex because I hadn't found someone willing to get lost in, I meant it. Usually, visions of that night repeat over and over in my mind when I try to get intimate, but they didn't with Luna.

Shaking my head, I acknowledge that it's taking over my mind now. That's because of the circumstances. I can't stop my eyes from glancing at the light fixture above her bed. It makes my blood boil that I'm connected to him.

"Parker, you joining us? Or are you going to stand there getting lost in your own mind?" Oscar asks, completely bringing me out of my memories.

"I'm here," I murmur, as my eyes catch up with what I've been missing out on.

Luna is leaning back against Oscar's chest, head propped against his shoulder as he caresses her stomach just under her top. I wet my lips at the sight of her, my hands itching to join in but not knowing where to start.

"Parker, you're wearing too many clothes for our girl. Strip for her, then we can trade places," Oscar orders, and the way Luna bites her lip in anticipation has me nodding in agreement.

Without taking my eyes off her, I kick my shoes off and throw them aside. As I pull the back of my top over my head, she instantly scans my chest with her heated gaze. Undoing the button on my jeans, she suddenly stops my movement.

"Let me." My dick pulses at her seductive tone.

Yes, please.

Oscar let's her go, and she drops to her knees in front of me. Pulling my zipper down, she makes slow work of taking my jeans off. She rubs the tip of her nose against my cock through the fabric of my boxers and I hiss in response.

She looks so hot kneeling in front of me like this. Tilting her head back, the smile she gives me is intoxicating. Encouraging her to her feet, I spin her around to face Oscar. Her back to my front, just like he had done. One hand cupping her pussy through her leggings while the other wraps around her waist.

We watch as Oscar rips his clothes off down to his boxers, not wanting to drag it out with a tease. That just leaves Luna to shed her clothes. Happy to assist, I slowly stroke my hands up her sides and over her rib cage, bringing her top with me.

"Fuck, Oscar. Come feel," I groan, wanting to share this moment, and make my angel feel good. Oscar steps toward us and places his palms on her bare waist. "Higher, Oscar. You're gonna need to move higher."

His hands slowly trail up her chest, causing Luna to moan. When his fingers scrape against mine I know he feels it too.

"Fuck, baby girl. No bra, just your bedazzled nipples screaming to be touched." He watches her reaction with a grin, as I scissor squeeze her jewels between my fingers, and he brushes his thumb over the peaks.

The whimper that passes her lips has my cock uncontrollably grinding against her ass. Oscar leans forward and bites her nipple through her t-shirt, and she's like putty in our hands. I need more. Releasing my grip for a moment, I pull her t-shirt off the rest of the way, while Oscar catches up and starts to slip her yoga pants down her legs.

"Holy shit, baby girl. No panties too? This is why I'm so damn hot for you," he whispers in awe. "Get on the bed, baby girl, flat on your back. Now."

She eagerly crawls on the bed, in all her naked glory. Oscar and I stand staring at her ass in the air, before she lays down like instructed with her legs parted. Never one to be completely at our mercy, she slowly trails a hand down her body, gasping as her fingers slowly circle her clit. Her other hand toys with her nipple piercing, and the whole vision is a wet dream.

"I think we won the lottery, man," Oscar murmurs to me, and I couldn't agree more. Patting his shoulder, I move toward her, bypassing any pleasantries and going straight for her core.

Forcing her legs wider, I bring my lips to her clit and

suck, hard. Her fingers still linger for a moment, before I nip at them to move. There's too much tension here for this to be soft and gentle, and the groan from her mouth as she grips my hair tells me she agrees.

"Fuck, Parker, more. I want more." Her hips lift up off the bed, trying to grind against my face as she takes what she wants.

"You'll get more, baby girl, when I say so," Oscar grunts, climbing on the bed beside me and taking her pierced nipple into his mouth. The scar down her chest glistens with sweat as her neck flushes pink with arousal. Nothing is more beautiful than this right here.

Squeezing her thighs, I slide my fingers to where she wants them. Tracing her entrance, as I continue to nip at her tight nub, I tease her, watching as she squirms beneath us.

"Do it, Parker," Oscar says, glancing at me with a wicked gleam in his eyes.

Thrusting two fingers straight into her core, Oscar matches my timing with a bite to her nipple and I swipe my tongue along her slit.

"Shit," she slurs as her back arches off the bed. That's all the encouragement I need. Swirling my fingers along her walls, I add pressure to her g-spot as I grind my palm against her pretty, swollen nub. Her hips work to match my pace as I bite down on her inner thigh. Feeling her legs tremble beneath me has me squeezing my dick to stave off coming too soon.

"Please, I need someone inside me," she pleads below us.

"Baby girl, I'm the boss around here," Oscar smirks down at her, but she growls in response.

"Only because I fucking say so, Oscar. Now get your cock in my mouth."

Not needing to be told twice, Oscar releases her breasts, drops his boxers and places his knees on either side of her head. Working himself up and down slowly, he braces his other hand against the headboard as he leans over her.

Damn. I'm not ashamed to admit how hot that is, the way his hips flex as he slowly thrusts into her mouth. I show how much I like it by pressing the pad of my thumb against her ass, as my fingers work overtime and my tongue presses against her clit. Her pussy clenches around my fingers and I hear her scream around Oscar's cock. His thrusts not relenting, continuing to fuck her head into the mattress, as she rides out her orgasm.

She liked that. It gives me an idea, but I don't know if it would be an option. It has always intrigued me, this level of intimacy, and being in here with Oscar gives me the confidence I need. When we played never have I ever, Roman mentioned it and she didn't bat an eyelid.

Let's see what my angel's got stashed away. I lean toward her bedside table, bedtime treats always go in the top draw right? Pulling it open, I'm not wrong, it seems she's stocked up better than I thought. Grabbing everything that catches my eye, I bring them to the bed with me as Oscar occupies her.

Watching as her hands squeeze his thighs, enjoying the position he has her in, encourages me to continue. Uncapping the lube from the drawer, I drizzle it onto my fingers, and the purple toy I just found in the drawer.

Teasing my fingers from her clit to her entrance, her legs widen for attention. I continue my trail down reaching her ass and I apply a little pressure, before circling her hole. I wait to see what her response is, and she doesn't disappoint when she nudges for me to do it again.

Oh god. The fact that she trusts us with this has my heart rate picking up. Adding a little extra lube to be on the safe side, I slowly push a digit into her backside as my other hand presses the vibrator into her pussy. I keep the setting on low as I slowly work it inside of her.

Her muffled cry breaks through the room, forcing Oscar to look back to see what I'm doing.

"Fuck, Parker, what are you doing to our girl?" As his eyes land on the vibrator they darken with need. "Yeah," he murmurs. Pulling himself from Luna's lips with a pop, he kneels beside her, searching her eyes to make sure she's okay.

Her lips are puffy, and her eyes are shot as she nods at him while trying to catch her breath. Sexy as hell.

His hand trails down her body, to meet mine at her entrance. I slip the vibrator out, so he can slip his fingers in, and that's when he sees I'm stretching her out.

He looks back in her direction, her hands gripping the pillows beside her head as she rides both of our fingers, loving it.

"Add another Parker," he orders, quickly glancing at me before turning back to Luna. "Baby girl, I have my medical records on my phone, I swear I'm clean. I've never... I've never done it how you and Parker did, but I want to. With you. As we take you completely between us." It's not exactly a question, but the intent is there. I add a second finger and scissor them as I work her over, while he waits patiently for her response.

She stares him down a moment, before lifting up to rest on her elbows. Her head falls back with the pleasure as a moan escapes her lips.

"You better mean that you're both going to fuck me. My pussy and my ass at the same time because I really want to try that right now."

Oscar doesn't respond, he just picks the lube up and coats his cock, his other hand still playing with our girl. Before handing me the bottle to do the same. He trails his hand up her body squeezing her breasts on his way, as he leans down to claim her mouth.

"Get up, Luna," he says against her lips. She doesn't stall for a second as she rises to her knees in front of me. My hands instantly go to her hips, my grip so tight her flesh beneath my touch is sure to mark.

Her hands stroke up my chest as my lips meet hers, the fact that they've just been around Oscar's cock only adds to my arousal. It's tantalizingly slow, but has my heart pounding out of my chest.

Oscar moves in behind her, trapping her between us. She releases my lips and reaches her head back to find

Oscar's, where he holds her face in place, dominating her mouth as I bite down on her neck.

Oscar blindly shuffles to stand beside the bed, and pulls Luna with him, lifting her straight into his arms and right on to his cock. She moans loudly as Oscar shudders with pleasure.

Holy fuck. No slowly easing into her, just straight up spearing her and she fucking loves it.

"I warned you, baby girl. I told you when I got to have you again it would be a pounding, did I not?" he growls, lifting her up and dropping her straight back down, impaling her again and again. Which only makes her cries louder. Sweat trickles down Oscar's brow with the force he's using and together they look amazing.

I've had my fill of watching, now I want inside her. Especially her ass, I love giving her my firsts. Stepping up behind her, I kiss down her back as I stretch her a little more, she trembles between us.

Oscar holds her by her thighs, so I grip her hip as I line myself up. Oscar gets the message and stops his movement, staying deep inside her as I penetrate her too.

"Fuckkk." She sighs, her head coming to rest on my shoulder. "So. Good," she stammers as I slowly push inside of her, all the damn way. Jesus Christ, my cock is on fire because of how tight she is. We're all breathing frantically, trying to hold off on this ending too quickly. Biting her shoulder, I attempt to stifle my groan. She's going to be covered in my marks at this rate, but that just makes my cock twitch inside of her.

I pepper kisses up her neck as Oscar works her mouth, we stay still waiting for Luna to move. When she grinds between us we take that as our cue, Oscar slowly pulls out and slams back in. Fuck me that rubbed right against my cock too. Sweat trickles down the back of my neck as I focus on all the sensations. My toes curl into the carpet, as my fingers dig deeper into her skin.

"Holy shit. Holy shit. Keep your cock there, Parker. Fuck." If I wasn't riding the same high I would chuckle at the surprise in his voice.

He does it again, and we all moan in unison. Lost to the moment until the door swings open.

"I have a few phone calls to make, you know, as the responsible one and you guys think it's okay to put on a sex sho…" Roman's growl comes to an abrupt stop. Looking over my shoulder to him, his eyes are trying to take in every inch of us all at once, as a gun hangs from his right hand.

Luna between us, with her legs wrapped around Oscar's waist as he fucks her pussy and my cock penetrates her ass. Our faces close together, enjoying the intimacy with Luna.

"Hey baby, come kiss me," Luna murmurs, her voice thick with lust, which has Roman nodding his head repeatedly in agreement. Kicking the door shut behind him, he throws the gun on the bed and moves toward us. Planting a punishing kiss to her lips, he slaps my ass which jolts us all, causing a ripple of moans throughout the room. The friction between us is like nothing else I've ever felt.

"Don't stop on my account," he says as he steps back to watch.

That's all the encouragement Oscar needs to start thrusting again. The tightness of Luna, and the rub of his cock has me too close. The quaking breaths coming from Luna tell me she's close too.

"Kiss him, Roman. Send me over the edge," Luna pants out, her hand resting on top of mine.

Within seconds he's in my face, his lips crushing mine, forcing me to thrust uncontrollably, but it seems that's all we needed. With Roman's tongue against mine, a few short strokes of my cock inside of Luna and the three of us are coming. I hear Luna's and Oscar's cries of pleasure as Roman swallows mine, only adding to my climax. When he finally pulls back, it's to whisper in my ear.

"You look hotter than I could have imagined when you're fucking, Parker. One day, I'm going to fuck you while you fuck our girl, how about that?" I can't answer as his words force another wave of pleasure through my body.

"I'll give you guys a few minutes, I think you're going to need it. I'm not happy about this little stunt. I get it, but I don't like eyes on what's mine. It doesn't happen again." Before anyone can respond, he picks his gun up off the bed, aims at the light fixture and pulls the trigger.

Nobody jumps at the noise, we all stare at the debris falling all over the bed.

"Guess you'll be staying with me tonight, princess." Without another word, he turns and walks out. Leaving us all standing in surprise at his actions.

"Fuck. That was sexy," Luna says, as she still stares at the mess.

"Yeah, even I'd have to agree. Plus, it was one hell of a statement," Oscar mutters, catching me off guard, and pulling my gaze to him.

From his words to the fact that we're all still connected, I can't help but chuckle at the state of us.

"Let me down, boys, my legs have gone numb, but so totally worth it," Luna giggles, and we do as she asks.

"Get a move on, Kai and Jess will be back from the coffee shop anytime and Rafe is twenty minutes out," Roman calls out from the other room.

All the laughter dies on our lips as, we remember what we were distracting ourselves from to begin with.

TWENTY

Luna

I managed to climb into the shower with a fresh set of clothes to change into, before Red and Kai get back, or Rafe arrives. Slipping into a pair of black skinny jeans and a ripped Iron Maiden t-shirt, I decide against any make-up. I can hear the guys and Red chatting in the lounge, but I can't bring myself to head back out there.

I refused to talk to anyone about what Veronica said, especially about Rafe. I wanted to wait for him to talk it through, it just seriously has my brain fried. Sitting on the vanity, I rest my head against the mirror, thinking it all over.

My father and Rafe were... together? I mean I don't care, go them, but how did any of this come to be? How am I even here? It kind of makes sense how I ended up with such a vile mother, and only loving memories of my father though. I can't explain the peace I feel knowing my father was never in a relationship with that bitch.

What did that make Rafe? I was racking my brain, praying for a memory to burst free from my mind. I could feel something hovering at the edge of my mind. Trying to encourage it to the forefront was proving harder than I thought.

How have I lived and grown up with this man and not remembered his importance? There have been so many times when I've wanted to call him dad yet I've always held my tongue. It came so naturally to my lips and I'd always assumed it was because he's my only true family. Now it seems there is more to the story, *our* story. I always pushed it back down, not wanting to make him uncomfortable. Did I ever call him that as a child?

Closing my eyes, I concentrate on repeating the words over in my mind. Rafe. Dad. Daddy. Papa. That's what kicks the memory forward, Papa.

"Luna, baby. I need you to have some water for me,

okay?" A rough hand strokes down my cheek, encouraging me to open my eyes. Blinking a few times, I look around to see the inside of a big car, possibly an SUV. It's a little blurry, but looking out of the window we're parked outside a gas station. There are two other cars and a tiny little kiosk, surrounded completely by dry land.

Rafe stands before me in the open door with a bottle of water in his hand.

"Hey darling, there's those pretty green eyes. Would you drink some of this water?" He stretches his arm out to bring it closer to me, and I hold my small hand out to take it. That's when I see the specs of blood on my hands, I start to tremble.

Tears begin to trickle down my face, my mind replaying why the blood is there, and why we're in the car to begin with.

"Hey, it's going to be okay, Luna. I promise you, darling girl, I will take care of all this. Me and you against the world, yeah?" I can see tears in his eyes too, he's trying his best to hold them back so he can comfort me. "Papa's got you, darling. We just have to keep going."

"Where's daddy?" I cry, as my body shakes with the pain the memories give me.

"It's alright, Luna. He's... He's..." Rafe starts to sob too, looking down at his hands at a loss for words. Taking a calming breath, he meets my eyes. *"Darling, I don't know where he is, but I hope he's in heaven where it's safe."*

"But I want daddy," I scream, swinging my arms and legs around in a tantrum. My foot hits the seat in front as my arm connects with Rafe's chest, knocking some of the water from the bottle onto his t-shirt.

"I know, baby. I know, we'll figure this out. Have a little water and we'll keep driving okay? You can be the Michelangelo to my Raphael, remember?" The mention of the Teenage Mutant Ninja Turtles distracts my train of thought.

"Cowabunga," I murmur, and it lifts a small smile from Rafe.

"Cowabunga, Michelangelo. Now, a little water." I take a sip, distracted as my imagination goes to TMNT, my favorite cartoon of all time.

"Okay, Raphael. Only code names from now on," I say, handing the water back and sitting up straight in my seat. He clips me in, and quickly walks around to the driver's side. When he starts to drive an idea comes to mind. "I think I'll call you Rafe for short." I decide, pleased with

my idea. I stare out of the window, making up adventures in my mind as a ninja, forgetting the horrors of my past.

A knock on the bathroom door pulls me into the present with a jerk, my head hitting the mirror behind me. Fuck. I rub my head as I hear Kai through the door.

"Sakura, Rafe is here." I can't bring myself to answer, not yet.

Standing, I look in the mirror to see tears streaming down my face. My shaking hands slowly lift to trace the wet track marks.

I feel like that little six-year-old girl again. Heartbroken. This time because that man out there lost his title of papa, to be the Raphael to my Michelangelo.

I need to see him. Rushing for the bathroom door, I don't swipe the tears from my face because they just continue to fall harder, faster. Swinging the door open, I step into the lounge, my eyes frantically searching around everyone.

They're all frozen in place, staring at me and my disheveled appearance. My naturally wavy hair is still wet and not contained with a hair tie, and I know my face is blotchy from the tears. The concern is clear on Red's face and the guys are looking at me on high alert. Oscar and

Parker are sitting on the sofa facing my direction, while Kai and Roman are sitting on the other.

Then, I see him. Standing by the main door, afraid to come in any further because he doesn't know what my reaction will be.

Fuck. Look what I did to him. His face is etched in fear and unnecessary apology because of me. He looks as much of a hot mess as I do. My feet move toward him on their own accord, carrying me past everyone as he stands as still as a statue. When I'm only a few steps away, I can't keep it in.

"Papa," I whisper, and his face crumbles at the crack in my voice, tears instantly streaking his face like mine. I throw myself at him, my arms wrapping around his neck as I squeeze with all my strength. He lifts me off the ground with his hold tight around me. I'm not sure if it's my heart pounding I can feel or Rafe's, likely both.

My tears flow freely, mixing with Rafe's and soaking his t-shirt. I can barely breathe, my emotions forcing me to hiccup against him as I choke on my sobs. My fingers hurt from the grip I have on him, but I can't let go.

We stay like this for what feels like forever. Locked in our embrace, sobbing uncontrollably and whispering apologies to each other.

Slowly putting me back on my feet, Rafe lifts my face to swipe his thumb across my cheek, just like the memory. This touch means so much more now, solidifying the father-daughter bond between us.

"Do you remember?" Rafe asks, his voice husky from our crying, with eyes searching mine as if he could see what I saw.

"Not a great one, but it was when you became the Raphael to my Michelangelo," I murmur in response, swiping my hands down the front of my pants. Who knew emotions could make you so sweaty? His eyes fall a little at the memory of that dreadful day, but he soon shakes it away. As a distraction, he looks to the others in the room, so I follow his line of sight.

They're all on their feet, looking in our direction. A mixture of confusion and relief crossing their faces, but no sympathy. Thank god, that is not what I need right now.

"Okay, we have a lot to talk about, darling. Do you want me to make some coffee?"

"No need, Rafe. I grabbed some from the coffee house, they should still be good," Red says with a soft smile, and Rafe nods.

"Great, thanks, Jess." He looks back at me, seeing the tension in my body. I catch the shift the moment it enters his eyes, the need to lighten the mood and ease it away. "Do I get to grill the boys properly before we have this chat? It would definitely improve my mood," he says with a cheeky grin on his face as he rubs his hands together in delight.

"You better behave, or I'll beat your ass." I give him a death glare with my hands on my hips, true Red style, but it only makes him smile wider.

"Hey, if he wants to know what my favorite parts of you are, then I'm more than happy to share." I know that's Oscar straight away and I turn to see him smile, as Roman smacks him across the head.

"Ignore him, Rafe. He talks a lot of shit, we don't pay him any attention," Roman grunts, pushing Oscar onto the sofa and making everyone chuckle.

"Roman, I swear to god, stop hitting me. Baby girl, tell him." He pouts, glancing backward at me. Just like that, the mood is lightened.

Red approaches me, melted Frappuccino in hand, and a soft smile on her lips.

"I'm sure it'll taste great," she murmurs, cringing at

the cup before wrapping her arms around me as tight as she can. I need this level of comfort from her right now. I'm emotionally drained, but there is still so much to discuss. Kai breaks the silence in the room as he clears his throat.

"Would everyone be okay moving this down to my room? There's a little more digging I want to do, and I can't do it on this thing," he says, waving Roman's laptop around. Everyone looks to me for an answer, which makes me roll my eyes.

"Of course, we need all the information we can get. Are you guys okay heading out first so I can have a chat with Rafe?" My voice is strong, but I find myself rubbing my arms nervously.

"Whatever you need, Sakura." Kai walks toward me, kisses me lightly on my forehead and heads for the door. It gets everyone moving and suddenly I'm like a conveyor belt, everyone rolling by me on their way to the door.

Red squeezes my arm and follows Kai. Parker pulls me into his arms and holds me close, placing a gentle kiss to my head, he stares into my eyes, peering at my soul.

"I see you, angel. Just as you see me," he murmurs before heading for the door.

Oscar's next, and in true Oscar style he swoops in and

lifts me off my feet. Twirling me around as he holds me tight, I soak up his fun aura as it brings a smile to my face. As he slowly puts me back on my feet, he raises a hand to my cheek, planting a swift kiss on my lips.

"Miss you already, baby girl," he mutters against my lip, before bopping my nose and disappearing after the others.

Wow. I don't know what that was but... Swoon.

Looking over to Roman, he's staring at me, hard. I can see his jaw working, as though he's trying to say something, but he doesn't know how. Before I can ask what's going on, he finally blurts it out.

"I thought you knew, princess." He must see the confusion on my face, making him continue. "I just thought yours and Rafe's dynamics had changed or something? I don't know, but I didn't think to tell you about this. I didn't realize how much you had suppressed. I just..."

Needing to make his rambling stop, I walk to him and throw my arms around his waist, crushing my face into his chest. His arms come down over me, squeezing me tight to him, as he rests his chin against my head. Inhaling his scent, I get lost in the familiar woodsy smell, feeling his heart beating fast against me.

My brain is slow to process what he's trying to say, but he must think I'm mad at him for not telling me. Tilting my head back I look up to him, his eyes are closed with his chin resting on his chest now that I've moved.

"Roman, this would never have been something I would expect you to tell me. When I said complete honesty, this doesn't count. I don't think I would have believed you anyway. Do I like how I found out? No, but I'm glad I remember now."

He peers at my face, trying to make sure I'm telling the truth. He slowly relaxes beneath me when he sees I'm not trying to put any of the blame on him. Stupid Acehole.

"Now, go boss everyone around, baby. Get your alpha vibes back, cos you're starting to sound like Red," I say, stepping back with a wink as I slap his ass into gear. The growl he gives me makes me chuckle at him. He crushes his lips to mine for a moment, not nearly long enough, before stepping back and heading for the door. My eyes stay on him, tracking his movements, and I already miss his touch.

Just before he shuts it, he turns to face me, Rafe still lingering quietly near the door watching us interact. I see the gleam in Roman's eyes and I instantly know he's got some smartass bitch comment on the tip of his tongue.

"Slap my ass again, princess, and I'll have to spank you. Rafe around or not," he grins and slams the door behind him.

Oh my fucking god. I can feel the heat in my face, not needing to see to know I'm bright red. Rafe turns to look at me with his eyebrows raised, and I shut him down before he can carry on too.

"Aceholes, the lot of them. Now, coffee?"

YOUR BLOODLINE

KC KEAN

TWENTY ONE

Luna

It's getting late as we stare across the kitchen table at each other. With my slushy coffee in hand I let the silence engulf us. Glancing at my watch, it's a little after five, I should be deciding what I want to eat but I'm not even a little bit hungry. I'm too busy churning over everything that's happened today.

"I'm sorry," we both blurt at the same time, which is cringy as hell and so cliché. I can't help but roll my eyes.

"I'll go first, darling," Rafe murmurs, taking a deep breath and squeezing my hand on the table. "I'm sorry that I never tried to tell you, Luna. After the therapists only made the situation worse, I didn't know what to do. You weren't remembering anything, so I made the decision not to push you any further. I wanted to wait for everything to come back to you naturally."

A soft smile plays across his lips, but I see the real pain in his dark brown eyes. Putting my watery Frappuccino down on the table, I place my hand on top of his, sandwiching it between mine. His hands are ice cold and it catches me by surprise. How do I even show this man how much I appreciate him, for everything he has done for me?

"Rafe. Papa. Shit." Sighing, I shake my head at myself. "I'm sorry, my brain is going to take a minute to catch up here."

"It's okay, Luna. The fact that you remember is all I've ever wanted," he says with the softest smile I've ever seen on his face. Nodding, I take a second to try again.

"I'm sorry I've put you through all of this. I can see the pain in your eyes, and it hurts me too," I whisper, pulling away from him to reach for my coffee again. I stir my straw through the slushy content, at least it still tastes good.

Leaning forward on crossed arms, Rafe meets my gaze.

"How about we stop apologizing and start trying to move forward? None of this is your fault, darling. I need you to accept that."

"I don't know how, I feel this ache in my chest that tells me I caused you too much unnecessary pain, but I would love to try and move forward." I smile weakly, surprised by the honesty in my words. "But to do that, I think we need to delve into the past a little more."

I push back from the table and rise to my feet. Thinking it, and actually saying it out loud are two very different things. My palms are sweating, and my heart is pounding in my chest, bracing myself for the conversation. I focus on taking some deep breaths to try and calm myself.

"We can talk about whatever you want," he says, watching me as I start to pace behind my chair. Glancing at the mess in the plastic cup on the table, I start the coffee machine instead, needing the time to get control over myself again.

Resting my hands on the countertop, I drop my gaze to stare at the marble patterns. Rafe stays quiet, giving me the time I'm asking for. I don't ask if he wants a coffee, he's getting one either way. I methodically go through the motions of making two cups, bringing them over to the table and taking a seat across from Rafe again.

He stares me down, looking between me and the mug in

front of him with humor in his eyes. It takes me a moment to understand what has his attention, and it makes me smile too. I hadn't been paying attention to the cups, I just pulled them from the cupboard. I've given him the one I bought for Red. It says, 'Back the fuck up sprinkle tits, today is not the day, I will stab you with my horn.' Whereas mine is just a picture of a rose, boring in comparison.

"Can you explain to me how an agreement was made between Steele and Hindman while you were in a relationship with Dad? I can't wrap my head around it." Tapping his fingers against the kitchen table, he nods a few times, gathering his own strength before answering.

"From before your father was born, there was an agreement in place between the Steeles and the Hindmans, that they would unite the families in marriage. When your grandmother, Maria, found out about our relationship she called off the arrangement. Maria believes in true love, she wanted us to have happiness in this dark world, and she approved instantly. This caused a lot of issues over the years, and eventually led us to agree to a new set up. The Hindmans and Veronica agreed to be our surrogate so we could have you."

I like my grandmother even more now. She accepted

the love between Rafe and my dad without question, and didn't force any of the betrothed agreement shit at them. Go, Grandmother! There is a wistful glint in his eyes as he talks about my father, the love still running through his veins.

"So how did that work? Her being my surrogate mother? It confuses the hell out of me because she shouldn't even be in our lives." He looks up to the ceiling, swiping a hand down his face. When he finally looks back at me, I can see the anguish in his eyes.

"Part of the terms were that Veronica would remain listed on the birth certificate, to show unity between the families. We agreed in an instant because we were just ready to have you and if it calmed the drama, then that was a bonus." He pauses to take a drink of his coffee, and I do the same. All this emotional shit has my mouth dry, I swear. "At the time, Veronica seemed happy to do it, she always wanted to please her family. They did the whole artificial insemination stuff."

"Eww, don't tell me about that bit," I cringe, shaking my head to push away the images, but ultimately glad my father didn't have to dick the bitch. I still shudder at the thought, gulping down my hot coffee to burn the visual from my mind.

"Sorry," he chuckles. "We supported her throughout the pregnancy, but she was never really interested. She didn't want to be a mother, so having her on your birth certificate wasn't an issue." He winces at his choice of words, and I stop the apology before it can even leave his lips.

"Rafe, don't apologize for the truth. We both know she doesn't have a maternal bone in her body. She showed up here today because someone asked her to. They clearly want me to stand with them, and they're using her as a pawn. She's too stupid to see it." I sigh, looking at the bottom of my empty cup. Damn it, I'm still thirsty.

"Honestly, Luna? I think that's always been the case. Someone has been using her for a very long time to try and get to you. I have my suspicions but no evidence to back it up. Which is why I have her monitored the best I can. When she goes off grid so easily it only encourages my thoughts."

I look into his deep brown eyes trying to search out the answer, he can't just throw me little cryptic lines and expect it to be enough.

"I need you to give me more than that. We're a team, Rafe, family. A team shares everything, even if it is just a suspicion," I say with a raised eyebrow, testing him and our new boundaries.

"She's definitely connected heavier to Rico than she lets on. Between the pair of them…" he pauses, as if the words cause him worry. "Between them, I think they're working with Totem."

I run my tongue along my teeth as I weigh up his words. Now that he's said it, I need to ask, to address the elephant in the room. Clearing my throat, I brace myself, and his back straightens at the look on my face. My resting bitch face is on full display as I try to not give anything away.

"I need you to give me the truth on this, okay?" He offers a simple nod, and I build up the courage I need to push the words past my lips. I square my shoulders and straighten my spine. "Am I the heir?" I ask the question so quickly I'm not sure he heard.

He sits staring at me with a completely blank expression, it's clear my inquiry has caught him off guard. The longer he says nothing, the longer I worry. My breathing starts to kick up a notch at the silence that engulfs me. My heart is about to beat out of my chest in panic, when he suddenly bursts out laughing.

I mean, he's sitting before me, leaning against the table

as a full belly laugh takes control.

"I think I'm going to take your reaction as a no, although simply saying the word would have sufficed," I grunt, scowling at him as his shoulders continue to shake.

He finally lifts his gaze to mine, and stops the bubbles of laughter from continuing. My face must give away how much he's annoying me. Clearing his throat, he stands from the table, putting his cup in the sink before turning to me.

"You are definitely not the heir, Luna," he says, a small chuckle leaving his mouth again, which he smothers with a cough. Acehole.

"Well thanks, Captain fucking Obvious. I think your reaction gave me that answer already," I say with a roll of my eyes.

His laughter dies out just as quickly as it started, leaving a look of seriousness to take over his features. I know something isn't right when his gaze flits around the room, looking anywhere but at me.

"But...?" I ask, and his eyes finally meet mine. He releases a heavy sigh as he pours another coffee into a new cup. Clearly he wasn't a fan of the unicorn, but the one he's pulled out has 'Fuck You' printed on the bottom.

"I hope you're going to do the dishes," I state, raising

my eyebrow at him.

"You have a dishwasher, don't you?" he snarks back with a grin, and I roll my eyes for the third time.

"Back to the conversation," I say, not wanting to get off track.

"Yes, sorry. When Veronica was here, it was mentioned that she was sent here by her lover. Something about him thinking you had the right attributes to stand beside the new movement. You may not be the heir, Luna, but they clearly want you on their side."

Taking a sip of his coffee, he thinks over his words, while I stretch, patiently waiting for him to continue. Lifting my arms above my head, I lace my fingers together and alternate between stretching to the left and right. A muscle pops at the top of my back, releasing some of the tension.

"When we were in high school, Veronica and Totem were a thing. There are a lot of arranged marriages within Featherstone, but you don't usually have to step up to that commitment until you are twenty-one. Although they had ended by the time we arrived at the Academy, your mother always thought the sun shined out of his ass. Following him around like a lost puppy all the time."

Wow. She's clearly crazier than I thought.

"We need to track her better, we need to know for sure," I say, determined, probably because I really would like to put a bullet through her brain right now after her little B&E. I can't help but slap my palm against the countertop in frustration.

"While she was up here, I had Maverick equip a device on her car. So we'll see how far that gets us," he murmurs. Hopefully, far enough to track this bitch down. Trying to get a bigger picture of what my life was like without my actual memory is proving difficult, but something does come to mind.

"Was she connected to Dad's death?" I whisper, blinking rapidly to keep the tears at bay. It doesn't stop my heart from beating brutally against my chest, or my hands from sweating profusely. Rubbing them against my pants, I focus on the motion as opposed to the fact my soul is dreading the answer. He doesn't answer straight away as he tries to control his own emotions too.

"A lot of things were happening around that time. That's when it was agreed that if anything happened to one of us, the other would run with you. Maria knew, and helped cause distractions so we," he gestures between us, "could get away." He takes a deep breath, making me sit back in my chair as he finally sits back down across from me.

"Tell me more," I mutter.

"That day, I was on my way home from a work trip." He shakes his head, huffing at himself, before meeting my eyes. "I was away completing an assignment for Featherstone. We always made sure we didn't accept jobs that overlapped. We may have only been twenty-four years old when you came into our lives, but we loved you so much. You were, and still are, our number one priority."

A soft smile graces his lips, and I can't help but smile back, which seems to be reassurance enough for him to carry on. My heart soars knowing I was never truly a lone ranger with the most amazing parents behind me.

"I'd managed to get back a day earlier than planned because it was Bryce's thirtieth birthday so I wanted to surprise you both." The little light that was in his eyes dims instantly, as the memory replays in his mind. "I err, I came up the driveway and the front door was open, which was odd. Your dad was crazy obsessive with security, worse than me if you can believe."

I reach my hand out to his, offering my support as he

did to me earlier. I may not remember that day, and part of me never wants to, but I can feel his pain.

"It's okay, Pops. If it's too much we can leave it for now."

"Pops, huh?" He smirks at my choice of words and it pulls him out of the memory for a minute.

"Yeah, I think I may need to trial all my name options because Papa just doesn't work for me now." He nods at that, and the fact I'm acknowledging his role in my life must spur him on.

"When I walked in, Luna, you were curled up in a ball in the back garden and your father was gone. I won't go into anything else because it doesn't matter, but Veronica's phone was in the entryway. As though it had been dropped by accident and she'd not been able to come back for it."

My father's body wasn't there? Why hadn't we gone looking for him? Why did we run? All of these questions are running around in my head, but I can't process any of them to ask him. I rest my head in my hands as I fight to stay in control of my mind. I feel Rafe's hand gently wrap around my wrist in comfort.

"Darling, I promised the love of my life, that if anything happened I would protect you, and Maria would search for him. I told you, priority number one was always you. We knew that, and I stand by our decision. Your father had a lot of surveillance set up around the house, and we were able to retrieve some of it. It just wasn't enough for a full picture."

Leaning back in my chair, I swipe a hand down my face. I think I'm at my limit.

"I've reached my breaking point," I mutter loud enough for him to hear me, and he nods in response. "I mean, it's progress for me to acknowledge that though, right?" I say, letting him see the pain in my eyes as I lose control of my emotions.

"Whatever you need. We need to plan, prep and monitor everything relating to Veronica. Whoever did send her here won't be happy she came away empty handed." I completely agree with him.

"Should we go meet the others so we can get a plan in place? I'd like to destroy these motherfuckers, and sooner rather than later. They've taken enough from us, and I refuse to let them take anymore," I growl.

Standing from the table, I run my hands down my pants as I try and shake the darkness from my mind.

"Come on then. I'm sure your *boyfriends* will help lift

your mood," he says with a grin, and I whack his arm as he walks past.

"Stop it, and quit with the cringy jokes too while we're at it. No dad should be saying them." I try to keep my voice stern and a glare on my face, but the smile he gives me makes it impossible. Wrapping his arm around my shoulder, he leads me out of the kitchen as he continues to tease me.

"No can do, darling. I promised your father I would forever be the cringy one, so he didn't have to be." He wears a smile on his face, but his eyes are welling up again. I feel like he's aged from the heaviness of this conversation. It seems we both need a break from all this heavy talk. Although, there is a new lightness in his eyes, likely because I know he's my Papa now.

"Whatever you say, old man." I head for the door, opening it dramatically for him to walk through.

He passes, giving me a fake glare. "I'm no old man. Call me that again and you're going in a time-out."

I stick my tongue out at his retreating form. Loving how our dynamics are exactly the same, yet our connection feels deeper at the same time.

If I've learned anything at Featherstone, it's that in

all the pain this world brings, we will protect our family, treasure them, love them and most importantly kill for them.

KC KEAN

TWENTY TWO

Parker

"What the hell is taking them so long?" Roman grumbles from the sofa across from me, his leg bouncing with anxiety.

"Would you stop? She needs a minute to wrap her head around a few things before we dig into everything else," Oscar grunts in response, but he's rubbing the back of his neck showing his anxiety too. Kai ignores us all as he works away in the kitchen on his own technology.

"Does anyone want a drink? I can grab some bottles of water from my room?"

I look to Jess who's trying to deal with us all moping

around waiting for Luna.

"There's some in the fridge," Kai shouts from the kitchen. He's adamant the blocker they used only covered the footage, not destroyed it.

"Please, Jess. That'd be great," I say with a smile, trying to relax the tense atmosphere with no luck. "What did your dad say, Roman?"

While Oscar and I were getting lost in Luna, Roman was trying to chase some leads. Protective should be his middle name, especially when it comes to family, and that's what we all are. Family.

"He was trying to get someone into the surveillance systems around town, so we could keep eyes on where Veronica goes from here. That way it allows Kai to focus on the Academy's security systems."

I nod in understanding, leaning back into the sofa and closing my eyes. Stretching my arms out along the back of the sofa, I try to relax. I don't want to worry about the impact my actions could have, but it's playing on my mind. My father won't be happy with the little show he got.

I've always done exactly what my father has demanded. Even though he didn't order me to stay away from Luna directly, I still feel the anxiety of going against his word.

I feel movement next to me on the sofa as a palm rests against my thigh. Rolling my head to the side, I expect to see Roman at my side. So I'm surprised when it's Oscar I find, looking at me with softness in his eyes, completely out of character for him.

"He's not going to get anywhere near you. Do you understand? Roman will kill him, possibly Luna too, but we're all in this together." His words are sincere and again, his actions take me by surprise.

Roman chimes in before I can respond. "For once I have to agree with Oscar. Whatever he tries to throw at us, we'll get through it," his usual nod of determination finishes off his statement.

"Can you say that again so I can get a recording?" Oscar asks, lifting his hand off my thigh to search out his phone.

Roman goes to hit Oscar as Jess steps back into the lounge handing out water to everyone. Without saying a word, she gets comfortable on the sofa beside Roman and flicks the tv on, unknowingly blocking his attack. Flipping through the channels, she settles on The Vampire Diaries, relaxes back, feet up beside her, and proceeds to ignore us. Okay then.

"Why didn't we wait in my room? We could have played some video games, instead we're stuck in Kai's boring room," Oscar moans, and I shake my head at the return of his whining.

"Shut up, Oscar," Kai shouts from the kitchen, always listening and observing even if it looks like he's not paying attention.

"Whatever, loser," he shouts back, as he lifts his legs over the arm of the sofa and rests his head in my lap. Who is this guy and what the fuck has happened to Oscar? Roman raises an eyebrow at me, just as surprised as I am, but all I can do is shake my head in confusion.

"Guys, I think my pussy is showing again," Oscar murmurs, looking up at the ceiling.

"What?" I don't move a muscle as we wait for him to explain.

"Have you ever been in love?" Really, who the hell is this guy? I look to Roman because I have no idea what I'm supposed to say here. This time it's Roman's turn to give his 'what the fuck' face. Luckily, Jess steps in.

"I haven't, why do you ask?" She looks at him out of the corner of her eyes, her focus still mainly on the television.

"I can't have this talk with you, Jessikins, you'll just

go and blabber your big mouth," he huffs, crossing his arms over his chest.

"Oscar, I helped you guys get Luna back without telling her, didn't I?" She turns her gaze back to the screen fully, acting indifferent and it works on him.

"I just wondered what the signs are? I did a quiz on Buzzfeed about it, but I feel like I need more specific examples." Nobody says a word as we all stare at him. His eyes are closed like it helped give him the confidence needed to say it out loud. Instead of feeling awkward, he continues, "Like, is insta love a thing?"

He lifts his head slightly to look at Jess who is openly gaping at him.

"Err, I mean some say so, but I guess it depends on you personally." She clears her throat and turns her whole body to face him, dropping her feet to the floor. "Is this related to Luna?" she asks gently, scared she'll spook him.

"Well, duh." He looks up at me, like it was obvious. Which I guess it is, but he's caught us all by surprise. Continuing to stare at him, I can't give him any further answers, because no, I've never been in love before.

"I read that if you can't stop thinking about them, and if you put their happiness before your own, they're signs, ya know?" Oscar says, looking to me for guidance. I shake my head at him, and now he has me questioning myself too.

I look at Roman for his help again, but he's sitting on the sofa, his arms braced on his thighs with his hands propping his chin up. I can see him trying to process his own emotions, which will be hard for Mr. hide-all-of-my-emotions-except-anger over there.

Kai suddenly appears, leaning against the door frame that leads into the kitchen. He looks at each of us, before finally resting his gaze on Oscar.

"Oscar, I don't think any of us know what love means, but I'm sure we'll figure it out. We just have to learn to understand our feelings, and consider each other's too." Always the wise one.

"Yeah, because she's dating us all exclusively, so you guys are practically my boyfriend-in-laws, right?" Oscar asks it so casually that I can't control the chuckle that leaves my lips. The others start to chuckle too, which makes Oscar frown.

"Shut up, Oscar," Roman says through his chuckle. Jess has her face hidden in her hands as her shoulders shake with her silent laughter.

A knock at the door has us all pause until we can hear the soft murmurs of Luna and Rafe on the other side of the door.

"Not a word, Aceholes," Oscar whisper-shouts as he glares at us. "Yeah, I know what she calls us," he adds, sitting up beside me. "You could have played with my hair you know," he grumbles, and my hand instantly rakes through his dusty blond hair. I'm surprised by how soft it actually is. The moan that passes his lips takes me by surprise, pausing my stroke, but the grin he gives is supposed to encourage me to continue.

Dropping my hand, I shake my head at him as Kai holds the door open for our girl and Rafe to enter. She looks lighter but weighed down at the same time. Kai is obviously the closest to her and wraps an arm around her shoulder, placing a delicate kiss to her temple.

"What did I miss then?" Luna asks, trying to break the little bit of tension in the room. Jess opens her mouth and Oscar sends her a death glare, which just makes her chuckle.

"Oscar's Team Damon," she finally says, pointing at the tv like we have any clue what that means.

"Err, what?" Luna responds in confusion, which makes

Jess roll her eyes.

"You haven't watched The Vampire Diaries have you?" It sounds like an accusation, and when Luna shakes her head that just makes Jess frown. "Girl, where have you been? Damon is the bad boy player, who eventually… Actually, no. I'm going to make you watch," Jess says, nodding to herself as she points her finger at Luna.

"That still doesn't explain me," Oscar interrupts, scratching his head trying to keep up.

"Whatever it means, you're still my big mouth, okay?" Luna smiles with a playful wink.

"Agreed, baby girl. As long as I'm your big mouth, I'm yours." A cheesy grin takes over his face as Rafe fake gags, making this whole thing even funnier.

I can see the relief in his eyes though, that no one blurted out what we'd just been discussing. I'm starting to notice that his party boy persona is a front for his deeper emotions. I hope Luna can help Oscar learn to be his true self, not this mask he always puts on.

"I've sorted the footage," Kai suddenly says, shutting the door and the room becomes a lot more somber waiting for the news. "Come, I'd rather show you."

That's never a good sign if he doesn't want to say it

out loud.

Kai makes us all take a seat on the sofas, as he fiddles with his laptop to get the images to come through the big screen. I remain seated with Oscar, and Rafe leans against the armrest, while Jess pulls Luna down in between her and Roman.

Roman's wearing a smug ass grin as he lays his arm behind her on the back of the sofa. So I slyly give him the middle finger. Oscar catches me flipping Roman off and proceeds to wrap his arm around my shoulder. He wags his eyebrows at Roman, who shoots daggers at him in return. He should know not to rise to Oscar's teasing, but he does every damn time.

Thankfully, Kai has the screen working before Roman and Oscar escalate their antics.

"Okay, so it's still a little grainy but everything is clear enough. Featherstone's surveillance system was fully disabled. They must have known there was a chance you'd have your own set up, which is why they must have come in with blockers. With that said, I haven't been able to retrieve the audio, only the video." Nobody says a word as he hits play and Luna's lounge comes into view.

It's only a few moments before the door handle wiggles and someone is stepping in.

Wren Dietrichson. Huh? We thought she'd gone off grid. Clearly she had to make it look like it wasn't her. They must be confident in their crappy blocker because they're not even attempting to disguise themselves. Although, it is strange to see her in jogger pants and a tank top instead of her usual get up, skimpy clothes and heavy make-up.

As she steps further into the room, her mother and a guy follow her inside. I'm sure he's from Heart's, but we'd have to check. I recognize him from Tech at least. Barbette Dietrichson has something in her hand which I'm guessing is the blocker Kai mentioned. Wren starts directing the guy around and he pulls the cameras out of his backpack.

They only spend ten minutes setting up before Veronica steps in. She hands them a duffel bag, presumably containing payment for their efforts, and they leave.

Surprisingly, Wren doesn't actually touch anything while she's there, likely because you can see her mother throwing her arms around aggressively at the two of them. Whereas, Veronica takes a stroll through every room, touching every surface before taking a seat at the kitchen table.

No one has uttered a word as we watch it unfold. When Luna enters the screen, Kai stops the footage and we all finally look around at each other.

"I'm going to gut them all," Luna growls, furious at the invasion of her privacy, especially because it was the Dietrichsons of all people. Her hand is gripping Roman's knee, turning her knuckles white, but Roman doesn't complain. Jess rubs her other arm, trying to calm Luna's fury.

"We need to play this smart, Luna. Let's assess everything and come up with a plan, okay? I'm sure you'll be gutting someone at some point," Rafe says, trying to pacify her, but the pain in his eyes tells me he's reminded of what we saw at The Pyramid.

I watch as she runs her hand back through her wavy brown hair, trying to understand that we need a plan instead of charging at them like a bull. She and Roman are too alike.

"Okay," she mutters, but it's clear the request has left a bad taste in her mouth. She looks to Rafe, waiting for a nod, which he gives, before she looks around the room at us all. "Rafe believes Veronica is connected to Totem."

Everybody continues to stare at her, likely as surprised as me by her statement.

"Okay, if that's the case then she may be more dangerous than we thought," Kai responds, tapping away on his laptop.

"Agreed, we need to try and have eyes on her at all times, we don't want her to go off grid again so easily," Rafe adds. "Your father called me, Roman. Said you'd called to put some emergency surveillance on her." Roman nods in response. "Good idea. I had Maverick plant a tracker on the vehicle she came in while Luna was in there with her. So, we are covering as many angles as possible."

"She also seems heavily linked to Dietrichson and Rico too. I have nothing set in stone yet, but it's clear from what she said and how she got in here," Kai adds, pulling up images on the screen of Veronica with Rico and Dietrichson at different times.

My father's face fills part of the screen, and my blood runs cold. I despise this man and everything he stands for, which is just himself. He feeds off the pain of others and destroys everyone in his path. After I joined Featherstone

Academy, I'm quite sure meeting Roman saved my life. When my father took me from my mother, I never got to see her again. I eventually worked up the courage to tell Roman my story, he had his father find my mother and place her somewhere safe.

"Parker, buddy. Parker." A shake to my shoulders pulls me out of my thoughts, and a concerned Oscar is leaning in beside me. "You okay?" he asks, and I nod lightly, looking around the room to find everyone staring at me with concern.

I clear my throat and try to muster up a half smile. "I'm fine," I say, but it's more of a croak. Clearly I'm letting this get the best of me. Within an instant Luna is sitting on my lap, her hands coming to gently hold my face up to hers.

"You are mine, Parker Parker, and nobody hurts what is mine." Her eyes search mine, but she must see the slight doubt there. It's not that I don't trust her abilities, she just hasn't seen my father at his worst yet.

Kai leans over the back of the sofa to squeeze my shoulder in support as Oscar stands for Roman to take his seat. Roman's thigh brushes against mine as Luna turns a little so he can move in closer. He lifts my hands to stroke my tattooed fingers, and I get lost in the motion.

A chuckle from the other sofa catches my attention. I look up to see Oscar winding Jess up, but she suddenly gets him in a headlock. It forces a little chuckle past my lips, and I feel myself start to relax again.

"Parker," Rafe says, and my eyes find his. "I was just explaining to Luna on the way down here that I think it's a good idea for us to make sure you aren't alone right now." Luna rubs my shoulder as she takes over the conversation.

"I don't think it's safe for you to be in your room alone when your father can access it so easily. Plus, you're the only one of us on the same floor as Wren, and I'd rather you weren't."

I understand what they're saying, but I don't want to be seen as the weak one. Roman's hand squeezes mine as he murmurs quietly in my ear.

"I can see your brain working overtime, Parker. This is us trying to protect you. We would be doing the same for anyone else. Family, remember? You can stay with me, it'll be like high school all over again." I hear the smile in his voice and it eases some of the tension from my body.

At Featherstone High School, the blocks were still the same, but the buildings were slightly different, and even in Ace we still had to share rooms. It was never an issue for us then, so I shouldn't make it one now.

"Alright," I say loud enough for everyone to hear, and they all visibly relax around me.

"Good," Rafe says, as he stands fully pulling his phone out. "I'd also recommend we don't piss Rico off right now. No offense, Parker, but I want to kill him myself. Nobody tries to watch my little girl, let alone touch her without her permission," he growls as he finishes his statement, and Oscar pipes up.

"Err, that might be an issue," he says, as he stands and glances between Luna and I. Yeah he's right about that. I'm not telling Rafe that I joined Oscar in tag teaming Luna in front of one of the cameras. No fucking way.

"That might be a problem, because I may have shot down the camera in Luna's bedroom," Roman grunts. "Accidentally on purpose of course." He gives Rafe a wide cheesy grin, which just has him shaking his head at us.

"Okay, well pissing him off is a little too late then, but I still call dibs on killing him. Agreed?" Rafe looks directly at me, nowhere else. His eyes trained solely on mine, as though my opinion matters the most.

"Whatever it takes to protect our family," I say, and my voice is surprisingly clear and strong. Luna kisses my cheek then stands from my lap.

"Okay, so I think we need some form of trap for Wren. She clearly knows more than we do, but we can't just grab her in the middle of the afternoon. We need some form of disguise, like a party or something." She rubs the back of her neck as she thinks for a moment. "Does Trudy usually host a Halloween party?"

She looks around at us and we all nod in answer.

"She does, they're usually pretty epic too. So, everyone goes," Oscar adds. I hadn't realized he'd stood up.

"Okay, I'll speak with Trudy. We also need to set a plan in motion for our second assignments, because I need to get that agent on record before the six weeks runs out. I've been too distracted lately. I'd rather not give Dietrichson any excuse to chop off my head."

"I can help with that, princess. I almost have his routine airtight. I can go over everything with you one day this week. I'm not adding to today's stress," Roman says with a clap of his hands, encouraging that conversation to an end for now.

"Thanks, baby," she says with a soft smile and an appreciative look in her eyes. I love how she looks at each of us differently. Like she shares herself between us, but only offers a small part of herself to us individually. I can feel the electricity between them from here.

She's so beautiful when she smiles.

"So, Maverick is going to help work on the tracking of Veronica, and I also advised him that Jess needs some extra training. Luna, I know you're putting the poor girl through her paces, but you need to tighten up your lessons to prepare for The Games. Maverick has agreed to come up with a training plan."

"What?" Jess squeals, as she jumps up from the sofa. "That's not necessary, one of these guys can help me, right?"

"Everyone else in this room is also entering into The Games, Jess. It's best for everyone to up their training. Besides, Maverick is the Combat tutor because he's the damn best," Rafe offers. She just gawks at him for a moment, before slamming her mouth shut and crossing her arms over her chest.

"I'm getting tired, can I go back to my room and lay down now?" She looks to Luna with pleading eyes, who nods in response and walks out of the front door with her.

What the hell just happened? I think we're all sitting here wondering the same thing. Who knows, but Red's room is only next door so Luna is back quickly.

"So, I need to set a plan in motion with Trudy for her Halloween party to corner Wren and get answers. Roman's going to help me with the agent, and Maverick is going to work with Red while we train our asses off. That just leaves West with the details he's been gathering for The Games," she summarizes.

"That's right, Sakura. I'll also keep up surveillance on Dietrichson's office too. We may need to possibly try and hack her phone because there is no activity today on her computer at all," Kai answers, from his spot on the floor next to his coffee table. His fingers working like crazy over his laptop.

"That's a good idea. I'll see what I can do too," Rafe adds.

Luna looks around us all with her hands on her hips, with a small smile on her lips.

"Perfect. Well, I just got cornered into watching some chick flick with Red." She rolls her eyes, but no one is surprised by how easily she gives into her. "So, Roman is going to get the debris on my bed cleaned up while I spend the night at Red's."

She chucks her keys toward Roman who manages to

catch them midair.

"Princess, that wasn't the plan. I said—"

"Baby, I know what you said, but we're a little more used to this level of crazy than she is. Big Daddy are you staying or heading back?"

Rafe turns toward her with his eyebrows raised. "Nope. No. Definitely not that one," he says with a chuckle, confusing us all, but neither of them explains their inside joke. "I'm going to head back, darling. Okay? I've got a lot going on at the shop and the gym at the minute, so it's probably best. If you need me for anything though, you call."

They embrace each other, and the newfound love for one another is clear. It warms my heart to see, and I'm not the only one watching.

What was it Oscar asked before?

I think we're all starting to develop feelings, in our own way.

TWENTY THREE

Luna

Monday morning arrives too quickly, and as I step back into my room I'm surprised to see both Roman and Parker asleep in my bed. When they'd brought the key to Red's last night, I thought that meant they'd left.

They look hot as hell in just their boxer shorts, sprawled out across the California king. Parker is lying on his back with one arm flung over his head and the other hand nestled in his boxer shorts. Whereas Roman is lying on his front, with his head half under the pillow and his left leg hanging off the side of the bed.

I'm a little disappointed that they're not snuggled up

together, that would have been amazing. Taking out my phone, I sneak a picture of them together, before tiptoeing into my closet to get dressed.

As much as I'd love to climb in and join them, I want to see Trudy this morning to plan for the Halloween party. This is her chance to show me we can really work together. Slipping into my blouse and skirt, I get my make-up done quickly. A light covering of foundation, a touch of bronzer, and coat of mascara and I'm good to go. Slipping my heels on, I grab my blazer and lip gloss and step back into my bedroom.

"Holy shit, how long have you been here?" Roman shouts, still half asleep and making Parker jump awake. I can't help but chuckle at the pair.

"Good night's sleep?" I ask, walking over to Roman's side of the bed. We have a free first period this morning, so they're obviously taking advantage and sleeping in. Red has L.F.G. (Laundering, Fraud and Gambling) so I left her room when she went to class. I had Ian drive her early, otherwise she'd be riding with Wren, and I refuse to let that happen.

"Err, yeah," he grunts, rubbing at his eyes. "You want to join us?" He grins up at me, not offering me any form of explanation as to why they're lying in my bed and not his.

"I would love to, but I've got Trudy coming over in thirty minutes to help with Project Ruin Wren." I lean over and plant a kiss against his lips, as his hand wraps around my wrist.

"Stay, princess," he murmurs against my lips, and it's oh so tempting.

"Yeah, angel. Come snuggle with us," Parker adds, and it takes all my strength to stand up straight again. Parker leans further over Roman to get closer to me and I chuckle at their antics.

"How about, you get your asses out of my bed, and come have breakfast with me before she gets here." Taking a deep breath, I look between them. "Yesterday was a complete cluster fuck, of epic proportions… and I'm still a little sore," I murmur the last bit, feeling slightly embarrassed even though I know I shouldn't be.

Parker instantly sits up in bed, swiping a hand through his hair.

"Angel, are you okay?" he asks with concern in his eyes. I nod my head but he's still not sure. "I didn't hurt you, did I?"

"I'm fine, Parker, I swear. I'm aching in the best

possible way." Searching my face, he must see the truth in my eyes.

"Move, Roman, let's give our girl what she wants," he says enthusiastically, and it makes me smile. Roman jumps to his feet beside me, wrapping me in his arms and grinning down at me.

"My princess wants to spend quality time with me, huh?" Parker lightly punches his shoulder, taking me by surprise as I feel his heat at my back.

"Quality time with *us*, Roman," he grunts at him.

"Well if you're going to be an Acehole about it, just forget it." I don't need him making a thing out of this.

Glancing over my shoulder at Parker, he's already looking down at me with his perfect smile.

"He's not being an Acehole, are you Roman?" Parker says, leaning around me to squeeze his arm.

"I'm playing, I'm playing. How about you give me a minute to shower and I'll come join you in the kitchen." After another sweet kiss to my lips, he's out of the door.

"Good morning, angel," Parker murmurs as he spins me in his arms.

"Good morning, Parker Parker." His hands clasp my face as he pecks my lips before sweeping me up off my feet, carrying me into the kitchen. He's casually holding me to the front of his body, our faces close together. It makes me a little giddy with how intimate it feels. Pulling a chair out, he places me into the seat before starting the coffee machine.

"Bacon and eggs?" he asks, glancing over his shoulder at me.

I'm too busy gawking at him standing only in his boxer shorts to respond. His curly hair is extra messy this morning, and the dimples at the bottom of his back have my full attention. Until I catch a glimpse of his feather tattoo on his bicep, making me instinctively touch my own. Yes, please. He's rocking my kitchen like he owns the fucking place. He smirks at me as I nod, but I stay silent, enjoying the view.

I want to ask him to stay with me instead of Roman, but I don't know whether it's too soon.

I'm not sure how much time has passed as I sit and watch Parker start cooking the bacon and eggs, when Roman strolls in. He scoops his hand around me, squeezing my breast and catching me by surprise. Damn, that's hot though. I grin up at him, to find him staring down at me in awe.

"I love it when you don't wear a booby holder, princess," he says casually, before patting Parker's ass and taking over the pans.

"Did you actually just say booby holder?" I ask. I'd expect that from Oscar for sure, but Roman? Clearly someone's playful this morning. He looks back at me, offering a wink and carries on preparing the food.

Parker fills my vision as he leans in to peck my lips, before heading to get ready. I don't care to push Roman for an answer, too lost in all the attention.

"I called Oscar and Kai, they'll be here in a minute," Roman says, but I'm still staring at his damp brown hair, tight white top and fitted black joggers. There are little droplets of water at the back of his neck, running down to the collar of his top. His skull tattoo that takes up his whole back peaks out of the top of his t-shirt and the dark outline can be seen slightly through it too. Topped off with bare feet, he looks fucking delicious.

I hum in response, not really paying any real notice to what he's saying. I just can't get enough of him.

"Fuck. Me." I slam my mouth shut. Holy fuck, I think I said that out loud.

"Princess," Roman says with a clap, making me lift my

gaze to his. Confident he has my attention, he continues, "I thought when you said you want to spend time together, that would mean you weren't going to picture me naked the entire time." He gives me a raised eyebrow and I can feel the flush creep up my neck.

Clearing my throat, I look to the ceiling. "I'm sorry, you just look so fucking hot." Trying to take a deep breath, I close my eyes. Only to have them blink straight back open when Roman bites down on my earlobe.

"Fuck, baby," I moan, loving the hint of pain.

"I didn't say stop, did I?" He grins down at me. "We'll just have to save it for another time. Just know that the longer we wait, you and me, the quicker it'll likely be over." Standing back from me, he squeezes himself through his joggers, giving me the perfect view of his outline, before turning his back to me. He lifts his t-shirt off over his head, offering me a full view of the piece of art that covers every inch of his back.

Fuck.

He looks over his shoulder at me with a cocky grin, and starts dishing the food out like he didn't just set my pussy on fire. Fucking Acehole.

A knock sounds from the front door, and Parker calls

that he'll grab it, while I just sit here and do nothing apparently. A girl could get used to this.

"Good morning, Sakura," I hear as soon as Kai steps through into the kitchen, Oscar hot on his tail.

"Hey, baby girl."

"Hey handsome, hey big mouth," I say in return with a smirk. A weird emotion settling over me at us all being together, in this happy kind of bubble.

Oscar charges past Kai, rolling his eyes at me as he pushes my cheeks together and slaps his lips against mine. Stepping back with a grin, he takes the seat beside me as Kai kisses my temple.

Parker steps in with another kitchen chair, which he must have grabbed from Roman's room. It doesn't match the rest of the set and it makes me smile, the dark wooden back standing out against my chic white chairs. Placing it at the table, he brings over a cup of hot black coffee while Roman puts a plate of bacon and eggs in front of me. It smells so good. I murmur my thanks, as the pair fill the table with coffee and food for everyone else.

We all sit in comfortable silence as we eat our breakfast, just happy to be in each other's company. I'm glad to have this moment with them, with everything that has happened in the past twenty-four hours.

When I finish eating, I sit with my cup in my hands, eyes closed and face lifted up to the ceiling. I could really do with pulling out my yoga mat. It's vital I train in the gym and with my weapons, but I could do with a relaxing session of yoga to help ground me some more.

"What's on your mind, Sakura?"

A small smile takes over my lips at the sound of the nickname he gave me the first day we met. I can't even understand why he had me tattoo my moon along with his own and his sister's, but I know I need to delve into that a little deeper at some point.

Releasing a deep breath, I tilt my head toward him directly across from me.

"I'm just thinking I could do with some yoga to try and relax my body and mind a little." The smile he offers in return fills me with warmth.

"I love yoga. I think we could get Parker involved, but alpha Roman and macho man Oscar are less likely." I can't help but chuckle at his choice of names for them. I glance at Oscar beside me who is pointing a piece of bacon around at everyone.

"I can do yoga, you say the word and I'll be there, baby

girl. You know how flexible I am." He gives me a wink before stuffing the bacon in his mouth. Parker is sitting next to Kai, and is already nodding in agreement with the plan to do some yoga. Looking to Roman, sitting on the chair from his room at the end of the table, I'm surprised to see him with a shit eating grin on his face.

"Princess, I'm there. Even if it's just to see your downward dog position."

I reach my arm out to hit his chest, but he grips my arm before I can. Prepared for the attack he knew was coming. His mouth comes down on mine in a quick and punishing move as a knock sounds from the door.

Reluctantly pulling away, I check the time on my watch. It'll be Trudy. Parker is already up and heading for the door before I can say anything. Roman keeps his hold on my arm as Oscar squeezes my thigh under the table.

"Are you sure it's a good idea letting her into your personal space, princess?"

"It's the only space I have that I have full control over," I answer, which has the three of them nod in agreement.

"Okay then. Let the planning commence," Oscar adds, rubbing his hands together.

God, please give me strength to deal with these crazy

Aceholes.

Roman

Damn, we may have the world against us, but after her chat with Rafe yesterday, my princess seems just a little bit lighter. There's a little more sparkle in her eyes, and her smile comes just that much quicker every time.

She goes to start gathering the dishes from the table, but Oscar beats her to it. Parker steps into the kitchen with Trudy and Aiden following behind. I can't control the growl at the sight of this asshole. I haven't seen this little shit since the party when he touched my girl. I want to pin him to the wall by his throat.

"Woah, big boy. No need to get growly, I was just testing your attachment to our pretty little Luna, that's all." He waves his hands up in surrender, the grin and waggle of his eyebrows only riles me up more, and he fucking knows it.

I go to step toward him, but Luna is up out of her seat and standing in front of me in a flash. Her hand is pressed firmly against my chest to stop me from going any further. I can hear Trudy telling her brother to shut the fuck up, but I'm lost in Luna's bright green eyes.

My heart is pounding in my chest and I have the urge to hit something, preferably him. Luna steps in closer, bringing her body flush to mine as she wraps her hands around my neck. My hands instantly find her waist, gripping tight.

"Baby, we need this to work. If he's still an annoying little prick to you when this is all over, you can beat the shit out of him then, just not now. Okay?" Her words are spoken softly to me, but it's likely everyone can hear her. From the second she calls me baby, I know I'm done for.

Squeezing her hips even tighter, I lean down and claim her mouth. She takes the brutality of my lips against hers, letting me claim her like my body screams too. I really need that alone time with my princess, and I need it soon.

Finally releasing her lips, she turns to greet our guests, a little flushed from the little taster I just gave her. My hands remain on her waist as she rests her back to my front.

"Thanks for coming, Trudy. We'll go into the lounge where there's more space. Aiden?" Hearing his name come from her lips spikes my anger again, until she continues.

"Don't poke the fucking bear, okay? I have way too much shit going on for you to add to it."

I fucking love being on a team with this girl.

Taking her hand, I lead us past everyone and into the lounge. I can hear Oscar grunt something at Aiden too, while Parker and Kai observe everything. That's not my priority right now. Sitting in the corner of the sofa with the best view of the room and outside, I pull Luna down onto my lap. I prepare for her to put up a fight, but she doesn't. Instead she settles in against me, as her left hand finds mine against the arm rest, and she threads our fingers together.

I give my fingers a gentle squeeze against hers, and she turns to offer me a soft smile. Parker takes the seat beside us, with Oscar on his other side, as Kai sits with Trudy and Aiden. Likely for the best, little prick.

"So, now my brother has got being a dickhead out of the way, shall we discuss what it is you need me for?" Yes Trudy, straight to the point, and the fact she knows her brother is a dickhead only makes me like her more.

"I hear you throw quite the Halloween party," Luna says, looking at Trudy who nods in response.

"It's my best party of the year, the big money maker.

What do you have in mind?" I can see Aiden wanting to jump into the conversation, but somehow he keeps his mouth shut.

"I basically need an event big enough to cause a distraction, and a space where I can hold someone for a little while." Trudy thinks on Luna's words for a moment, tapping her hands on her thighs as she does.

"In the orgy tent, I always have separate spaces set up for those who may want to get a little kinkier. I could hold one of those back for you?"

"That would be perfect. On the day, when you have everything set up, are you okay with me coming to do a walk through?" Luna asks, leaning forward slightly on my lap. I see Parker look at me from the corner of my eye, and he's smirking. Likely knowing what her little movements are doing to me.

"Of course, whatever you need, Luna."

"Are you not going to ask why?" Oscar blurts out, actually asking a reasonable question for once.

"There's no reason to ask why. If Luna wants me to know, she'll tell me. I owe her everything. If we'd been placed on Tyler's side of The Pyramid neither of us would be sitting here right now." Her mention of The Pyramid has everyone sitting in silence for a moment, reliving that eventful day. Luna is finally the one to break the silence.

"I'll need to have a few supplies at hand so I'll bring them over with me on the walk through," Luna says, not giving anymore away. Standing from my lap, Luna walks over to Trudy, who rises from the sofa too.

"I'm making a move against Brett, the asshole who touched me at the party," Luna's words confuse the hell out of me yet I manage to school my features. "I need to make sure I can get him there. Does he always show up at your parties?" I'd love to kill that fucker, but that's not what this is about, is it?

"He always shows," Aiden answers, and Luna nods.

"Perfect, the rest I can take care of while I'm there." Glancing at her watch, she speeds things along. "Thank you for coming over, I really appreciate your help with this."

Aiden stands from the sofa at the same time Kai does.

"Let me show you guys out," Kai murmurs, leading the way to the door.

"See you around, Luna pie," Aiden shouts as he steps out of the door, a wide grin on his face as he blows a kiss to Luna, and I want to punch him into next week. Parker has a hand on my thigh before I can stand, and they're out of sight with Kai shutting the door behind them.

"Why did you say this is about Brett, baby girl? And how do you even know his name?" Oscar asks, the question playing on my mind too, but it's Kai that answers.

"She's testing her, right?" he asks, looking to Luna who nods. "You want to see if she can be trusted and will keep her word." Luna smiles up at him as she stands in front of him, still over by the door.

"Ten out of ten for my handsome," she murmurs as she tips her head back for him to kiss her, which he does without question.

"So how do we get Wren into the orgy tent?" Parker asks, resting his chin on his laced hands.

"Roman," Oscar murmurs.

What? Feeling everyone's eyes on me I look to each of them, trying to find the question they're asking, and that's when it hits me.

"No. Hell no. Forget it." They can fuck right off. I couldn't stand the bitch to begin with, but I hate her even more now after what happened to my girl. "You can't be fucking serious!" I rest my gaze on Luna, who looks torn.

"Oscar makes a very good point, except I don't think I

can cope with her hands all over what's mine. I saw enough of it before this was really a thing between us, but now? No fucking way." Shit, the slight tremble in her voice has my dick hard. I love that she doesn't want anyone else touching me, except Parker of course.

"It wouldn't need to be like that, baby girl. Think about it. All Roman would have to do is approach her at the party and offer to take her somewhere private. We all know she'd jump at the chance in a heartbeat. He could lead her to the room you have set up, end of story," Oscar says, holding his hand out to her.

"That actually makes a lot of sense, and would work too easily," Parker adds, which does nothing to help me out here.

Luna places her hand in Oscar's as Kai moves around the coffee table, but everyone's eyes are on me. Luna sighs.

"Could we make it a two for one? Roman and Oscar maybe? I know it would only be a few minutes, but I think it would be better to double up. Then if she touches either of you, I'll torture the shit out of her even more," Luna adds with a slight smile at the thought. I release a heavy sigh. Oscar nods in agreement, so that's settled then.

"Fine, but you all owe me for this," I grunt, and

everyone nods in agreement. "Luna, you better get those pretty lips of yours on mine before I change my mind."

She throws herself at me, her mouth against mine as I forget everything, only knowing the taste of her lips.

YOUR BLOODLINE

TWENTY FOUR

Luna

Wren doesn't show her face at the Academy until Thursday morning. Walking out to the Rolls, this bitch is standing waiting for us with a smug ass look on her face. I want to chop her fingers off one at a time for invading my space.

It's a dull day with the sky filled with grey clouds, and it's too early in the morning to be dealing with her shit. Wren's got her little gang around her, including Becky, and they're standing by the fountain. She's in front, of course, always thinking she's a leader, with her little followers happily standing in her shadow.

This time, they're not trying to draw the whole damn Academy's attention to us. Wren seems quite happy to just stand and smirk. Clearly no one has told her we know about the cameras. Fucking idiot.

I need this Halloween party to roll around quicker. A week from Saturday, I'm on major countdown. I have plenty to do before then, but I'm ready to knock this bitch the fuck out. I want to know why they chose to break into my room and help Veronica, and I want to make her scream while I force her to crack.

Maintaining my resting bitch face, I stare her down as I step into the car with Oscar behind me.

"I fucking hate how bad her face smells," he grumbles, sitting beside me.

What? That doesn't make any sense. I glance at him in complete confusion, but the waggle of his eyebrows tells me he knows he just messed with my brain.

This is not the calm and relaxed atmosphere it usually is with Kai, but I laugh at Oscar's crazy presence.

Since Red is in Ace, my little clan of Aceholes refuses to let us drive alone. Everytime we're all going to the same lesson, they take turns escorting us both. I appreciate the level of care for Red, but I don't need it for me. We have

Weaponry this morning, which means Red is still in her room, and one of the guys will have to ride with Wren.

Placing my bag at my feet and buckling myself in, I get comfortable for the short ride. Oscar grabs my hand and laces our fingers together on the arm rest between us as I watch the Academy grounds drift by us through the window.

The campus looks even prettier now the leaves are starting to cover the ground. The trees blow in the wind as the leaves deepen in color every day. When I get a spare minute, I want to get a good picture of it. The mixture of yellows, oranges and reds is mesmerizing.

"You know, this is the first time I've been your car buddy, baby girl."

His words catch me by surprise, and I swing my head back around to him. A soft smile plays on his lips as I rack my brain to tell him he's wrong, but I come up with nothing.

"Big mouth, I—"

His hand squeezes mine, cutting me off.

"Baby girl, we're badass bikers. I love riding my Suzie nearly as much as I like riding you," he says with a wink. I smack his arm, but he just grins at me.

"You and your big mouth," I say, trying to get him again, except he catches my arm and pulls me closer.

"Baby girl, I like it when you're feisty. How about you come kiss me? Give me a taste of that sweet gloss on your lips."

I don't have a chance to respond before his lips are on mine, devouring me. He doesn't release my hands, holding me in place as he takes what he wants from me. His calloused fingers drag against my skin as he increases the pressure of his lips against mine. When he sinks his teeth into my bottom lip, I'm a goner.

I feel like a true teenager in this moment, making out in the backseat of a car. I mean it's a Rolls, so not your standard car for the classic teenage experience, but amazing all the same.

I expect him to eventually let go of me so he can touch my body, yet he doesn't budge. Not until we hear a throat clearing, and feel the sun shining in through Oscar's open door. Ian stands patiently waiting for us to step out, while we take a moment to gather ourselves. I hadn't even realized the car had come to a stop.

"What is it with you Aceholes distracting me so easily?" I mutter to myself, but I don't miss the grin on Oscar's lips.

Oscar's blue eyes are blown as he looks me over, likely seeing the same as me.

"Baby girl, I love your lips all puffy like this," he murmurs, pressing his thumb against my swollen bottom lip. I nip at the pad of his thumb, making him groan. "Let's go, baby girl, before I have Ian drive us back."

Oscar steps out of the car first, holding his hand out for mine. My hand feeling small and delicate in his, as I purposely brush up against him, inhaling his scent as I do. He's so intoxicating. Whatever he uses, it fucking works.

"You're playing with fire, baby girl," he whispers in my ear, pressing his erection into my hip and stepping back. Acehole.

Following him toward the others, he strokes his thumb lazily over my knuckles. I enjoy this tender side of him. He's usually wearing his metaphorical armor, blocking everyone from seeing the guy underneath all the jokes.

"Are you ready for this weekend with Roman?" he asks, glancing down at me as we near the others.

"Yes, I'm a little nervous with how I'm supposed to convince a Special Agent to join Featherstone's corrupt lifestyle, but whatever it takes, right?" I say, using my own 'fake it till you make it' mantra.

"Whatever it takes," he responds with a smile.

"What are you two muttering about?" Roman asks, throwing his arm over my shoulder from the other side as we come to stop in front of my guys.

"We were talking about you, not to you, Rome. You need to slow your roll," Oscar answers, simply trying to get a rise out of him as always.

Roman goes to swing his arm at him around my back, but Oscar's quick to release my hand and jump out of the way. Shaking my head at their crazy, I smile at Parker and Kai as we make our way inside, past the handful of students standing around. I like that Weaponry is a small group for the class, but it does make me wonder what West does the rest of the time.

Before we move much further, West is heading toward us, smiling as he approaches.

"Hey, Luna. Do you guys have a minute?" I slow my pace as we make our way toward him. Trying to embrace the peacefulness before he spills whatever news he has. Stopping in front of him, I nod for him to continue.

"I have a file for you to analyze regarding The Games. From people's experiences, to unauthorized files and rumors currently circulating." He holds out a small memory stick for me to take, but I indicate for him to give it to Kai, which he does. "It's all on there. I wanted to mention that there seems to be a lot of hearsay this year. I've heard quite a few say that they're trying to move The Games from December to early November. I don't know how true that is, but it's important you know."

"Thanks, West. I really appreciate this." Looking at my guys, I brace myself for some complaining over my next words. "Guys, can you just give me a minute? I'll meet you inside once I'm done."

Kai, Parker and Oscar nod in consent, and slowly head for the entryway, glancing back at me to be sure. Roman still stands with his arm over my shoulder, not moving a muscle. I look up to Roman, but he's staring West down, who seems unfazed by Roman's grizzly side.

"Don't give me an excuse to bury you, West the Pest," he grunts, finally stepping toward the others. He stops at the doors, arms crossed and stares us down. Other students are unable to step around him to get in the building, but he pays them no mind, his sole focus on me. I roll my eyes at his alpha beast coming through right now, yet a little part of me is turned on by it. Okay a large part of me. At least he gave me the space I asked for, progress.

"You okay, Moon?" West asks, running a hand through his short brown hair.

Glancing around us, I take in our surroundings as I process what I actually want to say. The flower bed to my left draws me in with the different colored flowers planted in it. The large oak tree behind it has us standing in the shade, with the cool breeze blowing around us. Separately these little things are inconsequential, but together they help ground me.

"Yes. I, err. I finally remembered Rafe is my father," I murmur, watching the surprise take over his face.

"Luna, that's brilliant," he says, his voice full of enthusiasm. I can see he wants to reach out and hug me, but he refrains. "Does he know? He'll probably have a breakdown over it." I nod in response, and look into his deep brown eyes.

"He knows, we had an issue with Veronica this weekend, so he ended up here anyway."

"Thank you for telling me," he says with a heartwarming smile. He squeezes my shoulder, unable to stop himself from needing the contact.

"Rafe also told me his suspicions about Veronica and her connections." I never asked if West knew, but my gut tells me he does. The nod he offers confirms I'm right. "If you hear anything at all, I need to know, West."

"I swear, Luna, whatever you need, remember?"

"Thanks." I offer a small smile, feeling Roman's eyes burning holes into the side of my face. A part of me wants to stand here longer just to piss him off, because I do what I want. The other part of me doesn't want to add any unnecessary stress onto our plates right now.

With that in mind, I step back, making his hand drop from my shoulder before I make my way toward the entry. He stays by my side every step, even when we get to Roman.

"I've set up a separate zone for you guys today. I managed to get my hands on some of the newest weapons on the market. I thought they might end up being useful for you all."

"Thanks," Roman grunts. I can see the relief in his eyes that West is following through on his word, and helping us like he said he would. With just as much surprise from West that Roman has manners. Patting his shoulder, West heads into the main space, while Roman guides me toward the changing rooms.

"Do you need any help getting undressed, princess?"

Roman murmurs, pulling me in close against him.

"Not this time, baby, but soon. Real soon." Placing a quick kiss to his lips, I step back and head inside. Wren is the only other girl who has this class, and she doesn't seem to be here yet. Likely still back at the fountain pretending to be the Queen of Featherstone.

There are wooden benches around the changing room with clothes hooks lining the wall too, but I always store everything in one of the blue lockers in the corner. Throwing on my classic black tight shorts and loose fitted black t-shirt, I choose to leave my hair in a bun today. Making quick work of getting changed and locking my stuff away, I get out of there before Wren does show up.

My brain is going into overdrive wondering what is on the flash drive West gave us, but for now, my goal is to get trigger happy with these new weapons. Maybe Wren would like to be my target for practice? A girl can dream.

YOUR BLOODLINE

KC KEAN

TWENTY FIVE

Kai

The guns West gave us are impressive. They are completely made of plastic, so they will pass through any security detectors. Overall, they are accurate soft shooting but hard-hitting pistols. We were all impressed with how they handle, and West was happy for us to keep them.

We aren't keeping them in the secure lockers here or in the vaults. Instead, we're going to keep them in our rooms so we can grab them at any time. No serial numbers are imprinted, which makes them the perfect ghost weapon.

Combat is extra brutal today with Maverick putting us

through our paces, but it'll be worth it to be in top form for when The Games come around. I sparred with Parker, who is getting much better with his left hook, while Roman was the only one willing to brawl with our girl.

I couldn't do it, spar with her. Yet the appreciation in her eyes when Roman does, shows how important that is to their dynamic. Oscar was running moves with some guy from Diamond, but it was just him showing off in front of Luna the whole time. Not that she didn't enjoy it, because the way she watched his every move told me she did.

After a quick shower, I take a seat in the back of the Rolls with Roman. I definitely miss being the only one who got to ride with my Sakura.

"Do you want to go through these files together?" I ask, twirling the stick in my hand.

"Yes, will it be easy enough to do in Luna's apartment or do we need to be in yours?"

"Luna's will be fine. I'll need to grab a few things from my room, but we should be good. Any reason why Luna's room specifically?" I question curiously, because it would usually always be Roman's room we gathered in.

"No real reason, I just like being in her space. Besides, she's most comfortable in her own room and my princess has enough to deal with. So, she should be able to relax when she can." He continues to stare out of the window as he says it out loud, but I'm impressed by his observation.

"I told her about Mia."

That catches his attention, and has his head whipping around to meet my gaze.

"You told her about your sister? When?" Roman looks surprised, although he shouldn't be. We're all trusting in her more and more each day.

"When we were at the garden on Sunday, before Veronica showed up," I sigh, frustrated by the families we are forced to deal with. I love my mother very much, but more for the person she was not the person she is now.

"Are you okay?" he asks, trying to soften his voice to offer me comfort, but it just makes me smile at his efforts.

"Yeah, the goal is to still take over my father's place in The Ring so I can find Mia. I need to get through The Games so I can get on with it."

"Did you tell her that part?" he asks, but I shake my head.

"No, Rafe was calling about Veronica, but she did say she would help me find her no matter what it takes. I believe her, besides, we all know if we survive The Games this is what is expected of us, right? To continue running our bloodline's specific skill sets, while holding a seat at the table for The Ring." He's quiet for a moment as he considers my words.

"I'm not sure she does, Kai. You have to remember, Luna wasn't a part of this life for a long time, and when she was, she doesn't remember anything from it. Plus, she was only a child then. I feel like we need to gauge how much she does know." The car pulls to a stop outside of Ace, but before we climb out Roman continues, "Sooner rather than later though. I hate her not knowing how this place fucking works."

I couldn't agree more. Stepping out of the Rolls, only Parker and Luna are waiting for us. Roman throws his arm around her shoulders as we step inside.

"Where are the brats?" he asks, leading us to the elevator.

"Oscar walked Jess back to her room, she said she wasn't feeling very well. To be honest, she did seem flustered all morning and her face was blotchy. I think we need to keep an eye on her," Luna says, concern written on her face.

Stepping into the elevator, I press for my floor and

Luna's. "I'm just going to grab a few of my devices, and I'll be up for us to go through this file West gave us, okay?"

"Thank you, handsome," she murmurs, offering me a soft smile. I love it when she calls me that. I hope this is what she feels like when I call her Sakura. Warm on the inside, like I'm actually living again. After Mia was taken, I completely shut down, numb to everything around me. Until now.

The elevator stops on my floor, and as I go to step out, Oscar is there ready to step in.

"Perfect timing," he says with a smile as we trade places.

"I'll be up in a minute, guys," I say over my shoulder as I rush to grab what I need.

Letting myself into my room I do a quick check of my security system. I have access to it from my phone, but I can't help but double check the actual system every time I step in. I make sure the footage hasn't stopped at any time and not been tampered with. When I'm satisfied everything is okay, I step into my room, pulling a duffel bag from my walk-in wardrobe. I quickly grab my personal laptops and a few connectors so I can link everything up, and I'm good to go.

Happy I have everything, I step outside just as Jess' door slams shut. I consider knocking but decide against it if she doesn't feel well.

Choosing to take the stairs up to the top floor, I knock on Luna's door and Parker lets me in. The smell of coffee fills the air as I step in to see Roman has Luna wrapped in his arms in front of the floor-length windows. I don't know what they're murmuring to each other, but they definitely need to fuck already.

Oscar walks in from the kitchen holding cups of coffee, and he whistles, cutting through the sexual tension growing around the pair by the window. The heat those two have is like a fireball surrounding them. Usually two people who are so alike would be awful for each other, but as much as they butt heads, there is a tenderness still between them. In the way she strokes his arm, and the sparkle that always appears in Roman's eyes when she's near.

"Okay, love birds, let's go through all this stuff relating to The Games, shall we? You've got plenty of time for foreplay later." Luna rolls her eyes at him as Roman glares.

"Before that, I want to show you guys something," I say, finally building up the courage to share something personal. When I start to undo my shirt, Luna instantly understands and smiles at me shyly.

"Yes, Kai. Any excuse to get naked and I'm involved," Oscar nods enthusiastically, as he too starts to undo the buttons of his shirt.

He stops the instant he sees what I'm trying to show them. All of the guys drift toward me as they look at my new tattoo, courtesy of Luna. She still hasn't said anything about it, but I'm sure she will eventually.

"Holy shit, did Luna do this?" Roman asks, as he leans in close.

"Yeah. They are the moons from when I was born," I say pointing to the one in the middle. "Mia's moon, and Luna's." I point to the left and the right in time with my words and everyone continues to stare.

I lift my eyes back to Luna who has little pink rosy cheeks. I offer her a gentle smile, not wanting to throw everyone's attention at her, but it seems she has it anyway.

"You did a brilliant job, angel," Parker mutters, kissing her pink cheeks before he sits back down. The perfect response, seeing as she's still not fully processed that it represents her.

I can see a cheeky glint in Oscar's eyes as he prepares to say something to her, but Roman must catch it too. He smacks him around the back of the head before anything can leave his mouth.

"Ow, Rome. Stop fucking doing that," he shouts, rubbing the marked spot.

I take a seat on the sofa, and start to set up my three laptops on the coffee table and download the file from West. The conversation ends there, and everyone is happy to sit in comfortable silence as I get to work, while they relax on the sofas around me. Luna presses a soft kiss to my temple, before sitting in between Oscar and Roman on the other sofa.

"Is it time for food yet? I'm starving," Parker moans, flopping down beside me on the sofa.

"Why don't we order something? It'll take a little while for it to be brought up," Luna offers.

"Pizza," Oscar says, not a question but a statement. He pulls his phone out and walks into the kitchen to call it in.

"How's everything looking?" Roman asks as I type away on my laptop.

"Good, just a second and it'll be up," I murmur, distracted by what I'm doing.

Parker leans in, trying to watch over my shoulder. His tech skills are good, but he's always trying to be better.

"Pizza's ordered. You suckers will get what you're given," Oscar calls walking back in, as Luna's tv screen fills with the main file. Spreading my laptops out a little wider, I separate the file between all the screens so we can dissect this a little easier.

Splitting the files into categories, I send each one to a different device.

"Okay, we've got four sections: experiences, academic knowledge, unauthorized documents and rumors. We'll get it done faster if we all focus on different categories, pull out the main points and then collate together." I glance around at the others who all nod in agreement. "Perfect, I'll take the unauthorized files, Parker can take the rumors and Luna the experiences. That leaves the academic files for Oscar and Roman, because there is a ridiculous amount."

"Do you want me to get my laptop so we each have a device?" Luna questions, standing to her feet and swiping her hands down her skirt. "I could do with getting changed while I'm at it too."

"Yes please, Sakura." I smile and she rushes off to grab her things.

"What are we expecting to find here?" Oscar murmurs, glancing at the screen in front of him.

"I don't really know, hopefully a heads up for what to expect from The Games. Especially, if they do move it up like West mentioned," Roman grumbles in response.

"Send anything that stands out to my encrypted email address, then we can look at it all together once we've sifted through it all," I say, as Luna steps back into the room, wearing a loose pair of grey shorts and a black t-shirt with fluffy socks. Stunning as always. It seems I'm not the only one to notice either, as we all sit gawking at her.

Luckily, my Sakura is confident as hell and doesn't falter at holding all of our attention. Looking at her hands, I'm surprised by the laptop she's carrying.

"That's not your usual laptop," I say, pointing to the one in her hand.

"Err, no. This is my personal one that I brought with me. The other I bought here, it's not safe for me to carry this one everywhere," she mutters, and I nod in understanding.

"Let's get started then, shall we?" I smile up at her, ready to get sucked in.

We all get comfortable and start digging through the files. It's tedious but we power through. Working in silence, and all focused on what we are doing, it doesn't take as long as I expect. The occasional grunt from Roman when he's reading something he's not impressed with is all that fills the room. Apart from Parker shuffling to readjust where he's sitting. Even Oscar hasn't complained once... yet.

I finish organizing the unauthorized files as a knock sounds at the door.

"I'll get it, I've finished anyway," I mutter, letting everyone continue with what they're doing.

Thomas stands on the other side of the door holding eight large pizza boxes. This is what we get for letting Oscar order. Thanking him, I take them out of his hands and shut the door behind me.

"Done!" Luna shouts, before standing to her feet and stalking toward me. "Now, feed me." She smiles, rubbing her hands together.

"Where do you want to start? Oscar ordered eight," I say with wide eyes, and she chuckles.

"Of course I did, we're growing boys, Kai," he adds from the coffee table, without lifting his eyes from the screen. "Two more minutes and I'll be done."

"That's what she said!" Roman hollers, not lifting his gaze from the monitor, catching us all by surprise and making us chuckle. I can tell he's pleased with the little outburst by the grin on his face.

Luna swipes the top few boxes out of my hands and carries them over to where the others are sitting. She makes space for the pizzas on the floor as all the tech takes up the coffee table. I take the other side of the space doing the same.

As she leans to place a box down beside Roman, he surprises her by pulling her down onto his lap, making her squeal and gaining our attention. Wrapping his arms around her waist, he just holds her against him for a minute. I know that feeling, of just wanting her close.

"Baby, let's eat," she barely whispers, as he peppers kisses along her neck, closing her eyes with the sensation. I can't stop staring, hot for my Sakura. I love being able to see her emotions on her face, when she hides them so well from the rest of the world.

Roman releases his tight hold around her, squeezing her hips for a moment before placing her back on her feet.

"You're a damn temptation, princess," he grumbles, picking the closest pizza box and chowing down without even looking at what flavor it is. "Who the fuck put pineapple on this pizza?" The disgust on his face has us all laughing, as Luna swipes the slice from his hands and starts to eat it. He quickly grabs another box and checks the content this time.

"Meat feast is my favorite, but I love me some hawaiian from time to time," she giggles, as Roman glares at her.

"You better mean the pizza, and not some guy," Roman grunts and she shakes her head, laughing harder at his response.

"Shall we eat and chat? My eyes are tired from all that," she says, calming down and yawning lightly as she settles back beside him.

"Yes of course, are you nearly finished, Parker?" I ask, glancing his way.

"Yes, I'll just send this last one now. Done. Now feed me too," he groans, stretching his arms above his head. Lightning fast, Oscar holds an open pizza box out to him, which he appreciatively takes.

"Okay, from the unauthorized files, I know that there are numerous trials that are a part of The Games, but only three will be selected. We can enter them together and work as a team, but some may enter alone." I glance at Luna, wanting to hear her choice. I know we're together, but she's mentioned being a lone ranger a time or two. I want to make sure we're all on the same page.

"Together," she says with a soft smile, understanding my silent question. I release the breath I didn't realize I was holding as I see the guys do too. Nodding, I continue.

"It doesn't state anywhere the location this all takes place," I say, flicking between a few tabs on my screen. Finally taking a minute to inhale some pizza, I take a break from the screen.

"From what the experiences say, you are blindfolded until you are on the property. Apparently they'll take us just like they did Red for The Pyramid," I mutter, hating the pain it puts on Luna's face at the mention of it.

"Everyone describes it as an old country estate. The land it sits on must be massive because everything is set up and takes place within the grounds," Luna adds, before grabbing another slice of pizza.

"Great, that's important to know. It looks as though it's spread out over five days, but nothing is mentioned about the duration of each trial or what happens in between, if anything," I continue to explain.

"The main trials mentioned are the Gas Chamber, the Shooting Range, The Maze, and The Slums. These are the ones people have experienced, but their recollections are a little varied," Luna adds, glancing around us all.

"So they're the same premise but adjusted occasionally to adapt to modernization," Roman says, and I nod in agreement. That sounds about right to me.

"Yeah, because it's definitely twenty-first century shit we're dealing with here," Oscar grunts, and I couldn't agree more. This whole thing is based on family agreements from years ago, and we have no choice but to participate for a chance at survival.

"I also found a few rumors mentioning something called The Static. There are no details surrounding it, but it's something to bear in mind," Parker adds, sitting on the floor with the laptop on the coffee table and the pizza box in his hands.

"Nearly every rumor mentions November too, but nobody seems to know why," Roman says, scrubbing a hand through his hair, sending the usually tamed strands all over the place. We like all the details, and as much as we are picking up new information, it's not the whole picture like we'd prefer.

"So, we're going to be blindfolded and taken, by surprise, to an unknown location, where we'll then spend the next five days competing in three trials as a group. Trials that we must survive or face death, and we may be dealing with this much sooner than expected," Luna summarizes, ticking each one off on her fingers, sadly hitting the nail on the head.

"Pretty much," Oscar says, staring down at the pizza box in his lap. Shit, this is hard for all of us, but most of all Oscar.

Luna must be able to sense the sadness wash over the room, as she looks around us settling her eyes on Oscar.

"What don't I know?" she quietly asks, not really wanting to pry but needing to understand his pain.

Clearing his throat and trying to slip back into party boy mode, he smiles at her across the table.

"My two older brothers died in The Games, baby girl."

"God, Oscar I'm so—" He stops her with a wave of his hand.

"Fuck pity, I don't need any of that. It's in the past, we're all good now." Stuffing a slice of pizza in his mouth, he brings the conversation to a halt.

I glance at Luna who is looking at him with pain in her eyes. I'm not sure if it's because of what he's dealing with, or because he just dismissed her so easily. Shaking her head, she stands to her feet. Looking down at the ground, hands on her hips, she responds to him.

"I don't pity you, Oscar O'Shay. I was six years old when my father was killed in front of me, so bad my brain refuses to remember the details. Speaking with Rafe last weekend, I've come to learn that my father's body was taken from the scene and my mother's phone was left behind." She sighs, lifting her gaze to him. "I know pain, Oscar, and I know we're never all good after loss like this. I'm here to talk when you're ready, okay?"

I look at her in awe. She didn't push him, pity him or tell him how he should feel. There is a lot of loss in this room. My sister, Oscar's brothers, Luna's father, even Parker's mother to some degree. We all deal with things in different ways, but she is right, the pain never truly leaves.

Taking my eyes off her to glance at Oscar, I see the appreciation in his eyes. Rising to his feet, he strolls over, wrapping her in his arms.

"Thank you, baby girl."

She hugs him back and the rest of us sit in silence, giving them their moment. Like magnets they lean into each other, their mouths connecting effortlessly. I can see him pour his feelings into her, his actions speak volumes without using any words, the gratitude in every brush of their lips.

Slowly stepping back, he lets her take a seat and throws himself down beside her. She stifles a yawn again, which Roman and Oscar notice. Oscar turns slightly and pulls her toward him, leaning her against his chest, which she does willingly. Roman lifts her legs onto his lap, and she doesn't complain, allowing them to position her while she relaxes.

"From the unauthorized files, I was also able to compile a list of recommended weapons. We should be able to get them from the vaults," I say, wanting to make sure we discuss everything.

Luna hums in response. "I don't know about you guys, but I can get us plenty of access to weapons from the Gibbs vault. If you print the list out, I could go down on Saturday to see what could be useful. From what their experiences said, they weren't given time to go to the vaults, only being able to take weapons they had in their room."

"I'll go with you, princess. We can go before or after we meet the agent, whatever suits you," Roman offers, and she smiles lightly as she rests her eyes.

"Great, then on Sunday I'm meeting my grandmother. It's about time, as I haven't seen her since Washington, and she might be able to add anything we've missed," she says, not opening her eyes and her voice getting softer.

Nobody responds as we all sit and stare at her. Oscar strokes his hand through her hair as we all watch her drift off.

"She's working herself too hard," I whisper, not wanting to disturb her.

"You're right. Between classes, the additional training and the mind-blowing revelations coming out of nowhere, she hasn't really had time to rest," Roman adds, staring down at her now sleeping form.

"While she's sleeping, now might be the time to tell you about what she asked me on the car ride over." Parker whispers, gaining our attention.

KC KEAN

TWENTY SIX

Roman

Saturday morning is finally here, and as I check myself over in the bathroom mirror, I quickly spray some aftershave and I'm ready to go. Wearing my tight black jeans and a plain black t-shirt with my combat boots, I look like a bodyguard or a bouncer, depending on who you ask. I somehow convinced Luna that we should all go with her and watch from the car when she meets with the agent, but we're heading to the vaults first.

The agent always goes to the same coffee house on Saturday afternoons and we agreed that was the best place to catch him off guard. Running my fingers through my hair, I sweep it to the side, leaving the gel out for today because I'll be wearing a cap later.

Stepping into the lounge, Parker is sitting back relaxing on the sofa in just his boxer shorts. His hair is all messy and he has a cup of coffee in his hands, watching some program about the devil. He hears my footsteps approach and looks at me with a smile.

"You shouldn't look so good in black, Mr. Rivera," he says, and I roll my eyes. "What? You know it's true, even Luna agrees." Does she? Good to know.

"I'm ready to head out. I don't know how long we'll be, but we'll bring the weapons back and split them between the rooms like we mentioned. Then we can leave to meet the agent." He nods in agreement and shoos me away.

"Go, the thought of you and Luna has my morning wood back, and I need to relieve myself in peace," he says with a grin, and I chuckle at him. He was never this confident in himself before Luna arrived, and even less sure of himself when we first met.

"You can picture me sucking you dry as Luna rides your face," I call out with a grin as I open the front door. The groan I hear in response is what I was going for, and I shut the door behind me.

I take a second to adjust myself, the visual runs through my mind too. As much as Parker and I would mess around together occasionally, our want for Luna has filled that hole. She's our main focus, but I love the fact that she likes to watch us. Not afraid to let us be who we want to be and explore our sexuality together, including Oscar too apparently. I can see the curiosity in his eyes, ever since his dick rubbed against Parker's when they both fucked our girl at the same time.

Knocking on her door, it takes a moment for her to answer, and when she does I'm left speechless, staring at her beauty as always. Her hair is thrown up in a messy bun at the top of her head, with loose pieces floating around her face. She's wearing denim skinny jeans with a loose fitted Rolling Stones tee and combat boots too. Her makeup is done, there's some black liner stuff around her eyes and her lips are painted red.

Hot. As. Fuck.

"Hey, baby. Are you ready to head out straight away?" she asks, rolling two small cases into view. They must be empty for us to use to bring the weapons back. I nod in response, and she raises her eyebrows at me.

I clear my throat and shake my head. "Hey princess,

you look gorgeous as always," I mutter, finally finding my voice. I grab the handles of the suitcases, pulling them toward me as a sign I'm good to go, and she locks up.

Moving the cases together in one hand, I hold the other out for her to take, which she does. It always warms me when I feel her delicate fingers in mine. She makes me sappy as shit.

"You okay?" she asks, as we step into the elevator and the doors close.

"I am, are you?" I look down at her as she squeezes my hand staring back at me.

"Yeah, I'll be better once I've figured out the agent, but for now I'm good." I love that she answers honestly, letting me see past the mask she always wears.

"It'll all be fine, princess, don't worry."

The elevator dings and we step into the lobby, Thomas offering a small smile in passing as we make our way outside to the waiting Rolls. It's Ian. I like how Luna has made a bond with this guy. He's willing to help her however she needs, and is the only guy outside of our group I'm not jealous of being close to her.

I throw the empty cases into the locked compartments in the trunk as Luna climbs in. When I join her, she's tapping away on her phone.

"Sorry, my grandmother was just reconfirming tomorrow," she says, pocketing her phone as she smiles at me.

"You don't have to explain to me," I respond, shaking my head. Lacing my fingers with hers, I bring her knuckles to my lips, her eyes tracking my every movement. When they are just a breath away, I show my teeth and bite them instead of kissing them like she expected.

The gasp that passes her lips makes me grin, and her eyes darken as she looks me over.

"We need to do something about this sexual tension, princess. Before my dick falls off from a severe case of blue balls." She smiles back at me, the seductive glint to her lips coming naturally.

"I agree. I wouldn't want anything to happen to your big cock because of me," she murmurs huskily in response, as her eyes trail down to where my dick is trapped against the inside of my jeans. Her other hand slowly starts moving to the spot she's staring at, when the Rolls pulls up outside the entry to the vaults, stopping her hand and ruining the moment.

Damn it, Ian. Does he not know what I'm dealing with

here? Luna grins at me knowingly as she steps out of the Rolls. Following behind her, I grab the suitcases while the first security guard checks her over.

"Swipe your hands any higher up the inside of her leg and I'll fucking chop them off," I growl murderously at the bastard who quickly steps away from her.

"Baby, he's just trying to do his job," Luna mutters, glancing over her shoulder at me as the guard steps inside the building.

"His fucking job is not to touch my girl," I grunt stepping inside with Luna following behind me. There is another guard in here with the dick from outside, who is quick to step toward me.

"I apologize for the confusion, Mr. Rivera. It won't happen again," he says, a slight tremble to his voice.

"You better hope it doesn't." I glare at the idiots, wrapping my arm around Luna's shoulder and walking her to the vaults.

"Do you need any assistance—"

"Do I look like I need any fucking assistance?" My temper is shot, and he shuffles his feet nervously, unsure of what to do.

The elevator door opens, and we step in. I press the

button for the Ace floor and the door shuts before us.

"Have you calmed down now, Mr. Alpha?" Luna asks, smirking at me from the corner of her eye.

"I'd be absolutely fine if people didn't touch what is mine," I grumble, swiping a hand down my face, but her smile just gets wider. Pulling her in with an arm around her shoulder fast, she giggles against my chest. "You're such a brat, princess." I grin against her head, and the door opens.

Ducking under my arm, she leads the way to the Gibbs Vault. Standing behind her as she swipes her keycard and the door opens, I'm stunned when all the weapons come into view.

"What the fuck?" I whisper, my eyes trying to take it all in at once. Stepping further into the room, I see the wall filled with blades too. "Holy shit, this is an assassin's wet dream, princess." Finally bringing my gaze to hers, I find her staring at me expectantly.

"How do you know that, baby?" she asks, curiosity in her tone but surprisingly no fear. Glancing around the vault, I try to find my words. When I can't think of anything to soften the blow, I blurt it out.

"Because that's my family skill. Well, that and business, but my father… my father is an assassin." My arms swing out to the side as I say it out loud to her, ready for the backlash, but all I get is silence. She stands looking at me with a new softness to her eyes, and the smallest dip of her lip.

"I feel like you're waiting for me to have a breakdown, to scream and shout at you," she murmurs, not moving from where she stands as she takes me in.

"I am."

"Is that what you want me to do, Roman?"

Releasing a heavy sigh, I shake my head, "No. No, I don't, Luna."

"Baby, do you need me to remind you what I did to Tyler? This is a very real game of survival. I'm never going to judge you for skills that are expected of you, just like I hope you don't base your opinion of me on mine," she breathes out, slowly walking toward me.

When she gets close enough, she slides her hands up my chest, bringing her body flush against mine.

"I don't want you to feel like you can't tell me these things, Roman." I nod in response, and I decide to rip the band aid off, remembering what Kai said the other day.

"We have to survive The Games to live, but the result of surviving is a place in The Ring. Unless there is an older sibling, then things fall a little differently." Wrapping my arms around her, I watch her reaction, but again she's not surprised.

"Juliana told me back in New York, when Rafe wouldn't. I understand that and I can deal with it, because, Roman? I'm going to tear these motherfuckers down, every single one of them that thrive in the darkness. To do that, it's best if I'm sitting at the top." The determination is vivid in her eyes and pulsing in every word she says.

"Whatever we have to do, princess. You know you have me, *us*." She nods and smiles up at me, squeezing me lightly on the shoulders before stepping back.

"Good, now let's get this shit done," she says with a wink, pulling the list out of her pocket. Laying it on the table in the middle of the room, she reads through it and starts scanning the rack.

Joining her, I set the suitcases on the table too, opened and ready to be filled. We work quietly and comfortably down the list, filling the cases up with a few of each weapon listed. From short blades, to handguns and assault rifles, this list can't be confused for groceries that's for sure. We're not far from being done, only a few more to search, when Luna breaks the silence.

"Check us out making a good team, we're getting this done quicker than I thought." I smile at her words.

"Damn right we make a good team, princess. I don't know what you expected," I say, raising my eyebrows at her, which just makes her grin wider.

"Well duh, I know. I'm just glad I'll have enough time to get changed into a different outfit and refresh my make-up before we head out to meet the agent."

I stand and stare at her as my brain short circuits at her words.

"What?" I ask, scrunching my face up in confusion.

"Err, I said I'll have enough time to get changed and freshen up my make-up. What's wrong?" She's just as confused with me as I am with her. She's standing on the other side of the table, closer to the blades while I'm near the guns. I brace my hands on the table as I stare her down, and try to rein myself in.

"Why the fuck do you need to get changed and touch up your make-up to see the agent, Luna?" I try to speak calmly, but it comes out as a growl. Her back goes up in defense instantly, her jaw tightening as she scowls at my tone.

"Roman, I need to be prepared to approach the agent

in any way possible. If that falls down to the clothes I'm wearing and the make-up on my face, then I need to be ready for that." She's failing at staying calm just as much as I am, her voice rising with every word.

"No fucking way, princess," I grunt, slamming my hand against the table, making the weapons rattle with the force. She fucking huffs at me as she shakes her head in irritation. Like I'm in the wrong.

"I'll do whatever I have to do, Roman, it's not up to you to decide," she spits back, as she turns to grab the next blade from the list, and storms over to put it in the case. Rushing around the table, I pull her arm back as she goes to get the next item. Fuck that. This needs to be discussed.

Trapping her between me and the table only makes her angrier, well fuck her.

"What exactly is 'whatever it takes', Luna? Hmm?" I sneer, feeling the tightness around my eyes as I try to not bare my teeth at her.

"Back off, Roman, if I have to show a little side boob and paint my lips red then I'll do it. I'm not going to let them kill me because I didn't complete my assignment," she hisses through her teeth at me. A pale pink flush creeping up her neck.

Fuck. A small part of me understands, and as much as I have a lot of control, there are certain things I can't intervene with. That doesn't mean she gets to offer herself up to any guy to survive.

"So when this agent catches a glimpse of you in your revealing clothes and red lips, only agreeing to your terms with a taste of your pussy. What are you going to do then?" I growl in her ear, and she scoffs back at me. "Would you use your sweet little body to get the agent to do what you desired?"

"That's not what I said, Rome," she tries to push against my chest, and look me in the face, but I don't budge.

"No, princess. Consider me intrigued. Please, tell me what you would do if Special Agent Dominic Bridge said, 'yes Miss Steele, whatever you wish, as long as I get a taste of your sweet sweet honey?'" Slipping my hand between us, I cup her core, not missing the slight moan she releases.

"It won't come to that," she whimpers, trying to lean back, but I grip my other arm around her back.

"But how do you know that? What if he takes one look at you and refuses to take no for an answer?" Lifting my hand from her denim clad heat, I run it under her t-shirt and grip around her ribs, just below her bare breasts. Fuck.

"Then I'd kill him, or you would, whoever had the clearest shot first. I don't want to use my body like that, Roman, but we both know I need to use whatever advantages I can. If I have to lower my standards a minute to stay alive, then I will."

Keeping my hand tightly gripping her rib, I bring the other around to tilt her chin back. Finally looking into her eyes, fire burns back at me.

"You think I'm going to let you step in there, showing him what belongs to me?"

"I'm not just yours, Roman, and I'm my own person first. Always," she grits out, her hands fisting against my chest.

"Clearly you need a reminder then." Her deep red lips tease me. Wetting my lips, I drop my hold on her and march to the door, slamming it shut and whirling back around to face her.

She hasn't moved an inch, still standing exactly where I left her watching after me. Her eyes are blazing and her chest heaves with each breath she takes. Good. I want to affect her as much as she affects me.

"Strip."

"Roman, I—"

"I said, strip."

She can't fucking lie to me. I can see the heat in her eyes mixed with the fire, and I'm done playing nice. I need to get this rage out of me, which is usually by sparring or sex, and I'm done with delayed gratification, so sex it is.

Looking around the room again, she eventually brings her eyes back to me, she can feel the sexual tension and my anger, and she wants it. The flair of her nostrils and her hands clenched at her sides, shows me how hard she's trying to fight my order.

Keeping her eyes trained on me, she turns her body toward the table. Lifting her combat boots up one at a time she unties the laces and kicks them off to the side. Turning her body toward me again, she unfastens the button on her jeans, and slowly slides them down her legs. I mean really, really slowly. My dick feels like it's going to burst from watching her teasing alone.

Stepping out of her jeans, she discards them without looking or caring where they go. I catch a glimpse of her bare pussy, not even a slight landing strip. Shit. I love it when my girl goes commando, but it still does little to calm my temper.

She pauses, looking at me, only her top left, and I stand and wait her out.

"Aren't you going to strip too?" she throws out. Clearly I'm not the only one mad here.

"Princess, this isn't my punishment," I smirk, and she lifts her eyebrow at me in surprise.

"If you think sex is punishment, maybe I should be naughty more often," she murmurs, but I don't answer her. She'll know the difference soon enough.

Sighing with an eye roll, she crosses her hands over her body, gripping the bottom of her t-shirt and pulling it over her head. There she is. My beautifully confident princess. Not afraid to stand in front of me with nothing covering her body.

"On your knees," I say, looking for the chair I spotted in the corner earlier. Not looking back, I grab it and turn to see she's still standing. I can't contain the huff that leaves my lips, but I don't say anything as I carry it over to where she stands.

Her eyes stay trained on mine as I brace my feet against the chair, undoing my combat boots just as she did. Not messing with my jeans like she did, I just drop them down my legs and step out. I can feel the heat from her stare, both of us getting pleasure from this crazy foreplay we've got going on.

Standing in front of her in my boxer shorts and black t-shirt, she raises her eyebrow at me, keen to see my next move. Sitting on the cheap metal folding chair I get comfortable right where I am. Leaning back a little, my erection is unmissable, the thick outline catching her attention.

Her hands clench at her sides in frustration. She wants me, but she doesn't want to do as I say. Deep down, really deep, a part of me loves this fight for power between us.

As I grip my cock through the thin fabric, a small whimper passes her lips, and it takes all that I have not to show my grin.

"We'll try again, princess," I grunt, "On. Your. Knees."

She still refuses to move but her eyes don't flicker away from between my legs. Deciding to give her more of a visual, I sneak my hand through the fly hole of my boxers and pull my dick free. She wets her lips as she continues to stare at my throbbing cock.

Out of nowhere, she slams to her knees in front of me.

I worry that she hurt herself on the concrete floor, but she doesn't even wince. Instead, she finds the strength to look up into my eyes.

"I can give you whatever control you need right now. I can let you punish me, but I'm warning you, don't get used to it." The fire burns brighter in her eyes with each word she says, making my cock pulse with excitement. I don't answer her statement, or even nod, I continue where we're at.

Reaching out, I wrap my fingers under her jaw, lifting her head back as my thumb pushes against the red paint on her lips.

"This lipstick is for me, and only me. Don't stand there and tell me you're wearing it for another man, no matter the circumstances. Do you understand?" I growl deep, my eyes blazing with the rage I'm finally unleashing.

She shakes her head frantically, ready to tell me she didn't mean it like that, but it won't change what I heard. She must see it in my eyes that it's not enough, stopping her movement to offer a single strong nod instead.

The grin that takes over my face is devilish, I know it.

"Good, now paint me red, Luna," I say, standing to my feet and feeding my cock to her mouth.

She instantly opens wide, eager to taste me. Her tongue licks her lips, ready to smear the lipstick all over my cock. The second my tip touches her tongue, I hiss at the contact, her hands resting against my thighs as she encourages more of me into her mouth.

I let her take me slowly at first, dragging her lips against every inch of me. A slight pink tinge rubs off in a few spots, but it's not enough. Raking my fingers through her bun, I release the hair tie, only to have another one underneath holding it in a ponytail. Perfect.

Wrapping my hand around her hair tight, I pull her head back to make her look up at me. Damn. Her puffy lips around my cock with her pretty green eyes wide with pleasure could make me cum from the sight alone. I hold her head in place, and she must see the question in my eyes as she releases me to murmur.

"Please."

Feeding myself back into her mouth, I don't pause, instead thrusting all the way in. She hums around my length which only adds to the pleasure. Slipping out, I push straight back in, making her deepthroat my cock. The moan she gives only adds to my pleasure. Not relenting I go again and again, fucking her mouth with a fraction of the anger I feel. Her hands run up the back of my thighs forcing me deeper, enough to make her eyes water, but she doesn't pause.

Scraping her teeth against my cock, I hiss in pleasure. Fuck me. My girl always likes to give me the illusion I'm in charge, but I'm not going to argue because I want her to do it again.

She tightens her grip on my thighs, holding me at the back of her throat for a moment, trying to test her own limits. My girl is always full of surprises. Swallowing around me, I nearly cum on the spot. Slowly pulling myself from her lips, nothing coats them anymore. Instead my cock has deep red smears marking it from root to tip, claiming me.

Pulling the back of my t-shirt up, I take it off and drop it to the ground, my boxer shorts swiftly following it. Her eyes burn trails all over my skin as she licks her lips.

"On your feet," I grunt, and she does as I ask the first time for a change. "Hands on the table."

"The rumble in your voice when you bark out these orders only makes me wetter you know," she taunts, doing exactly as I commanded. I grin at her words, but I don't respond, not wanting to get off track.

"Now spread your legs, princess. Nice and wide."

Just like that, she's on full display for me. Her fingers are spread wide on the table, her hair falling down her back, barely contained by the hair tie holding it together. The curve of her spine leading down to the globes of her ass sitting perfectly in the air for me. The strain in her calves and the tremble of her thighs only makes this sweeter.

Standing right behind her, I nestle my cock between her ass cheeks, and she pushes back with a moan. I shove the cases to the sides, giving us more space without knocking them off. Without warning I bring my hand down and smack my palm against the side of her left ass cheek. She jolts with the action but doesn't cry out in pain like I expect. Instead, her hands clench on the table as she pushes back for more.

Repeating the motion to her right side, she moans in pleasure this time. Stroking against the pink flesh, I repeat the motion again as she whimpers beneath me.

"Fuck, baby. Please," she cries, wanting more. That's my girl.

"You don't deserve my mouth on you this time, princess. I'll only devour you like that when you've earned it. I'm not impressed that your decisions came to this, because eating your pussy is my favorite pastime." I squeeze her hips tight, before stepping away to retrieve a condom from my wallet.

She doesn't utter a single word, but she tracks my movements from over her shoulder. Looking at what's in my hand she shakes her head.

"I'm on the shot, Roman. I've taken the others without condoms, I think it's about time you claimed me for real," she murmurs huskily, and I can't help but growl at the thought.

Fuck, I want that. I've never wanted that, but I do right now, with my Luna.

Tossing the condom to the floor, I step back into her space, pulling her hair to bring her body upright to mine so I can taste her lips. She lets my tongue explore her mouth from the awkward angle we're at, but my hips are pushing hers into the table so she can't turn.

"You're going to feel my true anger now, princess. You ready?" I ask against her lips, with her hair still tight around my fist and she attempts to nod. "Very well."

Pushing her back down to the table, I grip the back of her throat, holding her in place as I slowly enter her bare.

Holy. Fucking. Shit.

Sliding all the way in, I have to give myself a minute. No wonder she didn't complain at the no foreplay, because my girl is already dripping wet. The moan that passes her lips stretches out between us for what feels like forever.

Bringing my hands to her hips, I hold on tight as I slowly pull out and thrust back in. Hard. Her body drags against the table as her hands try to hold her up.

"More, baby. I need more," she groans out.

Never one to disappoint, I pull out and ram back in again and again, the brutal grip on her hips leaving fingerprints already. She tries to lift herself up again, so I let go of her hips and grip her wrists behind her back in one hand. The other coming down again and colliding with her already pink cheeks, as I slam into her.

Sweat glistens down her spine as her skin heats with the sexual need coursing through her veins. I continue to pound into her scorching core as her legs begin to tremble.

I want her to see my face when she orgasms.

Pulling her upright, I spin her in my arms and lift her up in the air, her legs wrapping around my waist. I go to move us closer to the wall, but her lips crash down on mine and I can't do both. Devouring her mouth, with my hands gripping her thighs I get lost in her. The feel of her fingers running through my hair and her nipples rubbing against my chest, only adding to the release I need.

When we finally part for air, I move us to the wall lined with old photographs near the door, slamming her against it. Taking her nipple into my mouth, she cries out in pleasure as I part her legs a little more and find my way home again. Her pussy clenching around my cock like a vice.

"Fuck, Luna," I grunt, tingles running through my body.

Holding her in place, I piston into her repeatedly as my movements start to stutter and her back arches. Her emerald green eyes catch mine and hold me captive. I don't remember a more intimate moment than this right here. Looking into her soul through her bright eyes as her body grinds against mine.

I see the moment she finds her ecstasy, her eyes barely remain open but stay glued to mine as she rides the waves. Her pussy squeezes around my cock and it's too much for me to take. My orgasm hits, starting in my toes and zapping through my whole body.

Pressing my forehead to hers we cum together, slowly dragging every gasp of pleasure from each other. As I hold her close to me, her hands cup my face, the delicate pads of her fingers stroking my cheeks.

"You're mine," I murmur, not moving a muscle as I wait for her response. She stares me down before finally offering a soft smile.

"And you're mine," she whispers, sealing it with a kiss to my lips.

I'll take that as a motherfucking win.

YOUR BLOODLINE

KC KEAN

TWENTY SEVEN

Luna

After splitting the weapons into duffel bags, Roman went to store them in each of the rooms while I got myself ready to leave. Each room now has blades and guns in all shapes and sizes in preparation for The Games. All except Parker's, we've kept his room empty. Understanding that his father could show up and get access to his room without question means we have to play this safe. We have added extra to the four remaining duffel bags to make sure we're covered.

I stash mine in my dresser beside the bag that sat waiting for me the first time I went to the vaults. The one with *Meu Tesouro* embroidered into it, which I've still not been able to bring myself to open.

After Roman's meltdown in the vaults, I try to meet him halfway with how I approach the agent. Keeping my jeans on, I switch my band tee for a white tank top that dips lower than usual. Kicking my combat boots off, I slip into a pair of sandals, and touch up my make-up, only applying gloss to my lips this time.

The image of my red lipstick smeared all over Roman's cock back at the vaults has my skin flushing and goosebumps trail up my arms. Fuck. The whole thing was so hot, even him forcing a little submission out of me. He better have believed me when I said it would be a rarity, but to see the burn in his eyes, I'd do it again.

I hadn't considered how my words would come across. I've never had to consider others before. I've also never had to do whatever it takes to corrupt someone either. I could see it in his eyes that he wanted to teach me a lesson, claim me, consume me, and I wanted to know what that felt like.

I took everything he asked, I gave him all of me. The peak of the intimacy was peering into his eyes as I climaxed around him. I want that feeling again, and again.

I can't put a name to the feeling that washed over me, but it was the difference between fucking for fun and fucking for feelings, that's for sure.

My fingers clawed into his back, his neck, anywhere they could grip as he powered into me against the wall. Small droplets of sweat beading along his brow line as he chased his orgasm too, he peered into my soul. Damn, I'll never be ready to leave if I don't stop replaying it through my mind on repeat.

"Are you almost ready, captain? The guys are here," Red calls from the lounge, kicking me into action.

"Coming," I shout back as I put everything away.

"Yeah, you were," Roman says from my bedroom door, catching me by surprise with a grin on his face.

The others must hear his comment, bickering between themselves that he got some of my candy, in Oscar's words. I don't hear anything else. I'm too busy watching Roman track his gaze up my body, his eyes stopping at my tank top and the peek of white lace showing underneath. His eyes darken as his fists clench at his sides.

"Baby, this is me compromising. Take it or leave it, but I'm not changing." My voice is firm as I walk toward him, stopping within an inch of his chest, making me have to tilt my head slightly to meet his stare.

His hand lifts to my breast, trailing a finger along the edge of the lace of my bra, as his eyes stay on mine.

"If I even catch him glimpsing at your perfect tits, I'll cut his eyeballs out," he grunts. His other hand finding my waist and holding tight.

These Aceholes are all leaving finger bruises along my hips and waist, and I'm not even sorry about it.

"Roman, looking isn't the issue, but if he tries to touch me, I'll kill him myself. Agreed?" I ask, lost in his bright blue eyes as he glares down at me. His hand cups my breast, as the other moves around to my ass and squeezes. His grip, forcing his knuckles white but my lust only kicks up a notch.

"Not agreed, princess. You're mine." Smashing his lips to mine with brutal force, he pulls away and steps back all too quickly. "Remember what we talked about? Don't make me go all assassin on your ass," he says before storming out of the room.

I have no idea if he's joking or not. My mind hopes so while my pussy wants to see him in action. Fuck me, she's an embarrassment. I glare down at myself, willing the sexual tension to go. Stupid lady parts.

"Let's go, baby girl. As hot as you look, I'm kind of on Team Roman with all this," Oscar says, peeking his head around the door and waving a finger up and down the length of me.

I roll my eyes at him as I walk past him into the lounge. The others are hovering by the door, while Red is sitting on the sofa with the television on and her assignments scattered all over the coffee table. Ignoring us all as she bounces her pen against the pad of paper in her hand, while her eyes are glued to the show playing on the screen.

"Red, are you sure you want to stay here on your own? You can come with," I offer, but she's already shaking her head.

"What, and spend my time sitting in the truck with this group? No thanks, I have better things to do with my time. Like eat all your snacks, pretend to do this work and watch tv." She looks at me with a wide grin, before turning back to the screen.

Taking that as my cue, I head toward the guys, and Parker holds the door open ready.

"Bye, Jessikins," Oscar shouts, but she doesn't respond. Instead she gives him the middle finger, making me laugh. I love all this confidence coming from her and Parker these days.

Now, I need to boost my own to get this Special Agent onboard and not give Featherstone any more reasons to kill me.

Roman puts the truck in park outside a small diner. It took us about twenty minutes to get here, on the outskirts of Innsbruck, and before us sits the most classic diner I have ever seen. I can see the fluorescent lights around the windows from here, and I'm a little eager to get inside. I love the leather seats and I'm secretly praying for a jukebox. It stands alone with a mall a little further down the road, desperately needing a fresh lick of paint. It's the biggest diner I've seen, and it breaks my heart a little that the sign is missing a letter.

For fuck's sake, Luna, this is business, not pleasure. Shaking my head, I focus on what actually matters here, which is not the milkshake board I can see at the entryway.

Sitting in the front beside Roman was the only way I would agree to not meet them here on Dot. I hate riding in a truck, but I always feel a little better being up front, than squished in the back. So, Oscar, Parker and Kai are all squashed into the back. Unclipping my seatbelt, I look over my shoulder at them, to see them all looking around for the agent.

Roman showed me a few pictures earlier of a middle-aged man, maybe late forties with grey-edged brown hair, and brown eyes. He seemed nice enough from the photos, like a classic all-American small-town hero, but we all know looks can be deceiving.

"There," Kai says, pointing a hand to the last booth on the left of the diner. You can only see his face from here, but it's definitely him.

Roman sighs beside me, gaining my attention as he looks down at his lap.

"On the way back to the Academy can we drive through Tuckahoe? Then when we get back and Jess asks where we've been, I can say to Tuck-a-Ho. Pleaseee?" Oscar says with a grin. His enthusiasm lightens my mood a little, as Kai tries to smack him around the head since Roman can't.

"Have you got everything you need, angel?" Parker murmurs, as he squeezes my shoulder from the seat behind me.

"Yeah, I'm good." I pick my backpack up off the floor,

and check I have everything one last time.

Roman has set me up with some photoshopped photos of this guy to use as blackmail if needed. As well as some forged contracts to put in his possession to cover all bases.

I haven't looked through them very much, but I know Special Agents can lose their jobs over embezzlement, contraband and bribery, and that's what all this is. I just hope I don't need to use them.

Not wanting to delay the assignment any further, I reach for the door handle when Roman grabs my arm.

"Princess, I want you to pull your phone out and type *pineapple*, so if you need to use it, it's ready to go. Okay?" I nod in understanding and open the door.

"Be safe, baby girl," Oscar adds as I step out, but I don't look back. Instead, I square my shoulders and head for the entrance.

I hold the door to the diner open, letting an old couple pass through before I enter. They murmur their thanks, but I'm not paying them any attention, I'm busy scanning the diner for all access points. Roman told me there are two backdoor entrances, which from here are beside the counter where the register is. The door I'm walking through and the one closest to the agent are the only other two.

It's not too busy here, eighteen people, not including the staff, are leisurely enjoying a late lunch. No one pays any attention to me as I walk through the tables straight to my mark. It's classic in here, deep burgundy leather seats and booths with cheap white marble effect tables. I fucking love it. It reminds me of the place near my home with Rafe where we would go once a week without fail.

The booth Dominic Bridge occupies is right in front of me, and I don't waver in confidence as I take the seat across from him. I place my backpack beside me as he finishes drinking his coffee, bringing the mug back to the table as he looks me over.

"Can I help you?" he asks wearily, as he scans my face but doesn't once glance down at my breasts. Good start, agent. He looks much more tired in person, with bags under his eyes and extra frown lines on his forehead.

"You can, although I don't appreciate having to take the seat without the best view of the vantage points," I offer in response, resting my forearms on the table in front of me and clasping my hands together.

A waitress approaches us with a wide smile as she looks to the agent. "Do you want a refill, Dom?" she asks, and he nods but his eyes stay on mine. "Would you like something to eat, sweetie?" I don't look at her, but I shake my head and she leaves.

Silence fills the space between us as we each size the other up. I don't want to give too much away, I want to see what he thinks this is about before I say anything. I struggle to keep my expression neutral when he finally breaks the silence.

"Are you the one who's been following me?" There's no anger in his voice, more curiosity, but he clearly knows Roman's been tailing him.

"Nope," I finally say, leaning back in the booth, trying to appear relaxed but the fact that he knows has me on edge a little.

"Are you linked to the reason why?" He raises his eyebrow at me, daring me to tell the truth.

"Yes." There's no reason for me to lie, not with what I need him to do.

"Are you from the Academy?" Damn, if I didn't know this guy was an agent, I would now. How am I the one answering all the questions?

"Are you going to continue asking irrelevant questions, or are we going to get to the point?" Blunt is all I can offer right now, I don't need to waste more time here than I need to. He leans back in the booth, matching my posture, and takes a drink of his coffee.

"I can only imagine you're here to get me to do Featherstone's dirty work, hmm?" He says it so casually, without even a blink, and I'm confused. There's something more going on here, something that I'm not aware of.

"Do you know how many kids from that place have been forced to come to me to do the exact same thing? They've set you up on an assignment they know you can't complete, do you understand that?"

Fuck.

Of course they have. How fucking stupid of me.

"I'm not surprised," I say, tapping my fingers on the tabletop. "Any excuse to kill me and they're all over it."

He stares me down, processing my words.

"What does that mean?" he asks, lowering his voice to make sure no one can hear us, but I'm furious right now. Trying to remain calm and relaxed is proving difficult.

"It means if I don't complete the assignment, I die. They've already forced me through some trial, scarred me and now this? I'm not surprised at all." And neither is he. Anyone else hearing what I just said would be panicked or at least stunned, but instead he curses.

"He said this would happen. Fuck. How long have you got left to complete this assignment?" His eyes search mine with a new light as he tries to piece everything together.

"Two weeks."

"Give me until next Sunday, I'll know what to do by then." Scanning around the table, he grabs a napkin from the dispenser and a pen from his pocket. "Write your contact number on here," he says, pushing them toward me.

"Sorry, do you expect me to trust you when my life hangs in the balance?" I scoff, this fucking guy. "No, thanks."

"Take it or leave it. It's more than I've offered any of the others before you," he says firmly while remaining calm. Searching his eyes, I don't know what makes me do it, but I scribble my number on the napkin. He quickly grabs it off the table and stands.

"I promise you, Luna, by next Sunday I'll have a way to figure this out." With that he's gone, leaving me to sit here reeling with this whole mess.

Wait.

He said, 'I promise you, Luna,' but I never gave him my name.

What the fuck?

Jumping to my feet, I grab my bag and rush outside. There's no sign of him. Swiping a hand down my face, I think I'm losing it.

Tires screeching to my side gain my attention. Roman is out of the truck and in my face in seconds.

"What the fuck happened?" he shouts, his eyes frantically searching mine as I try and process my own thoughts.

"Get back in the truck, baby. I'll explain on the drive home." He reluctantly releases me and climbs back in as Parker holds the passenger door open for me. I try to offer a smile in appreciation, but it falls flat.

Taking a minute to clip myself in, I rake my hands through my hair in frustration.

"He fucking knows, Rome. He pretty much knows everything. They set me up with an impossible task," I whisper, my brain hurting from trying to understand what the fuck actually just happened. I hear him slam his fists into the steering wheel in anger, but I don't pull my gaze from looking out of my window. I can hear the blood pumping in my ears and feel my heart pounding in my chest.

"Take us back, Roman. I'll tell you everything he said."

He slams the truck into drive, and we peel out of the car lot. Not wasting any time, I get straight to it.

…

KC KEAN

TWENTY EIGHT

Parker

Feeling the rays of sunlight hitting my face, I blink open my eyes, taking in my surroundings. We really need to just buy a bigger bed for Luna's bedroom. We arranged her sofas to the far walls of the lounge and pulled the mattresses off hers and Roman's bed again. Sprawled across them together we eventually fell asleep.

My angel was shaken yesterday. She told us every detail from the diner and the agent, who really did seem to know more than we expected. It seems Featherstone really wants to break her, but she won't allow that to happen. We won't either, she's too strong for these motherfuckers.

Now we have to do something we never would normally do, and that's trust in some guy we don't know nearly enough about. He has until next Sunday to get back to her, or we go in guns blazing and make him. It's as simple as that.

When we finally got back, Red had already left. She'd sent a quick text to Luna, so it was just us. Luna needed to numb her mind for a little while, and sex wasn't the answer this time. Instead, we sat together watching action movies and snacking on everything in sight.

We laughed, we joked, and we relaxed, but we didn't stress. It was perfect. Now today is a big day, I've got some alone time with Luna, which includes a trip into town and lunch with her Grandmother. The others are going to dig a little deeper into everyone trying to tear us down. Dietrichson, Veronica, my father, all of them.

Somebody needs to start paying for all of this shit they're putting us through, putting Luna through.

Needing to get up, I try to assess how to do so without waking anyone up. There's a leg draped over mine from behind, that is definitely too hairy to be Luna's. She's lying in front of me, her ass nestled perfectly against my dick, my morning wood loving it. My hand fits perfectly at her waist, but I slowly inch it from under her arm. She's still out like a light, so I glance behind me to find it's Oscar who's nestled against me.

When I've finally maneuvered myself out of the pile of body parts, I quietly slip into the bathroom. I grab my loose grey shorts from the coffee table on the way so I can change into them after a shower.

I make quick work of washing my hair and body, and it feels strange smelling of her. I use her strawberry shampoo and coconut body wash, but it's worth it to feel a little closer to her. Flicking the shower off I wrap a towel around my waist and look over the vanity for mouthwash or anything useful for my teeth.

That's when I see she's laid four toothbrushes still in their packaging out on the side, and I smile. I love it when she shows she cares without realizing, it helps solidify that she truly means it when she says she doesn't judge me by my father's actions.

Rubbing a towel through my hair, I slip on my shorts and roll my boxer shorts into my pocket. I'm surprised to see Oscar leaning against the back of one of the sofas as I step out of the bathroom.

"I'm going to put the coffee machine on, you want a

coffee too?" I ask, and he nods in agreement as he steps past me, shutting the bathroom door behind him. Okay then.

Glancing at the others still sleeping on the mattresses, I leave them be as I put the coffee machine on. Having a look through Luna's groceries, I decide on some French toast for everyone.

Pulling out everything I need, I set it all up beside the stove. Carving up the bread and measuring out the rest of it, I'm just about ready to heat the pan when Oscar strolls in. Glimpsing his way, I'm surprised to see a determined look on his face.

Before I can ask what's wrong, he's heading toward me and pulling the pan from my hand.

"What…"

"I need you to kiss me," he blurts out, taking me by surprise. He rubs the back of his neck, looking down at his feet, as the slightest pink tinge takes over his cheeks. I drop my hands to my sides as I look him over.

"I don't understand, Oscar." He probably thinks I sound stupid, but I don't know where this is coming from. He releases a heavy sigh as he glances back up at me.

"Ever since we shared Luna, I've felt different, and I

need to know if it's because I'm into guys too, or because your dick felt like magic against mine." He brings his hands to his hips, widening his feet a little as he relaxes his shoulders. "So, I need you to kiss me so I can figure it out."

Well, at least I understand where it's coming from now then. Is Oscar hot? Obviously, his dusty blond hair and blue eyes make him look like a surfer, and the one thing I've always been confident about is my sexuality.

"I get that, Oscar, but this isn't something I can help you with, without talking to Luna first." It's Luna we've all committed ourselves too. As much as she loves to see me with Roman, I don't want to do something that breaks some rule we haven't discussed. I might want to bite his pouty mouth when he whines, but I won't if she doesn't want me to.

"Luna is one hundred percent okay with it." My head whips to the door so fast I almost get a cramp. Oscar does the exact same and we say nothing as we stand and stare at our girl.

In nothing but her panties and a purple tank top, she stands before us running her tongue against her teeth as she looks us both over.

"Are you sure?" I have to ask, to make sure she's not

saying something she thinks we want to hear.

She slowly walks toward me, and her hand comes up to rest on my shoulder. Walking behind me, she wraps her hands around my waist, placing a gentle kiss to my feather tattoo on my arm.

"If Oscar wants to experiment, I'm never going to stand in the way of that within our circle, as long as I am your only girl. I understand the need for the big D though, and I can't refuse anyone that," she murmurs, with her lips dragging against my arm, as her eyes stay trained on Oscar.

He grins at her, as tension visibly leaves the set of his shoulders a little.

"Now, I want a front row seat for this," she says, holding her arm out to Oscar, who steps closer to us. Luna moves to stand beside us, as we stare at each other. There is very little difference between our height, so our faces align without any necessary movement.

I can see the curiosity in his eyes, mixed with a little uncertainty as he stares me down, needing me to make the first move. Glancing one last time to Luna, who nods in encouragement, I wet my dry lips and wrap my hand around the back of his neck. Stroking my finger along the hairline at the back of his head.

He keeps his arms at his side as the pulse in his neck increases. Moving my lips toward his slowly, I give him time to change his mind, but he doesn't. Softly brushing my lips against his, he keeps still, not moving an inch.

His lips are softer than I expected, softer than Roman's and fuller. I want to taste them a little more, but first, I pull back to check his reaction. His eyes are half mast, as he slowly blinks, I move back. Finally meeting my eyes, he wastes no time before he's crashing his lips back to mine. He touches his mouth to mine from different angles, as if imprinting the feel and dynamic of my lips to memory.

His tongue sneaks out and drags against mine a few times, before he tries to slip inside. Giving him the smallest of spaces, his tongue pushes past my lips, and I suck my mouth around it. The groan it forces from Oscar and Luna has heat coursing through me. I instinctively pull him closer to me, as the intensity increases.

Oscar's hand comes up to the back of my neck, pushing for more which I happily give him. Our tongues tangle together as we both push to overpower the other, and a moan slips past my lips. With Roman, he always controls the pace, whereas with Oscar, I feel the need to command him and it's a heady feeling.

The thought of Luna also watching us right now only increases the pleasure, and my cock is hard in my shorts, no real material containing it. Oscar pulls me closer and fuck me, I feel his solid dick touch mine again between us, and we both gasp.

A throat clears, and I pull back from Oscar, opening my eyes. When did I even close them? His eyes are blown and his pouty lips are extra puffy. I know the throat cleared from the door, but I look to my right first, seeking out Luna.

She stands before me, eyes as wide as Oscar's, her hand against her chest as her breathing comes in rapid bursts.

"That was fucking beautiful," she whispers, and I offer her a soft smile.

Finally turning to the door, I realize I have a hand on Oscar's hip and the other still gripping his neck. I can't even kick my body into movement as I take in Roman at the door, Kai standing with a grin behind him. I'm glad Oscar is taking a minute too, if his grip on my arm and waist are anything to go by.

I don't know what I expect Roman to say, but there's heat in his eyes too.

"I think he just went a little alpha there, Luna, what do you think?" he says, not moving his eyes from us.

"I think you are spot on with that observation. Anything you care to add, Kai?" she offers in response, as she remains frozen in place.

"What are the chances of a coffee?" Kai answers, finally pulling me through the sexual fog enough to function like an adult.

Meeting Oscar's gaze, he's smirking at me with a pleased look in his eyes.

"I'm not sure if I'm into guys or not, but I definitely need to explore that a little more at some point," he says, and I drop my hands from him. Searching his eyes there is no joke there, like a small part of me expects, so I offer a simple nod. He's completely caught me off guard. I would never have considered this with Oscar, but I am more than happy to help him experiment with his sexuality. Especially if Luna likes it too.

"Someone sort the coffees, Parker's making French toast and I need to go take care of myself." He offers me a wink and heads for the bathroom like his feet are on fire.

Kai chuckles and we all join him. Oscar, always the one to lighten any mood.

Luna steps up to me again, this time resting her chin against my chest as she looks up to me, wrapping her hands tightly around me.

"Are you ready for today, Parker Parker?" she murmurs, and I smile gently down at her. As ready as I'll ever be.

YOUR BLOODLINE

TWENTY NINE

Luna

"Do I look okay?" Parker asks, pulling at the sleeves of his white button up shirt. With his navy slacks on, and his curly hair crying out for me to run my fingers through it, he looks delicious.

"Parker, you look hot as hell, please stop worrying. You are my Parker Parker, that is always more than enough," I say, squeezing his arm in reassurance and loving the feel of the stretched material around his bicep. I follow his lead as we step into the lobby of the Jefferson Hotel, a bellman at the door ready to greet us. Maria somehow convinced us to boycott a normal restaurant to have Sunday brunch here instead, something about memory lane.

Parker was reluctant to hand the keys over to the valet attendant, but I eventually convinced him to, making the valet's day with the bright red Porsche 911 Carrera. I mean, I did understand his concerns, but I wasn't parking miles away to then walk the rest of the distance.

Roman was adamant it was Parker's car. Reggie Rivera had passed it on to him, but Parker being Parker, refused to accept it. Although he was more than happy to loan it from time to time. It drove like a dream. I hate going anywhere in cars, but this actually didn't take much convincing. The leather interior, the dashboard and the roar from the engine had me hot. I'd never been in a Porsche before, but I was fangirling over the twin-turbo flat six rear engine. Parker even gave me a little show of how it reaches 100mph in 4.2 seconds flat.

The lobby has a grand feel to it. High ceilings with a large red staircase in the center of the space. Marble pillars go all the way to the top, with balconies for each floor overlooking the area. Deep royal blue flooring and chairs mixed with the gold touches make it a lot more traditional than I'm used to. There's even a piano in the middle, with some guy dressed in a suit playing it.

"My hip is burning, angel. I think we did this the wrong way around, and I still don't understand why you couldn't be the one to do it," he mutters, as a few people lingering in the lobby stare us down. Clearly this isn't really the place for people with tattoos on their fingers and their neck. Staring the assholes down around us, I speak calmly as I repeat the words I've already said before.

"Parker Parker, honestly we've been through this. Traditions and all that…"

"Luna, you look fabulous." The sound of my grandmother's voice halts our conversation, and we turn to greet her. Why does she make me so nervous? "And Parker, I'm glad to see you in better spirits than the last time we met." The grin on her mouth shows her playful side, and it relaxes me a little. She looks stunning in a pink floral dress with white peep toe heels, a complete contrast to The Ring member we know.

She takes me in as I release my hold on Parker's arm to run my hands down my dress. It looks like a two piece, with full coverage over my chest and thighs, and an off-white lace overlay that holds it together over my stomach and falls a little lower on my legs. It was only right for me to pair it with the dusty pink heels I wore to the Fall Ball, the first time I laid eyes on Maria. I chose to leave my wavy brown hair down for a change, letting it fall to my waist.

"Thank you," I say as she steps in to hug me. I'm a little stiff for a moment, but I soon relax into her hold. My mind and soul become more familiar with her each time we meet. Kissing my cheeks like we're in Europe, she leans back and looks at Parker.

"And you, mister," she says with a little sass at Parker, who stumbles over himself to do as she says. It's a little comical watching him crouch down to hug her back. I can tell he's whispering something in her ear, but I can't hear what. She pats his back in response and squeezes his forearms before finally stepping back.

"Mrs. Steele, if you would like to follow me, please. I have the table you requested ready," a guy says with a polite smile. He's dressed smartly in a suit, and when I glance at his name badge I'm impressed that it's as swanky as the hotel itself. Apparently this guy is Richard, and it seems he's the manager, if I'm reading the fancy cursive print correctly. Maria smiles and waves a hand for him to take the lead. I follow behind her with Parker wrapping his arm around my shoulder, bringing me in close, and I smile up at him.

I notice a few faces around us as my grandmother's security men, none of whom offer any form of greeting. Their full attention on my grandmother's safety at all times, as their job requires. They're spread out watching the perimeter, exit points and the lady in question. All while blending in with the surroundings in their all black suits.

As we step into the dining area, the interior decor continues from the lobby. Marble columns frame the room, with high arched windows decorating the second floor and a rose stained-glass window filters light in from the ceiling. Making the whole space bright, even in the corners. Clearly, Maria is not down for a slice of pizza and an iced tea. I'm glad we're dressed for the occasion.

As we're led up the stairs to the second floor, my eyes stray to Parker who is already smiling down at me, and his hazel eyes warm my soul. He brings his hand from my shoulder to rest on my lower back, which tingles at his touch. I love the comfort and stability it offers me as we approach the only table that has been set up here. Only the three of us take a seat as Maria's men stand strategically around us, looking at the same access points as me.

It's strange none of us have spoken yet, but it feels comfortable and not forced.

The table is ridiculously big and filled with glasses in all different shapes and sizes, along with so much cutlery I don't know where to begin. The cream table cloth looks thicker than a duvet, and the plush grey chair is like sitting on a cloud.

"If you can bear with us for a few minutes, we are going to set up your own platter up here," the manager says, before stepping away from the table.

Looking at my grandmother, she has a sparkle in her eyes that wasn't there before. Noticing my curious look, she smiles.

"This was the first place your grandfather brought me on our first date," her smile only grows as the memory runs through her mind. "He was so cocky and full of himself to everyone, until we came here, and he showed me the version of himself nobody else got to see."

"He sounds like a good man, Mrs. Steele," Parker says in response, and her eyes dim a little.

"He was, he passed six months before Luna was born, but he will always be the love of my life." She runs her hands along the tablecloth to distract her mind from the heartache, and my heart hurts too. "You remind me of him, you all do," she adds, looking to Parker, who smiles at the comparison.

"I hope that's in a good way," he responds, tapping his fingers against his thighs nervously.

"It is in the best way possible. You showed me a true form of yourselves in that box while Luna took part in The Trials, and I'm sure you show an even more vulnerable side to Luna as well."

The mention of The Trials always catches me off guard, but it doesn't leave me on edge. Before I can ask what she means by that, a waiter approaches with a bottle of white wine, which Maria accepts. When he brings the bottle toward me, I cover my glass with a shake of my head.

"I would prefer a water, please."

"Me too, thank you," Parker adds. The waiter nods and rushes off to get the drinks.

Looking back to my grandmother, I ask, "Please, tell me more about this side you saw in the box. I'm intrigued." She smiles wide at me, as Parker looks to the ceiling with a groan.

"Well, Parker here kicked up the most fuss, I think. I'm sure you must have heard him banging on the window," she says, smiling in his direction. "They all showed loyalty and an intense level of protectiveness toward you, but most of all, they portrayed how much they believe in you. They are not above you, nor are you above them, but together you have a very special and rare bond, only bringing out the best in each other."

Her words hit me straight in the chest, and leave me almost breathless, I could float away. Looking to my left, I see Parker already staring at me with admiration in his eyes, and it grounds me. It scares me how true her words are after only knowing each other for two months. It's no time at all in the grand scheme of things, but this world we're in could kill us tomorrow too.

Parker lifts my hand off the table, bringing his lips to my knuckles and planting a delicate kiss there. As if he feels the effects of her words too.

The waiter chooses then to bring our waters over and the moment is broken. Clearing the glasses not required, he quickly leaves again giving us our privacy.

"I'm glad I showed such good qualities while having a meltdown and arguing with you," Parker says, catching me off-guard as Maria chuckles.

"It was your meltdown and argumentative state that

showed those qualities. It was rather refreshing. Do you know how many people actually make eye contact with me these days? Being a member of The Ring puts fear in everyone around you." She sighs, as food starts arriving. Platters of different varieties are placed around the table while a few side tables are set up around us with more choices.

Selections of seafood, carved meats, cheeses, fruit and so much cake I think I'm in heaven fill the space, and I'm suddenly pleased with Maria's desire to dine here. Everything smells amazing and looks super fresh, even though this isn't the pizza I would have preferred, I'm not complaining.

Not one of us continues any form of conversation as we dive into the food around us, which is beyond delicious. Come to think of it, none of these Aceholes have taken me on a real date outside of Featherstone's walls. They better bring me back here the next time we have five minutes to spare. Or maybe I need a girly day here with Red, either way, I deserve a fucking date.

"Are you okay, Luna? You seem mad," Maria asks, surprising me, I'm usually better at covering my emotions even without trying. She must be able to read my mind or something because she continues. "You get the smallest frown line on your forehead, just as your father did," she says with a soft smile, and I find my hand lifting to check. She's not wrong, it's definitely there, and it almost has me in tears.

I don't want to change my facial expression in fear of it going, a trait I have from my father.

"That son of a bitch," I mutter, my frown coming in full force this time.

"What?" Parker asks with concern, but I look at Maria when answering.

"Rafe always knew when I was mad or thinking too hard about something, but he would never tell me how. It's this, isn't it?" I ask dramatically, pointing at the frown line which only makes Maria chuckle at me.

"One hundred percent. Those two knew everything about each other, and there was always a running joke about that look," she says so casually, yet it gives me such an insight to their life. The joy and happiness they shared and brought me into.

One of Maria's men suddenly approaches the table with a cellphone in his hand and interrupts our conversation.

"Mrs. Steele, I apologize for interrupting but this is

urgent, and I think you need to know what's going on," he mutters, handing her the phone. She frowns at him as she looks down at the screen. Lifting the phone to her ear, she finally speaks.

"Hello." Her tone is measured and cold, not at all like the woman sat before us just moments ago. I can feel it in the pit of my stomach that something is going on, and my legs start to bounce nervously. I glance at Parker, who is looking at me from the corner of his eye and he places his hand on my thigh in silent support.

"Who authorized this? …No, it's not fucking okay…" She looks straight at me, and it instantly tells me I'm involved. "You tell that motherfucker I'm going to gut him with a rusty blade, chop his balls off and force them down his damn throat," she spits out furiously as she launches the cell phone across the room. Luckily not over the balcony, because that would have definitely done some damage with the force she just threw it with.

There is fire in her eyes as her shoulders shake ever so slightly. Standing to her feet, she smashes her fists into the table, knocking some of the food to the floor. Parker grabs my hand and pulls us back from the table, and the movement stops her tirade.

"I'm sorry," she mutters, looking to the ceiling as she takes a few deep breaths. "I'm sorry to cut our lunch short, but I think it's a good idea if you get back to the Academy and begin to prepare."

"Prepare for what?" I ask, as my heart starts to race, and the thumping starts to ring in my ears.

"Because, those cunts have moved The Games to November second," she growls, unable to contain her fury. Parker's hand tightens around mine as my blood pumps harder through my veins. It takes me a moment to get my brain in gear and catch up.

November second? That's a week from tomorrow. Fuck.

YOUR BLOODLINE

KC KEAN

THIRTY
Oscar

"Oscar, why do you have to play your video games in my room? What's wrong with yours?" Roman grumbles at me, but it doesn't stop him from watching. I don't know why he still bothers to ask me this every single time, I think he just likes to pretend to be irritated with me.

"Rome, this is where Luna will come when she gets back with Parker. She'll expect us to be here, so deal with it," I answer, not moving my gaze from the screen. He sighs heavily, like he knows it's more than that, but he also knows I'll only talk about it when I decide I'm ready to.

"You know he'll stop being grouchy when they get

back, you've only got an hour or two more to deal with him," Kai teasingly offers from the other sofa, where he's tapping away on his laptop... as usual.

"Fuck off, Kai," Roman snaps, only solidifying what Kai just said. "We've worked out, I've eaten and showered. They've been gone for ages," he says, as he goes to look out of the floor-length window again.

"Are you watching out for them or letting all the girls out there ogle your bod, man?" I ask, joking around but he just scowls at me from over his shoulder. "I'm just saying, before Luna did the whole ball and chains trick, I spent a lot of my time posing naked at the window to encourage the girls, ya know?" I waggle my eyebrows, but his frown only deepens. Spoil sport.

"Why would I fucking do that, you idiot?"

He continues to stand there, in only his loose grey joggers, watching the world go by. I go back to ignoring him as my game starts up and I can start shooting shit, I've barely landed when Kai distracts me.

"Holy fuck. Holy fuck."

"What?" Roman says, walking toward him. It must be something, because Kai is the one least likely to cuss. I drop my controller to the coffee table, as I watch Kai's face animated in disbelief.

"I've got some movement in Dietrichson's office," he murmurs, and turns the screen around for us to see.

"Holy shit," I say at the exact same time as Roman. "I mean, I'd call that a little more than some movement, but I understand your lacking knowledge, Kai," I continue with a grin. "That's what you call fucking my friend, and more specifically, that's what you would call Bitch Dietrichson being fucked by Parker's dickhead dad."

Bent over her desk with Rico slamming into her from behind, Dietrichson looks like she's having a good time, or at least pretending. We're all so surprised with this revelation, that Roman doesn't even smack me around the head for trying to get a rise out of Kai.

"You can turn it away now, Kai, her saggy tits are going to burn my retinas," I say as I fake gag, and Roman actually chuckles.

"Try having to listen to the audio too," Kai responds with a cringe, pointing to the wireless headphone in his ear, and I can't help but laugh.

Turning off the Xbox, I stand, stretching my arms over my head as I catch a glimpse of a familiar red sports car. I still can't believe Parker somehow convinced her to go in that thing.

"Hey Rome, they're here," I say pointing out of the window, and Roman hurries over.

"Why are they back already? It's too early for them to be here," he rushes out, confusion written all over his face.

"I don't know, quit whining. You should be pleased, all the moping you've done, but we need to be careful. Rico's on campus and we don't know what for. Well apart from the obvious," Kai adds, waving a hand at his laptop with a grimace and slight gag.

I look at Roman, but he's already moving to the door. "I'll meet them down there, something isn't right," he mutters, and slams the door behind him.

"Should we have mentioned he's shirtless and screams 'look at me', which is the complete opposite of being careful?" Kai murmurs, but I shrug in response.

"I think the slam of the door is a no, Kai."

"It's odd that Rico's here and they're home early, but don't stress, we'll figure it out, Oscar. We always do," Kai says, trying to calm me, but I'm fine. Totally fine.

Although my heart is beating a little faster and my forehead is sweating, it is completely unrelated to all this here. Rubbing the back of my neck, I head for the kitchen to grab a bottle of water. Gulping it down, I place the empty bottle on the counter and look for something heavier.

"It's okay to worry about others, Oscar," Kai murmurs from the doorway, catching me by surprise. I didn't even hear him approach.

"I'm not worrying, Kai," I say with a sigh, as I come up short on the alcohol front. Not even a fucking beer, absolutely useless.

"Hey, we're a team, remember?" he says as he steps toward me and squeezes my shoulder. "One day, you'll drop your persona you hide behind long enough for someone to actually see you, Oscar. I hope it's Luna," he says softly, before patting my shoulder and walking back into the lounge as I hear the front door swing back open.

"Where's Oscar?" I hear Luna ask, and she almost sounds frantic. Resting my palms on the kitchen counter, I look down at my feet and take a deep breath.

"Oscar, get out here now, it's urgent," Parker shouts. I shake my head as I move to the door, it's all going to shit, I can feel it.

Stepping into the lounge, Luna whips her head around to me and her shoulders relax when she sees me. Damn, why does seeing her calm at the sight of me, relax me in return?

"Hey," she murmurs as she steps toward me. "Are you okay, big mouth?"

I am now.

"Of course, baby girl. What's all the shouting about?" I ask as I wrap my arms around her, resting my hands at the bottom of her back while her hands stroke against my chest.

I glance down at her hands on me, and my heart beats rapidly in my chest. I know this is real now between us. She is ours, and we are hers, no matter what. I straighten my back as I push my worry aside. I want to be here, present and accounted for. Whatever she needs, I'm in.

"Oscar, they've moved The Games up," she whispers. I don't get a chance to answer her because Roman interrupts.

"We know that princess, that's what we've been trying to—" The shake of both hers and Parker's head cuts him off, as she looks back up into my eyes.

"The Games start in eight days."

Well, fuck me.

Luna

Oscar's arms tighten around me as I rest my forehead against his chest for a moment. As soon as Maria told us, we were out of there. I didn't want to tell them over the phone, I needed us to deal with this together, in person.

Leaning back to look at Oscar, my hands lift to his neck, gripping him like a lifeline. Parker drove us home with his hand in mine the whole way, I need to feel connected to them right now. To know we are the team they say we are.

I feel a body press in behind me, as arms wrap around my shoulders. Which leads to being blocked in from all sides in the best group hug ever. I feel Kai behind me, his gentle hands caressing my tummy soothingly. While Parker and Roman squeeze us in from the sides. I can't help the soft smile that takes over my lips as their presence alone comforts me. A kiss to the back of my head, one to each cheek and Oscar's to my lips, eases the stress from my body.

Pulling back, Oscar peers into my eyes with a gentleness I've not seen before. I won't say anything more of it, not wanting to rock his boat. I'll let him come further out of his shell when he's ready.

"We've got this, baby girl, but first I think it's best if we move this to your room. We have some news too, and your room has the best security," he says, and I hear Kai and Roman agree with him. Oscar's making sense? Something is definitely wrong, either way, I am liking this new side of him.

The others step back, as Oscar takes my left hand and leads me out of the room. His thumb stroking my fingers in a relaxing motion as he grins down at me. He grabs my room keys out of my grip with his other hand, and let's us in, throwing the keys in the dish by the door like it's completely natural for him.

"Do you want something to drink?" he asks, walking me over to the sofa.

"I would not say no to a coffee right now," I answer, pressing my fingertips into my temple.

"I'll do it," Parker calls out from behind me, making Oscar look at him for a moment and nod in response. What was that about? I turn to see what he was doing, but his back is to me as he steps into the kitchen.

Oscar takes a seat and pulls me into his lap, and I won't decline him. I'm a little worried about how he's acting right now, but that only makes me hold him closer.

"So, what's this news you have?" I ask, wanting something else to talk about before we have to get heavy into The Games.

"Err, it'll be best to wait for Parker too, princess," Roman says, taking the spot beside us.

Without moving his gaze from mine, he lifts my feet up into his lap and starts to undo my heels. Yes, please. I've had enough of those demons. The pads of his thumbs slowly start working into the balls of my feet, and I'm in heaven right now.

Kai places his laptop on the coffee table, and takes a seat next to it, waiting for Parker who strolls in with a steaming black coffee in his hands. Before I reach out for it, Kai blocks my hands and takes it from Parker. I can't help the whimper that passes my lips as I keep my arms outstretched for the cup.

"You'll want to hear our news without a burning hot drink in your hand," he mutters in response to the confused looks on mine and Parker's faces.

Roman shuffles closer to Oscar beneath me, keeping my legs over his thighs, and pulls Parker down in the seat next to him. Looking between the three of them, they clearly know something we don't, but none of them want to say what's going on. Before I can blurt out for them to get on with it, Kai sighs.

"We had some live footage today from Dietrichson's office." I nod for him to continue, and he braces his hands on his knees and taps his fingers nervously. "She had company," he mutters. Why is that a big deal? It's certainly not worth missing out on my coffee for.

"Okaaay, but what's the news?" I ask, frustrated it's taking them so long to spit it out.

"She was being banged from behind by Rico," Oscar blurts, rushing the words out as quickly as possible. I almost get whiplash as I spin to see his face. He's not lying.

"Holy shit," I mutter under my breath, but clearly not quiet enough.

"That's what we said," Oscar whispers in my ear, turning my face to Parker.

He stares at Roman, who nods in confirmation as he squeezes his thigh in comfort. This explains a lot, like how the Academy has been able to make sure that Parker doesn't find out his bloodline. Fuckers. Well screw them, he doesn't need any of this shit anymore.

"He's here on campus?" Parker finally says, paling a little as he speaks. He visibly gulps a few times, as he rubs his hands nervously over his knee caps.

"Yes," Kai answers. "But Oscar was right, being in Luna's room is the best idea. We'll all stay here tonight, drag in the mattresses and all that." I smile at his efforts to make Parker feel better. I may be the one they're in a relationship with, but it's clear they care for each other, and that's what makes this feel so much better.

"We're a team, Parker. He doesn't get through that door," Roman growls, and Parker relaxes. A little color coming back to his cheeks. Wow, the trust he has in Roman, and the effect it has on him blows my mind.

"Red," I murmur, my back stiffening, but Oscar strokes a hand down my arm, relaxing me.

"Don't worry, baby girl. I already spoke to her on the phone, and she was adamant she was okay. I can go and get her if you like?" I consider his words, and as hard as it may be, I have to trust her to tell me if she wasn't okay. She clearly wants her own space, and I have to respect that, begrudgingly.

"No, it's okay," I say quietly, my attention going back to Parker.

"Let's talk about The Games then, distract me." Parker says, determination visible in his eyes. Reaching over

Roman I squeeze his arm.

He lifts my hand to his lips, squeezing my fingers in his. Parker places our joined hands in between us on Roman's lap, who places his hands on top.

"The Games have been moved to November second, which gives us the next seven full days to train as hard as we can. I still want to grab Wren at the Halloween Party though. I sent a text to Trudy on the way over and we're still good on that front." Thinking over what little information Maria was able to give us, I push on. "Maria said it would be public knowledge tomorrow, so I'm glad we grabbed the weapons yesterday."

The others nod around me, my palms are sweating again. Not from fear, but the unknown. I'm not in control when these fuckers are making the rules.

"She also mentioned that a lot of rules have been broken to make this happen, but she didn't have time to explain what," Parker adds, and I nod in agreement.

"Now I need to hope Agent Dominic Bridge keeps his word, because when we survive The Games, it'll literally give me a day, two at most to track him down. If not, then Featherstone will take great pleasure in killing me for that instead." I frown at this shit.

Someone in Featherstone Academy clearly wants me dead while Veronica wants me to join some new movement. All I want to do is spend time with Red and my Aceholes while I draw my art on people's skin.

Oscar surprises me with a kiss to my cheek, "I'm pleased with your confidence, baby girl. We're going to tear these bastards down," he growls in my ear.

No truer words have ever passed his lips.

Game on, Motherfuckers. Game on.

THIRTY ONE

Luna

Tuesday morning, it's pouring down with rain outside as we make our way toward the waiting Rolls Royces parked at Ace. Ian has an umbrella raised above his head as he waits by the doors. Without a word he walks beside me, covering me with the umbrella too as he murmurs quietly.

"Miss Steele, they're going to officially announce that The Games will start next week." He glances down at me and the searching in his eyes tells me he has more to say. Although, he doesn't seem surprised that I'm not stunned by this information. I nod and he continues. "Can I give you my honest opinion, Miss Steele?"

"Always," I answer, as we come to a stop by the car.

"I've worked here for many years, and this feels different. I can't put my finger on it. I know they're pushing the date through earlier which is strange enough, but there is more going on, I can feel it." I offer him a soft smile, appreciating the fact that he's coming to me with this information, even if I do already know.

"Thank you, Ian. I always appreciate your insight, I'll bear this in mind." He sighs in relief and holds the door open for me.

"I also just wanted to mention a really nice drive for the next time you're out on your motorcycle, Miss Steele. It's about an hour up north called Beechwood Hall, you'll love it." I nod in thanks, before glancing over my shoulder to where Kai stands patiently behind us getting soaked by the rain.

"I'm so sorry, Mr. Fuse, I…"

"No need to worry, Ian, as long as my Sakura is taken care of, it's all that matters," he says with a smile, as he pats him on the shoulder.

Parker and Roman are riding together today. Leaving Red and Oscar to travel together, which I'm sure will be fun for them both.

We both climb in quickly, and Ian is suddenly at the open door with a towel for Kai, who takes it with a nod in thanks. He quickly wipes his face, ruining the visual I had watching the rain drops trickle down his neck under his shirt. I could totally be a raindrop all over him right now.

He clears his throat and I whip my eyes up to his, the grin on his lips tells me he caught what held my attention. Acehole.

Pulling my hand from my lap, he places it on the arm rest between us, caressing my fingers and palms. God, I've missed this. We really need to get all of this shit under control, so we can spend more time caressing each other.

Taking a deep breath, I find the courage I need to ask him what I've been too distracted to think about.

"Hey, handsome?" I say, getting his attention, and the smile that plays on his lips at my nickname for him has me all fuzzy inside. "Can we talk about your tattoo?" I ask quietly.

"I've been preparing for this, Sakura. Whatever you want to talk about," he murmurs calmly, but I can see the concern playing across his face.

"It's just that with everything that happened with Veronica, and the shit that came after, I haven't really processed the fact that my moon is on there too."

His fingers grip mine as he searches my eyes. "Are you mad?" he whispers, and I shake my head.

"If it made me mad, Kai, I wouldn't have done it. I just want to understand a little more, that's all."

He must be happy with that because I visibly see his shoulders relax.

"You're important to me, Sakura. I don't know what that means right now, but you've changed everything. I have hope, for the future and for my sister, and I have happiness. I haven't felt happiness in a very long time, and it's all because of you." The emotion swimming in his dark eyes floors me.

My pulse is throbbing so much I can hear it echo in my ears. Because of me? How did I do any of that? My mouth hangs open as I gape at him, he's left me speechless and I don't even know what to say.

I think my heart has stopped. Am I breathing?

He must be able to see my internal breakdown and brings his other hand to cup my face.

"I think your brain is short circuiting," he mutters, looking deep into my eyes. A giggle bubbles up out of me from nowhere, surprising both of us.

"I just, I didn't think it was possible for me to have that kind of effect on someone," I murmur, saying exactly what's on my mind. He gently kisses the corner of my mouth, his soft lips teasing mine.

"You're everything, Sakura."

Something catches his eyes as he glances through my window, and I follow his line of sight. There's a giant gazebo set up outside between the two academic buildings. "I don't know what's going on," he says, answering the unspoken question in my eyes, and I remember what Ian mentioned.

"Ian said the official announcement that The Games will begin on Monday is happening today. This may be for others to sign up, for those who aren't required to participate but want to." Why, I will never understand, but some people are just power hungry. Kai nods in understanding as Ian opens the door for us.

Stepping out of the car, Ian offers his umbrella to Kai who takes it, covering us both as we head for the others. As we near the gazebo, I'm surprised to see a small podium with Barbette Dietrichson standing front and center ready to address the crowd. All the other students stand gossiping in confusion, waiting for her to begin.

Her eyes instantly find me in the crowd, and she sneers at me openly, ruining whatever good looks she had going for her. I don't hide the disgust from my face at the sight of her. I knew we'd gone too long without having to see her in person and hear her drone on. She's got her hair scraped back in her classic botox look, as she stands in a bright red pant suit. Nothing has ever screamed cougar more than her right now. At least Rico isn't with her too.

Red steps up beside me, with the rest of my Aceholes behind her each carrying their own umbrellas. The tap of a microphone gains everyone's attention, forcing us to focus on Dietrichson.

"Good morning, my Featherstone students," she greets the crowd with a fake ass smile on her face. "I'm ever so disappointed in the dull weather, especially on such a day for celebrations." Of course she thinks this is a celebration.

I've already had enough of listening to her fake niceness. I know the real woman who I met the first day I showed up here, the power-crazy bitch who fumed at the fact I had a third bloodline. The one who apparently likes getting fucked by Rico, the king dildobasher. They really are made for each other.

Looking at Red to my right, she's frowning at

Dietrichson as she speaks, I'm glad it isn't just me. At least I was able to warn Red this was coming, otherwise she'd be having a panic attack right now.

"I wanted to be the one to announce to you all that The Featherstone Games have been rescheduled for next week. Monday, November second to be precise, and I'm so excited for those of you who will participate."

Holding her arms out wide, she draws everyone's attention to the tables set up around the edge of the sheltered space. Four white tables are decked out in full Featherstone Academy swag, each manned by a tutor with stacks of brochures and clipboards. I don't see West, but I spot Penny, our business tutor, and Maverick. The other two I'm not familiar with. They clearly take this very seriously.

"As you are all well aware, any member of The Ring's bloodlines will automatically be entered into The Games. Anyone else who wishes to participate may do so at their own risk. Surviving The Games will increase your reputation and bloodline within the Featherstone foundation if you are not an Ace."

Looking around at the crowd, there are actually a few of them eager for her to give the word, so they can sign up. I feel Kai's hand rest on my back, and I look up at him. He rolls his eyes as if this is all boring to him, but I find it completely fascinating that people would choose to do this.

"Hearing her talk is like someone is using a cheese grater on my actual ear," Red whispers, and I grin at the comparison. Dietrichson frowns at me, seeing the smirk on my face, but I don't shy away. I make sure she sees my pearly whites as I smile wide, even giving her a little encouraging nod to continue.

Kai pinches my side. "You'll be the death of me, Sakura," he murmurs in my ear, and I turn my megawatt smile at him. He just shakes his head at me, like I'm Oscar or something. I'm not acting *that* crazy.

"You have until the end of the day to complete the forms to be entered into The Games. Any submissions after midnight tonight will not be counted. First lessons have been cancelled this morning to allow you enough time to complete the necessary forms." Doing a final glance around the crowd, she claps her hands together. "I will be away on business for the rest of the week, so I wanted to wish you the best of luck." She gets a sparkle in her eyes as she says, "Try not to die." Offering me one more glare across the packed space, she is escorted to her car.

"Ace block, if you could come to my table, please. Anyone else wanting to participate go see one of the other tutors," Maverick shouts loudly over the chatter around us.

Perfect. Now would be a great time to talk to Maverick about a favor I have. I step out of Kai's space without glancing at the others, and make my way toward him. Once the guys notice where I'm heading, they'll be running in the opposite direction, trying to get as far away from Red as possible. They know the plan, and won't want to be near when she gets mad.

"What are you doing, Luna?" Red asks, trying to keep pace with me. I don't answer her because she'll just say no, and that isn't an option.

Coming around the side of the table to Maverick, he looks to me with a raised eyebrow, his green eyes filled with curiosity. Taking in his dark messy hair and his constant five o'clock shadow, I wonder if he even looks in the mirror before he leaves for the day, yet somehow it works for him.

"Hey, have you got a minute? I have a favor to ask."

He glances between the two of us, and nods for me to carry on.

"I was wondering if Red could come and stay with you while I'm in The Games?" There, I said it. I don't want to, I want her to be with me at all times but being in The Games would actually be worse than this.

"What?" they both say at the same time, like I'm crazy. I sigh as I look at Red.

"I need you to be somewhere safe, Jess. We both know the shit they like to pull. Maverick helped after The Pyramid, I trust him to keep you safe." Her eyes search mine frantically, wanting to argue with me. She must see the determination in my eyes as she leans her head back sighing heavily.

"I'm sorry, Luna. I don't think that's a good idea," Maverick finally says, and I spin my gaze to his.

"Oh." Well I was expecting him to be helpful, but apparently I was wrong. "Okay, no worries then. I'll speak to West instead." Red's hand is still in mine as I turn to go in search of West instead.

I'm surprised when a hand grabs my arm, stopping my movement.

Red looks all flustered, pink patches creeping slowly up her neck. Oops, clearly I should have mentioned this before now, but there hasn't been much time between all the training.

Looking at the owner of the hand, I meet Maverick's gaze.

"West? Why, West?" he asks, a frown taking over his face as he moves closer to stand at the side of the table with us.

"Why not? I need someone I can trust enough to keep her safe. My first choice was you, but you said no." His eyes burn holes in mine as he stares down at me. I feel Red's hand squeeze mine in discomfort, and he finally releases my arm.

"I'm standing right here, Luna," Red finally says, but neither of us take her on.

"So, what you're saying is, you trust me with Jess the most?" A grin slowly starts to take over his face, as he looks to Red beside me. I follow his line of sight, but she has her head down, blushing profusely. He's starting to get on my nerves, and he's making her embarrassed.

"Will you help or not?" I grunt out, fed up with wasting time.

"Yes. Yes, I will," he says, standing taller and nodding his head a few times.

"Good. I'd rather she came to stay on Sunday after the

Halloween party. I don't know when they're going to do the whole snatch and grab for The Games so I'd like to be prepared." I look to Red, whose face matches her nickname right now. She must be embarrassed but safety comes first. "Red, how about you give Maverick your number, that way it'll be easier to work things out more specifically, and we can sort out getting some of your things over."

She glares at me, as Maverick chuckles.

"Don't worry, I have her number… On file. On file, of course. We have all students' cell numbers in your profiles. I'll get it off there. Right?" He looks flustered too. I know I'm technically putting him out with my favor, but it's not that crazy of a request.

"Right. Thank you, Maverick. Now, show me what I need to do with all this shit here," I groan, waving my hand at the brochures and forms on the table.

One more thing ticked off my list, only a hundred more to go.

YOUR BLOODLINE

THIRTY TWO

Kai

By Saturday morning we've finally got a dry day. With the party tonight, and the uncertainty of when we will be taken for The Games, we decided to have our weekly diner breakfast today.

Sitting around the booth, it almost feels as though death isn't waiting for us in less than forty-eight hours. Oscar and Jess are sitting to my right, bickering over some television program, while Luna is sandwiched between Roman and Parker across from me.

She looks relaxed as she listens contently to what Parker is saying. Her hair is up in a messy bun on the top of her head, and denim shorts with an off the shoulder pale pink top covering her frame. Not a spec of make-up on, and my Sakura looks stunning.

I can see Roman's fingers trail patterns on the back of her neck as he listens to Parker too, who has his hand resting on the top of her thigh. They're looking at her like she hung the moon, and I'm quite sure she did. She embraces all of them, all of *us*.

"So, I have all of our Halloween costumes back in my room. You can grab them when we get back," Jess says, and we all stare at her, confused with what she's saying.

"I didn't agree to any costume," Roman grunts, not impressed by this idea.

"Roman, it's Halloween!" Jess exclaims with a roll of her eyes. "Besides, costumes will be best for acting cool and blending in. Right, Luna?" she asks, looking directly at her and nodding her head frantically.

"Right?" Luna responds, but I think that was more of a question than Jess'. Pleased she was able to get her way, Jess rubs her hands together in glee. The rest of us aren't really fussed. We would usually pour fake blood on our shirts and call it a day, but I'm open to seeing what she has in mind.

"Do you want to know what your outfit is, or do you want it to be a surprise?" Glancing around at the rest of us, she's not impressed that no one jumps at the chance to learn more. "Fine. Suit yourselves, surprise it is." She sticks her tongue out at us, and goes back to finishing the pancakes in front of her.

I feel a hand rest on top of mine on the table, pulling my gaze to the left. Turning my head, I instantly meet Luna's eyes, and I let myself get lost in them for a moment. I spend every minute of the day observing what is going on around me, but none of that matters when I see the sparkle of her deep green eyes, and the way the left side of her lip always quirks up when she first looks at me.

"Are you okay, handsome? I know you're Mr. Quiet and Observant, but it feels like more than that today," she says, full of concern. I place my other hand on top of hers as I offer a gentle smile in return.

"I'm absolutely fine, Sakura. I'm just running through all the scenarios we face, that's all."

Her pretty green eyes dim a little, fully understanding that everything is about to be turned upside down. Sometimes, it's hard to remember that we're only eighteen, well now I'm nineteen. As much as I want to join in with everyone having fun, enjoying the moment and not worrying about the future, I can't help it. It's not how my brain works, but I know she understands that.

Her phone vibrates on the table in front of us, and before she can reach to answer it, Oscar beats her to it.

"Hello, Luna's sex line. Ozzie the big-dicked Otter speaking, how may I help you?"

The booth is thrown into stunned silence at his straight face. He said all that with the most serious look I think I've ever seen on him. The rest of us burst into a fit of laughter, including Luna.

"Yep. Yeah. Alright. Give us one hour, we've nearly finished filming the reverse cowgirl scene. Chow."

Luna tries to reach over the table for the phone, but Oscar is too quick. She looks at Jess for help, who is doubled over in a fit of giggles. Even Parker and Roman are swiping at their faces as tears build in their eyes with laughter. She glares at me, expecting me to be the serious one, but I can't clear my throat properly without chuckling again.

"Oscar, who was that?" she cries out, still trying to reach for the phone.

"Chill out, baby girl. It was Trudy, she's got a space set

up and ready for you." She shakes her head at him, glaring for the phone to be passed back. As Oscar finally starts to hand it over to her, it rings again. The grin on his face tells us exactly what he's going to do.

"Big mouth! No, Oscar!" Luna shouts as we all continue to laugh.

"Hello, Luna's sex line. Roman the Rampant Rabbit speaking, how may I service you?"

Oh god. I feel like I can't breathe, I'm laughing so hard, while Roman's head is thrown back as his deep chuckle fills the whole diner. Other people in the diner are really staring at us now, but we don't care, unable to control our reaction to his silliness.

"Yes. Of course. I'll pass the message on." Oscar's voice becomes serious as he glances around the table. "Yes, sir. Five minutes. Bye now."

No one is laughing now, worried with the drastic change in Oscar.

"Oscar, who was that?" Luna murmurs, as worry sets in. He scrubs the back of his neck as he looks at her.

"Oh, nothing to worry about, baby girl. That was Rafe. He said for you to call him back when Roman the Rampant Rabbit has put his micro penis away," he cries out. His voice gets louder toward the end, as his palm slaps the table over and over again. None of us will ever truly know if that's what Rafe actually said...

"Fuck off, Oscar," Roman grumbles, but he still has a smile on his face. Eventually Oscar passes the phone back to Luna, and we are all calm enough to settle the bill. Heading out to where the truck and bikes are parked, Luna threads her arm through mine. Offering a gentle squeeze before looking up at me.

"When we get back, would you mind helping me set the space up at the party?" I nod in response, pleased to spend whatever time I can with her.

"Of course, Sakura. I'll bring a few cameras for around the rest of the party too," I offer, and she smiles up at me.

I'd agree to anything for a glimpse of that smile.

After we leave the others back at Ace, we grab the case Luna prepared for tonight with my duffel bag, and we have Ian drive us over to the gazebos that the Byrne's have set up.

The color coding for the tents is always the same so I know to head for the red tent. Luna somehow convinced the guys that we didn't all need to go. Likely because she didn't want to deal with Roman and Aiden at each other's throats for the next hour. I would have to agree.

Lacing my fingers through Luna's, I lift my duffel bag over my shoulder, and pull the case behind me in my other hand. Security is already scoping out the place, and manning the restricted areas even though the party doesn't start for another six hours.

Someone must have put the word out, because as we near the entry curtain the guy pulls it to one side to let us in without speaking a word. It's strange being in here without the music on, and without the giant orgy taking up the main space like it usually does.

"I have no idea where we are supposed to go from here, handsome," Luna murmurs beside me, as she too takes in the space around us.

"Hey Luna, this way," Trudy calls out from the far left side where there is another set of curtains, catching me by surprise. As we approach, she smiles at Luna in a friendly way, and my gut tells me we can trust her. We'll be able to confirm that more tonight, and whether she gave the wrong target a heads up.

"Thanks for doing this, Trudy," Luna says, and Trudy

claps her hands in delight.

"Not a problem at all. Are you guys ready for the party tonight? I love dressing up for Halloween." Luna rolls her eyes at her, which she catches, but it just makes her giggle more.

"We have no idea what we're wearing to be honest. Red set it all up, so it'll be a surprise I'm sure." Trudy shakes her head at us, like she can't understand why we don't love it like she does.

Walking down the narrow walkway lined with red silk curtains and dim lighting, she stops at the end and opens another set. How damn big is this place? It does not look this big from the outside. She's set up some tables and chairs in the far corner and even has a power cord available. Nothing has been placed over the concrete floor, it lays exposed at our feet. The walls are thick like the outside of the gazebo as opposed to the silk interior, thank god. This room has been left bare compared to what I assume the others look like.

"Will this be enough for you?" Trudy asks, watching for Luna's reaction.

"It's perfect, Trudy. Thank you," Luna says with a smile, as she steps around the space getting a better feel for the size. It'll definitely hold us all if needed, but we won't all be here.

"Right then, I'll leave you to it. Just call if you need me," Trudy offers a nod and heads out.

Placing the suitcase on the table, I pull out my bug scanner first, to make sure nothing has been set up to watch us. Luna watches me in silence, listening for a beep to say she's been played. There's nothing except silence. A pleased smile takes over her face, knowing so far she can trust the Byrnes.

"Let's get to work then, handsome," she murmurs as she approaches me, leaning up on her tiptoes and placing a gentle kiss to my lips. Damn, I could drown in her, especially when she touches me. Before I can catch up and wrap my arms around her, she's stepping back and opening the case.

Working side by side, we are set up in no time with two of Luna's micro cameras ready to go. One in the corner of the space, where the lining of the gazebo is. The other camera is placed in the handle of the suitcase which will stay in here. At least if anyone happens to take it, we'll know who.

Luna set's up a locked black box under the table,

containing the secret weapons she wanted to have close at hand, just in case. To say she didn't actually grow up in this life, she sure fits in like a damn queen.

"I think we're all set up in here now, Sakura. Shall we place a few more cameras around the rest of the space?" I ask, making sure the chair is placed perfectly in the middle where we need it.

"Yeah, then I think we're good. Red's already messaging about these damn costumes." She sighs, but if she really didn't want to wear one we both know she wouldn't.

Grabbing my duffel bag, Luna places her hand in mine. I enjoy the feel of her delicate fingers intertwined with mine as we enjoy each other's company. Slowing our pace, we relax as we follow the path we came down. Just like when we entered, the security guard opens the entrance to the gazebo for us to exit with a nod.

Taking in the area around us, we try to decide where would be best to put the other two cameras that will watch over the whole space.

"How about we place one in the tree over there?" I say, pointing to my right. "It has a good vantage point for the three open tents. We can have the other one more specifically covering the dance floor like we talked about."

Luna's eyes follow my hands pointing out where I'm talking about, and she nods in agreement.

"Have you got something to help get it up there in the tree?" she asks. The spot I'm considering is a little out of reach, but I don't need anything to help me.

"Sakura, I can climb that, no worries." She looks to me, mouth open wide as she takes me in.

"Kai, don't you think that's a little dangerous?" She has me staring at her with a slack jaw.

"Have you forgotten where we are? You've literally just set up a box of blades and a gun to potentially torture someone, and you're questioning my safety climbing up a tree?" I can't help but scoff at the irony as she sticks her tongue out at me.

"Well, it's not you I'm planning to torture now, is it?" She huffs, but it's too cute that she cares so much. Wrapping my arm around her shoulders, I kiss the crown of her head.

"You are too adorable, Sakura. Who knew?"

She back-hands my chest, as she tries to keep a glare on her face, but it doesn't help.

"Hand me one of the cameras, Acehole. I'll set the one

up on the dance floor while you tempt fate by hanging off a tree."

She holds her hand out between us, and I release her to grab one of the small devices from my backpack. They're a little bigger than Luna's micro cameras because mine have audio built in, whereas she runs separate systems to catch footage and audio.

She stomps off, an extra sway to her hips as she does. I don't miss her glancing over her shoulder with a smug grin to see me staring, like she intended. So hot. I can play that game too. Swiping my face with the bottom of my shirt, I flash my abs in her direction. It has the effect I wanted when I hear her call me an Acehole.

Shaking my head, I pull out a camera and drop my duffel bag to the ground, checking for the best access to climb the tree.

Digging my fingers into the still damp bark, I pull myself up high enough for my other hand to grab the closest branch. As if instinctively, my feet push off the tree to help lift me higher. Grabbing the branch I need, I'm able to wrap my arms around it, and pull myself up. There's a perfect split where the branches go off in different directions, and I secure the device in there.

Using my phone to make sure I have the view I want, I'm all set. It covers the view of the dance floor, the bar and the tables just like we want it to.

Getting ready to jump down, I glance over to where Luna is preparing the other camera, and she's not alone. Aiden Byrnes is leaning against the DJ booth saying something, and Luna's head is thrown back with laughter.

He's lucky it's me here and not Roman, otherwise he'd have lost his head by now. There's still a chance for that yet. Landing on the ground, I rub my hands down my jeans, before straightening my top and grabbing my bag to walk over to them. She's placed the camera just above the lights system directly in front of the booth, with the perfect view of the dance floor.

As I near them, silence falls over their conversation as they both watch me approach. I can't tell who has more lust in their eyes, Luna or Aiden. I'll never forget in high school when he tried to check out my junk in the bathroom, he's crazy. His level of confidence is on par with Oscar for sure.

"Sakura," I murmur as she smiles at me with a knowing look in her eyes. "What am I missing?" I ask, and they both begin to chuckle. I raise an eyebrow at her and she tries to calm herself, forcing her facial expression to be serious.

Holding her hands up parallel to each other, she begins to move them closer to each other before pulling them further apart.

"Nothing, handsome. It's just that Aiden wanted to know how hung you are, and I was trying to measure it out for him." They both start laughing as she holds her hands out exaggeratingly wide, making me roll my eyes at them. I can feel myself getting embarrassed at the topic we're discussing, but I refuse to look away.

"So gorgeous, Kai Fuse. It's a shame someone has caught my attention. Otherwise I would have been trying to convince you to let me rock your world," Aiden says, chuckling to himself.

"That's not funny," Luna jumps in, shoving him backwards a little and he laughs harder. Even though she knows he's joking, she can't help but get protective, and I definitely like it.

Her phone pings from her pocket, and she glares at him before retrieving it. Glancing over the screen, she turns her phone to me to read the message showing.

Rafe: Hey, darling. I still need you to call me.

Make sure your kits are ready to go, including spare clothes. Keep them near your front door or secure them in one of the Ace vehicles. I think it could be tomorrow.

Damn. I nod, and take her hand in mine.

"Let's go, Sakura," I murmur, and we head back to the Rolls waiting for us. Maybe we should ask Ian to hold some of the cases, they'd be secure then.

I don't know how any of this is going to go down, but we need to get through tonight first. Together as a team, we'll do whatever it takes.

THIRTY THREE

Luna

"Luna Moon Steele, will you get a move on?" Red calls from my dressing room, but I'm too scared to go in there. She's already done my make-up and I have no clue what waits for me in there. My lips are blue, like neon glow in the dark blue. She shaded my eyelids in green, matching my eyes, and added giant freckles across the bridge of my nose. I have no freaking clue what I'm supposed to be, and I'm a little concerned.

Stepping into the doorway, she catches me completely off guard. She's already dressed and damn does she look good. She's wearing denim shorts and a sparkly zip up shirt tucked in, but what catches my attention the most is the pink wig on her head. Topped off with an alien antenna headband. I think I can be onboard with this, although the thought of wearing a wig already has me itchy.

"Don't worry, Captain. No wig for you. I want to put your hair in two buns on the top of your head. Now get a move on," she says, rolling her eyes at me.

Following her lead, I find the clothes she wants me to wear on the stool near my dresser. Black leather looking leggings, a black sports bra and a cropped black netted overlay. Oh, well then I can deal with this.

"Red, we're aliens?" I ask, and she nods in response. Taking off my shorts, I step into the leggings. "I was expecting something super over the top like a skintight suit or a skimpy nurse's outfit covered in blood."

"Wait till you see the guys," she scoffs, and I don't even want to know. She turns to give me her back as I throw on the rest of the outfit, before checking myself over in the mirror.

"I thought you would be able to wear your combat boots with this outfit. Even I can accept that heels are not appropriate for tonight," she says, turning to see me with a smile.

"Well, I appreciate your thought process," I respond, as she ushers me to take a seat, diving straight in to drag a brush through my hair.

It surprises me how much I like it when she does my hair. It's not something I really recall anyone doing before, and it feels so good. Relaxing back in my chair, I close my eyes and let her do her thing.

"Is everything okay with you, Red? I know I kind of forced you to go and stay with Maverick while I'm away, but I hope you know it's to keep you safe," I murmur. I've been worried lately, she still has all her sass, but occasionally she just seems to be the super quiet girl I first met.

"It's not that, Luna, honestly I don't mind. It's just…" She pauses for a moment as she gathers her words. "I'm petrified. I know you're strong, Luna, the strongest person I know, but I'm so scared you aren't going to come home from these Games. You guys are my family now, and I don't want anything to happen," she breathes out, as I watch tears fill her eyes through the mirror.

Fuck. I didn't consider this would be playing on her mind. Standing from the chair, I turn to her.

"Red, I'll be damned if I let these fuckers get the best

of me," I say, holding her shoulders at arm's length and staring into her eyes as I speak the truth. "Can I promise nothing will happen? No, but I will do everything in my power to get back in one piece. Besides, we still haven't taken a trip together yet, and that's high on my to-do list, okay? Now, stop crying before you ruin your make-up and blame me."

I don't know what else to say. Actions mean more than words right now. She nods along with me, wrapping her arms around my neck and squeezing tight. I bring my hands around her back and hold her just as tight.

"Hey, you ladies okay?" Parker calls from the lounge. Red forced them into Roman's room to get ready so we could have a little girl time, but they must have given up on waiting.

"Yeah, we'll be out in a minute," I shout back. Red fans her face a little but straightens her shoulders, taking a deep breath.

"Fake it till I make it, right?" she says with a smile. I nod in agreement, loving that she still remembers the mantra I taught her when we first met.

She quickly finishes off my hair with a matching alien headband, and I secure my necklace beneath the netting before we walk into the lounge. The sight before me has me melting into a puddle at my feet.

Cowboys. Fuck.

There are four topless cowboys, chaps over their jeans, and Stetson's on their heads standing in my lounge. All the abs on display are messing with my brain. When I finally lift my eyes above their chests, Roman is frowning while Oscar is throwing his lasso around the room. Kai and Parker aren't fazed, likely because they're enjoying the heat in my gaze as I check them out.

"Red, this is fucking genius. My eyes are already pleased with your choices," I finally manage to say, which earns me a wink from Oscar.

"You are the hottest alien I ever did see, Sakura," Kai says as he approaches, kissing the top of my head. I blush at the compliment as always, but I'm too busy staring at his chiseled abs up close. His moon tattoo is on full display. I love it even more because a part of it represents me but not in the 'tattoo my girlfriends name on me' kind of way.

I place a gentle kiss to the center of it, and I feel his heart pounding underneath my touch.

"I feel like you guys need some baby oil on, you know, get the full effect going," I say huskily, making it clear how hot I'm finding this.

"Forget it," Roman grunts. "You're lucky I'm playing along as it is." His usually broody attitude makes me smile as he fidgets uncomfortably, tugging on the tight material around his groin.

"Ignore him, baby girl. He's just jelly because he doesn't look as good as me." Oscar struts in front of us all by the floor-length windows, twirling the rope around in front of him.

"God help us tonight, having to deal with you," Red sighs dramatically as she grabs her purse off the sofa, and passes mine over.

"This is your own doing, Jessikins," Oscar replies with a wink and a thrust of his hips at me, making everyone chuckle.

"Did you give Ian the cases?" I ask, breaking the fun atmosphere, but it's important. When we got back from setting up at the tent, I finally called Rafe.

From what he said, we need to stay alert. Everything happening has not been done following the correct procedures, Juliana is trying to keep us as informed as possible. It's definitely Rico and Dietrichson pulling strings, and The Ring is in total chaos. Changes are coming, and Rafe believes Totem must be involved somehow. We just don't understand how, and that leaves us in the dark.

He mentioned that when they take us we'll still be transported in the Rolls, which is why he wants us to have our belongings in there. If anyone gets crafty and doesn't let us get our things, we'll have them ready to go anyway. The Ring members will all be there as it's required, but Rafe will be there too. I still don't understand how this will run properly, but we have more information than others.

"We did, princess. It's all covered. Half of our belongings are in the cars, the others in the cases by our front doors, except Parker's," Roman says, and I nod. We are as prepared as we're going to be. Now to get any extra information we can from Wren, while also teaching her a lesson for breaking into my dorm.

"Perfect, thank you." I clap my hands and focus on tonight. "Let's get this show on the road then, shall we?" I'm so ready to finally take action, I've waited patiently and now it's my time. I feel completely energized.

"Lead the way, baby girl," Oscar says with a grin, as he scoops me up in his arms and carries me to the door. I feel him inhale against my neck as he whispers to me, "You smell like heaven, my favorite." I don't respond, but the compliment makes me smile.

Placing me on the floor, he holds the door open for me and pulls me along to the elevator as Parker locks the door behind us, throwing the keys toward me. My phone vibrates in my bag and I pull it out to find an unknown number calling. I glance at the others and Kai nods for me to answer it.

"Hello?" The line is quiet for a moment before a voice comes through the line.

"Luna? It's Dominic Bridge." I mouth 'the agent' to the others, who stare at me with wide eyes as the elevator arrives, and we step in.

"I hope you're calling with a positive outcome for me, agent," I murmur into the phone as everyone stares at me expectantly. I hear him sigh down the phone before he finally responds.

"I'll sign the contract, Luna." Thank fuck for that. I nod, and they understand my meaning behind it, the relief visible on everyone's faces. It's one less thing to worry about.

"Thank you, Dominic. I'll be occupied this next week, but I will meet you at the diner exactly the same as last time next Saturday, okay?" When I will also be able to quiz him on why he knew my name without me saying it too.

The elevator doors open up into the lobby, and Roman wraps his hand around mine, guiding me outside with the others. The line goes quiet for a moment before he finally breathes out his next words.

"Okay, Luna. I've also been told to tell you it's time to open the bag from the vaults." With that the phone line goes dead, but I stay frozen in space at his words.

Roman slows beside me confused with my sudden stop, but I can't process anything other than what Dominic just said. The bag from the vaults? The only one I can think of is the one that had *Meu Tesouro* embroidered into the material. It's been sitting in my walk-in closet this whole time because I haven't had the nerve to open it.

How does he know about it?

"What's wrong, princess?" Roman murmurs beside me, when I still haven't moved. He's standing in front of me as the others are all close by too.

"He's going to sign the contract, but he also said it's time for me to open the bag from the vaults," I mutter, still racking my brain with what he said.

"What bag?" everyone asks, including Red, at the same

time. Finally lifting my gaze from my phone, I look around at all of them.

"That's exactly my point, I haven't told anyone about that bag. On the Sunday after I arrived, before I ran into Roman the first time in the gym and met Red for lunch, I went to the vaults." Roman and Red smile, remembering the day I'm talking about. "I went to all three, and I saved the Steele one for last. When I finally went in, there was a duffel bag sitting on the center table with *Meu Tesouro* stitched into it. I brought it back here with me, but I've never looked in it. I haven't been ready to."

Roman's eyes frantically search mine at the mention of my father's nickname for me, but he relaxes a little when he sees I'm not breaking down. Shaking my head, I pull myself into the present.

"Let's not worry about that for now, we need to focus on Wren, but when we get back tonight will you guys help me?" It's barely a whisper but there it is, me officially asking for help on an emotional level. The soft smiles I get from everyone tells me it hasn't gone unnoticed, but they nod and agree like it isn't a big deal.

Ian holds the door open for the Rolls and I climb in with Roman behind me.

"We've got you, princess."

I truly believe those words, and it warms my soul knowing I feel less alone each day.

THIRTY FOUR

Luna

The decorations were clearly put up after Kai and I left earlier. Now we're surrounded by all the Halloween garland you could imagine. They've gone all out sugar skull themed and I actually love it. On the inside of the tents, neon skulls have been painted and shine brightly with the fluorescent lighting. Skull chains hang from the ceiling and brightly colored petals line the floor.

Every security guard we've seen has their face painted as a sugar skull, which only adds to their intensity. They've also lined up classic Halloween party games outside, but there is no way I'm bobbing for apples.

We're sitting in the exact same spot where the guys took the salt from my body before Tequila shots the last time we were here. The exact same spot. Roman and Parker are sitting on both sides of me, while Oscar and Kai are across from me with Red. I'm getting hot just thinking about that moment, and a quick look at my Aceholes tells me they are too. I just really can't let it distract me right now. I'm struggling to push the agent to the back of my mind as it is.

Sadly, no skin on skin teasing or Tequila shots this time. Instead, we're all nursing water, but in different glasses that look like we're drinking alcohol.

"Let's run through the plan one more time, I don't want anything to go wrong," Parker murmurs next to me, tapping his fingers against the table. We're trying to act natural, but we all subconsciously lean in a little more when he says that.

"Me and Parker will head into the red tent first, about fifteen minutes before everyone else. Kai and Red are going to hang back here with the monitors running on their phones to make sure we're not being followed. Roman and Oscar will approach Wren and hint at some alone time. *Hint* being the key word," I say, glaring at the two of them, but they both look at me like I'm the crazy one for suggesting anything more. I'm not jealous, just possessive.

"Then we'll take her to the room you guys have set up. Kai will direct us through the earpiece we'll each be wearing, and the micro camera on my cowboy hat," Roman adds, continuing the plan. "Then Luna and Parker will join us in the room. Where Luna and I will stay with Wren, and Parker and Oscar will head into the main area until we give the word."

Everyone at the table nods in agreement, except Red who has a frown on her face.

"I still don't understand why we don't have time to dance a little," she moans, downing her exciting glass of water, likely wishing it was a bit stronger.

"Fine, come on. One dance, but honestly, after that we need to get the ball rolling, okay?" I sigh, but the smile on her face makes it all worthwhile. Looking at Parker I point my finger, "Come save me soon, alright?" He nods with a surprisingly wicked grin on his face. Red wastes no time at all dragging me to the dance floor.

She times it perfectly for a more upbeat song to start as Demi Lovato's 'Confident' pours through the speakers. The floor is filled with other dancers, and all the girls are either bunnies or nurses with blood covering them to make it Halloween. These bitches haven't got a Red on their side with clever ideas.

Feeling the music start to fill my veins, we dance like no one's watching. Enjoying five minutes of being carefree before shit gets serious. Damn, the more I listen to this song the more it feels like this should be Red's theme song when she walks. The way her body moves, it's as if she knows it was written with her in mind.

As I glance around us, I notice there are actually a few tutors here this time. I don't know whether it's because it's Halloween, but they definitely aren't chaperoning when they're doing shots in the corner. Clearly, Featherstone Academy isn't set to usual standards for eighteen year olds.

That's when I spot Brett. I will never be more pleased to see his face than this moment right here. Trudy is really starting to show her worth, and I'm glad she's not letting me down. Looking at Red to tell her the good news, I'm surprised to see Aiden dancing behind her with his hand placed on her stomach.

My girl is grinding back against him with her head on his shoulder having the time of her life. He whispers something in her ear. Although I can't hear it, she smiles up at the ceiling, not stopping her movements. I consider how these two would know each other, and I remember when I stormed off at the last party she had helped him when Roman had gone crazy. He's dressed as the devil, wearing only jeans and devil horns. While someone's professionally painted his face to make it look as though his skin is being unzipped, and it looks amazing.

I'm not left to dance alone for long, when I feel hands wrap around my waist and pull me back against a solid wall. I freeze for a moment prepared to attack, but I'm instantly surrounded by Parker's classic woodsy scent, with a hint of sweetness. I feel the press of his hard cock against my back, and I grind against him.

"You owe me a dance, angel," he whispers against my ear, and I melt in his hold.

Moving with me, his arms land on my hips as we grind together on the dance floor. Holy fuck, he's got some moves that I didn't know about, and it makes me mad that we haven't done this before. The music changes, but I can't drag myself away from him. Loving the feel of him against me, his hands branding me with the punishing grip he has on my bare skin.

"As much as I wish I could dance with you all night,

angel, Wren is on the dance floor. I think it's time we put a little distance between us and the others," he whispers in my ear. I fucking hate Wren right now, ruining my moment with my Parker Parker, but then I remember why we're here.

Nodding in understanding, I glance at Red, who offers a smile acknowledging we need to move. Before I can try and walk her back to the guys, Aiden stops me.

"Let us dance for a few minutes, bossy pants. We're having a little fun," he says with a cheeky smile. I look to Red for confirmation and she nods with a smile on her face, which is enough for me. The guys know to watch her without me asking, and I have to remember she has a life too. It's nice to see Red feel just as confident around a guy as she does with us.

Squeezing her hand as I pass, she goes straight back to dancing as my Cowboy Parker wraps an arm around my shoulder leading me to the orgy tent. I pull my earpiece from my bag, and I assume Parker already has his in when he squeezes my shoulder. There are way more people at this party than the last one we came to. The pathways are filled with students everywhere, with candles lining the edges adding to the dark vibes.

The security guy at the entryway lets us in without question, cutting in front of the queue starting to form outside. I'm sure people are pissed about it, but I'm too pumped up to care. Who knew this would be so popular? From what I can tell it's still only Featherstone Academy students and tutors here, it just seems like a lot more showed up tonight.

We make our way to the open plan area, when Trudy approaches us.

"Hey guys, are you both okay?" she asks, but I'm too busy staring at her sexy Cruella DeVil outfit. She's wearing tight black cropped pants with a black top, which seem normal, until you add the bright red gloves, and dalmatian cape floating over her shoulders. She's even got her hair half white half black, it looks so real I can't actually tell if it's a wig or not.

"We're good. We're just going to relax in here a little while, if that's okay?" I finally answer, smiling up at Parker as I do.

"Of course. Although if you're going to be in the public area, I do have to warn you it's participation only. So if you don't want to, you'll probably be best in the space you set up earlier," she says with a smile, when someone calls her from the entry. "Sorry guys, business as always. Excuse me."

I watch her leave before glancing back to Parker to see what he wants to do.

"No way in hell, angel. I am not letting anybody in here see our girl like that," he grunts, surprising me with the firmness in his voice. I finally hear the others through my earpiece too. All of them growling in agreement with Parker, which makes me roll my eyes.

"I could give you a blow job, no one would see me then," I offer, but he only frowns down at me as he grips my cheek.

"Angel, if you think I'm going to let everyone here see you on your knees, you are mistaken. Nobody sees our queen on her knees but us." Holy shit, he's not helping because his words are making me hotter. "Change of plan, guys, we'll be in the room waiting," Parker says, pulling me to the side and ending the discussion.

I lead the way because I know where we are going. The dark red silk drapes look a lot more sensual now it's darker and filled with bodies grinding together. There are no Halloween decorations in here, but there are now some BDSM props hanging from the wall.

"How are things looking with Wren?" I ask quietly.

"They're with her now, they turned the earpieces off, not wanting you to hear any of it," Kai murmurs in my ear, and I don't know whether I appreciate it or hate it more.

Parker must be able to see the stress it's causing me, because he squeezes my hand tighter, and places a kiss on my head.

"Angel, they need to get her here. We all know it's you they want, they just don't want you to have to listen to it. They are doing this to get her here for you. Everything is for you."

His words calm me and the nagging in my mind, and it catches me by surprise how true they are. Funny how he can pull me from the darkness that feeds on the doubts in my mind.

Approaching the curtain at the end of the hall, I point it out to Parker.

"It's this one. The room I've set up is behind this curtain," I murmur.

As I pull the curtain back, everything happens in slow motion.

Staring down the barrel of a gun numbs my brain as my defensive instincts take over, but it's no use at all.

Something smashes into the back of my skull. It feels as though I'm falling forever before my body finally meets the ground. Parker lays beside me, our fingers still laced together. The only pain I feel right now is the helplessness of letting them get their hands on my Parker Parker. My soul aches as the darkness consumes me.

The last thing I see burns into my mind as I'm knocked out cold.

Dietrichson. Veronica. Rico.

Oscar

I'm sick of hearing this bitch's voice already. I bug my eyes out at Roman, hinting for us to get a move on, which he thankfully gets. He places his arm around her shoulder, but the cringe on his face at the contact is noticeable.

We're standing by the table she's at with her little fucking followers. Wren is pressed against Roman while her friends all sit and watch with delight. She is literally dressed in lingerie as a Playboy bunny. Fishnet stockings on her legs, and her ass cheeks hang out of the tight fitted bodysuit she's wearing. She didn't even waste time with any fake blood, instead going straight for the slutty look.

I'm beyond bored with all this already, so I turn my earpiece back on. Hoping to catch a hint of my Luna's voice instead, but I hear Jess screaming down my ear and Kai panicking. They sound frantic and I turn to search them out in the crowd, my heart pounding in my chest as adrenaline kicks in. What the fuck is going on?

"Rome, something's not right," I try to mutter quietly, and he frowns down at me. I tap my ear as I continue to scan the crowd, looking for that damn pink wig of Jess'. I don't have to look far as I see her and Kai running toward us, the fear clear on both of their faces.

Jess doesn't stop her pace as she charges at Wren, Roman steps out of the way just in time as she pins Wren to the table. Her head hits the surface with a lot of force as Jess screams down at her. Caging Wren in from behind, just like Luna did that time in the lunch hall. Everyone sitting at the table jumps back in surprise, but no one steps in to help.

"What have you fucking done? Where are they?"

Wren starts to laugh with her face pinned to the table, which only irritates Jess even more. She pulls Wren up off the table by her hair and slams her back down again, the thud booming around us. Luna and Parker, something's happening to them. I turn to Kai whose eyes are flitting between the screen of his phone and us standing in front of him.

"Kai, what's going on?" Roman growls frantically, and it takes him a moment to find the words to respond.

"Someone has them," he finally murmurs in response. "I'm trying to find them on the cameras we set up, but I think you two need to head in there now. Leave Wren with us," Kai says, darkness filling his eyes as fear kicks in, mixing with the anger already there, he's not dealing well with this.

"The Games?" I ask, needing clarification, but he shakes his head.

"I'm not sure, I don't think so. I heard Rico and Dietrichson, but there was a third person."

I can't breathe. I go to pull my collar away from my neck, only to not find one because I'm not wearing a top at all. Anger creeps into my bones, taking over my mind and pushing me to rush toward the tent. I'm not waiting around, and what the hell are all these people doing in my fucking way? Pushing through the crowd, I hope Rome is behind me because I refuse to stop as fear kicks in.

Fuck. Fuck. Fuck.

The security guy on the door goes to open the curtain for me, but he isn't quick enough as I pull it open the rest of the way. Stepping into the tent, I search frantically not knowing where to go. I finally look behind me for Roman, who is standing right there looking around as I am. Trudy, where's Trudy? I can't see her anywhere, everyone's too busy enjoying the fuckfest to be of any use.

"Please tell me one of you has turned your earpieces on," I hear Kai mutter in my ear, and I sigh a little in relief.

"Me, who knew I could be the smart one. Now tell me where to go, Kai," I bark, needing to get to them now. Roman glances at me with a confused look on his face, I point to my ear again and he finally understands, turning his on too. Kai directs us to the curtain of red silk which leads to a narrow corridor, pulling aside the material that conceals the room they set up, we come up blank.

"Fuck. Fuck, Kai. They're not here. Neither of them are here," I snarl down the earpiece. Not at him, but I can't contain the anger and the pain I feel rushing through my body. Throwing the cowboy hat to the floor, I run my fingers through my hair, gripping tightly as I can't stop the panic from setting in.

Roman crouches down beside me, venom in his eyes as he points to pools of blood on the ground at our feet. Someone's going to die for this, I'll kill them with my bare fucking hands.

"No. No get off him. Get off him!" Red screams through the earpiece, and I feel my world starting to crumble. "Roman! Oscar? Ozzie, they've got him. Please they're taking Kai," her cries spin me into action, running back out to where we just left them.

"Jess, I need you to focus, okay. This is really important," Roman grunts, as we try to get past the crowds of people in here.

It's as if they all know we are in a desperate hurry and they all want to delay our time. All I can see is a red mist of fury as I push through the tent to get back outside.

"Okay, I'm focusing," she whispers through the line, sobbing a little.

"What were they wearing? The people who took Kai?" he asks, and I'm thankful she answers straight away.

"Black tracksuits with the Featherstone emblem embroidered on the front. They had sunglasses on too." I sigh, only slightly in relief.

He's actually being taken for The Games, we knew this was coming, we just didn't know how soon. It still leaves a bad taste in my mouth, because I know if Rico was there when Luna and Parker were taken, they're not going to the same place as us. I can feel it.

"Good girl, Jessikins. You did brilliant, where are you now?" I ask, needing to make sure she is safe before anyone tries to come for us.

"I'm over by the DJ booth. They pushed me aside and took Wren too, and I didn't want to be alone with her crew," she mutters. "Maverick, what are you doing here? No, no they've taken Luna and Parker. I need to help them, Maverick. PUT. ME. DOWN!" God, I think I could hear her without the earpiece at that volume.

"Jess, go with him. It's the only way we can keep you safe if they're looking for us too." Roman sighs, swiping a hand down his face. As we finally get close to the exit, I see four men dressed exactly how Jess described moments ago. They're looking for us, but I can't go anywhere without finding Luna first.

Grabbing Roman's arm, I point them out and pull him in the opposite direction. We need a minute to think. Growling at anyone near us, they finally move out of the way, clearing a path. As soon as the Featherstone bodyguards are far enough into the tent, we slip out, quickly running around the corner where it's quiet.

"Fuck, Rome, I don't know what to do. How did we not consider the fact that Rico would use this as an opportunity to take them?" Rubbing the back of my neck, I pace the small patch of grass we're standing on.

"Fuckkk," he growls, pulling his hair just as I did earlier.

"We have our guns, Rome, but what are we going to do?" I ask, panicked.

I'm not the planner, I'm the go in guns blazing and hope for the best one of the group. When Jess gave us our outfits, they came with two plastic guns. Roman decided it would be a good idea to each switch one out and replace it with a real one. Which is great and all, but we still find ourselves in an impossible situation.

"Fuck, Oscar. Phone, where's your phone? Call her," Roman yells, searching his own pockets to do the same.

I try, and try again, frustration getting the better of me as it continues to ring without answer.

"Mr. Rivera? Mr. O'Shay?" someone whispers from the left, and we both pull our guns from the holster and aim in that direction. It's funny how pulling a gun out numbs my emotions as practice and precision takes over. My heart stops pounding in my ears as I train my gun on... Ian? What the hell is Ian the driver doing here?

His hands are raised in surrender, but I only lower my gun slightly, Roman doing the exact same. I step closer to him, and that's when I notice the panic in his eyes and the tremble in his hands.

"They took her, Parker too. In a big SUV, it's not the same people as The Games, but they are here. They just grabbed Mr. Fuse and Miss Dietrichson. I don't... I don't know what I'm supposed to do to help, they're in there looking for you."

I can see the pain in his eyes at the fact he's witnessing what's going on, and the fear he has for Luna. I lower my gun as I look at Roman, who remains standing with his gun trained at Ian. He slowly lowers his aim, staring him down.

"Luna mentioned that Rafe said we are taken to The Games in the same vehicles we use on campus. Does that mean you know where to go?" Roman asks quietly, placing the gun in his holster, and clenching his hands in anger. Ian nods slowly in answer, waiting for Rome to continue. "So, you could take us there without them having to knock us out, right?" he clarifies, and again Ian nods.

"They drug you, but yes, I could do that. It will put my life on the line, but whatever it takes," he says, standing taller before us. This guy right here is exactly who I want in Luna's corner.

"Then that's what we do, Ian. Let's get moving now, before they come back out here," I murmur, waving a hand for him to lead the way.

He's parked the Rolls around the corner. Roman marches ahead to open the door before Ian can, not wasting time on formalities. I shut the door behind me as Ian climbs in up front.

"The only person to get in the SUV with them was Miss Hindman and two Featherstone bodyguards. Rico and Barbette climbed into a separate SUV. I just hope Miss Steele took the hint I gave her last week," he breathes out, putting the car in driving and flooring it.

"What hint?" I ask, Luna hadn't mentioned a hint.

"I happened to mention the location in passing as discreetly as possible, but the fact that you don't know worries me even more." He slams his hand against the steering wheel, catching me by surprise.

"It's okay, Ian. Take us there. If Rico didn't get in with

them, he's gone straight to The Games to act like he had no involvement. That's the best place for us to go because we have no idea where they may be," Roman says with his head in his hands.

They're going to regret touching my family.

Blood really isn't thicker than water, and in a place where your bloodline matters so much it ruins me. They have my world in their hands, and I'm at a loss. I'll bring the violence, and destroy this whole fucking place if anything happens to them.

KC KEAN

THIRTY FIVE

Luna

The stench of cigarettes hangs in the air, my sense of smell being the first to come back to me. I'm lying on my front, but I'm not in the tent anymore. I can feel the rumble of an SUV beneath me. I try to clear the fog from my mind, but I can still feel the throbbing from the back of my skull where some fucker hit me. I have one arm trapped under me on the left as my right arm is thrown over my head. My legs are slightly bent at the knee, my feet propped up against the closed door. I don't feel any bindings around me, fucking idiots.

Parker.

Shit. My heartbeat kicks up a notch as I start to panic for his safety. I promised to protect him, now look at us. Taking a deep breath without drawing attention to myself, I smell his woodsy cologne. I pray it's because he's here too and not just my imagination playing tricks on me.

Calming the throbbing of my pulse bouncing around in my ears, I try to listen to what is going on around me. I can hear the crinkling of a packet of chips, followed by the munching of someone eating with their mouth open. Gross.

My phone vibrates in my bag, which I happen to be lyying on, but I don't move a muscle as I wait for it to end. I hear a female voice and I instantly know it's Veronica. That bitch is done, I swear to god.

"Answer the phone. Come on, answer the damn phone," she mumbles, clearly wanting to speak to someone. From the fact that her voice is coming from above me to the right, I know I've been put on the floor.

Assessing the rest of my body, I feel a small weight against the bottom of my back. Almost like a hand is resting on me from the seats to my left. Please be Parker, please.

"Finally, Pumpkin. I've been trying to get through for ages. Where are you?" Veronica demands. I'm guessing it's on the phone, but I refuse to open my eyes to check. "I have them. Luna and Parker are both knocked out cold with me. That girl gave them a sedative to make sure they are out for hours."

Girl, what girl? Trudy. I'll fucking ruin her when I get my hands on her.

"Yeah, we've just left the Academy. We'll be about four hours or so. Rico and Barb are heading straight to The Games." Just left? But she said they would be out for hours? What did Trudy do?

That's when I feel the smallest stroke against my back from the weight resting against me. It's Parker, I know it, and he's awake too. Fuck, okay. Trying to calm myself as best as I can I try to think, to control this situation.

My face is tilted in Veronica's direction so I definitely can't risk glancing around. She's not the one eating, whoever that is, is sitting in the front with the driver. I can't sense anyone beside Veronica, so that means there's three of them.

"Tony, you have nothing to worry about. I'll be with you soon and then we can be together, me and you, like you promised. Okay?"

Oh my god, she sounds like a lovesick puppy. Wait,

isn't Totem the nickname for Tony 'Totem' Lopez?

I've heard enough, I need to get us out of here before they take us too far. Remembering the fact that all the guys were carrying a real gun with a plastic one too, we may need to use that to our advantage.

Wiggling my toes in my combat boots, I make sure I have feeling throughout my body. The only body part I might have an issue with is my left hand, so it's a good thing I'm right-handed. Taking one final breath, I prepare myself for the fight that's about to come.

Bringing both of my hands to my shoulders, I don't stop to check if the movement goes unnoticed or not. I lift my knees under me, pushing myself into a crouched position facing Veronica. This bitch is staring at me like a gulping fish, but I don't waste any time bringing my arm across my front and hitting her in the face with my elbow.

She cries out in surprise with a mixture of pain, as the phone goes flying from her hands. I feel movement behind me as Parker sits up, aiming a gun at her head.

I can't risk taking my eyes off Veronica to check Parker over, I have to force myself to stay focused on the threats first.

The driver shouts, not lifting his pedal from the gas

as the passenger fumbles with his chips, not expecting to have to do anything right now.

Veronica sneers at me as she holds a hand to her cheek. "You stupid fucking bitch. Why the fuck are you not passed out?" she stutters, surprise written all over her face. "You're supposed to be out for the next six hours at least. Fuck. Sit down, Tony has plans for you, and I won't let you ruin it."

I can't help the laughter that leaves my lips, as if she thinks I'm fearful of her.

"Who's aiming guns at who here?" I murmur, nodding my head at Parker, and she chuckles back.

"I'm not scared of a plastic gun from a cowboy outfit, you dumb bitch," she cackles, and I love it even more when she underestimates me.

Reaching my hand out to Parker, he holds the gun in one hand as he passes the one still in the holster to me. Flicking the safety off, I aim it straight in between her eyes.

"I warned you the next time I saw you I'd kill you. You just made it easier without even trying," I say, as the passenger guy tries to grab hold of Parker from behind in a choke hold.

Shit, that little distraction is all Veronica needs to

throw herself at me, trying to wrestle for the gun. Out of the corner of my eye I can see Parker fighting off the guy, but I need to focus on Veronica wrapping her hand around the barrel.

"I really fucking wish you'd never been born," she spits in my face as we fall backwards with her on top of me. Kicking my legs out wide, I wrap them around her thighs as I struggle to keep my grip on the gun.

She pushes the barrel of the gun up toward the roof of the SUV as she tries to turn it on me. Forcing any panic deep down, I let my defensive mentality takeover. Thrusting our hands up above my head, it moves the gun out from between us, while forcing her face closer to mine. Without thought I throw my head back and smash it into her face, connecting with her nose, the blood instant. She cries out in pain, her eyes frantically tracking the blood dripping from her face.

Fuck, if my head didn't already hurt, it would now. That's a crack to the back and the front I'm dealing with. Maybe I should try to not do that again. I can hear Parker grunt beside me, and I know I need to put an end to this right now.

I don't give her a chance to move, hitting Veronica

around the head with the barrel of the gun, and she falls dramatically into the seats behind her. Without pause, I turn and aim the gun at the guy who has his arm wrapped around Parker's neck, my finger pulling the trigger with no hesitation.

Parker leans forward gasping for breath, his head dipped between his knees as my eyes search to check him over. The SUV screeches to a stop and I try to brace myself. The fucking driver, is all I can think as I'm thrown around the SUV. I try to grab on to the door handle, my fingers barely grazing against it as my head smashes the window beside me.

Fuck.

I feel lost, unable to register the state of my body, the pounding in my ears the only thing I'm sure of. Parker, where's Parker? I must have closed my eyes on impact, and it takes more strength than I'd like to force them open. The first thing I notice is the fact I'm still in the SUV. Thank fuck. My back is propped up against the door, tiny shards of glass shattered around me as I blink rapidly. I don't need to find the driver because he's leaning over the back of his seat, his sole focus on me.

"Luna!" I hear Parker shout, but my eyes refuse to

move from the end of the gun pointing in my face. Where's mine? This motherfucker thinks he can pull a gun on me, is he crazy? A gunshot goes off, and I just pray Parker can get out of here safely if this guy is intent on killing me.

My body stiffens, preparing for the bullet, but the gun in my face slips to the floor, as the guy's lifeless form hangs over the seat. Blood splatters against my face and I can taste it on my lips. Lifting a hand to my chest, feeling the pounding beneath my rib cage, I slowly digest that I'm alive.

Parker.

Swinging my gaze to him, he's kneeling on the floor of the SUV at my outstretched feet, gun still aimed at the dead body in my face. I can see the frenzy in his eyes as he continues to make sure this guy is not going to move again.

He just… killed someone, to save my life.

The SUV is engulfed in darkness, with only the sound of Parker and I breathing heavily.

Parker hits the overhead light above us as his eyes frantically search mine. Slowly lifting my hands to his chest, I feel his skin beneath my fingertips, making sure he really is here with me. An uncontrollable sob leaves my mouth as I inch closer to him, seeing the raw red marks around his neck.

"I'm okay, angel," he croaks out, and my lips find his in an instant.

The briefest of touches, but it grounds me like nothing else. He brings his forehead down to mine as we both try to calm our beating hearts. This is not the kind of action we expected tonight. Parker runs his fingers through my hair, pulling the tiny pieces of glass out while he checks my head over. When he's happy I'm not going to die from bleeding out, he cups my face and looks deep into my eyes.

"I'm sorry I got blood on you when I shot him," he murmurs, and I can't help but grin at his words.

Forcing myself to lean away from Parker, I finally take in the scene around us. My mother's still unconscious beside us, but for how long I don't know. Someone shouting in the distance has Parker and I frowning at each other in confusion.

Slowly, my eyes find Veronica's phone wedged between the seats on the other side of the SUV. I lean over her to get it, Parker grabs my other arm, concern etched all over his face, but I hit the speakerphone button.

"Veronica! Veronica! What the fuck is going on?" a man growls through the phone in frustration, and I know without a shadow of a doubt that it's Totem. The gravel in his voice sends a shiver down my spine.

"Veronica isn't available right now," I mutter, and he goes silent on the other end. I don't pull my gaze from the phone as I wait for his response.

"Well, well. If it isn't Miss Luna Moon Steele, you are a hard girl to get a hold of, aren't you? I love a little challenge, but you're starting to annoy me. Your mother promised you to me when you were a baby. Now I've waited patiently, and your time is up. Do as I say or it'll only be worse for you when I do get my hands on you."

The snicker that fills the air around us doesn't surprise me, but his words do. What is it with people promising me to others, it's getting on my last fucking nerve.

"It'll have to be a hard no from me, Totem, sorry for the inconvenience," I say, making him growl down the line.

"Whatever you want to think, little lady. Just remember, I'm coming for you."

The line cuts off and silence once again takes over. I toss the phone on to the back seat as Parker's fingers lace through mine, offering me the comfort I need right now.

We need to figure this out. Where do we go from here? The vibration of my phone buzzes from my bag on the floor again. I rush to grab it from the zipped pocket to see an unknown number flashing across the screen.

"Hello?" I answer in question, and relief floods me when I hear Maverick's voice come through.

"Oh thank god, Luna. Where are you? The others are on their way to The Games, but Jess said you had been taken by Rico?"

"Jess? Where is she?" I ask frantically. If the others have been taken to The Games that leaves her on her own.

"Don't worry she's here with us, safe. Focus on you right now. Is Parker with you?"

I glance at Parker, and he offers a soft smile. Even with all this chaos surrounding us we can still smile. I don't know whether that makes us crazy or blissfully happy, but I don't care either way.

"He is. I don't know where we are, but we need to get to The Games if that's where the others are. Where do we go, Maverick?" I ask, but he sighs down the phone.

"All I know is it's some estate about an hour's drive up north."

I process his words, and I've heard that before. Think, Luna, think. Ian! It was Ian, what did he say? There's a big estate called Beechwood Hall an hour's drive up north, plenty of roads for the bike. Holy shit, he was telling me where to go.

"I've got it, Maverick. Keep her safe for me," I shout before pocketing the phone. "Parker, I know where we need to go."

He nods in understanding, "Let's move their bodies to the back and we can get moving then, angel. Do you think they have something we can tie Veronica up with? As much as I'd rather toss them out here, I think we need to show up with a statement," he says, stepping out of the SUV, and I couldn't agree more. The road is dark around us, I have no idea where we are, but I can pull the directions up on my phone in a minute.

Without a word, we pull the dead bodies from the front and carry them to the back, unceremoniously piling them on top of each other. Luckily there are handcuffs in the glove compartment, and Parker even finds duct tape in the trunk, so I tape the bitch's mouth just in case. A little fishing wire from the tackle box in the trunk also comes in useful for her legs.

Parker takes the driver's seat as I climb in beside him. "Let's go get our family, angel." Yeah, let's do that.

We pull up slowly to the estate before us, we could see it from miles away. The land around here is nothing but farms and crops, leaving Beechwood Hall to fill your vision sitting on its own acres of land. Large wrought iron gates block us from getting any further, with a two man security booth to our right. Veronica woke up a little while ago but since she's handcuffed to the handle above her head, with her legs bound and mouth taped, I just turned the music up to ignore her whimpers.

I finally wind down my window, and the security guard raises an eyebrow at me.

"Can I help you?" he asks. His eyes take me in, but I haven't got time for this.

"I'm Luna Steele, and I'm here for The Games."

His eyes startle in surprise as he quickly looks to his clipboard, before glancing back at me.

"I do apologize, Miss Steele. Please take the main road, it'll lead you to the estate," he splutters, but I don't offer a response. Instead, Parker puts the SUV in drive as the gates open and I shut my window.

It takes another twenty minutes before we find ourselves

in front of the estate, neither of us saying much. My training tells me to assess my surroundings, but my mind can't see past anything except getting to my Aceholes. Our hands are joined on the arm rest between us, offering strength to each other.

He puts the SUV in park as we stare up at the mega mansion in front of us. At least five stories high with pillars creating a grand Mediterranean entrance. Large arched windows fill the ground floor, with balconies coming off the above floors. This place is ridiculously big.

"Are you ready, angel?" Parker asks, stroking his thumb across my knuckles.

"As I'll ever be," I murmur with a soft smile.

I can see his brain working overtime and I can feel what he wants to say in my soul, but I refuse to let him say it now under these circumstances.

"Don't you dare, Parker. You can tell me on the other side of this, and I can say it too. The chance of death will not be the reason, do you understand?" My heart pounds against my chest as it wants me to screw my logic and scream it at him, but I refuse to not believe in tomorrow.

He nods in understanding, but in complete silence he points to his eye, to his heart and to me. My heart melts, my hands shake and tears well in my eyes as I do it in return.

"Fuck you, Parker Parker, for making me feel," I murmur, pressing my lips against his as he gently lifts his hand to stroke my cheek.

Finally pulling apart, we both step out of the SUV and Parker drags Veronica out of the back. He doesn't give her a chance to fight as he quickly unlocks the handcuffs and tightens them behind her back. Tearing the binding on her legs, we head up the stairs to the entrance. Veronica struggles to move her feet to keep up, but Parker just drags her along beside us.

No one is around, but the noise coming from the door straight ahead tells us where people are. More specifically Roman, Oscar and Kai. I can hear the shouts and I know it's because they don't know where we are.

Picking up speed, I run for the double wooden doors, my feet pounding against the ground, deafening me. I push the doors open with a bang and they bounce off the walls on either side. The room comes to a halt with the noise echoing throughout the room. The guys whirl around to see what interrupted them.

The instant their eyes connect with us, the fury on their

faces melts away as they take us in. Making sure we're okay, their eyes trail to Veronica, whimpering in Parker's hold.

"Princess, why are you covered in blood? Parker?" Roman whispers, anger taking over his features, but before I can respond, Rico shouts from across the room.

"What the fuck is going on?" he snarls, and I force myself to step around my guys, pulling Parker with me, and Veronica trips over her own feet as he drops her in front of us. I refuse to let him hide in his father's presence any longer and Veronica can go to hell.

Getting a look at the room we've walked into, I see every member of The Ring sitting at a table set up on a small platform. My grandmother is on her feet, hands planted on the table, along with Juliana as they sneer at Rico. The room is massive, and smaller tables dot the main floor with families sitting around them. Thick red rope forms a partition between us and them, as if creating a walkway to where we stand.

Spotting Rafe in the crowd, I can see a mixture of emotions take over his face, relief that I'm here, but confusion over what's happened. Finding my voice, I take another step toward The Ring members, Parker's hand in mine and my other Aceholes behind us.

"Please, Rico. Do tell me where you thought we would be?" I question, raising my eyebrow at him as he continues to stare us down. "It wouldn't happen to be knocked out cold in the back of an SUV with Veronica, would it? On our merry way to see Totem?"

"I'm going to fucking kill you," Rafe growls as he stands, trying to control his breathing before he passes out with anger.

"It's okay, Dad. We're here now," I say softly, but loud enough for him to hear me. I watch as his hands clench at his sides, but eventually he nods in agreement. The room is silent around us as they look between Rico and us. "Still no response, Rico? I'm disappointed. I'm waiting for you to ask how we still made it here, and Barb, where's she? I'm sure she would love to know too."

I don't say a word as I look around the room for her in exaggeration. Parker squeezes my hand in his, a way of offering his support right now as everyone watches Rico. Bored with waiting and watching him snarl as he leans over the table at us, I decide to move this along.

"Okay, well you'll be glad to know the SUV is parked outside in one piece. Unfortunately, the other passengers are dead." Rico grins down at me, and looks at Veronica handcuffed at my feet.

"Not everyone, little girl," he sneers.

Perfect, I was waiting for him to goad me, and he's so predictable he doesn't disappoint.

"Hey, Veronica," I call, and she whips her head around to me, fear in her eyes as she frantically tries to get out of the situation she finds herself in. Mascara streaks down her face as tears continue to gather in her eyes. Dried blood stains her nose and cheeks, as she sobs against the duct tape. She knows what's coming, and that makes it even easier. Shaking her head frantically in protest, she tries to back away.

Now that I've got her attention, and not the back of her head, I raise the gun as I continue to stare into her eyes, and pull the trigger.

The room goes silent as they watch her lifeless body drop to the floor.

Rico slams the table in front of him, growling as rage builds inside of him, but he doesn't move from his spot, forcing himself to remain in place. Movement to my right catches my attention and it's Barbette Dietrichson trying to sneak off through another door to the right.

"Barbette," I call, pointing a hand in her direction. "Please, do stay." Forcing a megawatt smile on my face, I probably look manic holding the gun, especially with the blood splatter all over me. She stands frozen in place like a deer caught in the headlights, but I refuse to take the heat off her.

"That's enough, little girl," Rico growls, finally breaking his silence. "Parker, come here, son. Standing beside her does not help you earn your bloodline from me."

Fuck this asshole. I don't say anything, this is for Parker to do, to stand his ground. I don't panic as the silence stretches while he tries to find his words, but the grip on my hand tells me he's here, pushing through his usual barriers.

"I'm good where I am, thank you, Rico," he finally says, full of strength and determination. I could cry with joy.

"If you continue to stand there with her, you lose any right to my bloodline, and I don't need to remind you what happens in Featherstone to people who lose their bloodline," he threatens, and the grin on his face shows everyone how much he thinks he has this, but he motherfucking doesn't.

I look to Parker, who smiles down at me softly. I

squeeze his hand tight before releasing it to stand in front of him.

"I don't need your bloodline to survive, Rico," he says, crystal clear as everyone stares openly at the show we're putting on right now.

"Have it your way, you just signed your death wish," Rico throws back with a laugh, an actual laugh at the threat of his son's life.

"Nah, I don't think he did," I say with a smile of my own, as Parker unfastens the clasp of my necklace around my neck and places it in my hand. "You see, he doesn't need to be a Manetti," I say, looking at Parker to continue as I casually drop the bomb that we know his shitty fucking bloodline.

The ring from my necklace drops into my hand as Parker looks around the room. He dips down his jeans a little at the front to show off the full Steele family emblem. Diana the goddess of the hunt, an upside down crescent moon with three arrows pointing out of the top. While I wiggle my fingers like a sassy bitch for all to see my ring.

Offering that sexy smile of his to everyone, Parker's words flow from his mouth. My heart pounds with every syllable.

"Hi, my name is Parker Steele and this is my wife, Luna."

EPILOGUE
Parker

My wife.

Luna Steele is my wife.

I've wanted to scream those words from the rooftop since our day out and afternoon lunch with Maria.

This girl continues to save my life over and over again.

She is my everything, *our* everything.

The guys knew what was going to happen that day, and I think it's Oscar who has stared at that ring the most.

I'll make sure it represents all of us. I refuse to let it change what we already share all together.

Til death do we part, we both said, and I refuse for that

to be in The Games.

TO BE CONTINUED...

YOUR BLOODLINE

AFTERWORDS

What the actual F just happened .. Book Two that's what!!

Are you going to go back and see the little holes I left?

Are you screaming for answers?

If you threw your reading device I take no responsibility LOL.

I can't believe we are already here, and I could cry that you are here too.

Seriously, thank you! Thank you, for seeing something in this series to willingly pick it up and give it a try.

I'm so excited to continue Luna's story with her Aceholes that Book Three has already begun. It makes me sad mad that we are getting closer to the end.

I hope you love these Aceholes as much as I do!

Here's to a hot and steamy future people!

Much Love <3

THANK YOU

I have to start by saying the biggest thank you to my Handsome <3 No not Kai, my real Handsome <3 For telling me how proud you are of me everyday. For never holding me back and always wanting the best for me. You are my biggest fan, without even reading the books.

My b-e-a-utiful children! Thank you for putting up with me, and I don't mean when I hide out in the book cave while Daddy entertains you. I mean when I turn everything into a song and drive you cray cray, yet you somehow still love me!

High-five scuba-dive babies <3

Val the Alpha Queen.

You are by far the only person who could put up with me constantly everyday!

Your support is off the scale and my books would have no details without you LOL

Thank you for being a soundboard for all of this creativity, and loving Luna and the Aceholes just as much as me <3 and for just not being a tabby cat!

Thank you for making Roman cray-cray, Rico more

than just a snake and Oscar cheesier than ever LOL

Now I know it's your birthday this month, and I'm feeling extra cheesy, so …

CLEARS THROAT

Happy Birthday to you, Happy Birthday to you, Happy Birthday dear Valerie, Happy Birthday to you <3

Thank you to Hope, Katy, Emma, Kristin and Monica for being my BETA babes <3

You all have mega eyesight that puts me to shame LOL

You all offer such support and words of encouragement, I don't know how I'd get through this stage without your love for the story.

Without you everybody would be getting simulation instead of stimulation, awkward sentences, british meanings and a magic fucking door haha!

Thank you, thank you, thank you!

Extra special shout outs to my BAE's Noreah, Michelle, Rachel, Samantha, Nicola, Kathryn, Kelly, Caitlyn, Kyndal and Liv.

You guys are the bestest ever babysitters for these book babies LOL

Thank you for not getting sick of me yet!!

ABOUT THE AUTHOR

KC Kean is the sassy half of a match made in heaven. Mummy to two beautiful children, Pokemon Master and Apex Legend world saving gamer.

Starting her adventure in the RH romance world after falling in love with it as a reader, who knows where this crazy train is heading. As long as there is plenty of steam she'll be there.

ALSO BY KC KEAN

Featherstone Academy

(Contemporary Reverse Harem Academy Romance)

My Bloodline

Your Bloodline

Our Bloodline

Red

Freedom

The Allstars Series

(Contemporary Reverse Harem, Sports Romance)

Toxic Creek

Tainted Creek

Twisted Creek - September 14th

Printed in Great Britain
by Amazon